Summer BLOCKBUSTER 2024

MAISEY YATES

KATHERINE GARBERA

ALISON ROBERTS

MILLS & BOON

SUMMER BLOCKBUSTER 2024 © 2024 by Harlequin Books S.A.

ONE NIGHT IN PARADISE
© 2012 by Maisey Yates   First Published 2012
Australian Copyright 2012   Fourth Australian Paperback Edition 2024
New Zealand Copyright 2012   ISBN 978 1 038 93924 1

THE WEDDING DARE
© 2022 by Katherine Garbera   First Published 2022
Australian Copyright 2022   Second Australian Paperback Edition 2024
New Zealand Copyright 2022   ISBN 978 1 038 93924 1

Alison Roberts is acknowledged as the author of this work
A LIFE SAVING REUNION
© 2017 by Harlequin Books S.A.   First Published 2008
Australian Copyright 2017   Third Australian Paperback Edition 2024
New Zealand Copyright 2017   ISBN 978 1 038 93924 1

Published by
Mills & Boon
An imprint of Harlequin Enterprises (Australia) Pty Limited (ABN 47 001 180 918), a subsidiary of HarperCollins Publishers Australia Pty Limited (ABN 36 009 913 517)
Level 19, 201 Elizabeth Street
SYDNEY NSW 2000
AUSTRALIA

MIX
Paper | Supporting
responsible forestry
FSC   FSC® C001695
www.fsc.org

Printed and bound in Australia by McPherson's Printing Group

CONTENTS

One Night In Paradise

Maisey Yates

Maisey Yates was an avid Mills & Boon® Modern™ reader before she began to write them. She still can't quite believe she's lucky enough to get to create her very own sexy alpha heroes and feisty heroines. Seeing her name on one of those lovely covers is a dream come true.

Maisey lives with her handsome, wonderful, diaper-changing husband and three small children across the street from her extremely supportive parents and the home she grew up in, in the wilds of Southern Oregon, USA. She enjoys the contrast of living in a place where you might wake up to find a bear on your back porch and then heading into the home office to write stories that take place in exotic urban locales.

Also by the same author:

GIRL ON A DIAMOND PEDESTAL
HAJAR'S HIDDEN LEGACY
THE ARGENTINE'S PRICE

Did you know these are also available as eBooks?
Visit www.millsandboon.com.au

To my very best friend,
who I happened to be married to. Haven, I love you.

CHAPTER ONE

CLARA DAVIS LOOKED at the uneaten cake, still as pristine and pink as the bride had demanded, sitting on its pedestal. A very precarious pedestal that had taken a whole lot of skill to balance and get set up. Not to mention have delivered to the coast-side hotel that sat twenty miles away from her San Francisco kitchen.

Everything would have been perfect. The cake, the setting, the groom, well, he was beyond perfect, as usual. And everyone who had been invited had come.

There had been one key person missing, though. The bride had decided to skip the event. And without her, it made it sort of tricky to continue.

Clara eyed the cake and considered taking a slice for herself. She'd worked hard on it. No sense letting it go to waste.

She sighed. The cake wouldn't make the knot in her stomach go away. It wouldn't ease any of the sadness she felt. Nothing had been able to shake that feeling, not since the groom, who was now officially jilted, had announced the engagement in the first place.

Though, ironically, watching him get stood up at the altar hadn't made her feel any better. But how could it? She didn't like seeing Zack hurt. He was her business partner—more than that, he was her best friend. And also, yeah, the man who kept her awake some nights with the kinds of fantasies that did not bear rehashing in the light of day.

But secret fantasies aside, she hadn't really wanted the wedding to fall apart. Well, not this close to the actual ceremony. Or maybe she had wanted it. Maybe a small part of her had hoped this would be the outcome.

Maybe that was why she'd agreed to bake the cake. To stand by and watch Zack bind himself to another woman for the rest of his life. There wasn't really another sane reason for it.

She blew out a breath and walked out of the kitchen and into the massive, empty reception hall. Her heart hit hard against her breastbone when she saw Zack Parsons, coffee mogul, business genius and abandoned groom, standing near the window, looking out at the beach, the sun casting an orange glow on his face and bleeding onto the pristine white of his tuxedo shirt.

He looked different, for just a moment. Leaner. Harder than she was used to seeing him. His tie was draped over his shoulders, his jacket a black puddle by his feet. He was leaning against the window, bracing himself on his forearm.

It shouldn't really shock her that after being left at the altar he looked stronger in a strange way.

"Hey," she said, her voice sounding too loud. Stupid in the empty room.

He turned, his gray eyes locking with hers, and she stopped breathing for a moment. He truly was the most beautiful man on the planet. Seven years of working with him on a daily basis should have taken some of the impact away. And some days she was able to ignore it, or at least sublimate it. But then there were other days when it hit her with the force of ten tons of bricks.

Today was one of those days.

"What kind of cake did I buy, Clara?" he asked, pushing off from the window and stuffing his hand into his pocket.

She forced herself to breathe. "The bottom tier was vanilla, with raspberry filling, per Hannah's instructions. And there was pink fondant. Which I hand-painted, by the way. But the vanilla cake in the middle was soaked in bourbon and honey. And not a single walnut on the whole cake. Because I know what you like."

"Good. Have someone wrap up the middle tier and send it to my house. And they can send Hannah her tier, too."

"You don't have to do that. You can throw it out."

"It's edible. Why would I throw it out?"

"Uh...because it was your wedding cake. For a wedding that didn't happen. For most people it might...take the sweet out of it."

He shrugged one shoulder. "Cake is cake."

She put her hand on her hip and affected a haughty expression, hoping to force a slight smile. "My cake is more than mere cake, but I get your point."

"We've made a fortune off your cakes, I'm aware of how spectacular they are."

"I know. But I can make a new cake. I can make a cake that says Condolences on Your Canceled Nuptials. We could put a man on top of it sitting in a recliner, watching sports on his flat-screen television, with no bride in sight."

The corner of his mouth lifted slightly and she felt a small bubbly sensation in her chest. As though a weight had just been removed.

"That won't be necessary."

"That could be a new thing we offer in the shops, Zack," she said, knowing business was his favorite topic, aborted wedding or no. "Little cupcakes for sad occasions."

"I'm not all that sad."

"You aren't?"

"I'm not heartbroken, if that's what you're wondering."

Clara frowned. "But you got left at the altar. Public humiliation is...well, it's never fun. I had something like that happen in high school when I got stood up by my date at a dance. People pointed and laughed. I was humiliated. It was all very Carrie. Without the pig's blood or the mass murder."

"Not the highlight of my life, Clara, I'll admit." He swallowed. "Not the lowest point, either. I would have preferred for her to leave me before I was standing at the altar, with the preacher, in a tux, in front of nearly a thousand people, but I'm not exactly devastated."

"That's...well, that's good." Except it was sort of scary to know that he could be abandoned just before taking his vows and respond to it with an eerie calm. She reacted more strongly to a recipe that didn't pan out the way she wanted it to.

But then, Zack was always the one with the zenlike composure. When they'd first met, over a cupcake of all things, she'd been impressed by that right away. That and his beautiful eyes, but that was a different story.

She'd been working at a small bakery in the Mission District in San Francisco, and he'd been scoping out a new location for his local chain of coffee shops. He'd bought one of her peanut-butter-banana cupcakes, her experiment du jour. His reaction, like all of Zack's reactions, hadn't been overly demonstrative. But there had been a glint in his eye, a hint of that hard steel that lay just beneath the outer calm.

And he'd come back the next day, and the next. She'd never entertained, not for a moment, the idea that he'd been coming in to see her. It had been all about the cupcakes.

And then he'd offered her twice the money to come and work in his flagship shop, making the treats of her choice in his gorgeous, state-of-the-art kitchen. It had been the start of everything for her. At eighteen it had been a major break, and had allowed her to get out of her parents' house, something she'd been desperate to do.

In the years since, it had been a whole lot more than that.

Roasted's ten thousandth location had just opened, their first in Japan, and it was being hailed a massive success. Conceptualizing the treats for that shop had been a fun challenge, just like every new international location had been.

She and Zack hadn't had a life since Roasted had really

started to take off, nothing that went beyond coffee and confections, anyway. Of course, Zack was the backbone of the company, the man who got it done, the man who had seen it become a worldwide phenomenon.

They had drinks, coffee beans and mass-produced versions of her cupcakes and other goodies in all the major grocery chains in the U.S. Roasted was a household name. Because Zack was willing to sacrifice everything in his personal life to see it happen.

Hannah had been his only major concession to having a personal life, and that relationship had only started in the past year. And now Zack had lost her.

But he wasn't devastated. Apparently. She was probably more devastated than *he* was. Again, cake related.

"I didn't love her," he said.

Clara blinked. "You didn't...love her?"

"I cared about her. She was going to make a perfectly acceptable wife. But it wasn't like I was passionately head over heels for her or anything."

"Then why...why were you marrying her?"

"Because it was time for me to get married. I'm thirty. Roasted has achieved the level of success I was hoping for, and there comes a point where it's the logical step. I reached that point, Hannah had, too."

"Apparently she hadn't."

He gave her a hard glare. "Apparently."

"Do you know why? Have you talked to her?"

"She can come and talk to me when she's ready."

Zack would have laughed at the expression on Clara's face if he'd found anything remotely funny about the situation. The headlines would be unkind, and with so many media-hungry witnesses to the event, mostly on the absent bride's side, there would be plenty of people salivating to get their name in print by offering their version of the wedding of the century that wasn't.

Clara was too soft. Her brown eyes were all dewy looking,

as though she were ready to cry on his behalf, her petite hands clasped in front of her, her shoulders slumped. She was more dressed up than he was used to seeing her. Her lush, and no he wasn't blind so of course he'd noticed, curves complemented, though not really displayed, by a dress that could only be characterized as nice, if a bit matronly.

She did that, dressed much older than she needed to, her thick auburn hair always pulled back into a low bun. Because she had to have her hair up to bake, and it had become a habit. But sometimes he wished she'd just let her hair down. And, because he was a man, sometimes he wished she wouldn't go to so much trouble to conceal her curves, either.

Although, in reality, her style of dress suited him. They worked together every day, and he had no business having an opinion on her physical appearance. His interest was purely for aesthetic purposes. Like opting for a room with a nice view.

That aside, Clara was all emotion and big hand gestures. There was nothing contained about her.

"I'm fine," he said.

"I know. I believe you," she said.

"No, you don't. Or you don't want to believe me because your more romantic sensibilities can't handle the fact that my heart isn't broken."

"Well, you ought to love the person you're going to marry, Zack."

"Why? Give me a good reason why. So that I could be more broken up about today? So that I could be more suitably wounded if she had shown up, and we had said our vows, when ten years on the marriage fell on the wrong side of the divorce statistics? I don't see the point in that."

"Well, I don't see the point at all."

"And I didn't ask."

"You never do."

"The secret to my success." His tone came out a bit harsher

than he intended and Clara's expression reflected it. "You'll survive this," he said drily. "Breaking up is hard to do."

She rolled her eyes. "I'm worried about you."

"Don't be. I'm not so breakable. Tell me, any big word on the Japan location go up online while I was busy getting my photo taken?"

"All good. Some of the pictures I've been seeing are showing that it's absolutely slammed. And everything seems to be going over huge."

"Good. That means the likelihood of expanding further there is good." He sat down in one of the vacant, linen-covered chairs. They had pink bows. Also Hannah's choice. He put his hands on the tabletop, moving his mind away from the fiasco of a wedding day and getting it back on business. "How are things going with our designer cupcakes?"

"Um...well, I was pretty busy getting the wedding cake together." Clara felt like her head was spinning from the abrupt subject change.

Zack was in full business mode, sitting at the trussed up wedding-party table like it was the pared-down bamboo desk he had in his office at Roasted's corporate headquarters.

"And?"

"I have a few ideas. But these are pretty labor-intensive recipes and they really aren't practical for the retail line, or even for most of the stores."

"Cupcakes are labor intensive?"

She shot him a deadly look. "Why don't you try baking a simple batch and tell me how it goes?"

"No, thanks. I stick to my strengths, and none of them happen to involve baking."

"Then trust me, they're labor intensive."

"That's fine. My goal is to start doing a few boutique-style shops in some more affluent areas. We'll have bigger kitchens so that we'll have the capability to do more on-site baking."

"That could work. We'll have to have a more highly trained staff."

"That's fine. I'm talking about a few locations in Los Angeles, New York, Paris, London, that sort of thing. It will be more like the flagship store. A bit more personalized."

"I really like the idea, not that you'd care if I didn't."

"I am the boss."

"I know. I'm just the Vice President of Confections," she said, bringing up a joke they'd started in the early days of the company.

A smile touched his lips again and her heart expanded. "A big job."

"It is," she said. "And you don't pay me enough."

"Yes, I do."

She gave him a look. One she knew was less than scary, but she tried. "Anyway, go on."

"I had made an appointment to speak to a man who owns a large portion of farmland in Thailand. Small clusters of coffee and tea. All of his plants receive a very high level of care and that's making for extremely good quality roasts and brews. My goal is to set up a deal with him so we can get some limited-editions blends. We'll sell them in select locations, and have them available for order online."

Her mind skipped over all the details he'd just laid out, latching on to just one thing. "Weren't you going to Thailand on your honeymoon?"

"That was the plan."

Clara couldn't stop her mouth from dropping open. "You were going to do business on your honeymoon?"

"Hannah had some work to do, as well. Time doesn't stop just because you get married."

"No wonder she left you at the altar." She regretted the words the moment they left her mouth. "Sorry. I didn't mean that."

"You did, and that's fine. Unlike you, Hannah had no romantic illusions, you can trust me on that. Her reasons for not showing up today may very well have had something to do with a Wall Street crisis. There's actually a good chance she's at her apartment, in her wedding gown, screaming obscenities at her computer screen watching the cost of grain go down."

She had to concede that the scenario was almost plausible. Hannah was all icy cool composure, and generally nice and polite, until someone crossed her in the corporate world. Clara had overheard the other woman's phone conversations become seriously cutthroat in tense business situations. Threats of removal of tender body parts had crossed her lips without hesitation.

She admired her for it. For the the intense way she went after what she wanted. She'd done it with Zack. It had been sort of awe inspiring to watch. Mostly it had been awe-inspiringly depressing. Because Clara wasn't cutthroat, or intense. And she hadn't been brave enough to pursue what she really wanted. She'd never been brave enough to pursue Zack.

"I doubt that's what happened," Clara said, even though she couldn't be certain.

"There was a reason I asked how the designer-cupcake thing was going."

"Oh." Back to business.

"I was trying to make sure you didn't feel swamped by the amount of work you have to do."

"No. Creating recipes is the best part of my job. I've been having fun with this one. I've actually done most of the experimental baking and tasting with our panel, and I have a few standout favorites, plus some that need to be improved. And then I'll have to narrow down the selection, because it just won't be feasible to have too many different kinds on the menu at once."

"So that was the long, detailed version of you telling me you aren't too busy at the moment?"

She shot him a deadly look. Jilted or not, he didn't need to be a jerk. "No, I'm not too busy."

"Good, because everything was set for me to head to Chiang Mai tonight."

"And you need me to make sure everything is running smoothly at corporate?" That wasn't usually the role she fulfilled. She wasn't an administrator, not even close.

"No, I want you to get packed, because you're coming with me."

Her stomach honestly felt like it plummeted, squeezing as it made its way down into her toes. "You're not serious. You're not actually asking me to come on your honeymoon with you?"

"The trip is booked. I have appointments made. I'm not canceling the honeymoon just because my bride neglected to show up." He looked at her, like he had thousands of times, but this time felt… It felt different. The inspection seemed closer somehow, his gray eyes more assessing, more intimate. She swallowed hard and tried to ignore the fact that her heart seemed to be trying to claw its way out of her chest. "I think you'll make a more than fitting replacement."

CHAPTER TWO

IF HE HAD physically hit her he couldn't have possibly hurt her worse. A replacement? The consolation prize. The stand-in for tall, lean, angular Hannah who possessed the cheekbones of a goddess. Not that Clara had noticed, or compared.

Well, she had. And in some ways, on some days, the fact they were so different made it easier because there was no question of what the other woman had that she didn't.

But she had never, never put herself in the position of trying to vie for Zack's attention, not in that way. Because she'd known that she would be the consolation prize if he ever did decide to look in her direction. And she'd decided that was one thing she couldn't do to herself. The one thing worse than watching the man who meant the world to her tie himself to another woman. Being the one he'd settled for.

And now Zack was shoving her into that position. It made her want to gag.

"I'm not a replacement for anyone, Zack. And if you're suggesting I am, then I think we've become a little bit too comfortable with each other."

She turned and walked out of the reception hall. She left the cake. She didn't care about the cake. The staff of the hotel could have it for an early, sugary breakfast when they came in tomorrow morning.

She breezed through the hall and out the front doors, into the damp, salty air. It had been a cool day, but now, with the sun dipping down below the horizon, the air coming in off of the bay was downright chilly. Which was good, because now, if anyone saw her lip tremble a little bit, she could blame the cold.

She didn't want to be emotional, not over something that wasn't even intentional, and with Zack, she knew it wasn't. Zack wasn't mean, more than that; he simply wasn't all that emotional, so he never assumed that anyone else was.

Everything was so surface to Zack. Nothing seemed to get under his skin. Nothing seemed to throw him off, even for a moment. Not even a canceled wedding.

Anyway, she'd had enough intentional digs taken at her in her life to know that things could get far too dramatic if she didn't make people have to work at hurting her feelings.

But since her feelings for Zack were a constant jumble, her reactions to anything involving him were always strong. Most of the time, though, she managed to keep that fact hidden from Zack. A lot of the time, she kept the extent of her feelings hidden from herself.

"Clara."

She turned and saw him standing just behind her. She didn't say anything. She crossed her arms beneath her breasts and fixed him with her best glare.

"You're the second woman to abandon me today."

Her face flooded with prickly heat. "See, that comparison is not very flattering, considering you've already used the word replacement in regards to me."

"That's not what I meant."

"Then what did you mean?"

"That I need someone to come with me, and actually, under the circumstances you're a better fit than my ex-fiancée."

For a full second she could only think of one thing his statement could possibly mean. Images clicked through her mind like close-up still-shots. Tan hands on a pale, bare hip. Masculine lips on a feminine throat. Blood roared through her body, into her cheeks, making her face burn. She was sure they were the color of ripe strawberries, broadcasting her thoughts to anyone who looked at her.

"What?" she asked.

"Hannah's smart, don't get me wrong, but she doesn't know this market quite like you do. Prices on stocks, maybe, but it will be nice to have you on hand to offer an opinion about marketing and flavor."

Business. He was talking about business. And somehow, to Zack, business was more important than romance and making love on his honeymoon?

At least he was pretending it was. There was something different about his expression, a dark light behind his gray eyes. She'd seen Zack nearly every day for the past seven years. She knew his moods, his expressions as well as she knew her own.

And this was a different Zack. Well, she thought it was. For some reason, the hardness, the intensity, seemed more true than what she thought she knew of him.

Strange. But then, the whole day had been strange. Starting with the interminably long silence after the strains of the Bridal March had faded from the air and the aisle remained vacant.

All right, he'd made her mad. It wasn't the first time. He was bullheaded and a general pain in the butt sometimes. He was also the smartest man she knew, with a cutting wit that always kept her amused. He was one of the few people who'd never doubted that her ideas were good.

If she didn't go with him, she would spend her evenings hanging out by herself, reading and experimenting with cupcake recipes and licking the batter off the spatula. Fun, sure, but not the kind of fun she could have in Thailand.

Again, those images, erotic and explicit, assaulted her. No, that wasn't the kind of fun she would be having in Thailand.

Zack had never looked twice at her in that way and for the most part, she was fine with that. She'd had a crush on him at first, but even then she hadn't expected anything to come of it.

And, yes, Hannah had come in and stirred up some strange feelings. Because as long as Zack had simply been there, at work every day, and available for dinner meetings and a lot of other things, it had been comfortable. Zack was in every space in her life, at work and home.

But then along came Hannah, and she took up his time, and, Clara had assumed, that he loved her. And having to share Zack's emotion with someone else had felt... It had felt awful. And it had made her jealous, which didn't make sense because she'd never even tried to cross the boundaries of friendship with Zack. So it wasn't like Hannah had been encroaching on her territory or anything. But she'd been so jealous looking at Zack and Hannah she'd felt like her stomach was turning inside out, and she knew, that even if she could never have Zack, she didn't want anyone else to have him, either.

Which was just stupid and childish. About as stupid as going with a man on his honeymoon, platonically, in place of his bride, to conduct business with him. Platonically.

She needed her head checked. She needed some sanity. Maybe the problem was that Zack did take up all the spaces in her life. Maybe it would have to change.

Just the thought of that, of pushing him away, sent a sharp dose of pain through her system. She was addicted to him.

"All right. I'll go. Because I would rather have a paid vacation in Thailand than spend the week hanging out in the office and orchestrating the return of all your wedding presents."

"I'm not returning my wedding presents."

"You can't keep them, Zack."

"Of course I can. I might need a food processor someday. What does a food processor do?"

"I'll teach you sometime. Anyway, yes, I'll go with you."

The corner of his lip curved up into a wicked smile that made her stomach tighten in a way that wasn't entirely unpleasant. "Excellent. Looks like I won't be spending my wedding night alone, after all."

It probably wasn't nice of him to tease Clara. But he liked the way her cheeks turned pink when he slipped an innuendo into the conversation. And frankly, he was in need of amusement after the day he'd had.

But amusement hadn't been his primary goal when he'd given her the wedding-night line out in front of the hotel. He'd been trying to atone for his ill-spoken remark about her being a replacement. In truth, he had more fun with Clara than he did with Hannah. It wasn't as though he disliked Hannah; quite the opposite. But he hadn't been marrying Hannah for the company.

She'd needed a husband to help her climb the corporate ladder, a little testosterone to help her out in a male-dominated field. And a wife...well, a wife like her was a convenience for a lot of reasons.

But Clara was not his wife. In a lot of ways, she was better. And he hadn't intended to hurt her feelings. She'd been quiet on the ride from the hotel back to her town house by the bay, and once they'd gotten inside to her place she'd dashed into her bedroom to pack a few things "real quick" which, in his experience with women meant...not quick at all.

He sat in her white leather chair, the one that faced her tiny television. Not state of the art at all, nothing like his place. The home theater had been one of his first major purchases when Roasted had become solvent. Clara's had been an industrial-grade mixer for her kitchen. That was where all *her* high-tech gear was. She had a stove with more settings than his stereo system.

"Ready." He looked up and his stomach clenched.

Clara was standing at the end of the hallway, large, pink leather bag draped over her shoulder, dark jeans conforming to the curve of her hips, and a black knit top outlining the contours of her very generous breasts. He hadn't gotten married today, so he was going to allow himself a longer look than he ever did. He'd noticed her body before, but he'd never allowed himself to really look at her as a man looked at a woman. He didn't know why he was letting himself do it now. A treat in exchange for the day, maybe. Or exhaustion making him sloppy with his rules.

Clara was an employee. Clara was a friend. Clara was not a possible lover, and normally that meant no looking at her like she could be.

But tonight wasn't normal. Not by a long stretch.

"Good." He stood up and tried to keep his interest in her body sublimated. But he was just a man. A man who had been celibate for a very long time. A man who had been expecting a reprieve on that and had been sadly disappointed.

"Are we taking the company jet?" She smiled, her perfectly shaped brow raised.

She really was beautiful, and not just her curves. He didn't stop to notice her looks very often. She was like…not furniture, but a fixture for sure. Someone who was always there, every day, no matter what. And when someone was always there, you didn't stop and look at them very often.

But he was looking at her now. Her face was a little bit round, her skin pale and soft. Her eyes, dark brown and wide, were fringed with dark lashes, surprising given her auburn hair color. And her lips…full and soft looking, a very delicate shade of pink.

Looking at her features was a nice distraction, especially since he was about to make her very, very angry. Normally he didn't care for other people's feelings. Not enough to lose any sleep over. He was in command of his world, and he didn't question his decisions.

But Clara was different. She'd always been different.

"There's something I didn't tell you yet." And it might have been wise to save it until she was safely on the plane. And had had a glass or two of champagne.

"What's that?" she asked, eyes narrowing.

"I was supposed to get married today."

Her eyes became glittering, deadly slits. "Right."

"I was meant to be going on my honeymoon with my wife. And now, here I find myself jilted. No bride. Barely any pride to speak of."

She arched her brow, her mouth twisted into a sour expression. "What, Zack?"

"I need you to come with me. As more than my friend. Not really more than my friend, but more as far as Amudee is concerned."

She shook her head and let her pink bag slip off of her shoulder and onto the hardwood floor. "That's...that's insane! Who would believe you'd hooked up with someone else already?"

"Everyone, Clara. I'm a man who, as far as the public is concerned, is in the throes of heartbreak. Everyone knows about our business relationship. About our friendship. Is it so insane to think that, after suffering heartbreak, I looked to my closest friend and found so much more?"

Oh, it was sick. It really was. To hear him saying something that was...that was so close to her real-life fantasies it was painful to listen to the words fall from his lips. "No. No, I am not playing this game. That's ridiculous, Zack. Go on your own."

"I can't."

"Why?"

"Look, my pride will survive. But if I show up alone, and without my wife, looking the part of lonely loser who couldn't hold on to his woman...well, who wants to cut a business deal with that guy?"

"So offer him more money," she hissed.

"That's the thing with Amudee. Money isn't the main objective. If I could throw a bigger check at him, I would. But it's not only about that. It's about people, the kind of people he wants to do business with, and for the most part, I am that man. I care deeply about fair trade, about the work he has going on there in Thailand. I have to look like I call the shots in my own life, and I will not let an inconsequential hiccup like Hannah's cold feet affect that."

She shook her head. "No. Zack just..."

"If I lose the deal because of this..."

"I'm fired? I doubt it. And I can't imagine him passing this up just because you aren't getting married now."

"This growing project is a huge thing for him, his life's work. He's poured his entire fortune into this. He has high principles, and, yes, a lot of it does have to do with bringing money into Northern Thailand, for the people that live there, but he won't go into something if he doesn't feel one hundred percent about it. I can't afford to let it slip to ninety-nine percent. And if you tip the deal over, then I need you."

"So buy your beans from someone else," she said. "Someone who doesn't care what your personal life looks like."

"There is no one else. Not with a product like this. He understands the foundation I've built Roasted on. That it's always been my goal to find small, family run farms to support. He's a philanthropist and what he's done is give different families in the north of Thailand their own plots to cultivate their own crops. Tea and coffee is being grown there, of the highest quality. And I want the best—I don't want to settle for second."

Clara bent and picked her bag up from the floor. She really hated what Zack was proposing. Not just because she didn't exactly relish the idea of lying to someone for a week; there was that, but also because the idea of playing the part of his lover for a week made her feel sick.

She'd done a good job, a damn good job, of pretending that all she felt for Zack was friendship, with a very successful working relationship thrown into the mix. She'd pretended, not just for him, but for herself.

Because she didn't want to desire a man who was so out of

her league. A man who dated women who were her polar opposites in looks and personality. Women who were tall and thin, blonde and as cool and in control at all times as he was.

Wanting Zack was a pipe dream of the highest order.

Yes, it had been harder to ignore those sneaky, forbidden feelings when his engagement was announced, but she'd still done it. She'd baked his wedding cake, for heaven's sake.

But this, this was one ask too many. Even for him. To go to a romantic setting, pretend she was experiencing her deepest fantasy, all for show, just seemed too masochistic.

And yet, it was hard to say no to him, too. Not when, as much as it galled to be asked to do this, it would give her this sort of strange, out of time, experience with him.

And definitely not when the whole thing was such a big deal to the future of Roasted. Her wagon was well and truly hitched to the company, and in order for her to succeed, the company had to succeed.

Her wagon was hitched to more than the company, if she was honest. It was Zack. Zack and his wicked smiles, Zack and that indefinable thing he possessed that made her want to care for him, even though he never let her.

Zack was the reason she didn't date. Not because, as a boss he kept her so busy with work, though she'd pretended that was it for a long, long time. It was Zack the man. Because her feelings for him were more than just complicated. And she was... she was a doormat.

She'd baked the man's wedding cake. And then what had she thought would happen? She was going to stay at Roasted, after Zack married? Play Aunt Clara to his kids? Watch while he had this whole life while she died a virgin with nothing but her convection oven for company?

Sick. It was sick.

And now she was really going with him to Chiang Mai to play the part she knew he'd never really consider her for?

She needed to get a life.

She was right. What she'd thought earlier at the hotel had been right. A moment of clarity. It wasn't healthy to have him in everything. He was her boss, her best friend. He filled her work and personal hours, and even when he wasn't around, he was in her thoughts. Zack had dates, he had a life that didn't include her and she…didn't. She couldn't do it anymore.

"If I do this… If I do this, then it's going to be the last thing I do at Roasted." She thought about the bakery, the one she'd been dreaming of for the past few months. The one she'd drawn up plans for. It had been in her mind ever since Zack and Hannah got engaged. Just a mere fantasy of escaping that painful reality at first, but now…now she thought she needed to make it happen.

She needed to make some boundaries. Have something that was hers. Just hers.

"What?" he asked, his dark brows locking together.

"If I go with you and play arm candy then I'm done. It's not…it's not the first time I've thought of this." It wasn't. When he'd come into the office with Hannah and announced that the whole thing was official, well, she'd just about handed in her resignation then and there.

But of course his smile and his innate Zack-ness had stopped her. Because in her mind, it was better to have crumbs from him than everything from someone else. Because he was so enmeshed in her life, so a part of her routine. Her first thought in the morning, her constant companion throughout the day. And it was his face she saw when she drifted off to sleep.

He was everything.

And the real truth of the situation was that while Zack cared for her, and even loved her, possibly like some sort of younger sister figure, she wasn't everything to him. And he didn't want her the way she wanted him.

"What the hell?" he asked.

"I'm… I'm having a revelation, hold on."

"Could you not?"

"No. I'm sorry. I'm… I'm sorry, Zack. This really has been… It's been brewing for a while and I know it wasn't the best day or the best way to say it, but…it does have to be said."

"Why?"

"Because… Because it's eating my life!" The words exploded from her. "And if that isn't made completely obvious by the fact that I'm agreeing to drop everything at the spur-of-the-moment to fly to Asia to go on your honeymoon in place of your fiancée and pretend to be your *new* girlfriend…well… I can't help you."

"No. No, I don't agree."

"And what, Zack? You can't force me to stay at my job."

He looked like he was searching for some loophole that would in fact give him that authority.

"I need a good severance, too. I want to open my own bakery."

"The hell you will!" he said, his voice hard, harsher than she'd ever heard.

"The hell I won't," she returned, keeping her own voice steady, though, how she managed, she wasn't sure.

"Non-compete."

"What?"

"You signed a non-compete."

"A bakery would not compete with Roasted, not really," she said, planting her hands on her hips.

"It could, on a technicality, especially as we'd likely share a very similar desserts menu, seeing as you planned all of mine."

"I'm not talking about a worldwide bakery chain, I'm talking… I want to open one up that I run myself. Here in San Francisco. Something personal, something me. Something that would give me a chance to have a life."

"No."

It was shocking, Zack's transformation from unaffected, jilted groom, to this. She would have expected this kind of reaction from Hannah not showing up to the wedding, not to her asking to quit the business. Where was his control? Zack always had control. Always.

Except now.

"Then I won't go with you. And I get the feeling that a female companion is a bit more important than you let on. I know you too well for you to hide it from me."

His gray eyes glittered in the dim light of her apartment. "There is some competition. Sand Dollar Coffee is competing for the chance to get these same roasts, and Mr. Amudee, traditionalist he is, is very likely to give preference to their CEO. They were just there for a week in the villa, Martin Cole, his wife and their four children. Mr. Amudee was charmed."

"So you do need me. You need me to give you an edge. To make sure Amudee knows you're a macho man who can have his way with whomever, whenever. We're friends, Zack. I don't know why it has to be like this..."

"You were the one leveraging," he bit out.

"Because I can't do this anymore. The beck-and-call thing. I need more. *You* were getting married, you should get that."

"You want to get married?"

Her stomach tightened. "Not necessarily. But I don't even have a hope of it as long as I'm working sixty-hour weeks. And since I don't believe in practical arrangements, like the one you and Hannah have, that will keep me from having a successful relationship."

"Fine," he said, the word stiff. "But you stay on until the deal with Amudee is done. Got it? I'll need you to be around, at the business, my assumed lover, until the ink is dry on the contract."

It was cold and mercenary. And it was tempting. Tempting to play the part. To immerse herself in it for a while. Just thinking about it made her stomach tighten, made her shiver.

No. You can't forget. This is just a game to him. More business. "Yes. I won't let you down. If I say I'm going to do something, I'll do it."

"I know."

"And when it's over?"

"You can open your bakery. I'll make sure you're compensated for your time here."

Clara stuck out her hand, her heart cracking in her chest. "Then I think we have a deal."

CHAPTER THREE

ZACK WAS IN a fouler mood than he'd been when the double doors of the hotel's wedding hall had opened to reveal, not his bride, but a very panicked wedding coordinator who was hissing into her headset.

He leaned back in his seat on his private plane and stared at the amber liquid in the tumbler on his tray. Turbulence was bouncing the alcohol around, sending the strong aroma into the air. He wasn't tempted to take a drink. He didn't drink, it was just that his flight attendant had heard about the disaster and assumed he might be in need.

He looked across the wide aisle at Clara, who was, sitting on a leather love seat in the living-room-style plane cabin, staring fixedly at her touch-screen phone.

"Good book?" he asked.

Her head snapped up. "How did you know I was reading?"

"Because you always read."

"Books make better company than surly bosses."

"Do they make better company than bitchy employees? If so, perhaps I should read more."

She looked at him, her expression bland. "I wouldn't know."

"No. You wouldn't. Look, I gave you what you asked for."

"After a big ugly fight."

"Because I don't want to lose you."

A strange expression flashed in her brown eyes. "Right."

"You've been here since the very early days of Roasted, and you've been key to the success of the company, of course I don't want to lose you."

She looked back down at her phone. "Well, I can't live my entire life to make you happy."

He frowned. "That's not how it's been, is it?"

"No," she said, her tone grudging. She put her phone down and stretched her legs out in front of her and her arms straight over her head, back arching, thrusting her breasts forward. His body hardened, his blood rushing through his veins hotter and faster.

That was a direct result of the fact that he was supposed to break his long bout with celibacy tonight, on this very plane, and it wasn't happening now. Still, his body hadn't caught up with his mind yet. Damned inconvenient considering he was now fixating on his friend's breasts. Breasts that he was not supposed to fixate on. Basically two of the only breasts on earth that were off-limits to him.

More inconvenient, considering they were about to spend the week in Chiang Mai in a very secluded and gorgeous honeymoon villa. Even more when you considered that she was leaving the company soon after.

Well, that wasn't happening. He would make sure of that. He would offer her whatever he had to offer to get her to stay, and until then he would simply nod whenever she brought it up.

He wasn't sure how he would convince her, only that he would. He'd successfully stolen her away from her bakery job back when he'd only had a handful of coffee shops to his name. He had no doubt he could do an even better job of keeping her now that he had so many resources at his disposal. He could give her whatever she wanted, more freedom, more time off. And she was his friend. She wouldn't leave him.

She was just mad about the whole fake fiancée thing. But

she would get over it. She always did. It wasn't the first time he'd made her mad. Likely it wouldn't be the last. But that was just how it was. She wouldn't really leave him.

He was a master negotiator. And he didn't lose. He was good at keeping control, of his life and of his business.

"The property we're staying on is supposed to be amazing. It borders a Chiang Mai, and there's a spa right on site. It's more of a resort than anything else, but you have to be invited to stay there by the owner. Very exclusive." He got nothing but silence in response.

"They have unicorns, I hear," he continued, "with golden hooves. You'll love it."

He heard her try to stifle a very reluctant snicker.

He leaned in and looked at her face, at the faint shadows marring the pale skin beneath her eyes. "Are you tired?" he asked.

She leaned back in the chair. "You have no idea."

"There's a bedroom." His blood jumped in his veins again, like the kick-start on a motorcycle. "You could lay down for a while if you want."

"How long have we got?"

"Ten more hours."

"Oh, yeah, I need sleep." She stood up and did another little stretch move that accentuated her breasts.

Clara needed more than sleep. She needed to get out of the tiny, enclosed space with Zack and all of his hot, male pheromones that were wreaking havoc on her good sense. If she had any at all to wreak havoc on. Well, she did have some. She'd used it to ask for her out.

For a little bit of a chance to move on and forward with her life. Because Zack hadn't married Hannah today, which was fine and good, but he would marry someone. He'd decided to, and when Zack put his mind to something, he did it. That meant it would happen, sometime in the very near future, she imagined, now that she knew love wasn't necessarily on the docket. Heck, if he smiled just right at the flight attendant they would probably be engaged by the time they landed in Thailand. And then she could sleep in the guest room in the villa.

She snorted.

"What?" he asked.

"Nothing."

"The scariest word known to man when issued from the lips of a woman."

Her lip curled voluntarily at his statement. "Sexist."

"I prefer realist, but you're free to call it as you see it."

"So tell me this, Zack."

"What?" he asked, one dark eyebrow arched.

"I assume you'll attempt marriage again."

"If I find the right woman."

"And by that, you don't mean the woman you love?"

Something in Zack's posture changed, subtle but obvious to her, his shoulders straightening, his muscles tensing beneath his expertly tailored shirt. His eyes changed, too. There was something dark there, haunted, something she'd never seen before, not this clearly. She'd felt it before, an intensity lurking beneath his cool exterior, but she'd never seen it so plainly.

It was almost frightening in its intensity, transforming a man she'd seen every day for seven years into a cold stranger.

"I don't do love, Clara. Ever." He turned his focus to the newspaper that was folded on his lap. "Good night."

Clara turned toward the bedroom, exhaustion burrowing beneath her skin, down into her bones. Yesterday, everything had been the way it had always been. It had sucked; it had been heading in a direction she hadn't liked, but for the most part, it had been the same.

Today everything felt different. Most of it was her fault. And even though she wouldn't change it, she hated it.

"We just landed."

Clara sat up and pushed the wild mass of auburn curls out of her eyes. She blinked a few times and Zack's face came into focus. For a moment, she didn't do anything. She didn't move, she didn't breathe, she just concentrated on his face being the first thing she saw.

She'd never woken up next to a man before. And, yeah, this wasn't really waking up next to a man in the traditional sense. And he was more leaning over than next to her. But it was a really nice thought, and it was a very nice sight first thing in the morning. If it was even morning. She had no idea.

"What time is it?" she asked.

"It's 10:00 p.m. local time."

She flopped backward. "Oh, no. Why did you let me sleep?"

"I tried to wake you."

"No, you didn't."

"I did, you were out."

She felt a strange sort of disappointment curling in her stomach. She wished, well, part of her did, that he had woken her up. She swallowed hard. Her throat felt like it was lined with cotton. It was far too easy to think of a lot of very interesting ways he might have woken her up.

No. Bad.

"I'm going to be a wreck."

"Sorry."

"I take it you didn't sleep?" She looked down and realized she was still wearing her jeans.

"No. But then, I don't sleep all that much."

That didn't surprise her. She'd never really quizzed him on his sleeping habits, but honestly, he just didn't seem like the kind of man who could sleep at all. He had too much energy and drive to stop even for a moment. Whenever she'd thought of him in bed...well, it hadn't been images of him sleeping plaguing her.

"We're at the airport?" she asked, peering out one of the windows, confused by how dark it was outside.

"Don't know if I'd say airport so much as landing strip. We're on Mr. Amudee's property. It backs the city, but there's a lot of forest in between his land and civilization."

"Oh."

"There's a car waiting for us, and your luggage, such as it was, is already loaded in it."

She stood and her breasts nearly brushed his chest. She'd misjudged the distance. Her breath caught in her throat and nearly choked her.

Zack didn't seem affected at all. He just smiled at her, one of his wicked smiles, all of the ghosts she'd glimpsed in his gray eyes before she'd gone to sleep were banished now, leaving behind nothing but the glint that was so familiar to her.

"I didn't have—" she had to take in another breath because being so close to him had kind of sucked the other one out of her "—that much time to pack. Otherwise I could have had just as many bags as your high-maintenance ladies."

"You aren't like the women I date. You aren't high maintenance. I like that about you." He turned and headed out the bedroom and she followed him, her chest suddenly feeling tight.

What he meant was, she wasn't beautiful. Not like the women he dated. The women who were all high-fashion planes and angles. And cheekbones.

Her mother was like that. Her sister, too. Tall and leggy with hip bones that were more prominent than their breasts. And that was the look that walked runways. The look that was fashionable, especially in southern California.

And she just didn't have the look. She had curves. An abundance of them. If any of the chi-chi boutiques had bras with her cup size, they were very often too small around, meant for women who'd gone under the knife to give them what nature had bestowed upon her so liberally. And her stomach was a little bit round, not concave or rippling. She wasn't sure if she'd ever seen her ribs.

Standing next to the women in her family just made her feel…inadequate. And wide. And short. She'd tried to subsist on cabbage and water like her mother and sister, but frankly, she'd felt like garbage and had decided a long time ago that feeling healthy beat being fifteen pounds lighter.

Of course, that decision didn't erase a lifetime of insecurity. And that insecurity wasn't all down to weight, either.

"Great. Glad to be so...easy."

The door to the plane was standing open, and a staircase had been lowered to the tarmac. Zack stood and waited for her to go in front of him. She passed him without looking, trying not to show the knockout effect the slight scent of his cologne had on her as she moved by him.

"I wouldn't call you easy," he said.

She stopped, third stair from the top, and whipped around to look at him. "That's not what I meant."

"Not what I meant, either," he said, his expression overly innocent.

"Yeah. Right. Are you determined to drive me absolutely insane for this whole trip?" She continued down the steps and hopped onto the tarmac, the night air balmy and thick with mist, blowing across her cheeks and leaving its moist handprint behind.

"We are supposed to be a couple."

"Fair enough."

She was reluctant to get into the glossy black town car that was parked right by the plane. Because she'd only just gotten Zack-free air, and she didn't really relish the thought of getting right back into a tight, enclosed space with him.

She needed to be able to breathe. To think. And she couldn't do it when he was around.

That realization alone reinforced her crazy, spur-of-the-moment decision to move on with her life, and away from Roasted.

The idea made her slightly sick and more than a little bit sad. Roasted had been her life since Zack had hired her on. The day-to-day of it, the constant push to invent more and more goodies, to push the flavor profiles, to push her creativity...there would never be anything else like it.

But she needed to stand on her own feet. To move on with life. She'd gone from her parents to Zack, and while she didn't feel familial about Zack in any way, he represented comfort and safety. And other stuff that wasn't comforting or safe. But being with him, like she was, wasn't pushing her to move forward.

So she was pushing herself. It was uncomfortable, but that was the way it worked. She hoped it would work.

He opened the door to the town car for her and she slid inside, and he came in just behind her. "So, do you and your boyfriends have fights?"

He must know she never had boyfriends. The odd disastrous date that never went past the front door. Emphasis on the odd, since half the men picked her up while she happened to be in the flagship store. And, in her experience, men who picked you up at ten in the morning in coffeehouses were a bit strange.

"How many long-term relationships have I had, Zack?"

"Well, Pete was around a lot until he moved for work."

"Pete? He was a friend from high school. And I was not his type, if you catch my drift."

"You weren't blonde?"

"Or male."

"Oh."

"Point being, I haven't done a lot of long-term." Any, but whatever. "And if I'm ever going to...move on, go into that phase of life then I need to be less consumed with work."

A muscled in his jaw ticked. "But you won't make this kind of money running your own bakery."

"I know. But I have a decent amount of money. How much do I need? How much do you need?"

There was a pause. Zack's hand curled into a fist on the leather seat, then relaxed. "More. Just...a bit more."

"And then you're never done."

"But if not for that then what am I working for?"

She swallowed. "A good question. Good and scary. Though I suppose adding a wife will add...something. When you find a new prospect, that is. Did Hannah have an equally efficient and driven sister, by chance?"

"Not that I'm aware of."

She snapped her fingers. "Darn."

"Don't lose sleep over it."

"I won't be sleeping tonight, anyway. Because you didn't wake me up on the plane." She couldn't resist the jab.

"Because you sleep like a rock and snore like a walrus."

"Might be why my relationships aren't long-term," she said drily. Not that any man had ever heard her snore but she was so not admitting to that.

"I doubt that."

"Do you?"

His eyes locked with hers and something changed in the air. It seemed to crackle. Like a spark on dry leaves. It was strange. It was breathtaking, and electrifying, and she never wanted it to end.

"Why?" she asked, pressing. Desperate to hear more. A little bit afraid of hearing more, too.

"Because a little bit of snoring wouldn't deter a man who'd had the pleasure of sharing your bed."

She sucked in a sharp breath and looked out the window, and into the inky-black jungle. She felt dizzy. She felt...hot.

"Well, thanks," she said.

He chuckled, low and rich like the best chocolate ganache. Just as bad for her to indulge in as the naughty treat, too. "You seem uncomfortable with the compliment."

"You and I don't talk about things like that."

"Only because it hadn't come up."

"Do you snore?" she asked.

"Not that I'm aware of."

"Then your lack of long-term relationships doesn't really make sense at all."

He arched one dark brow. "Was that a compliment?"

"More a commentary on the transient nature of your love life."

"I'm wounded."

She winced. "Well, maybe in light of all that happened today it wasn't the best thing to say."

"You've never pulled punches before, don't start now."

"I don't know any other way to be."

"Now that may account for your own short-term relationships."

She whipped around to face him and her heart stalled. He was looking at her like she was a particularly interesting treat. One he might like to taste.

The car stopped and she nearly breathed a prayer of thanks out loud. She needed distance. She needed it desperately.

"Well," Zack said, opening the door. "Time to go and have a look at our honeymoon suite."

CHAPTER FOUR

THE HONEYMOON VILLA was the epitome of romance. The ante-rior wall of the courtyard was surrounded by dense, green trees, clinging vines and flowers covering most of the stone wall, adding color, a sense that nature ruled here, not man. There was a keypad on the gate and Zack entered a code in; a reminder that the man very much had his fingerprints all over the property.

"Nice," she said, as the gates swung open and revealed an open courtyard area. The villa itself was white and clean. Intricate spires, carved from wood and capped in gold, adorned the roof of the house, rising up to meet the thick canopy of teak trees.

"Mr. Amudee had planned on giving Hannah and I a few days of wedded bliss prior to meeting with me, so he made sure I had the code, and that everything in the home would be stocked and ready."

Clara tried not to think about Zack and Hannah, using the love nest for its intended purpose. More than that, she tried not to think of her and Zack using it for its intended purpose.

She really did try. There was no point in allowing those fantasies. Those fantasies had led to nothing more than dateless Friday nights and lack of sleep.

"Well, that was…thoughtful of him."

"It was. I believe he has some activities planned for us, too."

Oh, great. She was going to be trapped in happy-couple-honeymoon-activity hell.

She followed Zack through the vast courtyard and to the wide, ornately carved double doors at the front of the villa. She touched one of the flower blossoms etched into the hard surface. "These are gorgeous. I wonder if I could mimic the design with frosting."

"I will happily be a part of that experiment." He pushed open the doors and stood, waiting for her to go in before him.

"You do seem to hang around a lot more when I'm practicing my baking skills."

"I don't know how."

"I could teach you," she said. "Maybe sometimes after I can teach you how to use a food processor."

"I think I'll pass. Anyway, I'm a bachelor. Have pity on me. I wasn't supposed to be a bachelor after today, but I am, and now I still need my best friend to cook for me."

"And probably do your laundry."

"I wouldn't mind."

Basically he wanted her to be his wife with none of the perks. She nearly said so, but that would sound too much like she wanted the perks, and even if a part of her did, she'd rather parade naked through the Castro District than confess it.

"I'm not doing your laundry."

Zack closed the door behind them and a shock of awareness hit her, low and strong in her stomach. She felt so very alone with Zack all of a sudden that she could hardly breathe. And it wasn't as though she'd never been alone with him. She had been. Hundreds of times. Late nights in the office, at her apartment cooking, at his luxury penthouse watching a movie.

But this wasn't San Francisco. It wasn't their offices; it wasn't one of their apartments. It felt like another world entirely and that was…dangerous.

She looked up at the tall, peaked ceilings, at the intricately carved vines and flowers that cascaded from wooden rafters. Swaths of fabric were the only dividers between rooms, gauzy and sexy, providing the illusion of privacy without actually giving any at all.

And in the middle of it all was Zack. He filled the space, not just with his breadth and height, but with his presence. With the unique scent that was so utterly Zack mingling with the heavy perfume of plumeria. Familiar and exotic all at once.

This was like one of her late-night fantasies. Like a scene she'd only ever allowed herself to indulge in when she was shrouded in the darkness of her room. And now, those fantasies were coming back to bite her.

Because they were mingling with reality. This was real. And in reality, Zack didn't want her like she wanted him. But in her fantasies he did. There, he touched her like a lover, his eyes locked with hers, his lips...

She needed her head checked.

"I have a housekeeper, anyway. I was teasing," he said.

"I know." She hoped she didn't look as flushed as she felt.

"I don't think you did. I think you were about to bite my head off." He looked...amused. Damn him.

"Is there food?"

His lips curved into a half smile. "I can check."

He wandered out of the main living area, in search of the kitchen, she imagined, and she took the opportunity to breathe in air that didn't smell of Zack. Air that didn't make her stomach twist.

She walked the opposite direction of Zack, through one of the fabric-covered doorways and stopped. It was the bedroom. The bed was up on a raised platform, a duvet in deep red spread over it. Cream colored fabric with delicate gold vines woven throughout hung from the ceiling, shielding the bed. It was obvious that it wasn't a bed made for one, or for sleeping.

She swallowed heavily, her eyes glued to the center of the room.

She heard footsteps behind her and turned. "I found food."

"Good," she said, trying to ignore the fast-paced beating of her heart. Zack and the bed in one room was enough to make her feel like her head might explode. "There is... I mean, this isn't the only bedroom is it?"

"I'm not sure."

"Oh," she said.

"I set dinner out on the balcony, if you want to join me."

"Don't you want to go to bed?" she asked, then immediately regretted the way the words had come out. Heat flooded her face, and she was certain there was a very blatant blush staining her cheeks. "I mean...well, you know what I mean. That wasn't... I meant you. By yourself. Because I slept and I know you didn't."

"At least let me buy you dinner first, Clara," he said, his mouth curved in amusement, his eyes glittering with the same heat she'd noticed earlier. It made her uncomfortable. And jittery. And a little bit excited.

She laughed, a kind of nervous, fake sound. "Of course."

Zack ignored the jolt of arousal that shot through his veins. For a moment at least, he and Clara had both been thinking the same thing. And it had involved that bed. That bed that was far too tempting, even for a man who prided himself on having absolute control at all times.

Things with Clara had always been easy. No, he'd never been blind to her beauty, but their relationship had never been marked by moments of heavy sexual tension. Not until today.

And knowing that, even for a moment, she'd shared in the temptation, well, that made it all worse. Or better. No, definitely worse, because in his life, he valued boundaries. Everything and everyone had a place and a purpose. Clara had a place. It was not in his bed.

Or this bed.

It was important that his life stay focused like that. Controlled. That nothing crossed over. He'd been rigid in that, uncompromising, for the past fourteen years.

"This way, beautiful," he said, clenching his hand into a fist to keep from putting it on Clara's lower back. He would have done it before. But suddenly it seemed like far too risky of a maneuver.

Clara shot him a look that was pure Clara, his friend, and it made the knot in his chest ease slightly. Though it didn't do much for the heat coursing through his veins.

He was questioning why he'd thought bringing her was a good idea. And he never questioned his decisions. Not anymore. Because he thought everything through before he acted. Not thinking, letting anything go before reason, was a recipe for disaster.

And bringing Clara had been the logical choice. At least until thirty seconds ago.

He moved in front of her, under the guise of leading her to the deck, but really just so he wouldn't let himself look at her butt while she walked. Occasionally he allowed himself the indulgence of looking at her curves. Harmless enough. He was human, a man, and she was a beautiful woman. But it seemed less harmless after a moment like that.

"This is really nice," she said when they were outside.

Her words were true, banal and safe. He'd set the table and turned on the string of lanterns that were hung above the table. A moderate effort, but he had wanted it to be nice. Now it felt strangely intimate.

He couldn't remember the last time a dinner date had seemed intimate. He couldn't even remember the last time that word had seemed applicable to something in his life. Very often, sex didn't even seem all that intimate to him.

Of course, it had been so long since he'd had sex maybe that wasn't true. That was likely half of his problem now.

Clara wandered to the railing and leaned over the edge, tossing her glossy copper curls over her shoulder and sniffing the air. Or maybe the sex wasn't the problem. Because being alone with Hannah hadn't made him feel this way. And there were days when the scent of Clara's perfume hitting him when she walked past made his stomach tighten…

But he ignored that. He was good at ignoring it.

"What are you doing?"

"It smells amazing out here. Like when you bake bread and the air is heavy with it. Only it's flowers instead of flour." She turned to him and smiled, the familiar glitter back in her eyes.

The knot inside him eased even more.

"I would never have thought of it that way." He pulled her chair out and nodded toward it and she walked over to the table and took her seat.

He sat across from her, ladling reheated *Tom Yum Ka* into her bowl and then into his. She smiled at him, the slight dimple in her rounded cheeks deepening as she did.

Things seemed to have stabilized, even if her sweet grin did have an impact on his stomach.

"So, tell me more about this deal with Mr. Amudee."

He put his forearm on the table and leaned forward. "I think we covered most of it. Although, another reason it's nice to have you here is your palate. I'd like you to taste the different roasts and come up with pairings for them. It would be particularly nice to have in our boutique locations."

"Pairings!" Her eyes glittered. "I love it."

"Good coffee or tea really is just as complex as good wine. There are just as many flavor variations."

"I know, Zack," she said.

"Of course you do. You appreciate good coffee. It's one reason we get along so well."

Clara took another bite of her soup and let the ginger sit on her tongue, enjoying the zip of spice that hurt just enough to take her mind off the weird reaction she was having to Zack. Yes, being attracted to him was nothing new.

But this was different. The attraction she felt at home was

like a sleeper agent. It attacked her when she least expected it. In dreams. When she was looking at other men and contemplating accepting a date. It wasn't usually this shaky, limb-weakening thing that made her feel tongue-tied and exposed in his presence. Maybe it was the feeling of utter seclusion. Or maybe it was because she knew just what that big bed was here for, what he'd been planning on doing with it.

"That and I bake you cupcakes," she said, swallowing the tart and spicy soup.

"There is that." Zack looked toward the railing of the deck, off into trees, the look in his eyes distant, cold suddenly. "Tell me about your bakery."

"The one I hope to have?"

"Yes. And the life you're going to put with it."

Her chest constricted. "It will be small. I'll have regular menu items and daily specials. I'll have more time to make fancy little treats with a lot of decorations. I'll have a hand in everything instead of just conceptualizing and farming the instructions out to hordes of employees."

"And that's important to you?"

"It's how we started. Me in the flagship store, you going back and forth between your— What did you have when I met you? Fifteen stores up and down the West Coast? It was fun."

"Yes, but now we have money."

She nodded. "We do. And it's great. You've done this incredible thing, Zack. The growth has been...amazing. Way beyond what I imagined."

"Not beyond what I imagined."

"No?"

He shook his head. "It was always the plan. Planning is key. It's when you don't plan, when you drift, that's when things are a surprise. Good or bad."

"You didn't plan for Hannah to opt out of the wedding."

"I didn't plan for you to leave Roasted, either. Sometimes

other people come in and mess with your plans," he said, his dark eyebrows locked together.

"This doesn't mean I won't see you anymore," she said. Though she probably shouldn't. But the thought of that made her chest feel like there was a hole in it. Still, she'd baked the man's wedding cake. She was such a pushover, such a hopeless case, it was obscene. It had to end.

She didn't want it to. But if she didn't see him at work every day…it would be a start.

"I know you'll still see me," he said, his mouth curving. "You'd have withdrawals otherwise."

If only that weren't true. "Right. Can't live without you, Zack." She felt her throat get tight. *Stupid.* So stupid. But Zack really did mean the world to her, and she had a very strong suspicion that her statement was nothing but the truth. He had offered her support when no one else in her life had. He still did.

She regretted saying she wanted to leave Roasted. Regretted it with everything in her. But she couldn't change her mind. The reasoning behind the decision was still sound. And she really would still see him. He just wouldn't fill up her whole world anymore. She couldn't let feelings for him, feelings that would never be returned, hold her back for the rest of her life.

Zack's arm twitched and he reached into his pocket. "Phone vibrated," he said. He pulled out his smart phone and unlocked the screen, a strange expression on his face. "Hannah texted me."

"Really?"

"She's really sorry about the wedding."

"Oh, good," Clara snorted. The weird jealousy and protectiveness were back together again. She was still righteously angry at Hannah for what she'd done, even while she was relieved.

"She met someone else."

"What?"

"Yes." He looked up, his expression neutral. "She's in love apparently."

"And she's texting this to you?"

He shrugged. "It fits our relationship."

"No, it doesn't. Love or not, you still had a relationship."

"We weren't sleeping together."

Clara felt her stomach free fall down into her toes. "What?" That didn't even make sense. Hannah was a goddess. A sex bomb that had been detonated in the middle of her life, making her feel inadequate and inexperienced.

And he hadn't slept with her? She'd assumed—imagined even, in sadly graphic detail—that half of the meetings in his office had been rousing desk-sex sessions. And...they hadn't been? So much angst. So much stomach curling angst exerted over...nothing, it turned out.

"Why?" she asked, her voice several notches higher than usual.

"Hannah's kind of traditional. Because we weren't in love... well, she needed love or marriage. We were going to have marriage."

"Hmm. Well, then maybe texting is appropriate. I don't understand how you were going to marry this woman."

"Marriage is a business agreement, like anything else, Clara. You decide if you can fulfill the obligations and if they'll be advantageous to you. Then you sign or you don't."

"Cynical."

"True."

"Then why bother to get married? I don't understand."

He shrugged. "Because it's the thing to do. Marriage offers stability, companionship. It's logical."

"Good grief, Spock. Logical. That's not why people get married." She snorted again. "Did your parents have a horrible divorce or something?"

Zack shook his head. "No."

"You never talk about your family."

He looked down at his soup. "Not on accident."

"Well, I figured. That's why I never ask."

"This isn't never asking."

She looked at him, at the side of his head. He wouldn't look at her. "We've known each other for seven years, Zack."

"And I'm sure I don't know everything about you, either. But I know what counts. I know that you lick the mixer. Even if it's got batter with raw eggs on it."

She laughed. "Tell anyone that and I'll ruin you."

"I have no doubt. I also know that you like stupid comedies."

"And I know that you put on football games and never end up watching them. You're just in it for the snacks."

He smiled, his gray eyes meeting hers. "See? You know the real truth."

Except there was something in the way he said it, a strange undertone, that told her she didn't. She wasn't sure how she'd missed it before. But she had. Now it seemed blatant, obvious. Zack had a way of presenting such a calm, easy front. In business, she knew it was to disarm, that no matter how easygoing he appeared, he was the man in charge. No question.

Now she wondered how much of the easy act in his personal life was just that. An act.

His eyes lingered on her face for a moment, and she suddenly became acutely conscious of her lips. And how dry they were. She stuck out the tip of her tongue and moistened them, the action taking an undertone she hadn't intended when she'd begun.

This week was going to kill her. Eventually the tension would get too heavy and she would be crushed beneath the weight of it. There was no possible way she could endure any more.

"I'm really tired," she said, the lie so blatant and obvious it was embarrassing.

To Zack's credit, he didn't call her on it. "The inner sanctum is all yours. I'll make do with the couch."

She wasn't going to feel bad about that for a second. "All right, I'll see you in the morning."

Maybe by morning some of the surrealism of the whole day would have worn off. Maybe by morning she wouldn't feel choked by the attraction she felt to Zack.

Maybe, but not likely.

CHAPTER FIVE

"MR. AMUDEE HAS extended an invitation for you and me to have a private tour of the forest land."

Zack strode into the kitchen area and Clara sucked coffee down into her lungs. He was wearing jeans, only jeans, low on his lean hips, his chest bare and muscular and far too tempting. She could lean right in and...

"Coffee for me?" he asked.

"Oh, yes. Sure." She picked up the carafe and poured some coffee into a bright blue mug. "It's the shade-grown Chiang Mai Morning Blend. Really good. Strong but bright, a bit of citrus."

"I love it when you talk coffee to me," he said, lifting the mug to his lips, a wicked grin curving his mouth.

There was something borderline domestic about the scene. Although, nothing truly domestic could have such a dangerous, arousing edge to it, she was certain. And Zack, shirtless, had all of those things.

"All right, tell me about the tour," she said, looking very hard into her coffee mug.

"Very romantic. For the newly engaged."

Her stomach tightened. "Great."

"I hope you brought a swimsuit."

Oh, good. Zack in a swimsuit. With her in a swimsuit. That

was going to help things get back on comfortable footing. She looked at Zack, at the easy expression on his handsome face. The ridiculous thing was, the footing was perfectly comfortable for him. Her little hell of sexual frustration was one hundred percent private. All her own. Zack wasn't remotely ruffled.

Typical.

"Yes, I brought a swimsuit."

"Good. I'll meet you back here in twenty minutes."

"Right." Unfortunately it would take longer than twenty minutes to plot an escape. So that meant Zack and swimsuits.

She tried to ignore the small, eternally optimistic part of her that whispered it might be a good thing.

Clara tugged at her brilliant pink sarong and made sure the knot was secure at her breasts before stepping out into the courtyard, where Zack was standing already.

"Ready. What's the deal? Give."

"You have to wait and see," he said, moving behind her, placing his hand low on her back as he led her to the gate and out onto a narrow path that wound through a thick canopy of trees and opened on an expansive green lawn.

"Are you kidding me?" she asked, stopping, her eyes widening.

There were two elephants in the field, one equipped with a harness that had small, cushioned seats on top. He was large enough he looked like he could comfortably seat at least four.

"Elephant rides are a big tourist draw in Chiang Mai," Zack said, the corner of his mouth lifting. "And I've never done it before, so I thought I would take advantage of the offer."

"First time for you?" she asked. She'd intended it as a joke, but it hit a bit to close to that sexual undercurrent they'd been dealing with since they left San Francisco.

A slow smile spread across his face. "Just for the elephant ride."

"Right. Got it." She was sure she was turning pink.

"You?"

She just about choked. "The elephant?"

"What else would I have been asking about?"

Her virginity. Except, no he wouldn't have been asking about that. It wasn't like she had a neon sign on her forehead that blinked red and said Virgin on it. Unless she did. Maybe he could tell.

She really hoped he couldn't tell.

"Yes, first time on an elephant," she said drily, aiming for cool humor. She wasn't sure she made her mark, but it was a valiant effort.

"Mr. Parsons." There was a man in white linen pants and a loose white shirt approaching them, his hand raised in greeting. "Ms. Davis, I believe," he said, stopping in front of her, his dark eyes glittering with warmth.

"Yes," Clara said, extending her hand. He bent his head and dropped a kiss on it, smiling, the skin around his eyes wrinkling with the motion.

"Isra Amudee. Pleasure." He straightened and shook Zack's hand. "Very glad you could make it. Especially after what happened."

Zack put his arm around Clara's waist and Clara tried to ignore the jolt of heat that raced through her. "Really, it didn't take me long to discover it wasn't a problem. Clara...well, I've known her for a long time. I don't really know how I missed what was right in front of me."

Mr. Amudee's smile widened. "A new wedding in your future, then?"

Zack stiffened. "Naturally. Actually I've already asked."

"And she's accepted?" Amudee looked at her and Clara felt her stomach bottom out.

Zack tightened his hold on her. "Yes," she said, her throat sandpaper dry. "Of course."

"And you, I bet, will have the good sense to show up. Now,

I'll leave you to the elephants. I have to go and take a walk around the grounds. But I'll see you later on."

Clara watched Amudee walk away and tried to ignore the buzzing in her head as the man who was with the elephants introduced himself in English as Joe. He explained how the ride would work, that the elephant knew the route through the forrest and up to a waterfall, and she wouldn't deviate from that.

"They're trained. Very well. Safe. You'll be riding Anong." Joe indicated the elephant who was harnessed up. "And I'll follow on Mali. Just as a precaution."

He tapped Anong on her back leg and she bent low, making it easy for them to climb up onto the seat. Zack went first, then leaned forward and extended his hand, helping her up onto the bench.

"Seat belts," he said, raising one eyebrow as he fastened the long leather strap over both of their laps.

"Comforting," she said, a tingle of nerves and excitement running through her.

"Ready?" their guide called to them.

"I have no idea," she whispered to Zack.

"Ready," Zack said.

The elephant rose up, the sharp pitch forward and to the left a shock. She lurched to the side and took hold of Zack's arm while Anong finished getting to her feet, each movement throwing them in a different direction.

"I think I'm good now," she whispered, her fingers still wrapped, clawlike around Zack's arm.

"Just relax, he said this is a path she takes all the time. New for us, but not new for her."

She didn't actually want to know the answer to the question, but she asked it anyway. "Accustomed to calming the nerves of the inexperienced?"

"No. I don't mess around with women who need comforting in the bedroom. That's not what I'm there for."

She felt a heavy blush spread over her cheeks. "I guess not."

She was alternately relieved and disappointed by that bit of news. Relieved, because she didn't really like to think of her friend as some crass seducer of innocents, and she really couldn't picture him in that role, anyway.

If he was the big bad wolf, it would be because the woman he was with wanted to play Little Red Riding Hood.

But it was disappointing, too, because that pushed her even farther outside the box that Zack's "ideal woman" resided in.

Ideal bedmate.

Sure, maybe it was more that than any sort of romantic ideal, but she would like to just fit the requirements for that. Well, really, being the woman he was sleeping with was very far away from what she actually wanted, but it would be a start.

A wonderful, sexual, amazing start...

She jerked her thoughts back to the present, not hard to do with the pitch-and-roll gait of the elephant rivaling a storm-tossed boat. It was a smooth, fluid sort of motion, but it was a very big motion, to match the size of the animal.

It also wasn't hard to do when she remembered that, as far as their host was concerned, she and Zack were now engaged.

"A tangled web, isn't it, Parsons?" she asked.

"What was I supposed to say?" he countered. "Ah, no, this is just my best friend that I brought along for a roll in the hay."

"The truth might have worked. He seems like a nice man."

"Look, it's done. I'm sure his assumption works even more in my favor, in favor of the deal, and that's all that really matters, right? We know where we stand. It's not like it changes anything between us."

She felt like the air had been knocked out of her. "No. Of course not."

They moved through the meadow and down into the trees, onto a well-worn path that took them along a slow-moving river, the banks covered in greenery, bright pink flowers glowing from the dark, lush foliage.

She tried to keep her focus on the view, but her mind kept

wandering back to Zack, to his solid, steady heat, so close to her. It would be easy to just melt into him, to stop fighting so hard for a moment and give in to the need to touch him.

But she wouldn't. She couldn't. Nothing had changed between them, after all. His words.

There was a reason she'd never made any sort of attempt to change their relationship from friends to more-than-friends. The biggest one being that she didn't want to jeopardize the most stable relationship she had, the one closest to it being unable to stomach the thought of being rejected by him.

Of having him confirm that everything her mother said about her was true. Of having her know, for certain, that a man really wouldn't want her because she just wasn't all that pretty. Her mother had made sure she'd known men would still sleep with her, because of course, men would sleep with anyone. But she wasn't the sort of woman a man would want for a wife. Not the type of woman a man could be proud to take to events.

Not like her sister. Gorgeous, perfect Lucy who was, in all unfairness, smart and actually quite sweet along with being slender, blonde and generally elegant.

Lucy actually would have looked more like Hannah's sister than like *her* sister.

A sobering thought, indeed.

She should make sure Zack never met her sister.

The sound of running water grew louder and they rounded a curve in the path and came into a clearing that curved around a still, jade pool. At least twenty fine steams were trickling down moss-covered rocks, meeting at the center and falling into the pool as one heavy rush of water.

Anong the elephant stopped at the edge of the pool, dropping slowly down to her knees, the ground rising up a bit faster than Clara would have like. She leaned into Zack, clinging to the sleeve of his T-shirt as Anong settled.

"All right?" he asked.

She looked at where her hand was, and slowly uncurled her fingers, releasing her hold on him. "Sorry," she said.

He smiled, that simple expression enough to melt her insides. He was so sexy. Time and exposure, familiarity, didn't change it. Didn't lessen it.

Just another reason for her to leave Roasted. If exposure didn't do it, distance might.

Zack moved away from her, dismounting their ride first and waited for her at the side of their living chariot, his hand outstretched. She leaned forward and took it, letting his muscles propel her gently to the ground. Her feet hit just in front of his, her breasts close to touching his chest, the heat from him enticing her, taunting her.

"Do you want me to wait for you?" their guide asked.

Zack shook his head. "We'll walk back. Thank you for the ride. It was an experience."

He nodded and whistled a signal to Anong, who rose slowly and turned, going back with her owner and friend. She watched them round the corner, a smile on her lips. Yesterday, she was at a beachside hotel in San Francisco, expecting to lose half of her heart as Zack married another woman.

Today she was with him on his honeymoon. Riding elephants.

"An experience," Zack said, turning to face the water.

"It was fun," she said.

"Not relaxing exactly."

"No," she said, laughing. "Not in the least."

"Mr. Amudee informed me by phone this morning that this is a safe place to swim. Clean. They don't let the elephants up here and the waterfall keeps it all moving."

She made a face. "Good to know. I liked the elephants, don't really want to share a swimming hole with them. It looks pristine," she said, moving to the edge, looking down into the clear pool. She could see rocks covered in moss along the bottom, small fish darting around, only leaving the cover of their hiding places for a few moments before swimming behind something else. "Perfect."

Zack tugged his black shirt over his head, leaving him in nothing more than a pair of very low-cut white board shorts that, when wet, she had no doubt would cling to some very interesting places.

Her mind was a filthy place lately. And the sad thing was, it was hard to regret. Because it was so enjoyable.

"Swimming?"

"No." She shook her head and gripped her sarong.

"Why?"

"It looks cold."

He put his hands on his lean hips and sighed, the motion making his ab muscles ripple in a very enticing fashion. "It's so hot and muggy out here it could be snowmelt and it would feel good. And I guarantee you it's not snowmelt."

"It just looks…cold." Lame. So lame. But she didn't really want to strip down to her swimsuit in front of him, not when he looked so amazing in his. She was… There was too much of her for a start. She was so very conscious of that. Of the fact that she had hips and breasts, and that she could pinch fat on her stomach.

Zack's girlfriends had hip bones and abs that were just as cut as his.

"Ridiculous." He walked over to her and scooped her up in his arms, her heart climbing up into her throat as he did. His arms were tight and strong around her, masculine. Lifting her seemed effortless. His large hands cupped her thigh and her shoulder, his heat spreading through her like warm, sticky honey, thick and sweet.

She realized what was happening a little bit too late, because sexual attraction had short-circuited her brain. She put her hand flat on his chest, another bolt of awareness shocking her even as Zack took two big steps off the bank and down into the water.

The hot and cold burst through her, her body still warm from his touch on the inside, the water freezing her skin.

"Zack!"

He looked down at her, smiling. She sputtered and clung to his shoulders, his arms still wrapped tightly around her. His skin was slick now, so sexy, and it took everything in her arsenal of willpower to keep from sliding her palms down from their perch on his shoulders and flattening them against his amazing, perfect pecs.

She wanted to. She wanted to press her lips to the hollow of his throat, lick the water drops that were clinging to his neck.

She wiggled against him and managed to extricate herself from his grasp. Fleeing temptation.

She walked up to the shallow part of the pool, her pink sarong limp and heavy now, clinging to her curves like a second skin. She untied it and looped it over a tree branch. There was no point in it now.

She felt exposed in her black one-piece. It was pretty modest by some suit standards, but anything that tight tended to make her feel a bit exposed.

"Well, that's one way to get me in the water. Brute force," she sniffed, walking back to the water and sinking into the depths quickly, desperate for the covering it would provide.

"Brute?" Zack swam to where she was, treading water, his eyes glinting with amusement.

"Uh...yeah. You took advantage of me."

He paddled closer, his face a whisper from hers. "I didn't take advantage of you. If I had, you'd have known it, that's for sure."

Strangely, with her body half submerged in water, her throat suddenly felt bone-dry. "I feel um...taken advantage... You... picked me up and threw me in and I'm...wet."

His expression changed, his eyes darkening. "Interesting."

"Oh, *pffft*." She dunked her head, letting the cold water envelop her, pull the stinging heat from her cheeks. She paddled toward the waterfall, away from Zack. Away from certain mortification and temptation.

She surfaced again and looked back at Zack, still treading water where she'd left him.

Nice, Clara. Next time just tell him straight up that you're hot for him and would like to jump him, if that's all right with him.

She pulled a face for her own benefit and climbed up one of the mossy rocks that sat beneath the slow flowing falls, water trickling down, mist hovering above the surface of the cool, plant-covered stones.

She pulled her knees to her chest and looked up, squinting at the sunlight pouring through the thick canopy of trees.

"You're like a jungle fairy."

She looked down into the water and saw Zack, his hair wet and glistening.

"You're startling me," she said. More with his statement than with his presence, but she didn't intend to elaborate.

He planted his palms flat on the rocks and hoisted himself up, the muscles in his shoulders rolling and shifting with the motion. He sat next to her, the heat from his body a welcome respite from the cold. But that was about all it was a respite from. Because mostly he just made her feel edgy.

And happy. He made her so happy that it hurt. Just being with him made everything seem right. Like a missing part of herself was finally in place. Like some of her insecurities and inadequacies didn't matter so much.

And that was just stupid. Not to mention scary. Because it was an illusion. He would never be with her in the way she wanted, and watching him marry another woman, give someone else everything she longed for, *that* would turn her happiness into the bitterest pain.

The kind she wasn't sure she could withstand.

"You're beautiful," he said.

She turned sharply to look at him, her heart in her throat. "What?"

"Just stating a fact."

"It's not one you typically state. About me, I mean."

He put his hand out and brushed a water drop from her cheek with his thumb, the motion sending an electric shock through her body, heat pooling in her stomach and radiating from there to her limbs.

"Well, I thought it needed to be said."

It was so tantalizingly close to what she wanted. But to him it was simply an empty compliment, or maybe he even meant it. But not in the way she would. He didn't mean she was beautiful in the same way she found him beautiful. The way that made her body warm and her heart flutter.

"Thanks for that. You aren't so bad, either." She tried to sound casual. Light. Like a friend. Like she was supposed to sound.

He smiled and lifted his arm, curling his fist in, showing off his very, very impressive biceps.

"You're shameless," she said, somehow managing to laugh around her stubborn heart, still lodged firmly in her throat.

"Sorry."

"About as sorry as you are for dumping me in the water?"

"Yeah. About." He leaned in, his arm curving around her waist and everything slowed down for a moment. He tightened his hold on her, his face so close…

And then they were falling.

She shrieked just before they hit the water. And surfaced with a loud curse, unreasonable anger mingling with disappointment. "Zack! You jackass!"

She moved to him and planted her hands on his shoulders, attempting to dunk him beneath the water. He put his hands on her waist and held her still in front of him, her movements impotent against his strength.

"You can touch bottom here, can't you?" she asked, her feet hovering above the sandy floor of the pool while Zack seemed firmly rooted.

"Maybe."

His hands slipped down, resting on her hips, the heat from his touch cutting through the icy chill in the water. He kept one hand there, the other sliding around to her back, his fingers drifting upward, skimming the line of her spine.

She shivered, but she wasn't cold. And he didn't let go.

His eyes were locked with hers, the head there matching the heat he was spreading over her skin. Her hands were still on his shoulders. And since he'd just moved his hands, it seemed… somehow it seemed right to move hers.

Her heart thundered in her chest as she slid her hands down, palms skimming his chest hair, the firm muscles beneath, as she rested them against his chest. She could hardly breathe. Her chest, her stomach, every last muscle, was too tightly wound.

His fingers flexed, the blunt tips digging into her flesh. His hands were rough, strong, everything she'd ever imagined and so much more.

Zack loosened his hold, a muscle in his jaw jerking. She pulled away from him, the water freezing where his hands had been.

"We should go," Zack said, his words abrupt.

"I… We haven't been here very long." She felt muddled, as though the mist from the waterfall had wrapped itself around her, making everything seem fuzzy.

And she was glad. Because she had a feeling that when the reality of what had just happened, of how stupid she'd been, hit, it was going to hit hard.

"Yes, but I have some things to take care of before tonight. We have dinner reservations at the restaurant down in the main part of the resort."

He reversed direction and swam to shore, walking out of the pool, his muscular legs fighting against the water pressure, his swim trunks conforming to his body. A hard pang hit her in the stomach when she looked and saw the outline of his erection. Had she really gotten him hot? Was that about her?

He turned away from her and pulled his shirt on.

And was the arousal why they were leaving now?

So he felt something. Even if he was running from it. Something that was at least physical.

Her hart hammered, echoing in her head, making her temples pulse.

Maybe she did matter to him, like that, at least a little bit? Maybe... Yes, she knew men were excited by women but this had to be personal. It had to be about her, at least a little bit. Did he think she was sexy?

She followed him to shore, scrambling onto the sandy ground, her feet picking up grains of dirt, clinging to her toes. She shook her foot out, grateful to have something else to concentrate on for a moment.

She looked back up and saw Zack, his eyes on her, his jaw locked tight.

She swallowed hard and grabbed her sarong. "So we're having dinner out tonight?"

"Yes," he bit out. "I have to go and pick up a package down in town and then I'll meet you back up at the villa. The car will be by around seven."

"Okay." She wished she could come up with something better than the bland, one-word answer, but she just couldn't.

Something had changed. The air around them seemed tight, the way Zack looked at her new and strange. And for the first time, she felt power in her beauty, in her body.

And she wondered if maybe he could want her. If she could be the sort of woman he wanted.

Maybe tonight she would actually try.

It was criminal. The dress that Clara was wearing should be illegal. She certainly shouldn't be allowed out in public. It was tight, like that black, second-skin swimsuit, accentuating curves that, until this afternoon, he hadn't realized were quite so...lush.

Breasts that were round and perfect, firm looking. They

would overflow in his hands. And her hips were incredible, nothing like the androgynous, straight up-and-down supermodels that were so in style. Not even like Hannah, whose image he was having trouble conjuring up.

Today, at the river, with her body pressed against his, wet and slick, soft and feminine, he'd had a reaction he really hadn't counted on. He hadn't counted on touching her like he had, either. Exploring the elegant line of her back. Holding her to him. It had been a big mistake.

Getting out of the water, in front of his best friend, sporting an erection inspired by her, hadn't really been his idea of a good time.

He put his hand in his pocket, let his fingers close around the velvet box that was nestled there. The one that Hannah had had rush delivered to the resort. Because it was the right thing to do, or so she'd said. He hadn't really cared whether he got the engagement ring back or not. But he could use it.

The thing with Amudee, his assumption, had been unexpected. But Zack was good at reading people and the older man's delight at the thought had been so obvious, there had been no way he would disappoint him. Not with so much riding on things going well this week.

His other plans had all gone to hell. He wasn't sending this one there with the rest of them.

"What exactly is that?" he asked. They were in the car, being driven up to the main area of the resort, and being closed in with her when she looked like that and smelled, well, she smelled sweet enough to taste, was a bit of torture.

"What?" she asked.

"What you're wearing."

Her cheeks colored. "A dress."

"But do you...call it something?"

"A dress," she said again, her voice low now, dangerous.

"It's a nice dress."

She looked straight ahead. "Thank you."

The car stopped in front of an open, wooden building that had all the lights on despite the late hour. There were people sitting at a bar, musicians set down in the center of the seating area, and dancers out on the grass, candles balanced on their hands as they moved in time with the music.

He opened his door and Clara just sat, her posture stiff. "What?"

"Now I'm not sure if I should go back and change."

"I don't even want to understand women," he said.

"Why?"

"You just changed into that dress, so clearly you thought it was a good choice, and now you want to change back?"

"Because there must be something wrong with what I'm wearing. Although, you didn't seem to have a problem with my bathing suit, and it showed a lot more than this." She put a hand on her stomach. "It's too tight."

His body hardened. "Trust me, it's not. Every man in the bar is going to give himself whiplash when you walk by."

She frowned. "Really?"

She looked...mystified. Doubtful.

"Did you not look at yourself in the mirror?" he asked, completely incredulous that she somehow didn't see what he did. That she didn't realize how appealing a dress that was basically a second skin was to a man. It showed every bit of her shape, while still concealing the details. Made him feel desperate to see everything, the tease nearly unbearable.

She looked away from him. "That's the trouble, I did, and I chose to wear it anyway."

"What makes you think it doesn't look good?"

"You reacted...funny."

"Because I'm not used to seeing so much of you. But what I can see is certainly good."

"Really?"

He took a lock of her silky hair between his thumb and forefinger. A mistake. It was so soft. Like he imagined the rest of her would be. "Didn't I tell you any man would put up with your snoring for the pleasure of having you sleep with him?"

His eyes dropped to her mouth and he felt an uncomfortable shock of sensation when, for the second time in the past hour, she stuck her pink tongue out and slicked it across her lips, leaving them looking glossy and oddly kissable.

Clara felt like there was someone sitting on her chest, keeping her from breathing. The knot of insecurity that had tied up her stomach was changing into something else, something dangerous. A strand of hope she had no business feeling. A kind of feminine pride that didn't make sense.

Zack was a charmer. He could charm the white gloves off a spinster, and what he was saying to her was no different. Empty charm that had no real weight behind it. It was easy to say that some other man would like to share her bed. It didn't mean he did. Or that anyone he even knew would.

All right, in reality, she knew how men were about sex. If she was willing to put out they wouldn't care if she had a pinch of extra flesh around her middle, but that wasn't really the issue. She didn't want to be a second choice. Second best.

She was even second-guessing the physical reaction Zack had had to her down at the river. Because that could simply be a man overdue for sex. Nothing more. She'd made it personal because she'd been desperate for it. But in reality, he was supposed to be here, with his wife, having lots and lots of sex, and he wasn't. But she doubted he'd forgotten.

She was tired of being in the shadow of someone else. Even tonight, she was the consolation prize for Zack. Rather than spending the night with Hannah, he was with her, watching traditional dancing instead of having hot, sweaty, wedding night sex. Ah, yes, all fine and good for him to say those things to her, but he wasn't really backing it up.

She forced a smile. "You did. All right, let's go...drink or something."

He chuckled. "Sounds like a good idea to me."

They both got out of the car and walked over to an alcove, shrouded in misty fabric, like everything in the whole resort property. It was designed for people to take advantage of the perceived privacy. It was an invitation to some sort of heady, fantastic sin. Traditional values her fanny.

She sat down on one of the cushions, positioned in front of a low table. Zack sat next to her, so close she could feel the heat radiating off his body.

"So what about my comment spawned the dress edition of twenty questions?" he asked.

"I don't usually wear things that are this tight, so you…your reaction made me think it looked… You've met my mother, right?" She changed tactics.

"Yes."

"She's like a model. And my sister…well, she takes after my mom. I take after my dad."

"Something wrong with that?"

"Well, I'm just not…not everything Lucy is. And my mother let me know that. Let me know that I was second best in nearly every way. She didn't just get beauty, she had a perfect grade-point average without even trying. I was just average. I liked school, but I didn't excel at it. The only thing I've ever excelled at is baking, which in my mother's estimation contributes to my weight issues."

Zack swore and Clara jumped. "Weight issues? You don't have weight issues."

"I did. More than I do now, I mean. It was a whole…thing in high school. Remember, I mentioned the time my date stood me up?"

He nodded and she continued on, hating to dredge up the memory. "Asking me was a joke in the first place, not that I had any idea, of course. And I was supposed to meet him by the stage in the gym, which is where the dance was, and he walked up with his real date, and the guys doing the lights knew to put a spotlight on me right then. And I was all chubby and wrapped up in this silly, tight pink dress that was just so…shiny. That stays with you. Sometimes, for no reason, I still feel like the girl under the spotlight, with everyone looking at all my flaws."

He swore sharply. "That's bull. That's…kids are stupid and that's high school." He swallowed. "It's not real life. None of us stay the same as we were back then." His words ended sounding rough, hard.

"Maybe not. Still, even though I've sort of…slimmed out as I've grown up, as far as my mom is concerned, since I'm not six feet tall and runway ready, I'm not perfect. I have her genes, too, after all," she said, echoing a sentiment she'd heard so many times. "And that means I could be much thinner if I *tried*."

"Let me tell you something about women's bodies, Clara, and I know you are a woman, but I'm still going to claim the greater expertise. Men like women's bodies, and there isn't only one kind to like, that's part of the fun. Beauty isn't just one thing."

She tried to ignore the warm, glowy feeling that was spreading through her. "I know that. I mean, part of me knows that. But it's hard to let go of the second-best thing."

"Better than feeling like you're above everyone else," he said slowly. "Like nothing can touch you because you're just so damn perfect life wouldn't dare."

"I don't know if Lucy feels that way, my mother might but…" She trailed off when she noticed the look on his face. There was something, just for a moment, etched there that was so cold, so utterly filled with despair that it reached inside her and twisted her heart.

"Zack…"

He shook his head. "Nothing, Clara. Just leave it." The dancers had cleared the area out on the lawn and there were couples moving out into the lit circles, holding each other close, looking at each other with a kind of longing that made Clara ache with jealousy. "Care to dance before dinner is served?"

Yes and no. She felt a bit too fragile to be so close to him, and yet a part of her wanted it more than she wanted air. Just like in the water today, she'd wanted to run and cling at the same time. She was never sure which desire would win out.

He offered his hand and she took it, his fingers curling around hers, warm and masculine. He helped her up from her seat and drew her to him, his expression still strange, foreign more than familiar. He looked leaner, more dangerous. Which was strange, because even though Zack was her friend, she always felt an edge of danger around him, a little bit of unrest. Probably because she was so attracted to him that just looking at him made her shiver with longing.

"Just a warning," he said, as they made their way out onto the grass. "People will probably stare. But that's because you look good, amazing even. And you certainly aren't second to any woman here."

"Flatterer."

"No, I'm not, and I think we both know that."

"Okay, I suppose that's true," she said, kicking her shoes off and enjoying the feeling of the grass under her feet. Although, losing the little lift her shoes provided put her eyes level with Zack's chest.

He pulled her to him, his hand on her waist. She fought the urge to melt into him, to rest her head on his chest. This wasn't that kind of dance; theirs wasn't that kind of relationship. That didn't mean she didn't want to pretend. It was easy, with the heat of his body so close to hers, to imagine that tonight might end differently. To imagine that he saw her as a woman.

Not just in the way that he'd referenced, that vague, sweet, but generic talk about women and their figures. But that he would desire her body specifically. She kept her eyes open, fixed on his throat. She knew him so well, that even looking there she knew just who she was with. And she didn't want to shut that reality out by closing her eyes. She wanted to watch, relish.

For a moment reality seemed suspended. There wasn't time, there wasn't a fiancée, one more suited to Zack than she was, looming in the background. There was only her and Zack, the heat of the night air, the strains from the stringed instruments weaving around them, creating a sensual, exotic rhythm that she wanted to embrace completely.

She loved him so much.

That hit her hard in the chest. The final, concrete acknowledgment of what she'd probably always known. A moment that was completely lacking in denial for once. She loved Zack. With her entire heart, with everything in her. And she was in his arms now.

But not in the way she wanted to be. She breathed in deeply, smelling flowers, rain and Zack. Her lungs burned, her stomach aching. She wished it was real. So much that it hurt, down to her bones.

Maybe, just for a moment, she could pretend that it was real. That this was romance. That he held her because he wanted her. Because after this, after the fake engagement, after the ink was dry on the contracts, there would be no more chances to pretend.

She would go her way, and she would leave Zack behind. Why couldn't she ignore it now? Just for now.

She didn't want the song to end, wished the notes would linger in the air forever, an excuse to stay in his arms. But it ended. And that was why she shouldn't have said yes to the dance in the first place. Playing games wouldn't come close to giving her what she wanted with Zack. It just made her aware of how far she was from having what she really wanted.

He took her hand and pulled her away from the other dancing couples, and for one heart-stopping moment, she thought he might lean in and kiss her. His lips were close to hers, his breath hot, fanning across her cheek. Her body felt too tight, her skin too hot. She needed something. Needed him.

"I have something for you," he said. "For tomorrow."

"I like presents," she said, trying to keep her voice from sounding too shaky. Too needy. Too honest. "It's not a food processor, is it?"

He chuckled, a low, sexy sound that reverberated through her. "I told you, I'm keeping my food processor."

She tried to breathe. "All right then, I can't guess."

He reached into his jacket pocket and pulled out a small velvet box. Everything slowed down for a moment, but unlike before, when the gauzy, frothy film of fantasy had covered it all, this was stark reality. She shook her head even before he opened it, but he didn't seem to notice.

He popped the top on it and revealed a huge ring, glittering gold and diamonds. She sucked in a sharp breath. Such a perfect ring. Gorgeous. Extravagant. Familiar. The ring he'd given to Hannah. The exact same ring. The ring for the woman who was supposed to be here. The ring for the woman he should have danced with, the woman he would have kissed, made love to.

A well of pain, deep, unreasonable and no less intense for it, opened up in her, threatened to consume her. What a joke. A cheap trick. And the worst part was that she'd played it on herself. Letting herself pretend that he'd wanted *her* at the river, playing like he wanted her in his arms tonight.

Letting hope exist in her, along with the futile, ridiculous love she felt for him. Ridiculous, because for half a second, her breath had caught when she'd seen the ring, and she'd forgotten it was fake.

"No," she said.

"Clara…"

"I don't…" She was horrified to feel wetness on her cheeks, tears falling she hadn't even realized were building. She backed away from him, hitting her shoulder against one of the bar area's supporting pillars. But she didn't stop. "I'm sorry."

She wasn't sorry. She was angry. She was hurt. Ravaged to her soul. Maybe it had been ignorant of her not to think all the way to the ring. To think that the farce wouldn't include that. Of course it would. Zack didn't cut corners and he didn't forget details. So of course he wouldn't forget something as essential to an engagement as a ring.

But it hurt. To see him, impossibly gorgeous and, in so many ways, everything she'd always dreamed of, offering her a ring, a ring he'd already given to another woman, as part of a lie, it killed something inside her.

Maybe it was just the fact that it pulled her deepest, most secret fantasy out of her and laid it bare. And made it into a joke. Designed to show her that there was no way he would ever consider her. Not with any real seriousness. That she was nothing more than a replacement for the woman he'd intended to have here with him.

That she was interchangeable.

She was hopeless. She needed a friend to tell her what a head case she was. To tell her to get over him. To take her out to pie and tell her she could do better, have better.

But Zack should have been that person. *He* was her best friend. He was the one she talked to. The one she confided in. And she couldn't confide this, couldn't tell him that he'd just shredded her heart. Couldn't tell him she was hopelessly in love with a man she couldn't have, because he was the man.

The crushing loneliness that thought brought on, the pain, was overwhelming.

Her stomach twisted. "I have to... I'm sorry."

She turned away from him, walking quickly across the lawn, back to into the lobby area to find a car, an elephant, whatever would get her back to the villa the fastest.

She was running and she knew it. From him. From her hurt. And from the moment she knew would come, the one where she'd have to explain to him just why looking at the ring had made her cry.

It was an explanation she never wanted to give. Because the only man she could ever confide her pain in, was also the one man she could never tell. Because he was the man who'd caused it.

CHAPTER SIX

ZACK'S HEART POUNDED as he scanned the villa's courtyard. It was too dark to see anything, but he was sure this was where she was. Unless she'd called the car service and asked them to come and get her, which, if Clara was really upset, he wouldn't put past her. She could be on the next plane back to the States.

His plane.

Which, he had a suspicion he might deserve.

There was a narrow path that led from the main area of the courtyard into an alcove surrounded by flowering plants and trees. And he was willing to bet that, if she was still in the villa, she'd gone there.

He was right. She was sitting on the stone bench, her knees pulled up to her chest. She was simply staring, her cheeks glistening in the moonlight. The sight made him ache.

He was all about control, all about living life with as few entanglements and attachments as possible. But Clara was his exception. She had been from the moment he'd met her.

She was the one person who could alter his emotions without his say so. Make him happy if he really wanted to be angry. Make his gut feel wrenched with her tears.

"Are you okay?"

She dropped her knees and put her feet on the ground, straightening. "I'm sorry. That was stupid. I overreacted."

He moved to the bench and crouched down in front of it, in front of her. "What did I do?"

"I was just… I told you, it was an overreaction. It was nothing, really." She sucked in a breath that ended on a hiccup and his heart twisted. "I can't really…explain it."

The confusion he felt was nearly as frustrating as the pain he felt over hurting her. He didn't really understand exactly what he'd done, but not understanding it didn't make it go away.

Without thinking, he lifted his hand and curved it around her neck, stroking her tender skin with his thumb. It was a gesture meant to comfort her, because he'd upset her somehow, for the second time in forty-eight hours, and he hated to upset her. She meant too much to him.

But something in the touch changed. He wasn't sure exactly when it tipped over from being comfort to being a caress, he wasn't sure how her skin beneath his fingers transformed from something everyday to something silky, tempting.

She looked at him, her eyes glistening, the expression in them angry. Angry and hot. And that heat licked through him, reached down into his gut and squeezed him tight.

It was close to what he'd felt down at the river, but magnified, her anger feeding the flame that burned between them. And he couldn't walk away from it. Not this time.

Without thought, without reason or planning, without stopping to think of possible consequences, he leaned in and closed the space between them, his lips meeting hers. First kisses were for tasting, testing. They were a question.

At least historically for him they had been. This kiss wasn't.

Something roared through him, filling him, a kind of desperation he'd never felt before. He didn't ask, he took. He didn't taste, he devoured. The hunger in him was too ravenous to do anything else, so sudden he had no chance to sublimate it. He wrapped his arms around her, and she clung to his shoulders, her lips parting beneath his.

He growled and thrust his tongue against hers, his body shuddering as his world reduced to the slick friction, to the warmth of her lips on his.

Clara was powerless to do anything but cling to Zack. Powerless to give anything less than every bit of passion and desire that was pouring through her. To do anything but devour him, giving in to the hunger that had lived in her, gnawed at her for the past seven years.

This was heaven. And it was hell. Everything she'd longed for, still off-limits to her for the same reasons it always had been. Except for right now, for some reason, it was as though a ban had been lifted. For this one moment, a moment out of time. A moment that she needed more than she needed air.

His lips, firm and sure, were everything she'd ever dreamed they might be, his hands, heavy and hot on her back even more arousing than she'd thought possible.

This was why there had been no one else. Because the idea of Zack had always been more enticing than the reality of any other man. And the reality of Zack far surpassed any fantasy she'd ever had. Maybe any fantasy *any* woman had ever had.

She slid from the bench and onto the stone-covered ground, gripping the front of his shirt, their knees touching. He pulled her closer, bringing her breasts against his hard, muscular chest. She arched into him, craving more. Craving everything. All of him.

When they parted, he rested his forehead against hers, his breathing shallow, unsteady, loud in the otherwise silent night.

She didn't know what to say. She was afraid that he would try to say something first. Something that would ruin it. A joke. Or maybe he'd even be angry. Or he'd say it was a mistake. All valid reactions, but she didn't want any of them. She didn't want to deal with anything. She simply wanted to focus on the pounding of her heart, the swollen, tingly feeling in her lips.

On all the really good, fizzy little sensations that were popping in her veins like champagne.

Zack let out a gust of air. "Damn."

She laughed. She couldn't help it. Of all the reactions she'd expected, and dreaded, that hadn't been it. That he would allow an honest reaction, and that his reaction would match hers, hadn't seemed likely.

"Yeah," she said.

He braced his hand on the bench behind her and pulled himself up, then extended his hand to her. She gripped it and let him help her to her feet. She brushed some dried leaves from her knees, ignoring the slight prickle of pain and indents of small twigs left behind on her skin.

Her eyes caught his and held, and all of the good exciting feelings that had been swirling through her dissolved. The cushion of fantasy yanked from under her, there was nothing but cold, hard reality. She'd kissed Zack. More than kissed, she'd attacked him.

And there was nowhere for it to go from that point. If she leaned in again, if she kissed him again, then what? They might go to bed together. And where would that leave her after? Where would it leave them?

No, he hadn't slept with Hannah, but he'd slept with other beautiful women. Lots of them. She'd met a good number of them. And she was...she was inexperienced, unglamorous. And she was here as a replacement. If something happened between them now, on a night that was meant to be his wedding night with another woman, she would always feel like she'd been second.

He was a man, and the pump was well and truly primed. He'd been promised sex after what had been a lengthy bout of not having sex, so of course he was hot for it. But he was hot for it. Not for her.

He'd never kissed her before tonight. That, if nothing else, cemented the point.

She wasn't going to cry again. She wasn't going to let him know how vulnerable she was to him. Wasn't going to let him know how bad it hurt to pull away now.

"This has been a bit of a crazy day," she said.

"I can't argue with that."

"Sorry. About this." She gestured to the bench. "All of it... I don't... I don't really know what that was about."

The flash of relief she saw in Zack's eyes made her heart twist. She would finish now. Make sure he'd never want to talk about it again.

"I mean...how do you feel?" She'd said the magic feel word. Zack didn't like to talk about how he felt. Not in a way that went any deeper than happy, or angry, or hungry.

"Fine. Good, in fact. Kissing a beautiful woman is never a bad thing."

She felt heat creep into her cheeks. She shouldn't respond to the compliment. It was empty, an attempt to smooth things over. But it affected her, and she couldn't stop it from making her stomach curl in traitorous satisfaction.

"I might say the same. Not the woman part but the... You get it."

"I did something wrong. With the ring. I'm sorry. I'm not hitting them out of the park with you today, am I?"

"I don't think either of us is at our best right now," she said. That at least was true. Of course, she hadn't been her best since the engagement announcement. Her safe little world had been chucked off-kilter in that moment and she'd felt out of balance ever since.

"Probably need sleep."

She forced a laugh. "You probably do. I got that extra sleep on the plane, remember?"

"But you should sleep again. Otherwise you'll be off for even longer."

She did feel tired suddenly. And not a normal tired, an all-consuming sort of tired that went all the way down into her bones. "Yeah. You're right. I can sleep on the couch tonight."

"I'll sleep on the couch again. After being left at the altar, sleeping alone in the honeymoon bed is just a bit depressing, don't you think?"

For a moment, she thought about inviting him to join her. To play the vixen for once. To say to hell with all of her insecurities and just be the woman she wished she could be.

But she didn't.

"Yeah, maybe a little." She swallowed and stuck her hand out. "I'll take that ring though."

"You sure?"

"I told you, I was being stupid. Emotional girl moment. The kind specifically designed to boggle the minds of men. Actually, a little secret for you, they occasionally boggle our minds, too. So, ring, give."

She held her hand out and he took it in his, turning it over so her palm was facing down. He took the ring box out of his pocket and took the ring out of its pink silk nest, holding it up for a moment before sliding it on to her ring finger.

She looked down at it, then curled her fingers into a fist, trying to force a smile.

"Looks good," he said.

"It's a diamond, it can't look anything else," she said, trying to sound breezy and unaffected. Both things she wasn't.

"Perfect. And now we're ready for tomorrow. I hope you brought shoes you can walk in."

"Of course I did."

"That's right. I forgot."

"Forgot what?" she asked.

"That you're different. Come on, let's go try to get some sleep."

She followed him out of the courtyard, trying to leave everything behind them, all the needs, desires, pain, back in the alcove. But his words kept repeating in her head, and she could still feel his kiss on her lips.

And she felt different. Like a completely different woman than the one who had walked into the garden with tears streaming down her face.

One kiss shouldn't have that kind of power. But that kiss had. She felt changed. She felt a a tiny bit destroyed, and a little bit stronger. And she wasn't sure she would take it back. Even if she could.

Sleep had been a joke. An elusive thing that had never even come close to happening. Zack looked at the tie he'd brought with him for meetings with Mr. Amudee, and decided against putting it on. Not twice in one week.

He left two buttons undone on his crisp white shirt and pushed the sleeves halfway up his forearms. That should be good enough. They were spending the day looking at where the coffee and tea plants were grown.

Maybe spending the day outdoors would clear his head. Would lift the heavy fog of arousal that had plagued him since the kiss. Not just the kiss, since that strange, tense moment at the lake before the kiss.

But the kiss... A few more minutes and he would have had her flat on her back on the stone bench with more than half of her clothes stripped from her gorgeous curves.

He bit down hard, his teeth grinding together. He shouldn't be thinking of her curves. But he was.

"Zack?"

The sound of her voice hit him like a kick in the gut.

"Here," he said, sliding his belt through the loops on his pants and fastening the buckle as she walked around the corner, into the bedroom. Her pale cheeks colored slightly when she saw him.

"How did you sleep?" she asked.

"Great," he lied. "Thanks for letting me use the room to get ready."

"Yeah, no problem. I got up pretty early. Wandered around in the garden. There are so many flowers here."

And she'd put a few different varieties in her hair. It was silly. And it was cute. She had a way of making that work for her.

"I didn't know you liked flowers so much."

She shrugged. "I always have some on my kitchen table."

She did, now that he thought about it. He wondered if anyone ever bought them for her. He wondered why he'd never really stopped to notice before. Why he'd never bought her any.

Because, bosses don't buy employees flowers. And friends don't buy friends flowers.

Friends also didn't kiss each other like he and Clara had done last night. His pulse jump-started at the thought, his blood rushing south. He tightened his hands into fists and tried to will his body back under control.

"Ready to go?" he asked, his voice curt because it was taking every last bit of his willpower to keep his desire for her leashed.

She frowned slightly. "Yeah. Ready."

"Good. Remember, you're my fiancée, and we've been very suddenly overcome by love that can no longer be denied."

One side of her mouth quirked up. "Is that the story?"

"Yes. That's the story. As Amudee created it, so he'll believe it. He's the one who assumed."

"A romantic, I suppose. Either that or he just thinks you move fast."

"I'm decisive. And we've known each other for years." He studied her face for a moment, dark almost almond-shaped eyes, pale skin, clear and smooth. Perfection. Her lips were pink and full and, now he knew, made for kissing. And he had to wonder how he'd known her for so long and never really looked at her.

Because if he had he would have realized. He would have had to realize, that she was the most gorgeous woman. Exquisite. Curved, just as a woman should be, in all the right places. Beautiful without fuss or pretension.

"Yes, we have," she said slowly, those liquid brown eyes locked with his.

"So it stands to reason that after Hannah decided not to go through with things…"

"Right."

The air between them seemed thicker now, that dangerous edge sharpening. Now that he knew what it was like to touch her, to feel her soft lips beneath his, well, now it was a lot harder to ignore.

"So let's go, then," he said.

"Right," she said again.

He moved to her and slid his arm around her waist. It was more slender than he'd imagined it might be. "We have to do things like this," he said, his voice getting rougher as her hips brushed against his.

She nodded, her eyes on his face. On his lips. She would be the death of him.

"Lovely to see you again, Ms. Davis," Mr. Amudee said, inclining his head. "And with a ring, I see."

Her heart rate kicked up several notches.

"Oh. Yes. Zack…made it official last night. It's lovely to see you, too." She touched the ring on her finger and Zack tightened his hold around her waist. She nearly stopped breathing, her accelerated heart rate lurching to a halt with it. From the moment they'd arrived at Mr. Amudee's house, he had put his arm around her and kept it there. She'd assumed she would get used to it, to the warm weight of his touch. But she wasn't getting used to it. If anything, she was getting more jittery, more aroused with each passing second.

The sun was hot on the wide, open veranda that overlooked rows of coffee trees with flat glossy leaves and bright red coffee cherries. But Zack's touch was the thing that was making her melt.

"I had not met the other woman you intended to marry, Zack, but I must say that comparing the photos of the first one, to Ms. Davis, I find I prefer Ms. Davis."

Clara's heart bumped against her chest. "That's kind of you to say." She knew her face had to be beet-red, it was hot, that was for sure. Because it was nice of him to say, but there was no way it could be true.

There was no comparison between her and Hannah. Hannah was...well, sex bomb came to mind yet again.

"Not kind," Isra said. "Just the truth. I was married, a long time ago, to the most wonderful woman. I have a good judge of character. Unfortunately I was too busy to see just how wonderful she was. Don't make that mistake."

Zack cleared his throat. "Clara is also very knowledgable about our product. I know we'll both enjoy getting a look at the growing process today. And we're both excited about the tasting."

Back to business. Zack was good at that. Thank God one of them was.

"I'm excited to share it with you. Come this way." They followed him down the stairs that led to the lush, green garden filled with fragrant foliage. He moved quickly for a man his age, his movements sharp and precise as he explained where each plant was in the growing stage, and which family was leasing which segment of the farmland, and how the soil and amount of shade would affect the flavor of each type of coffee, even before it was roasted.

The tea was grown in a more remote segment of the farm and required walking up into the rolling hills, where the leaves were in the process of being harvested.

"A lot depends on when you pick them," Mr. Amudee said, bending and plucking a small, tender-looking cluster of leaves. "Smell. Very delicate."

He handed the leaves to Zack and he did as instructed. Then he held them out for Clara. She bent and took in the light fragrance. She looked up and her eyes clashed with Zack's and her heart beat double time.

"And this will be…what sort of tea will it be?" she asked, anything to get her mind off Zack and his eyes.

"White tea," Zack said. "Am I right?"

Mr. Amudee inclined his head. "Right. Ready to go and taste?"

Her eyes met Zack's again, the word tasting bringing to mind something new and different entirely. Something heady and sexual.

She swallowed hard.

"Yes, I think we are," Zack said slowly, his eyes never leaving hers.

And she wondered if he'd been thinking the exact same thing she was. And if he was thinking the same thing, if he wanted to kiss her again, she wasn't sure what she would do.

No, that was a lie. She was sure. She would kiss him again. Like nothing else mattered. Like there was no future and no consequences. Because she'd had enough of not getting what she wanted out of life. Quite enough.

She looked at Zack again and she wondered if she'd only imagined that momentary flash of heat. Because his eyes were cool again, his expression neutral.

She tried to convince herself that it was better that way.

Clara spent the next few days carefully avoiding Zack. It was easier than expected, given the cozy living situation. But during the day he had meetings with Mr. Amudee and when she wasn't needed, she took advantage of all the vacation-type things that were available in the resort.

There was a spa down in the hotel, and also some incredible restaurants. Her favorite retreat was up on the roof of the villa that gave her a view of the mountains, and the small town that was only a short walk away, the golden rooftops reflecting the sunlight like fire in the late afternoon. It was the perfect view for yoga, which kept her mind focused and relaxed at the same time.

She even managed to forget about the kiss. Mostly. As long as she made a concerted effort not to think of it. And as long as she didn't get into bed before she was ready to fall asleep instantly. Lying awake for any length of time was a recipe for disaster. And for replaying that moment. Over and over again.

Clara took a deep breath and tried to focus on the scenery, on the sky as it lightened. Orange fading into a pale pink, then to purple as the sun rose from behind the sloping hills. She would focus on that. Not Zack. Because that door was clearly closed. He hadn't touched her again, unless it was absolutely necessary, since the night in the garden. Since the kiss that had scorched her inside and out.

The kiss that didn't even seem to be a vague memory to him.

"Got plans for today?"

She turned and her heart lodged itself in her throat. Zack strode onto the roof in nothing more than a pair of low-slung jeans, his chest, broad and muscular, sprinkled with the perfect amount of chest hair, was streaked with dirt and glistening with sweat.

She had to remind herself to breathe when he came closer. And she had to remind herself not to stare at his abs, bunching and shifting as he moved.

"Do I..." She blinked and looked up at his face. "What?"

"Do you have plans? You've been busy. Remarkably so for someone on vacation."

"Well, down in the village they have these neat classes for tourists. Weaving and things like that. And one of the restaurants in the hotel has a culinary school."

"I thought you wanted to relax."

"Cooking is relaxing for me." And it had been conducive to

avoiding him. "Anyway, now I can make you some killer Pad Thai when we get back home."

"Well, I support that."

"What are you doing up so early?"

"Working. Before the sun had a chance to get over the mountains and scorch me. Part of the deal. I need to understand where it all comes from. How important the work is to the families. I'm really pleased we're going to be part of this process."

"Me, too," she said. Although, she wouldn't be. Not once everything was in place. This was it for her.

"I'm going up to Doi Suthep, to see the temple. I thought you might want to come with me."

She did. Not just to see the temple, although that was of major interest to her, but to spend some time with him. It was that whole inconvenient paradox of being in love with her best friend again. She wanted to avoid him, because she felt conflicted over the kiss. She wanted to be with him, confide in him, because she felt conflicted, too.

"I…"

"Are you avoiding me?" he asked, hands on his lean hips. "Well, I know you're avoiding me, but I guess I don't know why. Does this have to do with you leaving Roasted?"

"No!"

"Then what the hell is your problem?"

Hot, reckless anger flooded her. "My problem? Are you serious? You asked me to come here, and play fiancée, and I have. I don't have a problem."

"When you aren't avoiding me."

"I have done exactly what you asked me to do," she said. "I have played the part of charming, simpering fiancée, I've worn this ring on my finger, and you can't, for one second see why that might not be…something I want to do. And then you kiss me. Kiss me like…like you really are on your honeymoon, and you want to know what my problem is?"

He looped his arm around her waist and drew her to him, his

eyes blazing. She braced herself against him, her palms flat on his bare chest. "I think I do know what your problem is. I think you're avoiding me because of the kiss. Because you're afraid it will happen again. Or because you want it to happen again."

She shook her head slightly. "N-no. I haven't even thought about it again."

"Liar." He dipped his head so that his lips hovered just above hers. "You want this."

She did. She really did. She wanted his lips on hers. His hands on her body. She wanted everything. "You arrogant bastard," she said, her voice trembling. "How dare you?"

"How dare I what? Say that you want it again? We both know you do."

His lips were so close to hers and it was tempting, so tempting, to angle her head so that they met. So that she could taste him again. Have a moment of stolen pleasure again.

"You do want it," he said again, his voice rough, strained.

"So?" she whispered.

"What?"

"So what if I do?" she said, finding strength in her voice. "What then, Zack? We'll kiss? Sleep together? And then what? Nothing. You and I both know there won't be anything after that. We'll just ruin what we do have."

He released his hold on her and took a step back, letting his hands fall to his sides. "Sorry."

"You've been apologizing to me a lot lately," she said, her voice trembling. "You don't need to do that."

He nodded. "I'm going to take a quick shower."

"Not going to the temple?"

He smiled ruefully. "Still am. And you can come if you want. Provided you've worked the tantrum out of your system."

"That was your tantrum, Parsons, not mine."

"Maybe." He tightened his jaw, his hands curling into fists. "Just tense I suppose. Coming with me or not?"

She hesitated. Because she did want to go, but things

weren't…easy with him at the moment. And the scariest thing was she wasn't sure she wanted them to be easy again. She was sort of liking this new, scary dynamic between them. The one that made him touch her like she did something to him. Like he was losing control.

"I'll be good. I promise," he added.

She laughed, a fake, tremulous sound. "I wasn't worried."

Zack wasn't the one who worried her. She hesitated because she wasn't sure she trusted *herself* to behave.

"I was," he said, turning away from her and walking back into the house. She watched him the whole way, the muscles on his back, the dent just above the waistline of his jeans, and his perfect, tight butt.

She let out a slow, shaky breath. Yeah, it was definitely herself she didn't trust.

The temple at Doi Suthep was crowded with tourists, spiritual pilgrims and locals. Clara and Zack walked up the redbrick staircase, the handrails fashioned into guardian dragons with slithering bodies and fierce faces.

They were silent for the three-hundred-step trek up to the temple, Clara keeping a safe distance between them, in spite of the crush of people all around them. She was mad at him.

And fair enough, he'd been a jerk earlier. That was sexual frustration. Sexual frustration combined with the desire to give in to the need to kiss her again. To do more than kiss her.

Damn.

He could still remember the first time he'd seen Clara. She was working behind the counter at a bakery, flour on her cheeks. She was cute. Not the kind of woman he was normally attracted to. But she'd fascinated him. Utterly and completely. It had turned out she'd made great cupcakes, too. And that she was smart and funny. That it felt good to be with her.

The emotional connection to her, when he'd been lacking a connection with anyone for years, had been shocking, instant, and had immediately found him shoving his attraction to her away.

A friendship with her was fine. Anything else...he didn't have room for it. Anything else would go beyond the boundaries he'd set for himself. And he needed his boundaries. His control. He valued it above everything else.

Just another reason he'd intended to marry Hannah. Marriage brought stability, a sort of controlled existence that attracted him. One woman in his bed, in his life.

And now that that had gone to hell, it seemed his feelings for Clara were headed in the same direction. He'd done with her, for seven years now, what he did with everything in his life. She had a place. She was his friend. She didn't move out of that place in his mind.

His body was suddenly thinking differently. He'd made a mistake. He'd allowed himself too much freedom. He'd indulged his desire to look at her body. To touch her soft skin when they'd gone swimming. And that night, he'd given in to the temptation to allow her to feature in his fantasies. To find release with her image in his mind.

He'd allowed himself to cross the line in his mind, and that was where control started. He knew better. Yet it was hard to regret. Because wanting her was such a tantalizing experience. Just feeling desire for her was a pleasure on its own.

Her sweet, short, sundress was not helping matters. Though, thankfully she'd had to purchase a pair of silk pants to wear beneath it before they could head up toward the temple.

Still, even with her legs covered, there was that bright, gorgeous smile that had been plastered on her face since they'd arrived. She was all breathy sighs and sounds of pleasure over the sights and sounds. It was the sweetest torture.

"Incredible," she breathed, her voice soft, sensual in a way. Enough to make his body ache.

"Yes," he agreed. Mostly, he was looking at her, and not the immense, gold-laden temple.

He forced himself to look away from Clara. To keep his focus on the gilded statues, the bright, fragrant offerings of flowers, fresh fruit and cakes left in front of the different alters that were placed throughout the courtyard. A large, dome-shaped building covered entirely in gold reflected the sun, the air bright, thick with smoke from burning incense.

Monks in bright orange robes wove through the crowds, talking, laughing, offering blessing.

It *was* incredible. And still nowhere near as interesting as the woman next to him.

"Have you been enjoying yourself here?" he asked.

"More or less," she said, looking at him from the corner of her eye, color creeping into her cheeks. Probably not the smartest question to ask. Why was he struggling with his words and actions? That never happened to him. Not anymore.

"The less would be me being a jerk and planting my lips on you, right?" Might as well go for honesty. Clara was the only person in his life who rated that. He didn't want to violate it.

She blew out a breath. "Um...mostly the being a jerk. You're a pretty good kisser, it turns out."

"So you didn't mind that?"

"Not as much as I should have." Her words escaped in a rush.

"Glad to know I'm not the only one," he said, forcing the words out.

"Not sure it helps anything." She walked ahead of him, straying beneath the overhang of a curled roof, her eyes on the murals painted on the walls of the temple.

"Maybe not." He leaned in, pretending to examine the same image she was.

"So...is there a solution?" She put her hand on the wall, tracing the painting of a white elephant with her finger.

He covered her hands with his, his heart pounding, his hand shaking like he was a teenage virgin. "Let me see."

He leaned in, his mouth brushing hers. He went slow this time, asking the question, as he should have done the first time he'd kissed her. She didn't move, not into him or away from him. He angled his head and deepened the kiss and he felt her soften beneath him, her lips parting beneath his, her breath catching, sharp and sweet when the tip of his tongue met hers.

He pulled away, his eyes on hers.

She released a breath. "How do you feel?"

"I was going to ask you the same thing."

She looked up. "The roof didn't fall in."

"No," he said, following her gaze. "It didn't."

She leaned into him, her elbow jabbing his side, a shy smile on her face. "Good to know anyway."

"Glad it comforts you."

She laughed, her cheeks turning pink, betraying the fact that she wasn't unaffected. "Comfort may not be the right word."

He looked around the teeming common area, at the completely unfamiliar surroundings. And he found he wanted to pretend that the feelings he was having for Clara were unfamiliar, too.

But he couldn't. Because they had been there, for a long time, lurking beneath the surface. Ignored. Unwanted. But there.

"No. Comfort is definitely not the right word."

They'd spent most of the day at the temple, then taken a car back to Chiang Mai where they'd wandered the streets buying food from vendors, and watching decorations go up on every market stall for a festival that was happening in the evening.

Now, with the event coming close, the streets were packed tight with people, carrying street food, flower arrangements with candles in the center, talking, laughing. It was dark out, the sun long gone behind the mountains, but the air was still thick, warm and fragrant. There was music, noise and movement everywhere. The smell of frying food mixed with the perfume of flowers and the dry, stale scent of dust clung to the air, filled her senses.

It almost helped block out Zack. But not quite. No matter

just how much it filled up her senses, it couldn't erase Zack. The imprint of his kiss. It had been different than the first one. Tender. Achingly sexy.

It had made her want more. Not simply in a sexual way, but in an emotional way. It didn't bear thinking about. Still, she knew she would.

She kept an eye on the food stalls, passing more exotic fare, like anything with six legs or more, for something a bit more vanilla. Maybe food would help keep her mind off things. At least temporarily.

"I definitely don't need this," she said, stopping to buy battered, fried bananas from the nearest food stall.

"But you bought it," he said, breaking a piece off the banana and putting it in his mouth.

"Well, that's because sweets are my area of expertise. You're here for the beans and tea leaves, I'm here for the pairing, right? This is research. It's for work. I need to capture the new and exotic flavor profiles Chiang Mai has to offer," she said, trying to sound official. "Maybe I can write off the calories?"

They dodged a bicycle deliveryman and crossed the busy, bustling street, moving away from the stalls and toward the river that ran through the city. "You don't need to worry about it. You're perfect like you are."

She looked down at the bag of sweets. "You're just saying that."

"I'm not."

She sucked in a sharp breath and looked at the lanterns that were strung from tree to tree, glowing overhead. "We should do this more. At home."

"Eat?"

"No. Go do things. Mostly we work, and sometimes I feed you at my house, or we watch a movie at yours. Well, we do go out to lunch sometimes, but on workdays, so it doesn't count."

"We're busy."

"We're workaholics."

Zack frowned and stopped walking. He extended his hand and took a lock of her hair between his thumb and forefinger, rubbing it idly. "Is that why you're leaving me?"

She looked up at him. "I'm not leaving you. I'm leaving the company." And she was counting on that to put some natural and healthy distance between them. Roasted had brought them together, and because they got along so well, after spending the day at work together, half of the time it felt natural to simply go and have dinner together. Watch bad reality TV together. Once they weren't involved in the same business it would only be natural they would drift apart. And with any luck, it would only feel like she was missing her right arm for a couple of years.

"What do you need? I'll give it to you."

"You're missing the point, Zack. It's about having something of my own."

"Roasted isn't enough for you? You've been there from the beginning, more or less. You've helped me make it what it is."

"No. I just bake cupcakes. And there are a lot of people who can do my job."

"But they aren't you."

She closed her eyes and let the compliment wash over her. She'd say this for Zack; he gave her more than most anyone else in her life ever had, including her family. But it was still just a crumb of what she wanted.

"No," she said, "some of them are even better."

She wove through the crowd to the edge of the waterfront. People were kneeling down and putting the flower arrangements with their lit candles into the stream. The crowd standing on the other side of the waterfront was lighting candles inside tall, rice paper lanterns, the orange spreading to the inky night, casting color and light all around.

Zack was behind her, she could sense it without even turning around. "I'm glad we came tonight," she said.

Zack swept his fingers through Clara's hair, moving it over her shoulder, exposing her neck. He didn't normally touch her like that, but tonight, he found he couldn't help himself. Things were tense between them. The kiss at the temple certainly hadn't helped diffuse it.

He wondered if most of the tension had started in the bedroom back in the villa. That moment when they'd both looked at the bed and had that same, illicit thought.

If it had started there, they might be able to finish it there.

Temptation, pure and strong, lit him on fire from the inside out. She turned, and his heart slammed hard against his rib cage, blood rushing south of his belt, every muscle tensing. He could feel the energy change between them, like a wire that had been connecting them, unseen and unfelt for years had suddenly come alive with high-voltage electricity. He knew she felt it, too.

"We broke things, didn't we?" she whispered.

It was like she read his thoughts, which, truly, was nothing new. But inconvenient now, since his thoughts had a lot to do with what it might be like to see her naked.

"Because of the kisses?"

She nodded once. "I can't forget them."

"I can't, either. I'm not sure if I want to."

She took a deep breath. "That's just what I was thinking earlier."

"Was it?"

"Yes. I should want to forget it, we both should. So we can get things back to where they're supposed to be but…"

He leaned down and pressed his lips to hers, soft again. "Do you think we could break it worse than we already have? Or is the damage done?"

"I have no idea."

Everything in him screamed to step back. Because this was an unknown. A move that would affect his life, his daily life, and he couldn't see the way it would end. And that just wasn't how he did things. Not since that night when he'd been sixteen and he'd acted unthinkingly, impulsively, and ruined everything.

He wasn't that person anymore. He'd made sure of it. If he

didn't walk away from Clara now, from the temptation she presented, if he didn't plan it out and look at all the angles, he was opening them both up to potential fallout.

He stepped forward and kissed her again. Deepening the kiss this time, letting the blood that was roaring in his ears drown out conscious thought.

Clara knew she should stop this. Stop the madness before it went too far. It already had gone too far. It had gone too far the moment she agreed to come. Because the desire for this, for the week to turn into this, had been there. Of course, she'd never imagined that Zack would—could—want her.

The breaking of things wasn't just down to the kiss. It was the day at the river, the intense moment on the balcony. The fact that she'd realized she was deeply, madly, irrevocably in love with a man who was just supposed to be her friend.

He kissed the tip of her nose, then her cheeks. "Zack," she whispered.

"Clara."

"Are we trying to see if we can break things worse?"

"Actually, I'm not thinking at all. Not about anything beyond what I feel right now."

"What is it you feel?" she asked, echoing what she'd said after they'd kissed.

"I want you."

She hesitated, her heart squeezing tight. "Do you want me? Or do you want to have sex?"

He looked at her for a long time, the glow of flames across the river reflected in his eyes. "I want you, Clara Davis. I have never slept with one woman when I wanted another one, and I would never start the practice with you. When I have you, I won't be thinking of anyone else. I'll only have room for you."

His words trickled through her, balm on her soul. Exactly the right words.

The real question was, did she want to accept a physical relationship when it was only part of what she wanted?

You only have part of what you want now. A very small part.

"Just for tonight," she said, hating that she had to say it, but knowing she did. Because she knew for certain that there could be no romantic future for them. She loved him, she was certain of it now. She had for a long time, possibly for most of the seven years she'd known him. It had been a slow thing, working its way into her system bit by bit. With every smile, every touch.

And he didn't love her. Looking at him now, the light in his eyes, that wasn't anything deeper than lust. But if that was all she could have, she would take that. Right now, she would take it, and she wouldn't think about the wisdom of it, or the consequences.

Because she was staring hard into a Zack-free future, and she would rather have all of him tonight, and carry the memory with her, than be nothing more than his trusty sidekick forever, standing by watching while he married another woman. Watching him make a life with someone else, someone he didn't even love, while her heart splintered into tiny pieces with every beat.

"One night," she repeated. "Here. Away from reality. Away from work and home. Because… We can't keep going on like this. It can't be healthy."

The people around them started cheering and she looked around them, saw the paper lanterns start to rise up above them, filling the air with thousands of floating, ethereal lights.

"Just one night," he said, his voice rough. "One night to explore this." He touched her cheek. "To satisfy us both. Is that really what you want?"

"I want you. So much."

He kissed her without preliminaries this time, her body pressed against hers, his erection thick and hard against her stomach as his mouth teased and tormented her in the most delicious way. She wrapped her arms around his neck and gave herself up to the heat coursing between them. When they parted she felt like she was floating up with the lanterns.

One night. The proposition made her heart ache, and pound

faster. It excited her and terrified her. She didn't know what she was thinking. But one thing she did know: he wanted her. He wasn't faking the physical reaction she'd felt pressed against her.

The very thought of Zack, perfect, sexy Zack wanting her, was intoxicating. Empowering. She wanted to revel in the feeling. One night. To find out if her fantasies were all she'd built them up to be. One night to have the man of her dreams.

One night to make a memory that she would carry with her for the rest of her life.

CHAPTER SEVEN

BACK AT THE VILLA, Clara started to question some of the bravado she'd felt down in the city. It was one thing to know, for a moment, in public, fully dressed, that Zack was attracted to her. It was another to suddenly forget a lifetime's insecurity. To wonder if it would be Hannah on his mind.

They were in the bedroom. And her eyes were fixed on the bed, that invitation to decadence, to passion unlike anything she'd ever known. With the man she loved.

She sucked in a breath. She wasn't going to worry about how attracted he was to her, where she ranked with his other lovers. This night was for her. It was the culmination of every fantasy, every longing she'd had since Zack had walked into the bakery she worked at seven years ago and offered her a job.

He pulled her to him and kissed her. Hungry. Wild. She felt it, too, an uncontrollable, uncivilized need that had no place anywhere else in her life. No one had ever made her feel like this. No one had ever made her want to forget every convention, every rule, and just follow her body's most untamed needs.

But Zack did.

"I want you," she said, her voice breaking as they parted. She had to say it. Because it had been building in her for so long and now she felt like she was going to burst with it.

"I want you, too. I've thought of this before," Zack said, unbuttoning his shirt as he spoke, revealing that gorgeous, toned chest. "Of what it might be like to see you."

"To...to see me?"

"Naked," he said.

"You have?" she asked, her voice trembling now, because she'd hoped, maybe naively, that he would want the lights off. She didn't want him to see her. Touch, yes. Taste, sure. But see?

"Of course I have. I've tried not to think about it too hard. Because you work for me. Because you're my friend. And it's not good to picture friends or employees naked. In my life, everything has a place, and yours was never supposed to be in my bed. And I was never supposed to imagine you naked. But I have anyway sometimes."

"I have a hard time believing that."

"Why?" He shrugged his shirt off and let it fall to the floor, then his hands went to his belt and her breath stuck in her throat.

"Because I'm...average."

He chuckled, his hands freezing on the belt buckle. "Damn your mother for making you believe that garbage." He took a step toward her and put his hand on her cheek, his thumb sliding gently across her face. "You are exquisite. You have such perfect skin. Smooth. Soft. And your body." He put his other hand on her waist. "I thought of you last night. Of this. Of how beautiful you would look."

Reflexively she pulled back slightly.

"What?" he asked.

"I'm not... What was Hannah? A size two? I'm... I'm not a size two."

"Beauty isn't a size. I don't care what the number on the tag of your dresses says. I don't care what your sister looked like, or what your mother thought you should look like. I know what I see. You have the kind of curves other women envy." He reached around and caught the tab on her summer dress with his thumb and forefinger and tugged it down partway.

Her hands shook, her body trembling inside and out. She felt like she was back beneath the spotlight again. Just waiting to have all of her flaws put out there for everyone to ridicule.

"Wait," she said.

His hands stilled. "I don't know if I can."

"Please. Can were turn the lights off?"

There was only one lamp on. It wasn't terribly bright in the room, but she still felt exposed already, with the zipper barely open across the top part of her back. She felt awkward. Unexceptional. Especially faced with all of Zack's perfection. He didn't have an ounce of spare flesh, every muscle perfectly defined as though he were carved from granite.

He put his hands on her hips and pulled her to him. She could feel his erection again, hard and hot against her. "You are perfect." He moved his hands around to her back, to her bottom, cupping her. She gasped. She'd never been this intimate with a man. She wondered if she should be more or less nervous that it was Zack she was finally taking the step with.

No one had seen her naked, not since she was in diapers. She didn't even change in public locker rooms. She would hide in bathroom stalls, needing the coverage of four walls and a door. And Zack wanted...

"Please."

"Let me see you first." Her eyes met his and she drew in an unsteady breath. "It's me, Clara."

"I know," she said.

"When you're ready."

She took a breath and turned away from him, catching the zipper and tugging it down the rest of the way, letting her dress fall to the floor. Zack moved behind her, his arm curving around her, his palm pressed flat against her stomach.

He swept her hair to the side and pressed a kiss to her neck. "As I said. Perfection."

He turned her slowly, keeping his arms around her, holding

her against him, his hard body acting as a shield. Cocooned in his arms, she didn't feel quite so naked.

She looked at his eyes, so familiar, yet different at the same time. Zack's eyes, filled with a kind of raw lust she'd never had directed at her before. Not by him, not by any man. The enormity of the moment hit her then. She was about to be with Zack. About to make love to him.

She started shaking then, her hands, her entire body, from the inside out. He wrapped his arms around her and held her against him. "Are you okay?"

"Yes," she said, her voice shaking. "I'm okay."

"Why are you shaking?" She couldn't answer. "Be honest," he said.

"Because it's you."

He tilted his head to the side and kissed her. She closed her eyes determined to do nothing more than luxuriate in the moment. The heat of his mouth, the slide of his tongue. She was going to believe, in this moment, that she could be the woman he wanted.

He reached around and unhooked her bra. He pulled back from her for a moment so he could remove it the rest of the way, leaving her exposed to his hungry gaze. "I said you were perfection, but I didn't know just how true that was."

A hot flush spread over her entire body, heating her. Embarrassment battling with desire.

He cupped her breasts, sliding his thumbs over her nipples. And that was when desire won. She shook with pleasure, her stomach tightening, her internal muscles pulsing, her body ready, demanding, more of him. Demanding climax. She was close to finding it, with just the touch of his hands. Maybe it was because in her mind she had found pleasure with him so many times, in reality, it was effortless to get close to the peak.

A hoarse sound caught in her throat and she felt herself go over the edge. She gripped his forearms, her fingernails digging into his flesh. As soon as the numbing pleasure washed away, embarrassment crashed in on her. She couldn't believe she'd come so quickly. Telling in so many ways. She hadn't realized just how impossible it would be to keep secrets when they were like this, hadn't realized just how intimate it would be.

"I…" She looked at his face, and his expression stole the words from her lips. A look of pure masculine satisfaction, combined with total arousal. The embarrassment dissolved. She reached forward and put her hands on his belt buckle, undoing it and pulling his belt from the loops.

He pulled her to him again, kissing her like a starving man. She reached between them and undid the closure on his pants, pushing them down his hips, along with his underwear. She felt his bare flesh against her for the first time, so impossibly hot and hard.

She wrapped her fingers around him and squeezed. She wasn't sure why, only that she wanted to. That she wanted to touch him, taste him, everywhere. To make him feel half of what he'd made her feel.

So this would be about him, a little bit. But mostly, she was just going to enjoy having the man she'd dreamed of having for so long, completely available to her. For tonight, he was hers.

He put his hand on her thigh and pulled her leg up over his hip. She held on to his shoulders and he curled his fingers around her other thigh, lifting her off the ground and walking her to the bed, up the step, laying her down on the soft mattress, his body over hers, making her feel small. Feminine. Beautiful.

He dipped his head and slid the tip of his tongue around the edge of one of her nipples. She arched into him and he sucked the tip into his mouth, his eyes never leaving hers.

"You're so sensitive there," he said, his voice sounding different, strained. "I love it."

"I like it, too," she said. It was the first time she'd ever really liked her body.

He tugged her panties down her thighs and she helped kick them off of the bed. "I stand by what I said earlier. Perfection."

He kissed her ribs, just beneath her breasts, down to her belly button. "Designed to take pleasure. For me to give you pleasure. Exquisite." He moved lower, his lips teasing the tender skin. He parted her thighs and slid his tongue over her clitoris. White heat shot through her body, a deep, intense pleasure tightening her muscles. She gripped the sheets, trying to hold herself to the bed.

He slid one finger inside her and she thought she might explode. Then another finger joined the first and a slight stinging sensation cut through the pleasure. She held her breath for a moment and waited for it to fade. It would. She knew it would. And all the better if he took care of it this way.

He worked his fingers in and out of her body, each time, the discomfort lessened. And he didn't seem to notice. Which was fine by her.

"I can't wait anymore," he said, his voice rough, broken.

"I don't think I can wait, either."

He moved up so that the head of his erection was testing the entrance to her body, his arms bracketing hers, his biceps trembling slightly. He was as undone as she was. It was such a wonderful, incredible feeling. It made her truly believe that she was beautiful.

He pushed into her partway then pulled out completely, swearing sharply.

"What?" she asked, hoping it had nothing to do with her virginity. Because she couldn't stop. Not now.

"Condoms," he said, his hands unsteady as he opened the drawer to the bedside table. He opened the box and pulled out a packet, getting the condom out and rolling it on to his length quickly.

"Oh. Good." She didn't know why she hadn't thought of it. She should have. But there were so many things filling her head. So many emotions. She'd almost forgotten the most important thing.

Then he was back, poised over her, ready to enter her.

He slid back in as far as he'd already been, then pressed in the rest of the way. It was tight, but it wasn't painful, the evidence of her virginity likely dealt with earlier.

He flexed his hips, his pelvis pressing against her clitoris at exactly the right angle, the sensation of him being inside her as her muscles clenched tight around him so incredible she couldn't stop the moan of pleasure from escaping her lips.

She gripped his tight, muscular butt, so much more perfect than she'd even imagined. Everything so much more perfect than she'd imagined.

She wrapped her legs around his calves and held him to her, moving in rhythm with his thrusts, the pleasure building low in her stomach, emotion swelling in her chest, threatening to overflow. It came to a head, pushing her until she was certain that unless she found release, she would break apart into tiny little pieces beneath the weight of the pressure inside of her.

Then she was falling apart, splintering, release, pleasure, love, pouring through the cracks, filling her, washing through her. She dug her fingernails into his back, squeezing her eyes closed tight. She didn't even try to stop the sharp cry that was climbing her throat, couldn't feel embarrassed that she was arching and moving against him with no control at all.

Because he was right with her, his entire body trembling, his fist gripping the comforter by her head, a low, intense growl rumbling in his chest as he found his own release.

He lay above her, his breathing harsh, his heart pounding so hard she could hear it. And she was pretty sure he could hear hers, too.

"Wow," she said.

He moved to the side, withdrawing from her body, one arm resting on her body. He was watching her closely, like he wanted to ask her something. Or like he thought he should but didn't want to.

"You've never been careful about what you said to me before," she said. "Don't start now."

He huffed a laugh. "Clara..."

"Actually I changed my mind," she said. "We have one night. Why talk about anything?"

Something in his expression changed, hardened. "I think that's a good idea." He rolled to his side and stood up. "I'll be back in a minute."

He went into the bathroom and came back out a moment later. "What do you propose we do, if we aren't going to talk?"

She got up on her knees and went to the edge of the bed, wrapping her arms around his neck, uncharacteristic boldness surging through her. "I'm sure we can think of a few things."

This was her night to have all of the man she loved. And she wasn't going to miss out on a single experience.

Morning came too quickly, light breaking through the gauzy curtain that surrounded the bed, bringing reality in with the sunbeams.

She didn't want the night to end. She didn't want to face reality. She'd felt like a princess last night; beautiful, desired. She'd felt like her dream was in her grasp. And this morning she felt like she'd turned back into a pumpkin. Reality sucked.

She looked at the man sleeping next to her, the only man she'd ever really wanted. The only man she'd ever loved.

And today, she would have to get up and forget that last night had happened. She would have to consign it to the "perfect memories" bin along with other things she pulled out when she was feeling lonely, or when things weren't going well.

The thought made her whole body hurt.

"I arranged to have the plane leave in an hour or so," he said, his eyes still closed.

"Okay," she said, swallowing thickly and sliding out of the bed, clutching the sheet tightly to her breasts, desperate to cover herself now, in the light of day. It was one thing to feel sexy, to be all right with her nudity when he was looking at her like he was starving and she was a delicacy. A lot less easy when he seemed…uninterested.

"I'm going to take a shower real quick."

He made a noise that might have been a form of consent, but she didn't ask for confirmation before beating a hasty retreat to the bathroom. She turned the water on and sat on the closed toilet lid, letting the tears fall down her cheeks, hoping the sound of the water hitting the tile would drown out the sound of her sobs.

Zack sat up, a curse on his lips. Last night…last night had been an aberration. A hot, amazing aberration, maybe, but it could never happen again. He had been careless. He'd nearly forgotten to use a condom. And she'd been a virgin.

If he'd thought about it, if he'd thought at all, he would have guessed that. He knew her well enough to have picked up on how nervous she was, to understand what that meant. He also knew her well enough to know she wasn't really a one-night-stand woman. She was sensitive, emotional. Sweet.

His stomach twisted, nausea overtaking him, spreading through his limbs. She probably wasn't on birth control, and there was a possibility that in that moment, when he'd been inside of her without protection, that he'd made a very big mistake.

No, he knew he'd made a mistake. He hit his fist on the top of the nightstand and stood, stalking through the room collecting his clothes. Had he learned nothing? Was he as stupid now as he'd been fourteen years ago?

His heart froze for a moment, the events of what sometimes felt like a past life, playing through his head from start to finish. Like a horror film he couldn't pause.

No. He'd worked way too hard to leave that person behind. That boy, who had been so irresponsible. Who had caused so much damage.

Last night he'd lost control. With Clara, of all people. She shouldn't have tempted him like that. But she had. She'd made him shake like *he* was the virgin.

It couldn't happen again. It wouldn't. He might have lost his control for a moment, but he wouldn't do it again.

Clara appeared a few moments later, her face scrubbed fresh and pink, her hair wet and wavy. She was dressed, a fitted T-shirt and jeans meaningless now since he'd already seen her naked and his mind was doing a very good job of envisioning her as she'd been last night.

All pale skin and soft curves. Pure perfection. Better than he'd ever imagined.

"Hey," she said, trying to smile and not quite managing it.

"Are you all right?" he asked. He'd never slept with a virgin before, but that was only part of the foreign, first-time feeling he was dealing with. The other part of that was because it was Clara. And the rest was because of his carelessness.

Carelessness that had to be addressed.

"I'm fine," she said.

"Are you on birth control?" he asked.

She narrowed her eyes. "No."

He tried to get a handle on the gnawing panic in his gut. Condoms were reliable. He knew that. But there was the matter of his impatience, of his entering her, even briefly, without protection. He swore. "Why not?"

"What?" She crossed her arms beneath her breasts. "I'm sorry, was I supposed to start taking the pill just in case you invited me on your honeymoon and we hooked up? I was a virgin, you jackass."

"I know," he shouted, not sure why he was shouting, only that his blood was pumping too fast through his veins and his heart was threatening to thunder out of his chest. "I know," he said again, softer this time.

"You used a condom," she said, her cheeks flushing pink.

"Yes, I did, eventually. There's a chance that kind of carelessness could have gotten you pregnant. It's not a big chance, but there is a chance."

"I… I seriously doubt that I'm pregnant. Well, obviously I'm not pregnant yet since things take a while to travel and…well, that's high-school health, you know all that."

"But there's a chance. I'm usually more careful."

"Zack, I think you're overreacting."

"Is that what you think, Clara?" he asked, his voice deadly calm. "You think I'm overreacting because you think it can't happen. But then, you've never been pregnant, obviously. And I have gotten a woman pregnant, so I think I might be a bit more in touch with that reality than you are. Do you know what it's like? To know that everything in your life is going to have to change because for one moment you were so utterly selfish and consumed with one moment of pleasure that you didn't think about anything else?"

Clara's heart was in her throat. She felt like she couldn't breathe. It was like a shield had been torn away from Zack, like his armor had dissolved, crumbled around his feet, leaving nothing but the man he was beneath his facade. A facade she hadn't realized was there.

This was the man she'd seen glimpses of. The reason for the darkness that she saw in his eyes sometimes. And she was afraid to hear the rest. But she had to.

His chest rose and fell sharply. "I was sixteen. And I was more interested in getting some than thinking about using a condom. Turns out you can get someone pregnant after just one time, regardless of the idiot rumors floating around the high school saying otherwise."

She didn't ask him what happened. She didn't interrupt the break. She just let his silence fill the room, and she felt his pain. Felt it in her, through her. She didn't have to know what happened to know that it was bad. Devastating. To know that knowing it was going to change her. The way it had changed Zack.

"I didn't want a baby, but we were having one. She wanted

it. I didn't want him," he said. "But I got a job so that I could pay for the doctor bills. So I could help her raise him. Because at least I knew that I should do the right thing." A muscle in his jaw jerked. "He came too early. And by the time I realized how badly I did want him, it was too late. By the time I realized that a baby can very quickly mean everything in the world to you, he was gone."

She tried to hold back the sob that was rising inside her. His face was blank now, void of emotion, flat. Like he was reading a story in a newspaper, not telling her about his life.

"Another reason Hannah was so perfect for me," he said. "She didn't want kids."

"You don't... You don't want kids?"

"I had one, Clara. I would never... I will never put myself through something like that again. I nearly died with him. I don't make the same mistakes twice. I'm always careful now."

Except last night, he wasn't as careful as he usually was, obviously. And she wasn't sure how she felt about that. Or what it might mean. And right now, she wished they had never slept together. Because she wanted to comfort him as a friend. To tell him how much her heart ached for him. But she wasn't sure if it was her place now. She wasn't sure what she was supposed to do. What he expected. What he would allow.

Because now she saw just how much he had always hidden from her. She saw a stranger. She wondered if it was even possible that this man, hard and angry, was the same man she'd seen every day for the past seven years.

"How did you...how did you cope with it?"

"I don't need to talk about it, Clara. I don't talk about it, ever. This isn't an invitation for you to psychoanalyze me. But now you know why I insist on being careful. That's the important part of the story. And you'll tell me, if you're pregnant."

"I'll let you know," she said. "But I'm sure everything will be fine."

He turned away from her and shrugged his shirt on.

"Everything will be fine," she repeated. That assurance was just for her. And she wasn't certain she believed it.

CHAPTER EIGHT

THE PLANE RIDE back to San Francisco was a study in torture. Zack was hardly speaking to her and she felt battered from the inside out. Her body was a little bit sore from her first time, and her heart felt like it had been wrung out and left to dry.

Zack was acting overly composed. His focus on work, not on her. Not on the revelation that had passed between them, both in bed and out.

She didn't feel like the same person. She felt changed. She wasn't sure if Zack was the same person, either. Or maybe he was; maybe it was just that she saw him better now.

"I think I'll probably take a couple days off," she said, looking over at Zack who was engrossed in his laptop screen. "Recover. From the jet lag."

"Fine."

The chill in his response made her shiver. "And I'm thinking of buying a pony."

"You don't have anywhere to keep one," he said drily, still not looking up.

"Just a small one. For the rooftop garden."

He did look up this time. "Your neighbors would complain."

"I don't like my neighbors." That earned her a slight smile. "So, what's the plan when we get back to civilization?"

"With any luck, things can go back to normal."

Two questions flitted through her mind. Luck for who? And, what's normal? She didn't voice either of them. "Okay."

"I still need you there, at Roasted, until Amudee signs off on the deal."

"Right." She looked down at her hand. The ring was still there. "You'll want this back, I assume." She pulled the ring off and got up, walking over to his seat and depositing it on the desk in front of him. "Since we won't need it."

A relief. Wearing another woman's ring made her feel weighted down.

"No. We won't." His eyes met hers and held. She felt heat prickle down her arms, her nipples tightening as a flash of arousal hit her.

"Great. I'll um… I'm going to try to sleep."

As she drifted off in the plane's bedroom, she tried not to be disappointed that Zack didn't join her.

"Amudee is coming here."

Clara looked up and saw Zack. For the first time since they'd landed in San Francisco three days earlier. She'd taken a couple of days to get over her jet lag, and had sneaked around the office yesterday like a cat burglar, trying to get work done without encountering him.

Because ultimately, avoiding him was simply easier than trying to juggle all the emotions she felt when she saw him. Cowardly? Yes, yes, it was. But she felt a bit yellow-bellied after all that had happened between them, and she was wallowing in it.

"What?"

"He's coming here to see how we run our operation. He wants to talk to employees, to see where we work. If we truly do conduct business in an ethical manner."

Zack reached into his pocket and took out an overly familiar velvet box. He set it on the edge of her desk, his expression grim. "And now it continues. And every single person working in the this office has to believe it, too."

"Zack this can't… It has to end."

"It will. After. And you can take as much money as you need for a start-up. You can have my blessing, hell, you can have free Roasted coffee for the first five years. But I want this deal to go through."

"Ironic that you're trying to convince him of your business ethics by using a lie," she said, annoyance spiking inside her.

"Odd that it's necessary, too, don't you think?"

"He's a nice man."

"And a romantic, it seems. He loves you. He wants to make sure he sees us together as a couple again while he's here."

"Tangled web," she snapped, putting her pencil down on the desk.

"Isn't it?"

The air between them seemed to crackle, everything slowing for a moment, the silence so tense and brittle she was certain she could splinter it into tiny pieces if she spoke.

"Put it on," he said, looking at the ring.

"I gave it back," she said tightly.

"Clara, I need you to do this for me."

She fought the urge to make a rude gesture with a different finger than the one meant for a ring and grabbed the box, opened the lid and slid the ring on. "There."

"Come on."

"What?"

"We have to make an announcement."

"Zack…"

"We're going to see this through, right? Then you can leave. Whatever you need to do, you can go do it, but finish this with me."

"Fine." She stood up and rounded the desk, he wrapped his arm around her waist and drew her to him. Heat exploded in her, stronger than she remembered, more arousing than anything had a right to be.

Instantly she was assaulted by images of their night together. His mouth, his hands, the way it had felt when he was over her, in her. It was torture. She clenched her hands into fists and the heavy ring band bit into her fingers.

There was a small group of employees who worked on her floor, their desks clustered in the center of the room. Roasted's office had a social atmosphere, which Zack had always believed made for optimum creativity. Because Zack was a great boss, the kind who made everyone feel appreciated, all the time.

And he never, ever showed the dark, tortured side of himself she'd seen in Chiang Mai. He never showed the intense, sexual side of himself, either. But she'd seen it. She'd felt it.

"Clara and I have an announcement to make."

Ten heads instantly popped up, eyes trained on her and Zack. Her heart started pounding, her palms sweating. It was one thing to lie to a man she'd never met before. A thing she hated. But it was really quite another to lie to people she worked with every day. People who she considered her friends.

"We're getting married," he said.

"Pay up." Cynthia, a woman with gray hair and pronounced smile lines turned to Jess, a twenty-something computer whiz who did their online marketing.

Jess swore and took his wallet out.

"What is this?" Clara asked.

"Congratulations," Cynthia said, beaming. "We had bets placed on this. I bet you would get married. Most everyone changed sides when Mr. Parsons got engaged to someone else. But I held out. And now I'm collecting."

"Unbelievable," Clara muttered. She wasn't sure how she felt about this revelation, either. A little bit flattered that people believed it was possible.

"Clearly I'm not giving people enough work to do," Zack said.

"Kiss her!" This from Jess, who undoubtedly considered it a consolation prize.

Everything inside Clara seized up, her muscles locking tight. Zack looked down at her, his fingers brushing her jaw. He dipped his head and kissed her. A perfectly appropriate kiss to give her in front of his employees. Nothing scandalous or overly sexual. But it grabbed hold of her world and shook it completely. Shook her.

When he lifted his head there was a smattering of applause. "Feel free to spread the news," Zack said, lacing his fingers through hers and leading her toward his office.

He closed the door tightly behind him, taking long strides to the far window that overlooked the bay, his back turned to her.

"Good show," she said icily.

He looked over his shoulder. "You could have been a little less stiff," he said.

"You…" She strode across the room, embracing the anger, unrest and desire that was rioting through her. "You…" She grabbed the lapels of his jacket and stretched up onto her toes, kissing him with every last ounce of passion and frustration that she felt.

He locked his arm around her waist and drew her up tight against his body, his erection hard and hot against her. He spun them around and backed her against the wall, pressing her against the hard surface, his lips hungry as he tasted her, feasted on her.

She wrapped her arms around him, sifted her fingers through his thick brown hair, holding him to her as she returned each stroke and thrust of his tongue. The days of not touching him, thinking of him and denying herself the pleasure of even seeing in him, crashed in on her, fueled her desperation.

She growled in frustration, needing more, faster. Now. She pushed his jacket down his arms and onto the floor, grabbing the knot on his tie and tugging it down as he put his hands on her thighs and pushed the hem of her skirt up. She wrapped one leg around his calf and arched against him.

He tore his mouth away from hers and put his palm flat on the wall behind them, a short, sharp curse punctuated by heavy breaths escaped his lips.

The full horror of what she'd done hit her all at once, like getting a bucket of freezing water dumped in her face. She echoed his choice of swear word and ducked beneath his arm, leaning forward and bracing herself on his desk.

"That shouldn't have happened," she said.

"For more than one reason."

"Why don't you list them?" she said sharply.

"Fine. I'll list them. We said one night. And that kind of kiss doesn't stop at just a kiss. The second reason is that you mean more to me than this," he said.

"Than what?"

"Than an angry make out session against a wall. Than you sneaking around, avoiding me, because we slept together. You mean more to me than sex."

That cut. And maybe it shouldn't have, but she couldn't separate having sex with Zack from the emotions she felt for him. She loved him; sex had been an expression of that. Being joined to him, intimate with him, it had been everything.

But not to him. To him, the sex was separate from the feeling.

"Great. But I apparently don't mean so much to you that you won't use me as a pretend fiancée." Her argument was thin, because frankly, if her feelings for him were platonic, the engagement thing would be nothing big at all.

But her feelings weren't platonic. Not even close.

"Then leave, Clara. If you don't want to do it, don't do it. I'm not holding you hostage. But understand this. I will likely lose the deal with Amudee, and then I won't be able to get the product I need to start the boutique stores. And my search for an acceptable product will continue. It will cost everyone time and money, lots of it. That's just stating a fact—it's not emotional blackmail or anything else you might be tempted to accuse me of."

Clara looked at his face, at the familiar planes and angles. The mouth she'd seen smile so many times, the lips she'd kissed just now. She knew him differently now than she had a week ago. She knew his body, she knew his loss. And as hard as it would have been for her to walk away then, it was impossible now. Impossible to leave him when she'd promised she would see this through.

"I'll do it. I'll play the part, I'll keep playing the part, I mean. But I didn't expect for it to go this far."

"I know. But we had a deal." He probably thought she meant the farce, but she was thinking of the sex. Or maybe he knew what she was really talking about and he was content to leave it ambiguous, just like she was.

"When the ink is dry on the agreement, it can be finished. You gave me your word," he said.

"That's low, Zack," she said, sucking in a deep breath, trying to make her lungs expand.

"It's true. I've been there for you when you needed me. I held your hair while you…"

"I know. Food poisoning. Please don't bring that up." It was right up there with her high-school humiliation. Zack watching her vomit. But he had taken care of her. There hadn't been anyone else. Truly, they were the key players in each other's lives. They were there for each other, at work and at home.

"My point is, I've helped you. Help me. I'm asking you as a friend, not your boss. Your friend."

She gritted her teeth, raw emotion, so intense she couldn't identify it, flooded her. She swung her arms back and forth, trying to ease the nervous energy surging through her limbs. "So when does Mr. Amudee get here?"

"Soon. He'll be in the office tomorrow morning, so it would be good if we came in together."

If they spent the night with each other, it would be even easier for them to commute to Roasted together, but she didn't say that. And she wouldn't. One night, that was all it was supposed to be and that was all it would be. Make-out sessions against the wall would be immediately stricken from record and forgotten. Completely.

"Then I'll see you tomorrow."

"We should probably leave together, too," he said.

"Probably." That would mean an evening waiting around for him to leave. "I'm going to go down to the kitchens and fiddle around with some recipes."

"I'll see you down there."

"See you then." Hopefully a little baking therapy would clear her mind. Because if not, they were both in trouble.

By the time Zack made it down to the kitchen he didn't have a handle on his libido or his temper. He'd figured a couple of hours separation for him and Clara would be a good idea, but it hadn't accomplished anything on his end.

No, he wouldn't feel satisfied until he was in bed with her again. Or just against the wall. That was why he had stopped kissing her, though. He didn't have a condom.

As an adult he hadn't had all that many lovers, mostly because he believed in taking things slowly, and making sure everything was completely safe. He liked for the woman to be on the pill, and he still used condoms, every time.

Already with Clara he'd been lax, skipping steps he hadn't since high school, and then he'd been ready to forgo any sort of protection in his office so that he could be with her again. In her. Because the truth of the matter was, he hadn't stopped thinking about how amazing that night had been since they'd arrived back in California. Not even close.

He'd dreamed of it, or rather, fantasized about it since sleep had eluded him. And when he hadn't been thinking about making love with her, he'd been replaying the moment he'd told her about his son. Over and over again.

He never talked about Jake. Ever. Not since he'd died, still in the hospital he'd never had a chance to leave, only a couple of days old. Sarah had never wanted to talk about it, and they hadn't had a romantic relationship at that point, anyway.

His parents...they had been horrified that their star football-playing son was going to give it all up to raise a child. If anything, they'd been relieved.

That day had changed everything. He'd been nothing more than a spoiled brat. An only child, destined to skate through college on a football scholarship. He'd taken everything, the adoration of the girls at his school, the free passes the teachers had given him, as his due.

But when Jake was born, he'd felt the weight of purpose. And when he died, it hadn't gone away. He hadn't fit anymore. In one blinding, clear moment he saw everything he'd done that was wrong, selfish, careless. He saw how his stupidity had cost everyone so much.

And he'd left. Left who he was. Left everyone he knew. And every day that passed was one day farther away from that awful day in the hospital. That day that had felt like someone reaching into his chest and yanking his emotions out, twisting them, distorting them.

He had never wanted to feel that way again. Ever. Even more importantly, he'd never wanted to have anything unplanned happen ever again. He wanted control. To plan, to consider the cost of his actions. To be in charge of his life.

He wasn't sure why he'd told Clara about it. Although she had asked why the birth-control lapse was such a big deal to him. But then, a few of his girlfriends had wanted to know why he used every method he could think of to prevent pregnancy. It had cost him relationships since the women involved had taken it as a sign of just how much he didn't want to be with them.

And while it was true he hadn't been looking for forever, his reasoning hadn't quite been what they'd assumed. Still, he hadn't felt compelled to tell them the story. Maybe it was because Clara was… Clara. She was the one person who had been in his life with any regularity for the past decade.

And now he'd likely screwed it up by sleeping with her. Or by kissing her. Or maybe he'd screwed it up the moment he'd asked her to play fiancée and go on his honeymoon.

He pushed open the stainless-steel double doors that led to the baking facility and saw Clara, bending down and looking in one of the ovens.

He took the opportunity to enjoy the view, the way her skirt hugged the round curve of her butt. It was a crime that she'd been made to feel insecure about those curves. He flashed back to the heady moments in his office, when he'd had her skirt pushed up around her hips, when he'd been ready to…

She straightened and turned, her brown eyes widening. "Oh! I didn't know you were here."

"Just walked in. What did you make me?"

"I think you'll like them. I have some cooling. I'm going to pass them out at lunch hour tomorrow."

"No walnuts?"

"None. They're Orange Cream. Don't look at me like that, they'll be good." She handed him a vaguely orange cupcake with white frosting, coated in bright orange sugar crystals.

"It has orange zest in the cake, and there's a Bavarian cream in the center. And the frosting is buttercream."

"All things I like." He took a bite, relishing the burst of sweet citrus and cream. She really was a genius. She'd hooked him with her cupcake-making skills the first time he'd met her, and he'd known then he had to have her for his company. That with her, his line of baked goods would be a massive success. And they had been.

And now she was leaving him.

"Good," he said, even though now he was having a hard time swallowing the bite.

"See? I told you."

"And I told you you wouldn't be easily replaced. You're the best at what you do."

She smiled, a sort of funny smile that almost made her look sad. "I do bake a mean cupcake. I'm glad you like them."

He wasn't going to ask her what was wrong. Because he wasn't sure if he could fix it, and he was afraid he might be the cause of it. "Ready to go?"

"Yes, ready. Oh, wait." She stopped and moved toward him, her eyes fixed on his mouth. His entire body was hot and hard instantly. Ready for her touch, her kiss. She extended her hand and put her thumb on the corner of his mouth. "You had some frosting there," she said, her tone as sweet as her cupcakes, her eyes filled with a knowing, sexual expression that told him she was tormenting him, and she knew it. It was going to be an interesting few weeks.

CHAPTER NINE

"I'M NOT GOING to bite you."

Clara glared at Zack from her position in the passenger side of his sporty little two-seater. She was clinging to the door handle, her shoulder smashed against the window. As much space between them as was humanly possible in the tiny metal cage.

The first words that bubbled up were *well that's a shame*. But she held them back, because she was not going to flirt with him. Was not. And she was going to forget about that lapse in the kitchen when she'd wiped the frosting from his mouth. She hadn't licked it off and that had been her first inclination, so really, her self-control was pretty rock solid.

"I know," she said. Much more innocuous than an invitation to bite her, that was for sure.

"Then stop clinging to the door handle like you're planning on jumping out when there's a lull in traffic."

She laughed, somehow, even though most of her felt anything but amused by the entire situation. "I'm not, I promise." She relaxed her hold on the door.

"Good." They pulled down into the underground parking lot of Roasted and into the spot that was second closest to the elevator. He'd given her the closest spot years ago. Some sort of chivalrous gesture, silly, but at the time she'd loved it.

He put the car in Park and killed the engine, getting out and closing the door behind him. She watched him straighten his shirt collar through the window. He hated ties. He didn't wear them unless he had to. It was sexier when he didn't, in her opinion. It showed a little bit of his sculpted chest, a bit of dark hair. Of course, it was sexier when he didn't wear a shirt at all.

She felt the door give behind her and she squeaked, tightening her hold on the handle. Zack had opened it, just a bit, and was looking down at her, the expression on his face wicked.

"Are you going to sit in there all day? Because we have a meeting," he said.

"Creep," she said, no venom in her tone.

He winked and darn it all, it made her stomach turn over. "Only during business hours."

She released her hold on the door and he opened it the rest of the way, waiting for her to get out before pushing the up button on the lift. When they got in and the door closed, the easy moment evaporated.

The tension was back, and so thick she could hardly breathe. Judging by the sharp pitch of his chest when he drew in a breath, he felt the same. It made her feel better. Slightly.

"So, when is he coming in?"

"Soon," Zack said, his eyes fixed on the doors.

"Oh."

The elevator stopped and the doors slid open. Clara nearly sagged with relief as she scurried out of the elevator, eager to get back into non-shared air space.

When she and Zack walked into the main reception area the employees milling around, scavenging on last night's baking efforts stopped and clapped for them. She ducked her head and offered a smile and finger wave. She didn't know if Zack made a reciprocal gesture or not. She was far too busy not dying of humiliation.

The gleaming, golden elevator doors that would take them

up to their offices were just up ahead. She made a dash for it, and Zack got in behind her, the doors sliding closed.

"So many elevators," she said.

"Is that a problem?"

"Not at all," she said.

Two interminable minutes later they were on the floor that housed both of their offices. "I have work to do," she said, heading toward her own office. A little sanctuary would not go amiss.

"No time, Amudee is in the building. My office."

He put his hand on the small of her back and directed her into his office, closing the door behind them. A horrible, hot, tantalizing sense of déjà vu hit her. Their eyes clashed and held, his all steel heat and temptation. He took a step toward her just as the intercom on his desk phone went on.

"Mr. Parsons? Mr. Amudee is here to see you."

Zack leaned back and punched a button on the phone. "Send him in."

She wished she were relieved. She wasn't. She was just disappointed that she hadn't gotten to experience the conclusion of Zack's step forward. Of what he might have intended to do.

Zack's office door opened and the reason for their charade walked in, looking as personable and cheerful as ever, the lines by his dark eyes deepening as he smiled. "Good to see you again. Zack, I stopped by one of your locations here in the city on my way in, I was very impressed."

"Thank you, Mr. Amudee," Zack said, his charm turned on and dialed up several notches.

She watched Zack work, a sense of awe overtaking her. He was good, and she knew that, but seeing him in action was always incredible. He was smart and he was savvy. And the best part was, he really was a man of ethical business practices.

That, she knew, was the thing that made working with Amudee so important to him. Because he didn't just want to import coffee and tea from any farm. He didn't want to get involved in a share-cropping situation. He didn't want anyone being taken advantage of so that he could turn a profit.

Unfortunately Amudee seemed just as picky about who he did business with. And when money wasn't the be all and end all…you couldn't just throw dollars at it to solve everything. Dollars Zack had. It was the fiancée he'd found himself short of.

She toyed with the ring on her finger, her secondhand ring. The one that had belonged to Hannah. She would be a happy woman the moment she could get it off her finger and keep it off, that was for sure.

"So, dinner tonight, then?" Zack said. "Clara?" he prompted.

"Oh, yes. Tonight. Dinner."

"And as for today, I'd be happy to give you a tour of the corporate office. You can see how we run things here."

Mr. Amudee nodded in approval and started to head out the office door with Zack. "So," she said, "I think I'll go to my office and get some work done then."

"Great." He leaned in and kissed her cheek before walking out of the room.

She knew it was an empty gesture, all part of the show. But it still made her feel like she was floating to her office instead of walking. And no matter how much she tried to tell herself not to think about it, her cheek burned for the rest of the morning.

"What is this?"

When Zack had seen Clara's number flash onto his cell-phone screen, he'd heard her sweet hello before he'd even answered. So being greeted by a venomous hiss was an unexpected, unpleasant surprise.

"What is what, Clara? I'm currently battling traffic on North Point so I have no idea what you're talking about."

"This dress. This… Do you even call it a dress? I mean it's short and slinky and I think the neckline is designed to show skin all the way down to a woman's belly button."

"I saw it, and I liked it, so I had my PA send it over."

"I agreed to a lot when I agreed to play fiancée, but I did not," she growled and paused for a moment before continuing, "agree to stuff myself into a gown that has all the give of saran wrap like a Vienna sausage!"

"I like the visual, but your attitude needs work."

"Your head needs work," she shot back.

"Wear the dress." He hung up the phone and tossed it onto the passenger seat before maneuvering his car against the curb in front of Clara's apartment.

He didn't bother to wait for the elevator. He took the stairs two at a time and knocked on her door, beneath the pretty, pink flowery wreath thing she had hung there. A clever ruse to make people think the owner of the apartment was sweetness and light when, at the moment, she was spitting flame and sulfur.

The door jerked open and he met Clara's glittering brown eyes. And then he looked down and all of the blood in his body roared south.

She was right about the dress. A deep scarlet, it would draw the eye of everyone in the restaurant. And while it didn't show her belly button, it did put her amazing cleavage on display. The soft, rounded curves of her breasts were accentuated by the sweetheart neckline, the pleating in the waist showing off just how tiny she was, before her hips flared out, the fabric conforming to that gorgeous, hourglass shape of hers.

"I am not going out in this."

"It's too late for you to change," he said, barely able to force himself to raise his eyes to her face. He had to admit, the dress was counterproductive as when it came to trying to put Clara back into the proper compartment she was meant to be in in his life, he didn't want her to change.

He wanted to look at her in that dress for as long as he could. And then, he wanted to lower the zipper on the back of it and watch it slither down her body. He wanted to see her again, soft, naked and begging him to take her.

"Zack..."

"Do you have something against looking sexy?"

"What? No."

"Then what's the problem? If it honestly offends your modesty in some way, fine, change. But otherwise, you look…"

"Like I'm trying too hard?"

He took a step and she backed away from the door, letting him into the apartment. He shouldn't touch her. Not even an innocent gesture. Because with the thoughts that were running through his brain, nothing could be innocent.

He did anyway, and he ignored the voice in his head telling him to stay in control. He was in control. He could touch her without doing more. He was the master of his body, of his emotions.

He put his finger on her jaw, traced the line of it down her neck, to her exposed collarbone.

"You look effortless. As though bringing men to their knees is something you do every day of the week without breaking a sweat. You look like the kind of woman who can have anyone or anything she wants."

"I… I…well, I don't appreciate you dressing me," she said. "It's demeaning."

"I don't know if it was demeaning, but selfish, perhaps."

"Selfish?"

"Because I'm enjoying looking at you so much."

She bent down and picked up a black shawl from the couch, looping it over her arms before grabbing a black clutch purse from the little side table. "You shouldn't say things like that."

She breezed out the door ahead of him, clearly resigned to wearing the dress.

"Probably not," he said, his tone light.

"But you did anyway," she said, turning to face him.

"I did. There are a lot of things I shouldn't have said or done over the past couple of weeks, and yet, it seems I've said and done them all."

"I haven't," she said, turning away from him again and heading down the stairs, eager to avoid being in an elevator with him, he imagined.

"Oh, really?"

"Mmm. I have been virtuous. I've wanted to say and do many things in the past week that I haven't."

"Why do I feel disappointed by that news?"

"I don't know. You shouldn't be," she said, her stilettos clicking and echoing in the stairwell. "You should be thankful." She pushed open the exterior door and they both walked out into the cool evening air.

"I find I'm not."

"I can't help you there."

Something hot and reckless sparked in him. She must have noticed because she backed away from him until she bumped against his car. That was a picture, Clara, in scarlet silk, leaning against his black sports car. The fantasies that were rolling through his mind should be illegal.

"I wish you could," he said, taking a step toward her.

She shook her head. "There's no help for either of us."

"I'm starting to think that might be true."

He wanted to kiss the red off her lips. He wanted to take her back upstairs and do something about the unbearable ache that had settled in his body more than a week ago and hadn't released him since.

"Let's go. We have a dinner date," he said, his voice curt, harsher than he'd intended.

She nodded and went around to the passenger side and he let out a long, slow breath, trying to ease the tension in his body.

Being with her once hadn't helped at all. One night hadn't been enough.

But there wouldn't be another night. There would be no point to it.

CHAPTER TEN

"THANK YOU FOR doing that," Zack said, once they were back in the car and away from the presence of the man they were putting on the show for.

Dinner had gone well, and it looked like everything was on track for Mr. Amudee to sign the exclusive deal with Roasted. It turned out he was thrilled that Zack was marrying a woman he worked with, a woman who understood and shared his passion for the business. It was one of the things, they'd found out over dessert, that had placed Zack slightly ahead of his rival at Sand Dollar. Because Amudee felt Zack and Clara were working together, and the owner of the other coffee-shop chain would be spending more time away from his family.

So, just another way their farce had helped. She still didn't feel good about it.

"You're welcome."

"I'm serious. I should have thanked you before."

"Gourmet dinner after a week in Thailand? I'm not all that put out by it." A big lie, and they both knew it.

"I'm sorry about earlier," she said. "About freaking out about the dress."

"Not a big deal."

Tension hung thick in the air between them. She just felt...

restless and needy. The kiss, the one they'd shared in his office, still burning her lips.

It was only supposed to be the one time. Just once. In Chiang Mai, not here.

"I really liked my...salmon," she said. It was lame but she didn't want to leave Zack yet. Didn't want to get into her cold, empty bed and slowly die, crushed beneath the weight of her sexual frustration.

A dramatic interpretation of what would actually happen, but she felt dramatic.

"You didn't have salmon."

"I didn't?" she asked.

"No. You had... I think you had chicken."

"Oh."

The only thing she could remember about dinner was trying not to melt every time Zack looked in her direction.

"So... I guess I'll see you tomorrow, then," she said slowly, reaching for the door handle.

"Wait." She froze. "I have a nice vintage wine at my house. I've been meaning to have you come and try it," he said.

She moved away from the car door, letting her back rest against the seat again. "Really?"

"Yes. Do you want... You could come over and have some?"

Zack could have cut his own tongue out. As pickup lines went, it was a clumsy one. He shouldn't be handing her pickup lines at all, clumsy or otherwise. They'd committed to only sleeping together one time, and the fact that he was so turned on his entire body had broken out into a cold sweat shouldn't change that. Once should have been enough. But it wasn't.

He watched her face, watched her eyes get round, her mouth dropping open. As if she'd just realized what the hidden question was.

It was hidden. If she said no, they could both pretend that it wasn't another night he was after. They could brush it under the rug. Simple.

"Now?" she asked.

He nodded once.

"I don't…" She looked at her apartment building for a moment, her hands folded in her lap, toying with the fabric of her skirt, twisting it. "I'd love some wine."

"Good."

He turned the key over and the engine purred as he pulled away from the curb and headed out of the city, toward the waterfront.

Zack's house was a marvel, grand and pristine, massive windows with views the bay and the Golden Gate Bridge. It was a physical testament to the wealth he'd accumulated since he started his business. How much he had done. How far he had come on his own.

Every time she came over, she stopped and looked at the gorgeous, stained-glass skylight in the entryway. Not this time, though. This time, she didn't have energy to focus on anything beyond Zack and the desire that was roaring through her body. Desire that was finally going to be satisfied tonight.

A week without him, without him inside of her body, had been far too long of a wait.

He closed the door behind them and stood still, poised near the door. He looked like a predator lying in wait. The thought of it, of being the object of his desire, heated her from the inside out.

When he moved, it was quick and fluid. He wrapped his arms around her, kissing her deep and long, his tongue stroking against hers, the evidence of his arousal hard and tempting against her body.

"You're sure?"

"No," she said.

"I'm not, either."

"But I want to."

"Me, too. You know where the bedroom is," he said.

"I do. But I haven't spent that much time in it."

"You'll be lucky if I let you out of it tonight," he said, his voice a low growl. Feral and uncontrolled. It sent a shiver of pure need all the way down to her toes.

It was crazy. Stupid crazy and not at all what they'd agreed to. *Just one more time. One more night.*

"I don't mind."

She walked ahead of him, to the winding staircase that led up to his room. She heard him following behind her as she walked up the stairs, and she knew the action was making her dress ride up, made it hug the curve of her bottom, and barely covered it at all.

He grabbed her arm and turned her to him. He was on the step below her, which, with her heels, made them close to the same height. He put his hand on her lower back and pressed her to him, kissing her again, his mouth hot and hungry on hers.

She cupped his face, his stubble rough on her fingertips, a potent, sexy reminder of his masculinity. He reached up and took her hands, lacing his fingers through hers and backing her against the wall as he stepped up onto the stair she was on.

He pressed his body against hers, hard and long, perfectly muscular. She started working the buttons on his shirt, popping a few of them off in her haste to get him undressed. He helped with the sleeve cuffs and tossed the shirt down to the bottom of the stairs.

"Oh, yes," she breathed, running her hands over his bare chest, the crisp hair tickling her palms. "You're so hot."

He chuckled. "I could say the same." He gripped the zipper tab of her dress and tugged it down, letting her dress fall off her body. She hardly had time to think about it, to worry about how she looked to him.

She kicked the dress down to the next stair, still wearing her heels, a strapless bra and a pair of underwear that may as well not exist for all that they covered.

But tonight, she really did feel sexy. She didn't feel the need to cover herself, to hide anything. And she really didn't want him hiding anything. She made quick work of his slacks, pushing them down his muscular thighs, her body heating when she looked at him, dressed in nothing more than a pair of tight black boxer briefs that revealed the outline of his erection in tantalizing detail.

She put her hand on him, sliding her palm over his cloth-covered length, reveling in his harsh, indrawn breath.

"Do you know how many times I thought of you?" she asked, the question requiring a whole lot of boldness she hadn't realized she possessed. "Of touching you. Having my way with you. You've kept me up a lot of nights, Zack. Imagining what it would be like if you kissed me."

"You thought of me?" he asked, his words rough.

"I did."

He didn't have to ask why she hadn't acted on it. Because what would the point have been? They didn't want the same things. He wanted a loveless marriage, no family. She wanted more. There was still no point to this. No point beyond trying to satisfy the sexual hunger that was burning between them.

And the burning hope in her that she couldn't quite snuff out that wondered if he could change his mind...

"Do you know what *I've* thought about?" She pushed his underwear down and he kicked them down with the growing pile of clothes on the staircase. She started to kneel down in front of him and he forked his fingers through her hair, halting her for a moment, the sting from the tug on her hair sending a sharp sensation of pleasure through her.

"Careful," he said. "I'm close."

"We have all night. I'm not worried. And I've had a lot of fantasies about this. You wouldn't deny me a little fantasy fulfillment, would you?" She leaned forward and flicked the tip of her tongue over the head of his shaft. He sucked in a breath, his hold on her hair tightening again.

She took him into her mouth, loving the taste of him, the

power she felt. That she could make his thigh muscles shake, make his hands tremble. He kept one hand in her hair, one on the staircase railing, bracing himself as she continued to explore him.

"Clara... I need...not like this."

She raised her head, her heart nearly stopping when she saw his face. He had sweat beads on his forehead, the tendons in his neck standing out. He looked like a man who'd been tortured with pleasure.

And she'd been the one doing the torturing.

"I don't mind."

"I do. I need to have all of you."

"Maybe we can make it the rest of the way up the stairs?"

"If we hurry," he growled.

So she did, walking in front of him, knowing her thong and high heels were making a provocative visual for him. The feeling of confidence she felt, the absolute certainty that he enjoyed looking at her, that, for now at least, she was the woman he desired, was amazing. New.

His bedroom door was open, and she walked inside and sat down on the bed, waiting for him. He stood in the doorway, his eyes hot on her. The lights were off, moonlight filtering through the window. The darkness felt like a cover, made her feel more confident.

"Take everything off," he bit out.

She undid the front clasp on her bra and was gratified by the sharp rise and fall of his chest as she revealed her breasts to him. She stood and tugged her underwear down her legs, leaving the high heels for last.

"Want to help with these?" she asked, sitting again, holding her foot out.

He smiled and walked over to the bed and knelt in front of her, putting his hands on the curve of her knees, sliding them down her calf, he bent his head down and kissed her ankle as he took one of her shoes off and dropped it onto the carpet.

He did the same with the other one, slow, erotic movements making her shiver all over. And when he leaned in and pressed his mouth between her thighs she nearly came apart with the first stroke of his tongue.

"I'll confess, I didn't think about this very much until recently," he said. "But I haven't stopped thinking about it since last week. Every night, I dream of you," he said, his voice rough as he continued to pleasure her with his hands.

"Me, too," she said, panting, her body on the brink of climax, so close she felt it all through her, tension drawing all of her muscles tight.

Zack stood up, his smile wicked as he looked at her. He leaned over and took a condom from the nightstand. He tore the packet open and rolled a condom onto his length before joining her on the bed.

He put his hands on her thigh and pulled her over him so that her legs were bracketing his and his erection poised at the entranced to her body. Her eyes locked with his, she lowered herself onto him, a low moan climbing in her throat as he filled her.

She gripped his shoulders, enjoying the feeling. Enjoying the moment of being joined with him completely.

She moved slowly at first, trying to find the right rhythm, her confidence increasing as his grip on her hips tightened, as she started to move closer to the edge of climax.

She was saying things, words, about how good it felt, how much she cared about him, but she wasn't sure what she was saying exactly. She didn't care. She couldn't think, she could only feel.

Could only hold on to Zack as her orgasm pushed her over the edge and into an abyss of light and feeling, where there was nothing, no one, except for her and Zack. There was no past, and there was no future. There was only the two of them.

In that world, in that moment, everything could work. Everything was perfect.

The ascent back to reality was slow and fuzzy, and she almost regretted it when it happened. But even reality, his skin hot and sweaty beneath her cheek, his chest hair a little bit scratchy, was pretty near perfect.

She didn't have the assurance of a future. But for now she had Zack. And she would take him. She felt tears sting her eyes and she squeezed them shut, trying to hold them at bay.

She had him tonight. And it would be perfect. She wouldn't ruin it by crying.

"I'll go and take care of things," he said.

Clara sat up and let Zack get out of bed and go into the bathroom. He came back a couple of moments later and slid back into bed. She looked at his profile. Strong, set. So handsome, so special to her. For so long she'd imagined that she knew everything about Zack. Now she found out there was a huge piece missing.

"Zack…" She knew she probably shouldn't say what was on her mind, but they were naked and in bed together. If they couldn't be honest now, when could you be honest with anyone? "What happened?"

"I told you," he said, his voice stilted. He knew what she meant. No need to clarify.

"Sort of."

"You want to hear more?"

"I want to know what happened. Have you ever told anyone?"

There was a long pause, Zack shifted next to her. "I don't talk about this, Clara. Not ever. Not with anyone."

She put her hand on his shoulder. "And I don't let men see me naked. Not ever. But I let you. So tell me."

He paused and she thought, for a moment, he wasn't going to say anything. "We named him Jake. He lived for forty-eight hours. No one at the hospital thought, even for a moment, that he had a chance. But I did." Silence hung between them, heavy and oppressive. She didn't interrupt it.

Zack breathed in deeply. Faintly, in the dim light filtering in through the windows, she could see a single track of moisture shining on his cheek. "I was wrong. There was no miracle. No beating the odds. I'd thought... I was sure he'd have to be okay. I'd changed all my plans, in my head, my whole future was different. And then it was back to being the same, except it wasn't. It never would be again. And my parents... I think they were relieved. They'd been so angry that I was throwing my future away. I think they were relieved when my son died, Clara."

"Zack..." She started to offer something. Comfort maybe. But she wasn't sure if there was any comfort for that kind of pain. She wasn't sure if it was a wound that could heal.

"Sarah didn't want to talk to me again and I don't blame her. Every time I looked at her I just remembered. I think it was the same for her. So I just left. I couldn't stay there." He paused for a moment. "He would be fourteen now. Just two years younger than I was when he was born. Maybe he'd play football, like I did. He'd be close to the age where I would be teaching him how to drive and telling him about girls. I think about it still. About him. I didn't understand how one person could, even for such a short amount of time, became my whole world. For those two days, I breathed for him. And when he stopped, I almost forgot why I was still trying. Rock bottom is...something else. There's a lot of alcohol there, let me tell you. But not even that fixes it. It just makes you pathetic. But I got hired on at a coffeehouse here, even though I was an aimless wreck. Once I had that job, I had a new focus. I got my GED, I found out I loved coffee. I worked my way up in the company, and I bought it from my boss when he retired. I think that's the beginning of what you, and everyone else, already knew."

She wiped at a tear that was sliding down her cheek, her heart aching, her entire body aching, real, physical pain tearing at her. She turned to the side and rested her head on his shoulder, her hand on his face. He wrapped an arm around her and held her to him.

"But that changed me," he said, his voice strong. "It made me grow up. Made me move forward. It taught me to value control. Responsibility and planning. It's why I'm here. Why I'm so successful and not some burned out, ex-college football star has-been."

He believed it. She could tell he did. But the road to success had been hard. It had hurt. And along with conviction, she heard the pain in his voice, too.

"Arrogance, impulsiveness. That leads to disaster. It creates grief. Needless grief," he said.

She wished she could tell him how much she loved him, but she knew that it was the last thing he wanted to hear. So she just held him, and let him hold her. Let him offer her comfort, so that he didn't realize she sas offering him everything.

"So," she said after a while, "do you want me to go?"

"I want you here," he said. "Spend the night with me."

"Sure, Zack," she said, breathing a sigh of relief.

He tightened his hold on her and neither of them spoke.

Tonight they were together. She hoped she didn't fall asleep. She didn't want to miss a moment.

Clara rolled over and stretched in the morning, her eyes opening to a familiar sight. Zack's room. Though, it wasn't familiar at all to wake up in Zack's room. Even less familiar to wake up in Zack's room after making love with him all night.

A slow smile spread across her lips, followed by a pang of sadness when she remembered their conversation. When she remembered his story about his son.

She looked at Zack, his eyes still closed. She wished, more than anything, that she could take his pain from him. His grief was something she couldn't begin to understand, the kind of cut it would leave so deep she wasn't sure if it could heal. She knew it couldn't, not really. It would never disappear. He'd said himself it had changed him. Had changed the course of his entire life.

His eyes opened and he smiled. "Good morning."

"Morning."

"So, I guess we should get ready to go to work," she said.

"You think so?"

"Well, it's almost time."

"True," he said, wrapping his arms around her and rolling her beneath him. "But you might be able to go in late today. I know the boss."

"So do I," she said, wiggling underneath him. "He's kind of intense about people being at work on time. A bit anal, even."

His eyebrows shot up. "Really? Well, I have a feeling that he'll look the other way today."

CHAPTER ELEVEN

"I GOT AN invitation in the mail. For me and my wife." Zack walked into her office and tossed a cream-colored envelope onto her desk.

She grimaced. "Don't people read the news?"

"Well, I called the charity putting the event on and I explained to them what happened. Of course, they would still like me to come and buy two dinners at four hundred dollars a plate, so my new fiancée is more than welcome."

"Well, hopefully the deal will be finalized by then," she said, looking down at the spiteful ring. "And I'll be off the hook."

"Good for both of us, but even if you are, you still might like to come. As my friend."

"Right." Yes. They were friends. First and foremost, before the sex stuff. At least in his mind. She was his friend, and he was hers, her very best friend. But he was so much more to her than that.

"It's for charity. Something I've been planning on for a while, though, thanks to everything that's been happening the timing slipped my mind. And I can't take anyone else until all of this is finished."

She noticed he didn't say that he didn't want to take anyone else. Only that he *couldn't*.

Being a bit oversensitive, aren't we? Maybe. Or maybe not.

"When is it?" she asked.

"Thursday. How are things going today? Have you come up with anything to go with the white tea from Amudee's? I'm thinking of a gourmet tea cake. Wondering if we could start making our own preserves. That has definite mass-market appeal. Are you closer to reaching a deal?"

"It looks that way. I'm optimistic. He's a hard man to read but he seems reasonably satisfied that Roasted is run to the sort of standards he likes to see."

"Good." She fought the urge to reach out and touch him, to forge a connection. That would just come across as needy and she didn't want to seem needy. Even if she did feel a little bit needy.

"What's this?" He took a sheet of paper off her desk and she cringed.

"Uh...a list I was making. For my bakery."

Her bakery. The dream that wasn't really her dream. She loved her job at Roasted, but if things didn't work out with Zack she was going to need her escape more than ever.

"Oh. Right." He set it back down. "Working on it during business hours?"

"Or during lunch. Or maybe during business hours, but you know I put my time in," she said stiffly.

"I'm not going to give you special treatment just because we slept together."

His words hung in the air, too loud in the small office, and far too harsh for her already-tender insides.

"Of course not. That would be ridiculous," she said, picking up a stack of unidentified papers from her desk and walking over to the industrial stapler. She punched it down in three places and hoped that they were at least documents that went together. "Why would you do that?"

The truth was, he had always treated her like she was special, and having him say something like that made her feel demoted.

"You know what I meant."

"I guess I don't."

He rounded her desk and cupped her chin with his thumb and forefinger, tilting her face up so that she had to meet his eyes. He leaned in and pressed a light kiss to her lips. He didn't apologize. He didn't say anything. Even so, all of the fight drained out of her.

"I'm going to be busy tonight," he said.

That was probably for the best. Distance was probably a really, really good idea. Because she desperately didn't want it, and that meant she very likely needed it. Because last night was proof neither of them were thinking clearly where the other was concerned.

They'd done it again. And there could be no more sex. None. It was too dangerous for her, too stupid. Too little. It was physical only for Zack, and she wanted more. She needed more.

"All right. Me, too, actually." She'd find something to be busy with. She would. Except, the only people she ever hung out with, besides Zack, were the people she worked with. And it would be hard hanging out with them now when she was lying to them.

Maybe she'd work on some of the tea pastries she'd been thinking of.

"See you tomorrow, then. At work," she said, feeling very accomplished that she was managing to seem cool and aloof about the whole thing.

"See you then," he said, nodding and walking out of the room.

When he left she blew out a breath. The affair, fling, whatever, was supposed to ease some of the tension between them. But if anything, it seemed more intense than it had before.

She looked back down at her list. The items she was choosing for if she opened her own bakery. For if she had to leave Roasted so she could get away from Zack.

She was starting to hope she wouldn't need it.

* * *

Clara put a pan of twelve cupcakes into the oven and closed the rack with her foot. They were pineapple cupcakes which she was intending to pair light, whipped frosting and candied mango on top. They might very well taste like a Caribbean vacation gone wrong, but she was feeling risky.

She was also feeling restless and sad.

It was Monday and normally Zack would come over for a football game neither of them would pay attention to. He would bring takeout, she would provide all things baked and sinful.

She missed that. And she wondered if the status quo hadn't been so bad after all.

Right. Because you were such a sopping, sad mess you made his wedding cake even though it destroyed you to do it. And you've barely had a date since you met the man.

All true.

She growled into the empty room and turned her focus to whipping her frosting. That, at least, was physically satisfying. She dipped an unused spoon into the mix and tasted it. She hit Play on her kitchen stereo system and turned to the pantry humming while she rummaged for a can of pineapple juice.

She heard a sharp knock over the sound of her acoustic-guitar music and she stopped rummaging. She frowned and walked over to the door, peeking through the security window at the top.

Zack was there, looking back down the hall, like he was thinking about leaving. He had a brown paper bag in his hand, his work clothes long discarded in favor of a gray T-shirt and a pair of dark fitted jeans.

Her heart crumpled. Seeing him was almost painful. A reminder of how close they'd been physically. How far apart they were emotionally.

She braced herself for the full impact of his presence and opened the door.

He turned to her, smiling. "Hi."

"I thought you were busy."

That wasn't what she'd intended to lead with, but it had sort of slipped out. Things just seemed to be "happening" around him without her permission a lot lately.

"It turns out it could wait." He slipped past her and stepped into her apartment, depositing his bags of food on the counter and pulling white boxes from it without even asking for permission.

"Why are you…here?"

"It's Monday."

"And?"

"Football." He shrugged as he opened the first container, revealing her favorite, Sweet and Sour Pork. Like nothing had changed.

It was comforting in a very bizarre way. And a tiny bit upsetting, too. She wasn't sure which emotion she was going to let win. She'd give it until after dinner to decide.

"Right." She turned and made her way around the counter, taking plates and utensils out of the cupboard and drawers. Zack dished up the food and neither of them spoke as they took their first few bites.

"You could turn the game on," she said.

Zack walked across the open room and took her remote off the couch, aiming it at the TV and putting it on the local channel broadcasting the event.

"Who's playing?" she asked.

"No idea." He tossed the remote back where it had been and crossed back into the kitchen, taking a seat at one of the bar stools that lined the counter.

"Important enough to come over for, though," she said, looking down at her plate and stabbing a piece of meat with her fork.

"I missed you," he said, his voice rough.

"What…me? You missed me?"

"Yes. We always get together Monday. And I found myself wandering around my house. Thought about turning the game on. But you're right. I don't really care about football, probably a side effect of coming down from the high of being the world's most entitled high-school jock. I didn't really want to watch sports, but I did want to eat dinner. With you."

"I missed you, too, Zack," she said.

His smile. His presence. His arms around her while she slept. But she wasn't allowed to miss that last part. That had to be done. Over.

As for their friendship…she didn't know what she would do without him. But she didn't know if she would ever get over him if he was always around, either.

But she had to be with him, at least until she left Roasted. She would worry about the rest then.

"Making cupcakes?" he asked.

"They're going to be very tropical." She took a bite of fried rice and stood up, walking back into the kitchen to grab the can of pineapple juice she'd been after when he came to the door. "Not sure about them yet."

She punched the top of the tin and drizzled some juice into her frosting, stirring it in slowly.

Zack leaned over the counter and stuck his finger in the bowl. She smacked the top of his hand. "I will frost your butt, Parsons. Keep your fingers out of my mixing bowl."

He held his finger near his lips and gave her a roguish smile. "Is that what the kids are calling it these days?" He licked his frosting-covered finger and her internal muscles clenched in response.

She snorted. "No. I don't know. You know what I meant."

"Yeah."

Her heart fluttered, but it was a manageable amount. "Behave."

He arched one eyebrow. "Can't make any promises."

She rolled her eyes and sat back down to her dinner.

"Heard anymore about the store in Japan?" she asked.

That got Zack rolling on statistics and sales figures and all sorts of things he found endlessly fascinating. She liked that about him. Liked that his job sometimes gave him a glint in his eye that made him look like an enthusiastic kid.

Then he launched into a story about the street performers that had been out in front of the restaurant tonight when he'd picked the food up, which reminded her of the time they'd been all but accosted by a street mime on their way to lunch one day.

She really had missed this. Sharing. Laughing. She loved that he knew her, that he knew all of her best stories, her most embarrassing moments.

The timer pinged for the cupcakes and she got up to check them.

"Finished?" he asked.

"Yes," she said, pulling them out with an oven mitt and setting them on the counter. "But hot." She nearly laughed at his pained expression. "I have some cool ones, though. I know you don't bake, but if you want to frost them you're welcome to."

"I think I can handle that."

"Bear in mind they are highly experimental."

He smiled. "Sounds exciting, anyway."

"Or a potential disaster of epic proportions, but we won't know until we taste them."

She loaded up a frosting bag and handed it to Zack while she set her own up and got started on leaving little stars all over the surface of one of the cupcakes.

Zack sneaked his hand past her and dipped it into the bowl again. She grabbed the spatula and smacked the back of his hand, leaving a streak of white frosting behind. "I said stop!" she said, laughing as he examined the mess she'd left behind.

"But the frosting is the best part."

"You didn't try the cake yet."

He shrugged and raised his hand to his lips cleaning off the frosting she'd left behind, then he moved his finger near her mouth. "Taste?" he asked.

In that moment, it felt like her vision tunneled, reduced to nothing but Zack. The game, the sounds of the whistle, the crowd, the announcers, faded, blood roaring in her ears.

It was innocent. Or it should have been. She tried to tell herself that for about ten seconds. Because there was no female friend on earth, no matter how close, who would have offered what Zack was at the moment.

So it wasn't innocent. She looked up, her eyes clashing with his.

They were dark, intense. Aroused. The air between them seemed to thicken, the only sound her breath. Too loud. Too obvious.

It wasn't innocent at all.

She'd promised herself it wouldn't happen again. That their last night together had been exactly that: their last night together.

It won't happen again. I just need a taste.

She leaned in and slid her tongue along the line of his finger and her entire body tightened when a rough groan escaped his lips. The salt of his skin gave bite to the super-sweet frosting. If her cupcakes were a bust maybe she could just spread it all over Zack...

No.

She pulled back sharply, shaking her head. "Sorry. Just... sorry, I..."

He wrapped his arm around her waist and kissed her, deep and long, his tongue still coated in icing. When he released her, she felt dazed in the very best way.

She licked her lips. "You taste like a pineapple," she said, her breath erratic, her heart pounding.

"Is that a good thing?" His voice sounded strained, like each word was an effort.

"I might have to...test it out again."

He smiled and her stomach curled in on itself. "I'm more than willing to aid you in the testing."

He dipped his head and she closed the distance between

them, sliding her tongue over his bottom lip, reveling in the rough groan that rumbled in his chest.

He dipped his fingers back in the bowl and tugged at the hem of her shirt, drawing it over her head. "I feel at a disadvantage," he said, sliding his fingers over her stomach. "Because you got a chance to taste me this way, and I haven't gotten to do the same."

He bent down and slid his tongue over her stomach. She shivered, gripping his shoulders, knowing they were going too far, not sure if she wanted to stop.

He stood and reached behind her, unhooking her bra with one hand. "You're better at that than I am," she said, her voice shaking.

"Good. That's kind of the idea. I'd hate to think you'd be better off doing this for yourself." He cupped her breast and slid his thumb off her nipple, leaving a faint dusting of icing covering her there. He bent his head and circled the tightened bud with his tongue before drawing it into his mouth.

She forked her fingers through his hair, holding his head to her as he continued to lavish attention on her breast.

"Oh, no... I could not do this by myself," she breathed.

He lifted his head and captured her lips, sweetness clinging to his tongue, his grip tight on her hips as he tugged her body against his. "You're beautiful," he said, abandoning her mouth to skim kisses down her neck, across her collarbone.

"You make me believe it."

He raised his head, his expression serious. "You should never doubt it, not for a moment. You make me lose control."

The words hung between them, an admission that held power. Because she knew Zack, and she knew what he prized. His control. Above everything. She knew why now, too. She even understood it. And he was saying that her beauty, her body, took it from him.

"Me?" she asked.

"You," he repeated, his voice hard. "Everything about you."

He moved his palm over her breast and she shuddered. "Now that I'm allowing myself to look... I can't stop myself. I can't stop at just looking, I have to touch you, then I have to taste you. And it's still not enough."

Zack's heart raged out of control. It was more than just arousal. His chest burned, the need going so much deeper than sex. It was pleasure and pain, heaven and hell. But he couldn't turn away from any of it. He didn't want to.

This wasn't what was supposed to happen tonight. He'd missed Clara, Clara his friend. The companionship she provided, the safety. She was the one person he ever let his guard down with. The one person he laughed with. Relaxed with.

It wasn't supposed to turn into this. But his desire for her was like a storm, devastating everything in its path. Devastating his control.

And he'd admitted it to her. Because what else could he do? She'd brought him to his knees.

"It's a nice apartment," he said, trying to lighten the moment, to bring himself back to earth. "I bet the bedrooms are really nice."

She snorted a laugh and buried her face in his neck. "You've been in my bedroom."

He sifted her hair through his fingers. "I've never slept in your bed."

"Do you want to?" She posed the question as though she was asking if he wanted something purely innocent.

"After we get some other business taken care of."

"I'm in complete agreement with that."

He swung her up into his arms and she squeaked, looping her arms around his neck and laughing as he dashed to her bedroom.

Zack set Clara down when they got inside her room. A room he'd been in more times than he could count. But never like this. She kissed him, her mouth hungry, pulled his shirt off him in one swift motion. Trading piece of clothing for piece of clothing until they were both naked, limbs entwined, her full breasts pressed against his chest.

It was almost enough for a while, to simply lay on the bed with her, moving his hands over her bare curves, kissing her. Doing nothing more than kissing.

It was almost enough, but not quite.

He swore sharply. "I don't have anything. I didn't plan this."

"It's okay," she said, wrapping her hand around his length, squeezing him. He groaned, her soft flesh against his almost making up for the fact that he couldn't be inside her. Almost.

He put his hand between her thighs and drew his fingers over her clitoris, then repeated the motion.

She gasped and arched against him, tightening her hold on his arms, fingernails digging into his skin. "Oh, Zack," she breathed, his name on her lips like balm to his soul.

Everything after that was lost in a frenzy of movement, sighs and graphic words that he'd never heard come from Clara's mouth before. But it was only more exciting, because it was her. Because he knew that he was able to do that to her, to make her say things, feel things no other man ever had.

They reached the peak together, his body shaking down to his bones as he found his release.

He held her soft body against his afterward, a sort of strange contentedness spreading through him that he'd never felt before.

"You're beautiful, you know?" he asked, pushing her hair to one side and kissing her neck.

She turned to look at him, rolling to her side, making the curve of her hip rounder, her waist smaller. And her breasts...

"You keep saying that."

"So that you can't doubt it."

"I'm starting to believe you, actually," she said, a smile curving her lips. She reached out and put her finger on his biceps, tracing a long line up to his shoulder. "You're not so bad yourself."

"I'm flattered." He leaned forward and kissed her nose, the

contentedness morphing into something else. Something that felt light and...happy.

He wrapped his arms more tightly around her and rolled onto his back. She planted her palms on his chest, her body half on his.

"Hi," she said, smiling.

"I just want you to know that you're not second to anyone," he said, cupping her cheek. "There's no other woman on earth I would rather be with."

Her brown eyes glistened. "You really are good for my ego."

"I'm glad. Someone has to be."

He wanted to say something. Something bigger than he should, than he could. He just wanted more. In that moment, with her body, so soft and bare and perfect, pressed against his, with her smiling at him like he could solve all of the world's problems, he wanted to offer her the world. He wanted more than temporary, more than distant for the first time in his memory.

She rested her head on his chest, her fingertips moving lightly over his skin until her breathing deepened and her eyes fluttered closed.

It wasn't until she was asleep that panic slammed into him. The full enormity of what had happened. He'd lost control. More than that, he'd been letting go of it, inch by inch, with Clara for the past seven years.

With everyone else he was guarded. He never dropped his defenses. He never talked about his past.

He'd cried in front of her. He had allowed real, raw weakness and emotion to escape in her presence when he never even let himself give in like that in private. She was under his skin. So much so she felt like she was a part of him.

A necessary part.

What if he lost her? No, it wasn't even a matter of if, it was when.

The terror that thought evoked, the absolute, gut-wrenching horror was a sobering as a punch to the jaw. He was playing a game he had no business playing, flirting with things he shouldn't be. Tempting feelings he couldn't risk having.

He slid out of her hold and she stirred briefly, stretching, arching her back. His mouth dried. He shook his head and bent to collect his clothes, dressing and walking out of her bedroom, closing the door quietly behind him, ignoring the continual stab of pain in his chest.

He paused in her living room for a moment, the weight of the familiarity of his surroundings crushing him, a feeling of claustrophobia overtaking him.

He had to leave. He had to think. He had to find his control.

He walked out her front door, closing it behind him and making sure everything was locked so that she would be safe. He walked out into the cold night, sucking in a deep breath and blaming the cold for the pain that came with it.

"Where were you this morning? When did you leave?" Clara whispered the words when she went into Zack's office in the early afternoon. He'd been out of the office all morning, and he had been very noticeably not at her apartment before that.

"I had some things to do," he said, his voice flat. "Could you bring me a coffee?" His phone rang and he picked it up. She stomped out of the room and picked up the freshly brewed pot that was sitting in the main area of the office. She poured a half a cup and dumped powdered creamer in, no sugar, and stirred it halfheartedly with one of the little wooden sticks that was on the coffee station.

There were still little lumps of powder floating on the top.

She went back into his office and plunked it onto his desk, letting some of it slosh over the side. He didn't flick her or the coffee a glance as he continued his phone call. He picked it up and took a sip then grimaced and set it back down, shooting her an evil look. She responded with a wide, saccharine smile.

"I'll call you back," he said into the phone, hanging up. "Do you have something on your mind?"

"Yes. Where were you this morning, and do not give me another half-assed answer."

"Clara, there's a way I conduct physical relationships. I don't always stay for the whole night."

She felt like he'd slapped her. Like she was just the same as every other physical relationship he had. But she wasn't. She knew she wasn't.

Anger made her scalp feel prickly. "Don't give me that. Don't even try. I made you shake last night. Made you lose control." Boldness came from anger, and she could't regret it.

His eyes glittered and he looked like he might pounce on her. But he didn't. "I just went home, so that I could get a good night's sleep. I have to go over some legalese in the contract I'm having drawn up for the deal with Amudee. That's all."

That wasn't all. She knew it wasn't all. But she didn't know what the rest of it was, either, so that didn't help.

"And that looks like it's going to go through?" she asked, looking down at the ring again, the ring she was starting to hate, willing to let the subject drop, for now.

"Looks like, but nothing is finalized. So we're still in this until the ink is dry."

She nodded. "I know."

It was all about the contract to Zack. Last night...she could have sworn that last night something had changed. There had been more in their lovemaking. There had been fun. Their friendship had been in it.

It had been special.

Well, today things felt different. It just wasn't the sort of different she'd been hoping for.

"I'll be down in the kitchen," she said, eager to get away.

It was going to take a whole lot of cupcakes to make this day feel okay.

* * *

The next few days Zack really did manage to be busy and stay busy. He didn't stop by her apartment late at night, or any time of day. Her head hurt and her bed felt empty. Which was silly, since her bed had been empty of anyone other than her for twenty-five years.

It was just the past couple weeks she'd had Zack sometimes. And she found she really liked it, and it wasn't just because of the orgasms. It was just listening to him breathe. Feeling his body heat so close to hers. Just being with him, finally, finally able to express how much she wanted him. To not have to hold such a huge part of herself back from him anymore.

She loved the way he made her feel about herself. That he wanted her in a sexy red dress, or yoga pants, or nothing. That he made her feel beautiful. That he made her see things in herself she hadn't seen before.

And if she told him that he'd undoubtedly run away screaming.

Tonight, the contracts remained unsigned and that meant they still had plans to go to the big charity event. Something to do with a children's hospital. She wondered if that was by design. If it would bother him. Make him think of his son.

Her heart hurt every time she thought of Zack's past. Of what that false front of his was created to hide. To hide what he'd been through, who he really was. He had perfected a persona, controlled, light, charming, and even she had bought into it. Not even *she* had seen everything.

But she was starting to.

Tonight was going to feel more like a real date. A public event with just the two of them, not with Mr. Amudee sitting by, watching their performance as a couple. She was dressing up in a dress she'd selected this time. Something between her usual fare and that screaming, sex-on-a-hanger number Zack had picked out for her.

It was a full-length gown with a mermaid-style skirt that

conformed to her body before flaring out around her knees. It swished when she walked, and a halter-top neckline showed her cleavage. And she felt sexy in it. She felt like a woman who was ready to conquer the world. One who could outshine other women, at least for the man she was with. And that was what mattered, anyway.

She heard a knock on her door and she tried to shove her feet into stilettos, while standing, and fastening dangly diamond earrings. "Coming!"

She opened the door and all the air rushed out of her body. Zack was a wearing a suit, black jacket, crisp white shirt and a perfectly straight black tie. He was the epitome of gorgeous. He always was, half dressed, all dressed or completely naked. But there was something about a man in a suit...

It sort of reminded her of his wedding. The wedding that wasn't.

"You look...you look great," she said.

"So do you. I brought you something," he said.

There was something strange about his tone, something formal and distant. It matched his clothing. Cool, well-tailored, nothing out of place. And yet, that in and of itself felt out of place. Zack wasn't formal with her. Why should he be? They'd known each other for years. They had slept together for heaven's sake.

She held her hand out and smiled, trying to make him smile. It didn't work.

He took a flat, black box from his jacket and opened it.

"Oh, my... Zack this is...it must have cost..." None of her words would gel into a complete sentence, everything jumbling and stalling half thought through.

It was a necklace, a truly spectacular necklace, not the sort you saw under the display case of just any department store. Not even the sort of thing you saw at Saks. It was too unique, too extravagant.

She reached out and touched the center stone, a deep green

emerald, cut into the shape of a teardrop and surrounded by glittering diamonds.

"I don't think I can accept this."

"Of course you can," he said, his voice still tinged with that unfamiliar distance. "Turn around."

She did, slowly, craning her neck to look at him. He swept her hair to the side and took the necklace from the box, draping it over her, the stone falling between her breasts, the chill making her shiver. He clasped the necklace, his fingers brushing the back of her neck as we worked the tiny clasp.

"This isn't…this isn't a friendships gift," she said, her voice trembling.

That did earn her a short chuckle. "Maybe tonight friendship isn't what I want."

His words made her shiver, the sensual promise in them turning her on. The underlying, darker meaning she couldn't quite grasp making goose bumps break out on her arms. "It really is too much," she said, turning to face him, her nose nearly touching his.

He straightened putting some distance between them. "It's a perfectly fitting gift for a lover. Are you ready?"

"Yes," she said, turning his choice of word over in her head. Yes, she was his lover, in the sense that they'd slept together. But there was something in the way he said it, something that seemed cold, when a lover should be something warm. Something personal.

She touched the necklace, the gems cold beneath her fingertips.

CHAPTER TWELVE

THE CHARITY BALL was crowded already when they arrived, a sea of beautiful people dressed in black positioned around the ballroom, chatting and eating the very expensive canapes.

Heads turned when she and Zack walked down the marble staircase and down into the room. Everyone was looking at Zack, because it was impossible not to. She was fully appreciating just how he was viewed in the community now. A man of power and wealth, a man of unsurpassed beauty. If you could call what he possessed beauty. It was too masculine for that, and yet she wasn't sure there was another word for it, either.

Pride flared in her stomach, low and warm. All the women in the room were looking at Zack with undisguised sexual hunger. And Zack was with her. Touching her, his hand low on her back, possessive.

She turned and pressed a kiss to his cheek. He looked at her. "What was that for?"

"Because," she said.

He looked at her for a moment, a strange light in his eyes. "Let's go find our table."

"Okay," she said, trying to ignore the tightening in her throat.

There was a table, for two, with place cards set on each empty plate. Zack held her chair out for her and she sat, her heart slamming against her ribs as she read the name that had been written in calligraphy on her place card.

Hannah Parsons.

With Zack's name tacked on to hers, even. Clara felt dizzy. She looked down at the ring. Hannah's ring. Hannah's seat. Hannah's man. She had to wonder if the necklace had been meant for Hannah, too.

She wrapped her fingers around the card and curled them into a fist, crumpling it and tossing it onto the marble floor.

"What the hell?" Zack asked.

"It had the wrong name on it," she said stiffly.

"Does it matter?"

That hit even harder than seeing the name. "I suppose not." She put her foot over the crumpled paper and squished it beneath the platform of her stiletto.

"You're the one who's here with me." He stretched his hand toward hers, covering it, stroking her wrist. "No one else."

She knew it. And in some ways she knew his words were sincere. But there was also something generic in them. There was something strangely generic to the whole evening and she couldn't quite place what it was or why.

"Of course." She looked into his eyes, tried to find something familiar now. Something of her friend. But she didn't see it. She only saw the man as he presented himself to the world. Aloof, put together, charming. But there was no depth there. No feeling or warmth.

It was frightening.

Dinner was lovely, tiny bits of sculpted beauty made to be admired before being eaten. Of course it was marked up extravagantly, because the whole point of the evening was that the charity received donations.

A woman in a long, flowing dress walked up onto the stage, her air of authority making it obvious that she was the coordinator of the event, and a hushed silence fell over the crowd.

"Thank you all for coming tonight," she said. "And for the

very generous donation of your time and money to the Bay Area Children's Hospital."

She turned and looked toward their table, a smile on her face. "And tonight, we would also like to give special acknowledgment to Mr. Zack Parsons, who has donated enough money to revamp the entire Neo-Natal Intensive Care Unit. Everything in the unit will be state of the art. It will be the best equipped facility in the state of California. There have been major advances in the field of Neo-Natal medicine over the past few years. We're able to offer hope to babies, to families, who wouldn't have had any as little as five years ago. And now, we're able to offer even more. So, thank you, Mr. Parsons."

The room erupted into applause and everyone stood. Except for Zack. Except for her. Her eyes stung, her entire body feeling numb.

Zack lifted his hand and nodded once, his acknowledgment. Her heart broke for him. What a wonderful gift he was giving to so many families. A gift he hadn't been able to give to himself, to his own son.

She wanted to howl at the universe for the unfairness of it all. And yet there was no point. And Zack was there, broken, and probably in pain. She could be there for him. It was all she could do. And she would. Because she was his friend. His lover.

The speaker went on to talk about some more donations and then invited everyone to stay for dancing and an open bar.

After the applause died away, people started to wander around the room, talking and laughing, some people came to talk to Zack. She wanted to tell them to go away. Because she could feel the dark energy, the grief, radiating from him like a physical force. How was everyone else missing it?

She didn't understand how they could miss what was so clear to her.

"Let's go." She put her hand on his, felt his pulse, pounding hard in his wrist. She ran her fingers along his forearm. She didn't think he would accept loving words, but she could offer him comfort in another way. A way he could accept.

There was no question where things would end up tonight. No fighting it. They both knew it.

He nodded once and stood, she stood, too, and went to him, putting her hand on his back. He wrapped his arm around her waist as they headed out of the ballroom.

Zack's chest felt too full. Everything felt like too much. The whole day. He shouldn't have brought Clara with him tonight. It was one thing to sit in a room full of strangers and have them talk about his contribution to the NICU, but it was another to have someone sitting there, knowing why he'd done it. Someone else thinking of Jake. It was hard enough to be alone in it. Sharing it made it seem more real. It made him feel exposed.

It made him feel like everything, his failures, his pain, was written on him. Something he couldn't hide, or scrub off no matter how many layers of control he tried to conceal it with.

Clara saw him.

When he'd picked her up tonight, he'd fully intended on keeping her at a distance, putting her in her place. A new place. Because he had mistresses, women who were with him for the sole purpose of warming his bed and accompanying him to events.

He wasn't friends with those women. He didn't eat their baked goods, he didn't know that they wore yoga pants to bed when there wasn't a man around. He didn't know that they were insecure about their bodies, or that their favorite band was still that group of long-haired teenage boys that had been so popular in the nineties.

He didn't know anything about them beyond what they looked like naked.

He knew the other stuff about Clara. And he knew the naked stuff. And tonight he'd been determined to focus only on the latter. If he couldn't keep her as only a friend, and he'd proven he wasn't doing a very good job of that, then he would have her as a mistress. Because what had happened at her apartment, the way they'd shared dinner, jokes, then made love, him holding her while she'd slept...he couldn't do that. It was too reckless. To out of his control.

He had to move her into the compartment he could deal with. And she seemed determined to push her way back out.

The expression on her face when she saw the wrong card in her spot had been so sad, stricken, as though someone had slapped her.

And he'd felt it in him. As though her emotion was his. He'd always felt connected to Clara, but this was different. Sharper. Impossible to deny. Beyond his control.

He should have taken her home. Yet he'd still taken her back to his house. Because he had planned on having her tonight, had been obsessed with it all week. If only to prove that he could sleep with her without having his insides flayed. Sex was only sex. It didn't have to be personal, it didn't have to mean anything. It didn't have to be related to the awful, tight feeling in his chest.

She was beautiful tonight, incredible in that form-fitting black dress and the gem, enticing in the valley of her cleavage, drawing his eye, tormenting him.

She was standing by the massive living-room windows, the bay in the background, city lights glittering on the inky surface of the waves. He wanted her. Here and now. A good thing he'd planned for it. It wasn't spur-of-the-moment, it wasn't beyond his control.

He had condoms and everything else he needed. He was in control. He desperately needed the control. He tightened his hand into a fist, steadied it, ignored the tremor that ran through his fingers and skated up his arm, jolting his heart.

Ignoring the strange tenderness he felt when he looked at her. This wasn't about feeling, not in an emotional sense. This was physical. It was sex.

"Take off your dress," he said.

She reached behind herself and unzipped the gown, letting it fall to the floor. She wasn't wearing a bra, only a small triangle of lace keeping her from being completely bare. That and the necklace, the emerald heavy and glittering between her breasts.

She reached around to remove it, her breasts rising with the action, pink tipped and perfect.

"No," he ground out. "Leave it on." A reminder. A reminder that she was the same as every other woman he'd ever been with. The exchange of gifts, jewelry, that was how it worked. It was invariable, it was safe. It was unchallenging.

She dropped her hands to her sides and he walked closer to her, loving the way the moonlight spilled silver over her pale curves. The way the deep shadows accentuated the dip of her small waist, the round fullness of her hips and breasts.

She was a woman. There was no denying it. And he was starving for her.

But he would wait. He would draw it out. Because he was the master of this game. He was always in charge. He had forgotten that sometimes over the past few weeks, had allowed her inexperience, the nature of their friendship, to change the way he approached it.

Not now.

She's a woman. Only a woman. The same as any other.

No. Not the same. His mind rebelled against that thought immediately. There had never been a more exquisite woman, that much he knew for certain. There had never been a figure, not since Eve, better designed to tempt a man.

She was the epitome of sensual beauty, more seductive simply standing there than any other woman could have been if she'd been trying.

Clara.

Her name flashed through his mind, loud, a reminder.

No. He didn't need it. He wasn't thinking of her. Only of his own need and how she might fulfill it. He would pleasure her, too, as he did all of his lovers. But it wasn't different. It couldn't be different. Not again. Not after that night in her apartment.

"Turn around for me," he said. "Face the window."

She obeyed again. She was like a perfect hourglass, the elegant line of her back enticing. He walked over to her, extending his hand and tracing the dip of her spine. She shivered beneath his touch.

"Do you like that?" he asked.

"I've liked everything you've ever done to me." Her voice, so sweet, a bit vulnerable. Not a temptress.

Clara.

He put his hands on her hips and tugged her back against him, let her feel the hard ridge of his arousal, the blatant, purely sexual evidence of what he wanted from her. Her indrawn breath, the short, sweet sound of pleasure that escaped her lips, let him know that she was tracking with him. Important.

He would never do anything she didn't want.

He put his hand on her stomach, soft, slightly rounded. He liked that about her, too, that she was so feminine, curved everywhere. Absolute perfection.

He cupped her butt with his other hand, her flesh silken beneath his palm. "You're beautiful," he said. She leaned back against him, her head against his chest. Her slid his hand up to palm her breast, teasing her nipples as he continued to stroke her backside.

He gripped the side of her panties and drew them down her legs.

He move his hand back behind her, moving it forward, teasing her slick folds before parting them and sliding his fingers deep inside of her. She gasped, spreading her thighs a bit wider to accommodate him.

The line of her neck was so elegant, irresistible. He bent his head and kissed her there, tasting the salt of her skin, so familiar now, as he slid his free hand up to her breast and squeezed her nipple tightly between his thumb and forefinger. She arched against him, her breathing growing harsher, more shallow.

He had her pleasure in his hands, how he touched her and where, dictating everything she did. Everything she felt. This was like everything else. Every other sexual encounter he'd had as an adult. He was in charge of their pleasure, both of them. He decided when things happened and how.

This thing with Clara hadn't been right from the beginning, because he hadn't managed to put her in her place for their affair. He hadn't separated their friendship from it. That was why he'd shared with her, held her while she slept. That was why he'd started feeling things.

But he knew it now. He knew what he had to do. He could still have her. He could get a handle on everything, and then he could have her. He touched the necklace between her breasts, fingers sliding over the gem. A reminder of exactly what they had between them.

She tried to turn and he held her so she was facing the window, away from him. He reached over and picked up a condom sheathing himself and turning her to the side so that she was standing in front of the couch.

"Hold on to the back of it," he said. She obeyed, bending at the waist, gripping the back of the couch. She looked back at him, her eyes round, questioning. Familiar.

He chose not to focus on her face. He gripped her hips, looked at the curve of her hips, how her body dipped in beautifully, perfectly, at her waist.

He positioned himself at the entrance to her body.

She made a short, low sound that vibrated through her. "Okay?" he asked, his teeth gritted tight, every ounce of control spent on moving slowly, on not thrusting in to her the rest of the way and satisfying the need that was roaring inside of him.

"Yes," she said.

He pushed into her the rest of the way, her body so hot and

tight it took every ounce of his willpower to keep from coming the moment he was inside.

"Oh, Zack," she breathed. "Zack."

His name on her lips, her voice, so utterly Clara. So familiar and still so exciting.

Clara. Her name was in his head on his lips, with each and every thrust, with each sweet pulse of her internal muscles around his shaft.

And suddenly there was no denying it. It didn't matter that he couldn't see her face. Her smell, the feel of her skin beneath his fingertips, the way it felt to be in her body, all of it was pure, undeniable Clara Davis.

The woman who baked orange cupcakes and had a pink wreath on the door. The woman knew about his past, about the darkest moments of his life. The woman who smiled at him every morning. Who could always make him smile, no matter what. Who put powdered creamer in his coffee when he made her angry.

The woman who lit him on fire, body and soul.

He couldn't pretend she was someone else, or that it didn't matter who she was. There was no way. No one had ever been like her before, no one ever would be.

He had no control. He had nothing. He was at her mercy. If he'd had to get on his knees and beg her for a kiss tonight he would have done it, because he needed her.

Not just in a purely sexual sense. He needed *her.*

His climax built, hard and fast, the pitch too steep, too unexpected for him to control. He put his hand between her thighs and stroked her, trying to bring her with him. Her body tightened around him, her orgasm hitting hard and fast. When she cried out her pleasure, then he let go.

"Clara," he whispered, resting his forehead on her back as he gave in. As he let the release crash through him, devastating everything in its path.

He released his hold on her hips, his body shaking, spent as though he'd just battled his way through a storm. Sweat made his skin slick all over. His hands were trembling, his breathing sharp and jagged.

He looked at her. At Clara. There were red marks on her hips where his fingers had pressed into her flesh. Where he had lost all control. He brushed his fingers along the part where he'd marked her, his chest tightening, regret forming, a knot he couldn't breathe around.

She turned to look at him, a smile on her lips. She straightened, naked and completely unconcerned about it. Nothing like she'd been at first. Her confidence, the fact that she felt beautiful, shone from her face.

Her beautiful face. Unique. Essential. So damn important.

"I'm sorry," he said.

She blushed, looking away from him. "Didn't I tell you not to apologize to me all the time?"

"What about when I need to?" he asked, moving toward where she was standing, brushing his fingertips over her hips. "I was holding on to you too tightly," he whispered.

She met his eyes and they held. He saw deep, intense emotion there. A connection, affection. Something real. It wasn't part of a facade, or a game. It was the way she always looked at him, whether they were in his office, in her living room or in bed. She was the same woman. She cared for him. She looked at him like he mattered to her.

The realization rocked him, filled him. Every piece and fiber of his being absorbing it. It made it easier to breathe, as though he hadn't truly been drawing in breath for years and now he was again.

For the first time in fourteen years. Since he'd lost his reason for breath, his desire to give any sort of emotion, to give of himself. He felt like he'd found it again. In Clara's eyes.

"I didn't mind," she said.

The moment, the tiny sliver of freedom he felt evaporated, chased away by a biting, clawing panic that was working from his stomach up through his chest. He had felt this way before and it had ended in utter destruction.

He knew what this was. And he knew he couldn't have it. Wouldn't allow himself to have it. Not ever. Not ever again.

He took a step away from her and bent down, picking her dress up from the floor, rubbing his fingers over the sequins. He felt choked, like his throat was closing in on itself, like his chest was too full for his lungs to expand.

He could do it. He could have her still, keep her where she belonged in his life. In his bed.

He had been careless again. He had lost control. He could find it again. He had to.

"Get dressed," he said, handing her the gown.

"What?"

"I'll drive you home."

"What?" she said again.

He didn't look at her face. He couldn't.

"You and I are having an affair, Clara, I made that clear the other day. I don't cuddle up with the women I'm having sex with at night, and I damn sure don't have their toothbrush on my sink. That's just how it works."

"And I think I told you, I am not just one of your mistresses."

"When you're in my bed...or my couch, you are."

"I am your friend," she said, her voice ringing in the room.

"Not when we're here, like this. Now, you're just the woman I'm sleeping with. We aren't going to curl up and watch a chick flick after what just happened."

She jerked back, pulling her dress over her breasts. "I'm going to go get dressed. Send the car. I'm not riding back with you, and I'm not staying, not now so I think the decent thing to do, if you still remember decency, would be to arrange me a ride."

"Clara..."

"We'll talk tomorrow. I can't now."

She turned and walked away, her steps clumsy. She ducked

into his downstairs bathroom and closed the door. He heard the click of the lock.

And he didn't blame her. But he had to define the relationship, as much for her benefit as for his. Yes, he had lied. She was different. But she couldn't be. It couldn't happen.

He would fix it. He'd gotten it wrong tonight, by denying the one thing that had been there from the beginning. His feelings. The sex...he would pretend it hadn't happened. Whatever he had to do to fix it, to have her never look at him like that again. As if he was a cold stranger, as if he'd physically hurt her.

It would have to go back to how it was. Because he could live without sex. He wasn't sure he could live without Clara.

It was the longest car ride in the world. No one was on the streets, and it technically took half the time it normally did to get from Zack's place to hers, but it seemed like the longest ever.

Because everything hurt. And she was wearing a really fabulous gown that had already been torn from her body once, during the most intense, emotion-filled sexual encounter they'd ever had. There had been something dark in Zack tonight. A battle. She wasn't stupid. She knew something had changed, she knew, at least she hoped, that he wasn't as horrible as he'd seemed when he'd sent her away.

She bunched up the flaring skirt of her gown when the car stopped and she slid out, letting the dress fan out around her. She gave the driver a halfhearted, awkward wave. He knew her. She'd used his services quite a few times with Zack. Having him be a part of this, the most awful, embarrassing, heart-wrenching moment of her life wasn't so great.

Because it was two in the morning and it was completely obvious what had just happened. That Zack had had sex with her, sex, at its most base, and had her go home rather than have her spend the night in his bed.

She curled her hands into fists and let her nails cut into her palms, tears stinging her eyes. She almost hated him right now. It almost rivaled how much she loved him.

Almost.

If she didn't love him, it wouldn't hurt so bad.

You're my mistress.

Like hell she was. He might be the only man who'd seen her naked, but she was certain, beyond a shadow of a doubt, that she was the only woman who'd ever seen him cry.

CHAPTER THIRTEEN

SHE REALLY HOPED everyone wanted cupcakes for lunch. Because there were cupcakes. Nine varieties of them, and someone had to eat them.

She didn't think she could eat and she was *not* sharing them with Zack, which meant they would be going straight into the break room. On the bright side, she'd found a few new varieties that had worked out nicely.

The sea-salt caramel one was her favorite. She just couldn't force down more than two bites at a time. Anything beyond that stuck in her throat and joined the ever-present lump that made her feel like she was perpetually on the edge of tears.

She was just too full of angst to eat anything. She hadn't been able to eat anything since she'd been dropped at the front of her building by Zack's driver.

Zack.

She put her head on the pristine counter of the office kitchen and tried to hold back the sob that was building in her chest.

Something had broken in him last night. It had started after their time together at her place, the night he'd left. And last night it had snapped completely. But she didn't know what it was. She didn't know how to pull him out of it. If she could, or if she even should.

"Clara."

Clara looked up and saw Jess standing in the doorway of the kitchen. "Zack is looking for you."

"Oh," Clara straightened and wiped her eyes. Normally Zack would come and find her himself. Because there was a time when he'd wanted to be with her simply to be with her. Now she wondered if she had any value when she wasn't naked. "I'll be there in a second. Take..." She gestured to the platters of cupcakes. "Take some of these with you. I can't eat them by myself. If Zack comes near them, tell him they have walnuts."

Jess's eye widened. "They all have walnuts?"

"No. But tell him they do. All of them."

Jess gave her a strange look and picked two of the platters up, heading back out the door.

She had no choice now. She had to go face the man himself. And figure out exactly what she was going to say. As long as it didn't involve melting into a heap, she supposed almost anything would do.

"You sent Jess after me?" She looked inside of Zack's office, waiting to be invited in. Silly maybe, since she hadn't knocked on his office door in the seven years since she'd started working at Roasted. But she felt like she needed to now.

"Yes. Come in." His tone was formal, like it had been the night before when he'd given her the necklace. Distance. Divorced from emotion.

That was the strange thing. He'd been aloof the night of the charity, until they'd made love. Then he'd been commanding, all dark intensity and so much emotion it had filled the room. It had filled her. It hadn't been good emotion. It had been raw and painful. Almost more than she could bear.

It had caused the break. That much she knew.

But he was back to his calm and controlled self now, not a trace of last night's fracture in composure anywhere. She almost couldn't believe he was the same man whose hands had trembled after they'd made love.

She almost couldn't believe he was the same man she'd known for seven years. The same man she'd watched movies with, shared dinners with.

But he was. He was both of those men.

He was also the cold man standing before her, and she wasn't sure how all of those facets of himself wove together. And she really wasn't sure where she fit in. If she did at all.

She stepped into the office, watching his face for some sort of reaction. He had that sort of distant, implacable calm he'd had on his wedding day, standing and looking out the window as though nothing mattered to him. As though he had no deeper emotion at all.

She knew differently now. She saw it for what it was now. A facade. But she wasn't certain there was a way through it, unless he wanted her to break through.

"I'm about to sign the final paperwork for the deal with Amudee. I wanted to thank you for your help."

For her help. "Of course."

They were talking like strangers now. They'd never been like strangers, not from the moment she'd met him. They'd had a connection from the first moment he'd walked into the bakery.

Now she couldn't feel anything from him. Now that they'd been so intimate, she felt totally shut off from him.

"Once everything is finalized we can let everyone know that our engagement has been called off," he said.

"Right," she said, clenching her left hand into a fist.

"That's all." He looked back at his computer screen for a moment, then looked back up. "Are you busy tonight?"

Her heart stopped. Did he want sex? Again? After what he'd done last night?

"Um…why?"

"Because I thought I might come over and watch a movie."

His words were so unexpected it took her brain a moment

to digest them, as though she was translating them from a foreign language. "And?"

He shrugged. "Nothing."

He was behaving as if…as if nothing had changed. As if they'd gone back in time a few weeks.

He was pretending, she was certain of it, because he certainly wasn't acting normal, whatever he might think, but she was insulted that he was trying. After what he'd said to her last night. After the way he'd objectified her.

She wanted to yell at him. Maybe even hit him, and she'd never hit anyone in her life. But she wanted a reaction. She didn't want his control.

"Are you going to pretend last night didn't happen?" she asked, her voice low, unsteady.

Zack remained calm, his control, that control he claimed to have lost, the control she witnessed in tatters last night, firmly in place. "I think we both know that's not working out. But you're right. You're my friend, and I didn't treat you like a friend last night."

"An understatement," she spat. "You treated me like your whore."

She saw something, an emotion, faint and brief, flicker in his eyes before being replaced by that maddening calm again. That same sort of dead expression he'd worn when he'd been jilted on his wedding day.

"I apologize," he said. "I wasn't myself."

She curled her hands into fists, her fingernails digging into the tender skin on her palm, the pain the only thing keeping her from exploding. "Do you know what I think, Zack? I think you were yourself. This? This is the lie. This isn't you. It's you being a coward. You can't face whatever it is that happened between us last night and now you're hiding from it."

"It isn't working. That element of our relationship." The only thing that betrayed his tension was the shifting of a muscle in his jaw. "But we've been friends for seven years. That works for us. We need to go back to that."

"Are you...are you crazy?" she asked, the words exploding from her. "We can't go back. I've been naked with you. You've been... We've made love. You can't just go back from that like it never happened. I don't care what we thought, we were wrong. That one night, that one night that's turned into four, it changed everything. You can't just experience something like that with someone and feel nothing."

"I can."

"Do you really think this is nothing? That we're nothing?"

"We're friends, Clara. You mean a lot to me. But it doesn't mean I want to keep sleeping with you. It doesn't mean I want this kind of drama. We need things back like they were so that the business can stay on track..."

"I'm leaving Roasted. You know that."

He tightened his jaw. "I didn't think you would really leave."

"What? Now that we've slept together? You can't have it both ways. Either it changed things or it didn't."

"I care about you," he said, his tone intensifying.

"Not enough." She shook her head, fighting tears. They weren't sad tears. She was too angry for that. That would come later. "I am your sidekick, and that's how you like it. As long as I give you company when you want it, eat dinner with you when you're lonely, bake your wedding cake when you decide it's time to have a cold, emotionless marriage, well then, you care about me. As long as I'm willing to pretend to be your fiancée so you can get your precious business deal. But it's on your terms. And the minute it isn't, when I start having power, that's when you can't handle it."

He only looked at her, his expression neutral.

"I'm done with it, Zack," she said, pulling the ring, the ring that wasn't hers, from her finger. "All of it."

She put the ring on his desk and backed away, her heart thundering, each beat causing it to splinter.

"We have a deal," he bit out.

"You'll figure it out. If that's the only reason you don't want me to go…if that's all that's supposed to keep me here… I can't."

Zack stood, his gray eyes suddenly fierce. "So, you're just going to walk out, throw away our friendship over a meaningless fling?"

"No. It's not the fling, Zack, it's the fact that you think it's meaningless. The fact that I've realized exactly where I rate as far as you're concerned."

"What do you want?" he exploded. "Why is what we have suddenly not good enough for you?"

"Because I realized how little I was accepting. That everything was about you. I'm just willing to take whatever you give me, whether it's a spot in your bed or a job baking your wedding cake and it's…sick. I can't keep doing this to myself." She turned to go and he rounded the desk, gripping her arm tightly.

"I'll ask you again," he said, his voice rough. "What do you want? I'll give it to you. Don't leave."

"So I can wait around for you to decide you want to try a loveless marriage again? So I can bake you another cake? Maybe I'll help the bride pick out her dress this time, because, hey, I'm always here to do whatever you need done, right?"

"Does it bother you? The thought of another woman marrying me? Then you marry me." He reached behind him and took the ring off the desk, holding it out to her, his hand shaking. "Marry me. And stay."

She recoiled, her stomach tight, like she'd just been punched. "For what purpose, Zack? So I can be the wife you don't love? Your stand-in for Hannah, different woman, same ring. Doesn't matter, right? You're still doing it. You're trying to keep me from leaving, trying to keep control. You'll even marry me to keep it. That's not what I want."

He took her hand in his, opened it, tried to hand her the ring. She pulled back. "Don't," she said, her voice breaking. "Don't. I'm going to clean my desk out now."

"Clara."

Zack watched as she turned away from him and walked out his office door, closing it sharply behind her. Everything was deathly silent without her there, his breath too loud in the enclosed space. The ring too heavy.

Had he truly done that? Offered her Hannah's ring? Begged her to marry him just so she would stay?

He had. She had gone anyway and there had been nothing he could do to make her stay. All of his control, all of his planning, hadn't fixed it. He had lost the one person in his life who had given things meaning.

He'd been pretending, from the moment he'd met Clara, that she was only his friend. Only one thing. Because he'd known she could very easily become everything. How had he not realized that she'd been everything from day one?

Pain crashed through him, a sense of loss so great it stole the breath from his lungs.

His chest pitched sharply, his body unable to take in air.

He dropped the ring and it fell to the floor, rolling underneath his desk. He left it. It didn't matter.

He'd just broken the only thing in his life that did matter.

Control. She spoke of his control, how he tried to control her, keep her in his life on his terms. And she was right. Because he'd known instinctively that if he ever let go of that control she would take over.

She had. His control was shattered now, laying around his feet in a million broken pieces he would never be able to reclaim.

And if finding it again meant losing Clara, he didn't want it, anyway.

He hadn't chosen to lose his son, it had been a tragedy, one that had painted his life from that moment forward. He'd let Clara leave, because he'd been too afraid to give. Too afraid to let his barriers down.

Because he'd been certain he couldn't live with the kind of pain love would bring, not again. But now he was certain he couldn't live without it. Without Clara. He loved her so much his entire being ached with it.

And if he had to lay down every bit of pride, every last vestige of control and protection to have her back, he would.

CHAPTER FOURTEEN

CLARA HAD LOOKED at nine buildings in the space of four hours.
She'd hated them all. The idea of having her own bakery…it
had been so great before. But she realized now that when she
pictured it, when she saw the image of a shop filled with people
enjoying her cupcakes, Zack was there. At a table that she knew,
in her imagination, anyway, was the one he sat at every day.

And she would come and sit with him when she took a break.
And ask him what his favorite confection was. How his day
had been. If he'd run in to any mimes. Because in her mind,
in her heart, she'd never truly thought he would be gone from
her life altogether.

The truth was, a life without him had been impossible to
imagine.

In the three days since she'd walked out of Zack's office, it
had changed. She didn't have a vision when she viewed the potential bakery locations. She saw nothing more than brick and
wood. There were no visions. No warmth.

There was no Zack.

When he'd handed her the ring…the temptation to say yes
had been there, and it had sickened her. That she would continue to be the void filler in Zack's life, while she let him be
her everything. It was wrong. And she knew it.

Still, a part of her wished she could go back and say yes. She despised that part of herself.

She sighed and walked up the narrow staircase that led to her apartment. She hadn't taken the elevator in three days, either. Because it reminded her of the elevator rides with Zack, the ones rife with sexual tension. It was almost funny now.

Almost. She'd discovered a broken heart made it mostly impossible to find things funny.

When she reached her floor she walked slowly down the hall. She was exhausted, but going back to her apartment wasn't a restful thought. Because he was everywhere there. Memories of him. On her couch, in the kitchen, most recently, in her bed.

She stopped midway down the hall, her eyes locking on the small pink and brown box placed in front of her door. She eyed it for a moment before making her way to it, kneeling down and lifting the lid.

Her breath caught in her throat when she saw the contents. Cupcakes.

The ugliest cupcakes she'd ever seen. The frosting was a garish orange, the cake a sort of sickly pale gray. There was a note tucked into the side and she took it out and unfolded it.

I know I said I don't bake. I did, though. For you. Because it means something to you and I wanted to try it. It made me feel close to you to do it. Please don't eat them, they're terrible. I miss you.
Zack

She traced the letters with her fingertips, his handwriting so familiar. So dear to her. The note was scattered, funny. Sweet. She could hear him reading it to her.

A tear slipped down her cheek. "I miss you, too," she said. "But I couldn't let things stay the same."

"Don't cry. I know they're awful, but they aren't that bad are they?"

Clara looked up and saw Zack standing in the doorway of the elevator. He looked tired, the lines around his mouth deeper.

She wiped her cheeks. "They're pretty bad."

"Almost as bad as their creator." He took a step toward her. "I'm sorry. About the other day. About the past few weeks."

"Zack can we not do this? I don't think… I don't think I can."

"Well, I can't walk away. I won't. So if you don't mind me camping out here in front of your door until you're ready, then I can wait."

Clara crossed her arms beneath her breasts, curling her hands into fists, trying to disguise that she was shaking, trembling from head to toe. "What is it?"

"I told Amudee that I lied."

"And?"

"We still have a deal, but not based on how he feels about me as a human being. More about my corporate track record."

"Why did you do that?"

"Because I had to clean this up. I used you. I didn't want to gain anything from that."

Clara tried to smile. "I appreciate that, Zack, but…"

"I'm not finished."

She blinked and tried not to cry. She wasn't ready for this. Wasn't ready for him to try to repair their friendship, not when she needed more.

"You were right. About me," he continued. "I have been trying to control everything in my life, including you. Because I felt like there was safety in control. I felt like it was responsible, and I never wanted to deal with the consequences of a lack of control again."

He took a step toward her, put his hand on her cheek, and her heart stopped. "Clara, from the moment I met you I felt a connection with you. And I had to make a very quick decision about where to put you in my life. It was conscious. It was controlled. So I decided you would be my friend, my employee, but never anything more. Because I think part of me knew that if I let you, you could mean everything to me. If I didn't keep you in your place you would fill my life, every part of me. That I would love you. But then in Chiang Mai, being near you like that, I couldn't deny it anymore. I couldn't pretend I didn't want you. And we gave in. I lost control. So then, I thought maybe if I put you in that same place in my head I put my lovers, I could have you in my bed, without risking anything more. Without things getting deeper."

Clara's entire body trembled as she looked up at Zack, as she watched his face, so tired and sad. Mirroring her own, she knew.

"But they got deeper," he said, his voice rough. "And I couldn't stop it. Then I tried to reset things, and that didn't work, either. Not just because you told me where to stick it, which I absolutely deserved, but because things changed too much. Because knowing what it is to be skin to skin with you, has changed me. And it terrified me to admit that, even to myself."

"Zack…"

"You have every right to be angry at me. To hate me."

"I don't hate you."

"That's good, because it makes this next part easier. Because as terrified as I was the first time we kissed, I'm even more afraid now." He took a deep breath, his nerves visible, his control absent. "You're right, Clara Davis, you do make me tremble. You have been my friend, my partner, my lover. I want you to be all of those things to me for the rest of my life. I'll understand if you don't want the same from me. But no matter what, you have to know that I love you."

Clara felt dizzy, her fingertips numb. "You…you love me?"

"With everything. After we made love at my house, the last time, I felt like I could breathe again for the first time in fourteen years. For the first time since I lost Jake, I felt something real, something bigger than myself. Do you have any idea how much that scared me? But I realized something, the other day as I was reaching for a bottle of alcohol, to drink away the pain for the first time in fourteen years. That love can make you strong. I've always thought of it going hand in hand with loss, with weakness. But being with you…it makes me better. That's just one reason I love you so much. One of the reasons I had to tell you. Because all of my control, all of my pride, was just to cover up how scared I was. How weak I was. You've made me stronger. You've made me stop hiding."

A sob worked its way up her throat. "Zack, I thought I knew you. For seven years I thought I knew you. I thought you were this suave, together guy who had an unshakable calm that I really, really envied. And then I found out how broken you were, how messed up. I loved you before. I loved that guy I thought I knew. His jokes, his company, everything."

She pressed on, her voice cracking. "But do you want to know something? I love this man more." She stepped forward and put her palm flat on his chest, her hand unsteady. "Because this is you, and this is real. And I know you've been hurt. I know you've hurt in ways I can't imagine. And I know you aren't perfect. But you're perfect for me."

And then he was kissing her, his lips hot and hungry on hers. Her chest expanded, love, hope, filling every fiber of her body. When they parted, they were both breathing hard.

"Do you really love me?" he asked, wiping away tears she hadn't realized were on her cheeks.

"From the moment I met you."

"What a fool I was."

"I wouldn't trade the time, Zack. I wouldn't give back those years of friendship, not for anything. They made us who we are. They made us right for each other."

"I don't know if you can ever know how much your friendship has meant to me, how much your love means to me now. You're the only person I've shared myself with in so long, the only person I've wanted to share with. Without you…there would have been nothing in my life but work. You brought color, flavor."

"Cupcakes."

"That, too. And as you can see, I need someone to provide them for me because I'm useless at doing it myself. You make my life worth living, Clara. You make me better."

"I can say the same for you. I never felt beautiful, never felt special, until you."

"You're all those things. Never doubt it."

"I never will again."

"I have something for you," he said.

She smiled through a sheen of tears. "I love presents."

"I know." He reached into his pocket and pulled out a box. This one wasn't black and velvet. It was pink silk with orange blossoms. "Because you like flowers. And pink." This was for her. Only for Clara.

"I do," she said, opening the lid with shaking fingers. The ring inside was an antique style, a round diamond in the center and smaller diamonds encircling the band.

"It reminded me of you," he said. "Mostly just because it's beautiful. And so are you."

She laughed through new tears and held her hand out. "That's so lame, Zack."

"I know. It is. It's really lame. I make bad jokes sometimes, but you know that. You know everything there is to know about me, and if you can do that and love me anyway, I consider myself the luckiest man on earth."

"I do," she whispered. "Put it on me."

He took the ring out of the box and got on his knee in front of her. "Will you marry me? Clara Davis, will you be my wife, in every way. Will you understand that you are first for me, in every way. Will you love me, and let me love you?"

She wiped a tear away that was sliding down her cheek. "I will."

"And will you bake me cupcakes for as long as we both shall live?"

A watery laugh escaped her lips. "Without a walnut in sight."

He stood and kissed her on the lips. "I love you. As my friend, my future wife, my everything."

"I love you, too." She kissed him again.

"Would you mind if I stayed the night with you?" he asked, his lips hovering near hers.

"One night only?" she said, turning to him.

"No. It would never be enough. I want you every night for the rest of our lives, does that work for you?"

"Yes, Zack. I think a lifetime sounds about right."

EPILOGUE

CLARA PARSONS LOOKED at the mostly uneaten cake. Three tiers of blue frosting that had been perfectly smooth just a few hours earlier, before two, chubby hands had taken some fistfuls out of the side.

"That was the most extravagant cake I've ever seen at a one-year-old's birthday party," Zack said, looking down at the crumbs all over the kitchen floor. "And I don't think Colton ate half of it. He mostly just spread it around."

"That's what kids do, Zack."

"He's asleep. I think we put him in a sugar coma. Anyway, you only get one first birthday, I suppose. You might as well live it up."

Clara looked at the cake again. "This reminds me of another cake I made that didn't really get eaten. A wedding cake."

"I'm still very thankful that one didn't end up being used for its intended purpose."

"Oh, so am I. Because then we wouldn't have had our wedding cake, or our wedding."

"Or our son," Zack said.

"So, all things considered, it was a pretty important uneaten cake."

Zack advanced on her and pulled her up against his body,

resting his forehead against hers. Her heart stopped for a moment, like it always did when she looked at him. Like it had from the moment she'd first met him.

"A lot has changed since that day," he said, dropping a kiss on her lips.

"A whole lot," she agreed.

"Do you know what's stayed the same?"

"What's that?"

"You're still my best friend."

She kissed him, deeper this time, love expanding her chest. "You're my best friend, too."

* * * * *

The Wedding Dare

Katherine Garbera

Katherine Garbera is the *USA TODAY* bestselling author of more than ninety-five books. Her writing is known for its emotional punch and sizzling sensuality. She lives in the Midlands of the UK with the love of her life; her son, who recently graduated university; and a spoiled miniature dachshund. You can find her online at www.katherinegarbera.com and on Facebook, Twitter and Instagram.

Books by Katherine Garbera

One Night

One Night with His Ex
One Night, Two Secrets
One Night to Risk It All
Her One Night Proposal

Destination Wedding

The Wedding Dare

Visit her Author Profile page at
millsandboon.com.au,
or katherinegarbera.com, for more titles.

Dear Reader,

I'm so excited to bring you to Adler and Nick's wedding! There is so much going on and, in each book, a new part of the secret and scandal is revealed. I hope you enjoy this sexy, scandalous ride.

Logan and Quinn have a past and it's not necessarily a bad one. They grew apart as Logan became more obsessed with beating his competitors and taking over as CEO. Quinn is as competitive as Logan is but felt that their relationship was one place they shouldn't be trying to best each other.

Now she's a top reality television producer and on Nantucket to cover his cousin's wedding. His family is falling apart as more secrets from his parents are revealed, and Logan turns to her for comfort and distraction. Quinn tells herself that they are hooking up for old time's sake but her heart isn't so sure. As much as Logan has changed, she's not sure she can trust him.

I love a summer wedding and getting to be on Nantucket with its beaches was so much fun.

Also, as this is my twenty-fifth year writing for Harlequin Desire, I want to say thank you for reading my books.

Happy reading!

Katherine

For Georgina Mogg.
Our entire family got lucky when Lucas met you.
Thanks for all the laughs and good times.
I'm looking forward for more to come.

Thanks as always to my brilliant editor, Charles,
who always sees what I'm trying to do
and how to make it better!

CHAPTER ONE

SUNSHINE AND BLUE SKIES. It was the kind of June day that made most people happy to be on Nantucket. But Logan knew the cell phone signal would be iffy at best and that he was on the island to attend the wedding of his business rival. Not exactly his idea of fun.

And having arrived at his grandmother's large "cottage" on Nantucket to find his brothers all gathered in the study secretly conferring instead of socializing with other wedding guests, Logan couldn't help but hope that it meant his cousin Adler had come to her senses and jilted Nick Williams.

His family was large and the connections were complex but they were all here on Nantucket for the wedding of his cousin Adler Osborn. Adler's father was the rock star Toby Osborn and her mom was Logan's aunt Musette, who had died when Adler was a baby. His mom had been a surrogate mother for Adler and honestly his cousin was more like a sister to them all.

Nick Williams was another story. For as long as Logan could remember Nick and his father, Tad Williams, had been rivals to Bisset Industries. Logan had probably spent more time with Nick than any of his siblings and personally couldn't stand the guy, who was always trying to outmaneuver him.

In fact, Logan had been late arriving on Nantucket because

he'd wanted to one-up Nick and had been negotiating to buy a patent out from under him.

"What's going on?" he asked his brother Zac, who'd been on the island for several days with his new girlfriend and the maid of honor at the wedding, Iris Collins.

"Dad's just admitted to having an affair with Cora Williams thirty-five years ago. Nick is our half brother," Zac informed Logan as he handed him a whiskey and Coke.

"Are you f-ing kidding me?" he said. Not the news he was hoping for. Maybe he'd heard Zac wrong.

Logan didn't need another brother. He already had three—besides his younger brother Zac, there was Leo—also younger—who had left Bisset Industries and started his own successful company after butting heads with Logan. Then there was their eldest brother, Dare, who was a United States Senator. And their little sister, Mari, who was engaged to the Formula One driver Inigo Velasquez.

"I wish I was. Mom is...well, very upset. Cora and her husband are with her and Dad in the study, with Carlton," Dare said, pouring more whiskey into his own glass and offering more to Zac and Leo as well.

"Am I the last to learn?" he asked. He wasn't surprised that his dad had brought in Carlton Mansford—the family PR person and his father's assistant.

"Mari's not here yet," Leo said, mentioning their youngest sibling and only sister. "But she is on the ferry. I texted her the deets."

"The deets?"

"Stop acting like you don't know what it means," Leo said.

"I just prefer it when we talk like we're adults," Logan said, feeling angry and spoiling for a fight.

"Thanks, Dad Junior, should we expect any surprises from you too?" Leo asked.

Logan lunged for his brother, fists clenched. He could use a fight; it would give him something to do with all the anger welling up inside him at the thought of Nick Williams being their brother.

"Stop it," Dare said, wrapping his arm around Logan and physically hauling him back. "Us fighting is the last thing Mom needs right now."

"You're right," Logan said, pushing away from Dare and looking out the window at the neatly manicured gardens that spread toward the ocean in the distance.

Family.

It was the one thing that had made him the man he was, but it was also the most difficult thing for him to navigate. Logan took pride when people said he had his father's tenacity and his mother's charm. Arguably, he was the best blend of his parents. Though he knew that Leo might argue, but his youngest brother just liked to debate. And Dare would argue there weren't any good qualities in their father, a sentiment shared by Zac. Marielle adored their father, so she'd side with him.

"How is Mom?" Dare asked.

Only Zac had been in the conservatory when the news about their father's affair had been revealed.

"She looked broken," Zac said. "I didn't want to let her be alone with Dad, but he wasn't going without her."

"He won't hurt her," Logan said. "He would never do that."

"Well, other than sleeping with another woman while Mom was pregnant with you and then finding out thirty some odd years later that her niece's fiancé is really our half brother," Zac said sardonically.

"Right. Aside from that," Logan said. "This isn't like Dad."

"It's exactly like Dad," Leo said. "You just don't see it because you want to be like him."

"I don't want to be like him, I am like him," Logan said.

"At least the good parts," Zac said.

Dare snickered under his breath. "I've seen him at the negotiating table, Z, he's got some of Dad's tougher qualities too."

"So? I pair it with Mom's charm," Logan said.

"Or try to," Leo added.

"Are you looking for a fight?" Logan asked.

"Yes. I'm not you. I can't go out there and be all broody, I have to be the one who's smiling and friendly. But I don't want Nick Williams as a brother. The man has a reputation that's almost as bad as yours, Logan."

"Now we know why," Dare said. "He's a victim just like us. From what Zac said, Nick seemed blindsided by the announcement too."

"This is a complete cluster f—"

"Watch your language, boys. There's a lady in the room," Mari called out as she entered. Their sister wore her blond hair flowing past her shoulders to the middle of her back. She looked like she'd just stepped off the runway at Fashion Week instead of the ferry, and the smile on her face was genuine and not forced the way it used to be before she'd fallen in love with Inigo Velasquez.

Everyone turned to greet and hug her. Logan went last. He and Mari had always been close due to their relationship with their father.

"So, Dad did it again," Mari said. "I knew that affair he got busted for before I was born couldn't have been the only one."

"Yeah, so what are we going to do about Nick?" Dare asked. "Carlton and Mom and Dad will deal with the outside world."

"I had dinner with Nick the other night. I'll be the one to feel him out and see what he wants," Zac said.

Yeah, of course, they'd have to see what Nick wanted.

Logan had arrived on Nantucket prepared to play nice all weekend with his business rival and archenemy Nick Williams. Only because the bastard was marrying Logan's cousin by marriage, Adler Osborn. She was his mom's only niece. Adler's mother had died when she was a toddler—and his mom had assumed the role of mother to her. He adored his cousin, but thought she had horrid taste in men.

He was still reflecting on her horrid taste in men three hours later in the bar at the hotel. The wedding guests were gathering on the beach for a clambake with all the wedding attendees for the weekend's festivities. Apparently, the wedding was still on. Logan sat sullenly in the bar—he could admit when he was being a brat—until he saw Quinn Murray walk through the lobby.

His college lover—and the producer in charge of filming Adler's celebrity wedding for a television network. He hadn't expected to feel anything when he saw her. But there she was walking through the hotel like she owned the place. There was no mistaking her long red hair and her brown eyes, which had a way of boring past the bullshit he used to charm most people to the truth beneath his comments. And of course, that petite, curvy body of hers that no matter how many lovers there had been since they'd been a couple, he couldn't forget.

She was the one woman he'd never been able to charm or figure out. There was something about her that mesmerized him. And he hated that. He prided himself on seeing a problem and solving it. And tonight, when his entire world was off its axis, he could use the distraction that Quinn would provide.

He wasn't kidding himself that she'd fall back into bed with him—that wasn't Quinn's way—but she'd give him the distraction he needed. He told the bartender to put his drinks on his tab and followed her out into the summer evening.

Quinn was already on the path that led down to the shore, moving quickly, as if in a hurry. When wasn't she? She was just as ambitious as he was and had never let anything throw her off her path—even their brief love affair. She'd said he was too driven for her, but she had always had the same drive.

When he got to the beach, Zac and Nick were drunkenly singing and looking over at Adler and Iris. The last thing Logan wanted to do was get to know his new half sibling. He and Nick were business rivals of the worst kind, both always trying to one-up the other. Zac had somehow come back from Australia, where he'd been training for the America's Cup to start his own team and raise money to fund his next Cup run, and, in the course of a week, managed to start dating Iris, who was smart, sophisticated, and seemed to enthrall his normally free-spirited brother. He shook his head.

The Nick thing.

How the hell was he going to be cordial to a man whose business he was planning to undercut? How the hell was he going to convince everyone that he'd put those plans in motion a long time ago and that they couldn't be stopped? How the hell—

"So, you've got a new brother," Quinn said, breaking into his thoughts. "That must have thrown you for about half a second."

He glanced over at her. In the shadowy light from the clambake he could barely make out the freckles that dotted the bridge of her nose and her cheeks.

"Yeah, not what I was expecting to deal with today," he said acerbically.

"I figured. You probably were coming in all magnanimous and then—wham! Your enemy is actually your brother."

"Is there a point to all of this, Quinn?"

"Nah, just seeing if you are rattled or ticked or have already figured this out and made a plan to manage it," she said. "Plus, you looked a bit like Heathcliff staring broodingly over at Nick and Zac."

"You like Heathcliff," he said. She liked books with angst and drama in them.

"Not my point. You okay?" she asked, sitting next to him on one of the chairs the hotel had provided.

He looked over at her. It had been years since he'd let anyone close to him. He had his brothers and sister, and sometimes he relied on his assistant, but most of the time he kept his own counsel and he liked it that way.

"Yeah."

She arched one eyebrow at him. "That didn't even sound real."

"It didn't? I thought it was convincing," he said.

"I don't buy it," she said, reaching over and putting her hand on top of his. A zing went straight through his body and right to his groin. He straightened his legs. He'd wanted to be distracted from his own internal debate about this new brother he didn't want. But he knew that Quinn was complicated. It was okay to be turned on by her. She was hot as hell and they'd always had this kind of reaction to each other.

But that was it. She was complex and real to him. She wasn't a woman he'd picked up in a bar and could take back to his room for one night. He liked Quinn, respected her, and she was very good friends with the women in his family. He knew this couldn't go anywhere, but that didn't stop him from turning his hand over and running his finger along her wrist and up her arm.

She shivered and leaned in closer to him. She still wore that faint vanilla scent that always made him think of her. She tipped her head to the side, studying him. He wasn't sure what she'd see, but he knew that tonight he didn't want her realism. He needed to believe the image he always presented to the world.

So he leaned in slowly to see if she'd allow him to kiss her, and she licked her lips, putting her hand on the side of his jaw, her fingers moving along the side of his neck before she squeezed his shoulder as she came closer to her.

Her lips brushed his and he pushed aside all of the worries of the day and took the kiss he hadn't realized he'd been missing for ten long years. Her mouth opened under his and he forgot about complications and messed-up family relationships. He forgot about the wedding and the merger he'd already set in motion. He forgot about everything except Quinn Murray and the fact that she kissed him the way she did everything else in life. With passion and need. And she made him realize how busy he'd been with his business life and how he'd neglected this side of himself.

But this was Quinn Murray. The one woman he'd never been able to resist. He needed a distraction, so he lifted her out of her chair and onto his lap to deepen the kiss. She pushed both hands into his hair, holding him close to her. He had found the distraction he was looking for in the fire of her kiss and knew that, for tonight at least, he didn't need to figure out anything other than pleasing this woman.

Logan. He'd always been the one problem she'd never been able to solve. The one guy she couldn't just leave in the past. He was hot, anyone could see that, with his dirty-blond hair, chiseled jaw and ice-blue eyes. He'd always had striking looks. He was muscled because he had an amazing amount of energy. She knew from his sister, Marielle, that he still got up every day at five to work out and then went into the office, staying until almost midnight.

When they'd been in college, it had been attractive to be with a man who was so driven, so determined to succeed, but then she'd realized that he'd never stop competing with her over everything. And she'd liked the challenge at first. But soon it was more than who got the better grades, it was…well, everything, and when she started to realize that no prize was ever going to be enough for him, she'd walked away. But a part of her, the part that had her climbing all over his lap like it had been nine months since she'd made love to anything other than her vibrator…well, she wanted him. Even if it was just because of the long weekend they were both spending in Nantucket.

He tasted good. *Addictive.* She had to be honest and say he was the best man she'd ever kissed. There was something unhurried and yet raw and sensual about the way he kissed her. He took his time, but she felt completely laid bare by it. The passion between them hadn't waned in the years they'd been apart and, as much as she wished it had, she was glad it hadn't.

She liked being in his arms, feeling his hard-on under her hip and his hands roaming up and down her back.

Quinn knew that this wasn't real. She didn't kid herself that it was anything more than Logan distracting himself from finding out that a man he considered his rival and enemy was now his brother. But that didn't mean he hadn't turned her on.

She broke the kiss and opened her eyes to find herself looking into that icy-blue stare of his. The honesty there, the unfettered need, struck a chord deep within her. She'd always been able to see past the ego and the arrogance that he wore like a haughty cloak. But tonight, what she saw there mirrored what she wanted.

They needed this night. They'd never really had any closure, and this could be it. Just a night of burning up the sheets and, in the morning, he'd go back to the mess that his family was and she'd go to work producing *Adler's Destination Wedding* for the television network she worked for.

"That was unexpected," she said.

"Unwelcome?" he asked. "I know we broke up a long time ago, but I have to be honest, Ace, every time I see you, I think about kissing you."

Ace.

He was the only one who called her that. It had been years since she'd heard him use the nickname, though.

"I think about it sometimes too," she admitted.

"But not more than me, right?" he asked. "I know I was too much at the end and, hell, I probably still am…"

It was there in the way he paused. He wanted to hook up, but he didn't want to appear to be the one to suggest it in case she said no. This was why their relationship hadn't worked. Quinn believed with her entire heart that when she found a man to spend the rest of her life with, she'd feel comfortable being vulnerable to him. But with Logan she'd had to keep her guard up. He was always competing, always trying to win, and after a while she'd realized she couldn't compete all the time.

"That kiss was hot and a nice trip down memory lane," she said. "But I don't think either of us need the complications a hookup would bring."

"Does it have to be complicated?" he asked.

"I'm not sure, but you are hedging like you can't admit you want me, and I'm way past that," she said. Turning thirty had burned away a lot of the artifice she'd used in the past. "I'm not interested in being your dirty little secret."

"It wouldn't have to be a secret," he said. "I don't mind if it's a little dirty."

A shiver went through her and she knew she didn't mind if it was dirty either. The thing about Logan was that once he committed to something, he never backed down. Maybe commitment was the wrong word, because the only thing he was dedicated to was his career.

"Why me?" she asked. "There're tons of women here you could hook up with."

"Sometimes I wake up in a sweat thinking about you and me together. I know we don't work for more than a few nights, but I still want you, Ace. I always have. And I'm not sure I have the strength to deny myself tonight. I'm not trying to push you into anything. If you say no, I'll let you walk away. But I'm praying you'll say yes because, after this day, I need you."

He needed her.

Was there a more powerful aphrodisiac in the world?

For other women, maybe, but having a man like Logan need her was all it took to crack her resolve and make her want to give in to the cravings that had been awakened the moment she'd seen him tonight. He was strong—a titan of industry. A man who left nothing but gobbled-up companies and bemused people who weren't sure how they could like a man who was so arrogant. But tonight, Logan Bisset, who had never needed anything or anyone, needed her.

And she needed him too.

Needed to remember what it was like to be in his arms and forget about competitions and standing on her own.

She stood and held her hand out to him. He looked at her, those ice-blue eyes hard to read in the flickering light of the bonfire. But his hand when it engulfed hers was warm and he tugged her slightly off balance and into his arms. She inhaled the scent of his spicy aftershave and closed her eyes, hoping she wasn't making the biggest mistake of her life.

CHAPTER TWO

SHE SMELLED OF summer and sunshine and something pure. Quinn was the kind of distraction he longed for. She was familiar. She knew his faults better than anyone and she had no expectations from him. He tugged her back down onto his lap.

He lowered his mouth to kiss her, but she put her hand on his lips. A tingle went straight through to his groin and he groaned.

"What?"

"Are you sure about this?" she asked. "I mean I know you—"

"Do you?" he countered. The last thing—the very last thing— he wanted to do was to talk. He wanted her to just be some hot lay so he could forget. But when had Quinn ever been that?

He had the feeling that he was on the cusp of making a big mistake. But then everything he'd ever thought he knew about his life had changed. His enemy—he knew that made him sound like Machiavelli but didn't give a crap—was now his half brother. Everyone was going to expect him to make nicey-nice, except he'd already put in motion a plan to crush Nick and his family's company, Williams, Inc.

Quinn shifted on his lap, settling closer to his chest and rubbing her finger over his lips. "Talking about it will help."

"I don't think so, Quinn. I can't. I can screw. I can drink. But I don't want to talk."

"You're being a douchebag, Logan."

"It's kind of my thing," he said, not at all joking. He looked into Quinn's brown eyes and realized that he was seconds away from spending this night alone, listening to his younger brother Zac sing off-key lyrics about love, and stewing in his own ruthlessness.

She sighed.

He was losing her. He put his hand lightly on her thigh and took a deep breath. "I don't want you to think I'm easy."

She threw her head back and laughed. She laughed so hard and loud, her entire body shook with it, and he smiled himself because he'd been the cause. After a day filled with anger and uncertainty, he needed this.

He needed her.

Damn.

Only for tonight, he promised himself.

He was Logan Bisset. He didn't need anyone. Especially a curvy, determined redhead who had always beaten him at his own game. But then she turned, putting her hands on his shoulders and straddling him on the beach lounger.

She lowered her head, the sides of her hair swinging forward to brush against his cheek a moment before her lips brushed over his. Her breath was sweet-smelling and warm, and he put his hands on her hips to hold her to him just in case she changed her mind and decided to leave.

She tipped her head to the side, deepening the kiss, her tongue thrusting into his mouth. He groaned as he felt his erection growing, exercising every amount of control he could muster to keep from rubbing it against her. He knew she didn't want to go to bed with him. And he respected her and wouldn't push. But he hadn't really had a kiss like this in too long.

He avoided women like Quinn, who could make him feel as well as turn him on. It was easier to just hook up. But tonight when he felt like he was shattered and knew that the worst of the fallout over the Nick situation wasn't over due to his own actions in stealing a patent out from under Williams, Inc., he needed this. Needed her.

She pulled back, sitting on his thighs.

Their eyes met and he saw compassion in her gaze. It was probably one of the things that made her so successful at her job. She was driven and competitive, but she also had empathy, which he knew he lacked.

Please, he thought, *don't ask me anything else.*

"Is it a whiskey or beer night?"

"I was thinking serious drinking," he admitted.

"Whiskey then. I think there is a bar set up down at the clambake. Want to go grab some food and drinks?"

No. But he knew that if he said he wanted to go back to his room, she'd leave.

"Sure. But I'm not going to be socializing."

"Duh," she said with a wink as she hopped off his lap. "When are you ever?"

He shook his head as she held her hand out to him. He stood and took her hand. She linked their fingers together and then looked up at him. "Don't think this is more than friendship."

He nodded. They had always been like oil and water and he was pretty sure that would never change. "Why are you doing this?"

"You need a friend tonight. Someone you can let go and be yourself with, and you can't with your family right now," she said.

"Thank you," he said.

"Don't thank me yet. We still have to navigate the clambake," she warned.

Where his entire extended family and a bunch of friends of his parents' and cousin, whom he'd known his entire life, were. Only the inner circle of his family and the Williams' siblings knew the truth about Nick.

He could bullshit and keep secrets with the best of them. But he'd never been good at hiding his emotions. When he was mad, everyone knew it. He doubted that was going to change tonight. But as they approached the bonfire, his brother had given up singing and now Adler's father, the rocker Toby Osborn, was singing his number-one hit song about rebellion and making his own path. Logan, who had always been the model Bisset son, listened to the lyrics. *My path could have been easier if I had been a different man.* Damn but those words resonated. He shook off that thought as he just followed Quinn.

Logan went to the bar, ordered two Jack and Coke, and then turned and bumped into Nick Williams. The groom, his business rival and, as of today, his half brother. The other man's eyes were bloodshot, and he looked…well, like Logan felt. Nick had the worst of the news and if Logan were a better man, he would have tried to comfort him. But at the end of the day, Logan was still himself.

"Fuck," Nick said. "Of course, I bump into you."

"Ditto," Logan said.

Nick gave a little half smile. "The only silver lining to this entire shit storm is the fact that I know you hate it as much as I do."

Logan fought to keep from smiling. He'd never spent any time with Nick other than on the other side of a boardroom table negotiating to outbid him. Now he regretted it. There was something familiar in the other man; probably that DNA his father had contributed.

"Exactly my thought," Logan admitted. "Let me buy you a drink."

"Like hell," Nick said. "I'll buy the drinks."

"You're buying them all," Logan pointed out gently. "This is your event. Where is your bride?"

"Listening to her dad sing," Nick said, shaking himself and then standing taller. "And waiting for her drink. So move it, Bisset. I don't want to keep her waiting."

"You say Bisset like it's a curse but you—"

"Don't. Don't say it out loud. I'm not ready to hear it, especially from you," Nick said. He pushed Logan out of the way and Logan let himself be moved.

As hard as this was for him, it had to be at least the same if not more so for Nick. The family had gathered for his wedding and on the eve of everyone they knew arriving on an island, he'd learned he was the biological son of his business rival and the man who'd raised his worst enemy. Logan just nodded and turned to go find Quinn.

He knew that over the next few days things would more than likely get worse as the news broke in the press, despite Carlton's best public relations spin. And at some point, Logan realized, he was going to have to come clean with his dad and with Nick about the patent he'd purchased out from under him after Nick had beaten him to the punch on another deal three months earlier.

Damn.

Quinn danced in the moonlight near his sister, Iris Collins and Adler. Logan stood there in the shadows wanting to join the women but also knowing he should let them be. Let Quinn help Adler adjust to the news that was rattling her as well. His cousin had been born into a world of paparazzi and tabloid headlines. Her mother had been the younger lover of a famous rock star known for his debauched lifestyle. Then, when Adler was two, her mom had died of a drug overdose, which had simply fanned interest in her. All of Adler's life, she'd been struggling to stay out of the spotlight but televising this wedding was the kind of media attention Adler wanted. The kind that would give her legitimacy and take away the tabloid headlines—until today.

Until her very respectable fiancé turned out to be the bastard—was that a word that anyone used anymore?—son of a business rival. How fucked up was that?

He had to wonder sometimes if fate was just having a massive laugh at his entire family. His dad had certainly stirred up some bad karma in the business world over the way he stabbed associates in the back and undercut rivals. And, of course, in his personal life he'd slept around on his wife, had affairs and lied to them all.

Was he any better? Logan wondered. He tried to be the charming and kind person that his mother was. Tried hard to balance his ruthlessness with a softer side, but it wasn't all that easy.

"Dude, you're bringing me down by standing in the shadows and brooding," Leo said, coming over and taking one of the drinks from his hand. "It's a party. Even a workaholic like you should know what that is."

"That drink was for someone else," Logan said, taking a swallow of his own. At least Leo would prove a distraction. His youngest brother and he had always been competitive with each other. If Leo had been born earlier, closer to his own age, Logan had often thought that Leo would have challenged him for the CEO position of the family company. Instead he'd struck out on his own and created a business that was quickly expanding.

"No one was going to want to drink with you until you lost that dour expression," Leo said.

"You are so annoying," Logan responded. "Why are you such a little prick all the time?"

Leo raised his eyebrows at him. "Because you're such a big one. Everyone else gives you leave to be an ass, but since I'm a lot like you, I know better than to feed that need. You need someone to cut you down."

He smiled. "As do you. You know there's a company I've been hearing about that does American-made leather goods that's gunning for your market share."

"That little Etsy shop owner?" he asked.

Logan nodded. Danni Eldridge was making all sorts of waves in the business community and one of the board members at Bisset Industries had forwarded Logan a prospectus recommending they invest in her company. He'd turned it down. They weren't going to buy a company that would put them in direct competition with Leo and his niche of the leather goods market.

Leo's company had started out small and his online presence had grown it into a multi-million-dollar business.

"Danni Eldridge is a fad. I know because I grew my business from Instagram followers by showing consumers a lifestyle they wanted. It takes a lot of acumen, determination and drive to turn that into a real business. I don't think she'll last," Leo said.

"Fair enough," Logan said.

"I thought you were getting drinks for both of us," Quinn said, coming up to them.

"I stole yours," Leo said. "I'll grab you a fresh one."

As Leo turned away and left, Quinn grabbed Logan's hand, pulling him toward the bonfire. "Dance with me?"

"Yes."

Quinn had noticed Logan talking to his brother. Given Logan's mood tonight, and the fact that Mari had mentioned they'd almost had a fist fight earlier, she thought it would be a good idea to interrupt. And she was glad she had. Dancing with Logan was almost as good as sex. And about a thousand times safer for her heart and soul.

Or so she'd thought until Toby and his band slowed things down with the ballad that everyone said he'd written for Adler's mom after she'd died. It was the love song he'd never written when she was alive, and it spoke of love and longing. It was a sensual bluesy-sounding song that had Quinn pulling Logan into her arms and closing her eyes.

His hands fell naturally to her hips and he pulled her close enough that she felt the brush of his chest against her breasts as she twined her arms around his neck. It had been over three years since she'd danced with anyone. She just felt like she was too old to go clubbing. That had to be the reason why every touch of Logan's hand was sending tingles all through her body.

His legs brushed against hers. Since it was hot and summery, she'd dressed in a flirty little sundress instead of her typical khakis, so she felt the brush of his thigh against her bare skin. He wore a pair of Bermuda shorts, so it wasn't skin-on-skin—thank God for that.

He swayed with her to the music, their bodies finding a natural rhythm, the one they'd always had. No matter how out of sync they'd been emotionally, physically they'd always just had this link. This bond that had been hard to shatter and break.

Quinn knew that a smart woman would turn and walk away. Go back to her hotel room and work or do something else—anything else. But under the full summer moon, she didn't want to do the smart thing. Her entire life had been about following the practical path and, for this one night, she knew she wanted to be impulsive.

To follow her hormones or her lust-filled self and indulge in everything Logan was offering. Just pretend that she could sleep with him and walk away unscarred even though deep inside— *Shut up.* She pushed the logical, thinking part of herself to the back of her mind.

She wanted something fun to remember about this night, a night when the people she loved were hurting and struggling to make sense of something that was hard to wrap their heads around. But then, August Bisset had always thought he was above the rules everyone else followed and he'd never really worried about those he wounded with his actions.

Her eyes met Logan's and she saw the hurt and pain in his eyes, the need and want as well. He didn't want to talk, and that said everything. He wasn't processing this at all; he needed to forget and she needed to remember. She wanted a night of passion without the pain that had always followed when they'd been a couple in college. She wanted a night that could just be about this feeling of rightness they'd always had physically.

And she was going to take it.

She didn't care if she regretted it the next day or if there were consequences. She'd deal with them. She would have regrets either way.

She pulled his head down to hers and kissed him. Not the tentative way she had earlier on the beach chair, but in a way that said *Take me. Take me now.* She undulated against him in time to the music and it took Logan a split second before he reciprocated.

His tongue tangled with hers as his hands cupped her butt and lifted her more fully into his body. They danced until the music stopped and then Logan raised his head and looked down at her.

The questions in his eyes weren't ones she wanted to answer. But she hadn't exactly said yes earlier and he didn't want to read her wrong again. He needed to hear the words.

"Walk with me on the beach?" she asked. "Let's go somewhere where we can be alone."

"Only if you're sure," he said. "I don't need something else to regret tomorrow."

"I don't want to be something you regret," she answered. "I want you, Logan. No strings. Nothing but the summer night and this moment."

"Me too," he said.

He slipped his hand in hers and led her away from the bonfire, stopping to grab a blanket from the pile the hotel staff had set out for the guests. They walked away from the crowd and the music. The night got darker and the breeze a bit stronger, but she grew more confident.

For too long she'd ignored the fact that she'd never had the closure she'd wanted with Logan. She'd given him an ultimatum—stop turning everything into a competition or leave—their senior year of college and had expected that he'd give in to her. Instead he'd walked away. She hadn't had a chance to end things the way she'd wanted.

And this, of course, wasn't an ending but it was one last time in his arms so she'd be able to finally put that chapter of her life to rest. Mark it ended and move on from Logan Bisset once and for all. It was past time that she did it, and tonight seemed the right moment.

A moment when they could just be Logan and Quinn and forget about the rest of the world.

CHAPTER THREE

THE FARTHER AWAY they got from the bonfire, the more relaxed
Logan seemed to be. It was as if, in the darkness, with only the
moon to light their way, he could let down his guard. A part
of Quinn, the part that, if she were honest, probably still loved
him a little bit, softened. She had always thought that Logan's
biggest problem was the fact that he thought he had to be invincible. She knew he'd never change. There was too much August
Bisset in him for that to happen.

The walk gave her time to think. The thing about Logan was
that he was better to deal with as an impulse and then move on.
As soon as she started worrying about his happiness—seeing
the broken man she wanted to fix no matter that she knew she
couldn't—she should walk away.

For her own sanity.

He stopped and let the blanket drop to the sand at their feet,
pulling her into his arms with his chest to her back, just holding her.

"I'll deny it if you ever repeat this, but there are times when I
agree with Zac. I totally understand his love of the sea. There's
something soothing about the ocean that tempts me to forget all
my problems," he said. His voice was a low rumble and there
was a softness to his words that surprised her.

This wasn't the Logan she'd dated in college; she'd do well to remember that. And it was a good and bad thing, she thought.

"Why wouldn't you want anyone to know that?" she asked, putting her hands over his wrists where they crossed over her stomach.

"Because I'm always giving Zac a hard time about being a sailor. I mean I know he's so much more than that, as he is a captain for the America's Cup and it's highly competitive and he's very good at it. But he's my little brother…"

She shook her head. As an only child, she'd never really understood the sibling dynamic—especially the Bisset siblings— but she knew that whatever it was meant a lot to all of them. "Well, I doubt I'll have a chance to speak to him, so your secret is safe with me."

He sighed then.

"What?"

"Why is it that you're the one woman I can trust?" he asked.

"I don't know," she admitted. "I think if we dwell on this, then we will be heading back to the bonfire."

He moved to stand next to her. They were facing the inky-dark ocean and the gentle sound of the waves wasn't as soothing as it had been a few moments ago. This was what she'd hoped to avoid. There was no closure in talking to Logan. He was always going to be the guy he'd been. He was always going to let her down, not through a fault in him—he could only be the man he was—but in her own expectation of the man she wanted him to be.

"That would be the safe choice," he said. "But I've never been one to avoid a risk and if you are anything like the woman I used to know, you're the same."

She groaned.

He laughed.

She shrugged. "I'm not that woman anymore, Logan."

"Sure you are, Ace. That's why you're standing with me down

the beach from the crowd. And if you are anything like me, you remember how good we were together," he said.

They had been good together. Physically they'd always had that spark. There was something in him that drew her like a moth to a flame, ignoring the danger for the chance to get closer to him for a short amount of time. She wanted to turn and walk away. She was thirty. Smarter now than she had ever been. Well, if not smarter, at least wiser.

Wiser.

What a dumb thought. She wanted Logan and was trying to justify it, but no matter what she did tonight—walk away or stay—she'd have regrets in the morning. The only difference would be what she regretted.

He bent and straightened the blanket, sitting on it and looking up at her as he pulled a bottle of Jack Daniel's from his pocket. "Drink?"

She almost shook her head and left.

Wiser.

Instead she sat next to him. He'd sit there by himself and drink the entire bottle and, as much as she knew she should probably leave, she couldn't let him do it. Plus, it had been a long time since they'd been this close, and she wanted him. She'd forgotten the potency of his appeal when they were apart, living their own lives.

But up close with his bright, light blue eyes and strong, square jaw that she knew was a harbinger of his stubbornness, she couldn't resist him. She couldn't even pretend that she was going to leave the beach without having him. But she promised herself she was doing it on her own terms. Not his.

This was for her.

Quinn snatched the bottle from him and took a drink. She loved whiskey, which was why she resisted drinking it whenever she could. But it felt right tonight. She leaned back on her elbows after she handed the bottle over to him.

"The night sky on Nantucket always seems bigger and

brighter to me. Especially out here. I remember the first time I visited..."

"I do too. You were so nervous to meet Gran and she immediately fell in love with you when you sided with her," Logan said.

She smiled. Logan was used to bullying his way through life but his grandmother, though she loved him, wouldn't have any of it. The two women had bonded over not taking Logan's bullshit. That relationship was one of the things she'd missed when they'd broken up.

"Gran still thinks the world of you," Logan said, as if reading her thoughts. "She'd love to see you."

That was nice to know, but was there anything worse than an ex-girlfriend who didn't move on? "We're not a couple."

"I know. I guess that's why we are talking and drinking instead of hooking up."

"Definitely."

Talking and drinking.

It wasn't what he wanted to do. He wanted dirty, mind-numbing sex. But he wasn't interested in going back and finding another woman. He wanted it with Quinn. Only Quinn.

And she wanted to talk.

"What's it like to work in television?" he asked, going along with her wishes. "I thought you wanted to direct movies and be the next Kathryn Bigelow."

She took a sip of the Jack instead of answering.

"I thought you wanted to talk," he said gently.

He had the feeling she wanted him to talk. He wasn't going to. Maybe he'd feel like discussing this new half brother when he was dead, but probably not any time before that.

"I did. I do. That's a complicated question. So TV... I like it. It's pretty exciting doing destination weddings. There are always a million things that don't go to plan, but it keeps me on my toes. And I have a travel series on YouTube...kind of a side hustle."

He hadn't realized she was a YouTuber. "Does producing not pay enough?"

"No, why?"

"You said 'side hustle.'"

"Yeah, I don't know. Seems like everyone has one now and I figured it was a way to monetize my downtime."

He looked over at her. "You know a lot of people in my life give me crap for being a workaholic, but you pretty much just admitted to being one."

"When you look at it that way, I guess, but the thing is, I'm at these really great locations and I sort of explore them with my drone camera and then do a voice-over... I know it sounds like work, but it gives me the freedom to create my own content, which is what I originally wanted to do. TV pays the bills, the YouTube stuff lets me make little mini documentaries. Does that make any sense?"

It sort of did. It was so like Quinn to be practical about taking her degree and using it, at the same time finding a rewarding way to fulfill her dreams. He envied her. She'd even made working all the time sound balanced and fulfilling. The one thing he'd never been able to achieve.

He shoved his hands into his hair and looked up at the starry night. His mind was a beehive of activity and the one thing he'd hoped to calm it wasn't working. He could smell her perfume drifting to him each time the breeze shifted in his direction. If he rolled over, he could touch her, they were sitting so close on the blanket. But she wanted to talk.

And talking was making it worse, reminding him of all he'd chosen to walk away from. Would he be a different man if they'd stayed together? Duh, right? But would he be any happier? Frankly, in his mind—

"What are you thinking?" she asked.

"Just about if you would have made my life better or if I would have ruined yours had we stayed together," he said, honestly.

"Logan, don't do that. We aren't the kind of couple who are

meant for anything but competing. We're really good at putting together the best debate and then trouncing each other. Or making everything into a game… you know it and I know it."

"I do. It's just when you talk, I'm tempted to let myself believe I could be a better man."

"You're a good man," she said. "This isn't like you. Why do you think you need to be better?"

"No reason," he said. "Just the thing with Nick and Dad is throwing me."

Yeah, right, his conscience jeered. Like he hadn't spent the last few months plotting to dismantle everything Nick Williams had built over the last few years. As if he wasn't a vindictive man who had lost one too many times, so he'd gone for the jugular and now…now he knew that when what he'd done to take Nick down came out, his father's extramarital affair was going to pale in comparison.

"You okay?" she asked. "When I said talk and drink, I thought we could do something fun."

"Like what?" he asked.

"Find out what we'd been up to since the last time we chatted," she said.

"Like a girl's brunch?"

She punched him in the shoulder, and it was harder than he'd expected.

"No, asshole. Like two friends catching up."

He reached over and squeezed her hand. "I'd like that. Tell me about the videos you make. How did that start?"

She groaned.

"What?"

"You won't like the answer," she warned him.

"It's my night for not liking things," he said. Honestly, there wasn't anything she could say that would hurt more than knowing he was going to drive a wedge in his family that would make welcoming his new half brother impossible.

"It started after you and I broke up. I took a job on one of those catamaran cruise tours and worked my way around the Caribbean."

"Why wouldn't I like that?" he asked.

"Because I went with Cruz," she said.

She was right. He didn't like it. Cruz and he had competed for everything in college, including Quinn. Of course the other man would have made a play for her when they'd broken up. "We weren't together anymore."

"I know. That's why I went with him," she said. "Not my best moment. But Cruz guessed that's why I'd said yes. He actually is a really decent guy. We had fun and he suggested I do travel videos."

"It was a good suggestion. I'm glad something came out of our breakup."

"Me too. Mainly, that's why I'm afraid to hook up now," she said. "It wasn't easy getting over you, Logan."

"You broke up with me," he reminded her.

"Only because I knew you'd never stop competing with me. I know it sounds silly but that morning you suggested we see who could get their Starbucks order first was it. Then when we got back, you were trying to tell me that our latest exam results, which were the same, weren't really and you had done a longer essay so essentially you'd won. Well, I realized it would never be enough for you to tie with me. You have to be number one," she said.

"What's wrong with that?" he asked.

"Nothing, but I wanted something different."

Something he couldn't deliver. So instead of sex with him, she was talking, and it wasn't going to get either of them what they wanted.

He should leave. Just get up and go.

When he rolled to his side to do so, she stopped him.

Quinn tugged Logan down next to her on the blanket and rolled so she was facing him. He was complex and always made her...

well, feel a million and one things at once. She should let him go. But she didn't want to.

"Don't. I can't do this. I wanted to be chill, but it's not me," he said. "I want you. I don't want to talk or rehash the past. I just want sex and maybe to hold you the rest of the night so I can pretend for a few short hours that things are normal. I know that's not what you want, and I completely appreciate where you are coming from, but I can't turn it off. I never have been able to around you."

God.

This was the one thing she'd never been able to understand about Logan. He played to win but he played from a place of total honesty. Maybe that was why it was so hard to walk away. Even though she knew that if she stayed, she could get hurt, his honesty made her want to try. Try to figure out a way to get what they both wanted.

"I'm not trying to make this harder on you," she said.

"I know," he said. "Let me leave. You can go back to the party and I can do what I do best."

Quinn wondered what he thought he did best, but didn't ask. There had been too much talking and it hadn't moved them any closer to sorting anything out. She moved quickly, straddling him and putting her hands on his shoulders.

She saw the surprise on his face, yet couldn't really read the emotions in those bright blue eyes of his. She didn't need to. "I want this too. I think I was trying to justify it to myself, but the truth is, it's been a long time and I've missed you, Logan."

He put his hands on her waist; she felt his fingers squeeze her. "If this isn't what you want…leave now or let me leave."

She leaned down then, her lips brushing his before she kissed him long and deep. She pushed her hands into his thick hair and held him underneath her. Pretended for the moment that he was in her control.

His tongue brushed over hers and she shifted on his lap, taking the kiss deeper. She had been kidding herself when she'd thought that she wasn't going to have sex with him on the beach.

This was Logan. The one man who still haunted her. The guy she'd never been able to really stop judging every other man by. And she needed this. She needed to have sex with him as an adult so she could stop idealizing that college relationship.

She was sure that sex with him would be as mediocre as it had been with all the other guys she'd dated in the last few years. That something had changed in her and there was no going back to those wild years. But she quickly realized how wrong she was as Logan's hands slipped down the backs of her thighs and he raised himself up, his abdomen tightening underneath her. She wrapped her legs around him and he paused, resting his forehead against hers.

Quinn opened her eyes, stared into his, then closed them again. It was too intense. She felt him all around her, his exhalations brushed over her face as his chest bumped her breasts.

She opened her eyes again and this time he was watching her. "I know what you said, but are you sure?"

That old hurt that had lingered for so long inside her soul started to melt a little bit. He'd given her more chances to walk away than any other man would. "I'm where I want to be tonight."

"I'm so glad," he said as he tugged her T-shirt up in the back.

She felt the cool summer breeze on her skin a moment before his warm palm was on the small of her back, just holding her with that one touch as he shifted underneath her. "Are you on the pill? I know that question seems awkward, but I'd rather know now than find out you aren't at the wrong moment."

She nodded. "Me too. Yes, I am. Also, I'm healthy, so nothing to worry about on that front."

"Me too. Just had my yearly physical for the board so I can keep my job as CEO," he said.

"Glad to hear it," she said, putting one hand on his shoulder. He looked into her eyes again and something changed inside her. She knew she'd told herself this was to close the door on the past and finally move on from him, but there was something about this that felt new and different. And if she were being honest with herself, it had absolutely nothing to do with the past.

Quinn shoved the thought aside as she felt his hand in her hair, cupping the back of her head as he kissed her again. It was slow and seductive. Not the starter gun at the beginning of the race, but more of a tentative testing of the waters.

CHAPTER FOUR

THE JACK DANIEL'S hadn't really made a dent in his temper or caused him to forget anything, but the touch of Quinn's lips was doing just that. He shoved everything aside but the fiery redhead in his arms and focused on her as if she were a million-dollar deal he didn't want to lose.

Her lips were full against his; her hair was soft and smelled like spring when the blossoms in his mother's orangery bloomed. He held her gently though what he really wanted was to roll her beneath him and let go of all his inhibitions. But he knew that would be too much.

No matter that they had always gone full-on when they competed, Logan had always been smart enough to keep the darkest part of himself from her. His intensity when he was trying to be normal was off the charts, so there was no way going all-out wouldn't overwhelm her.

She sucked his lower lip into her mouth and bit him lightly. He ran one hand down her back, cupping her thigh as he thrust his hips toward hers. Her skin was soft and smooth, her legs bare. He ran his finger up underneath the hem of her shorts, caressing the back of her legs as she drove him out of his everloving mind sucking on his lip.

Finally he tore away from the kiss and rested his forehead

against hers. She put her hands on his cheeks and ran her thumb along his jaw, causing him to grapple for self-control. He wanted this night with Quinn to last forever so he needed to be more than a five-minute man with her right now. Because he wasn't fooling himself that he'd get more than this one night with her.

In the light of day, given his current fucked-up life situation, this was all the two of them could have. And it was so good that he wanted to binge on all of Quinn. Just give in to the fire that was burning between the two of them. But he liked the slow burn.

"What are you doing?" she asked, rubbing her finger over his bottom lip and making his dick even harder.

He was getting harder and harder and, for the life of him, it wasn't easy to remember why he was trying to go slow. This was Quinn, for fuck's sake. She'd always rendered his control nonexistent.

"Trying to make this last. But damn, woman, I forgot how fast you get to me," he said. His words were meant to be calming—for himself. But his voice was low, guttural with need, and he stopped trying to hold back. Stopped pretending he could be anything other than his most basic self.

"I didn't," she said, pushing her hands between their bodies and undoing the buttons of his shirt, parting it to drop a kiss in the middle of his chest next to the chain holding the gold coin medallion his father had given him when he'd become CEO. "You make me hotter and wetter than any other guy ever has. I was sort of hoping time would have dulled this, but…"

No such luck, he thought.

He reached for the hem of her dress and lifted it over her head. She shivered as the night breeze brushed over her skin and he wrapped his arms around her, drawing her against his chest to warm her up. Her hard nipples pushed into his chest and the lace of her bra was soft against his skin. She wrapped her arms around his neck and twined her fingers together there.

Their eyes met and, for a moment, he forgot everything but Quinn. She shifted again and his erection hardened as she rubbed herself against him. He groaned and sprawled one hand wide against the small of her back, holding her, guiding her as she rocked against him, trying to get her to rub herself against the tip of him. When she did, his head dropped back and he said her name softly like a refrain in time with the movements of her hips.

She laughed softly and he felt her mouth against the column of his neck as she sucked and kissed her way down his body. She shifted, the exquisite movements of her hips stopping as she did so. But he felt her fingers, long and cold, grazing over his stomach and down the center of his body.

He flicked the catch of her bra open with two fingers and then pulled it down her arms. She lifted one and then the other to allow him to remove it. She started to reach for the fastening on his shorts, but he stopped her.

He put his hands on her waist and shifted back so he could see her. In the dark of night, with only the moon and stars, he couldn't see her skin clearly but knew she had freckles all over her body and that her nipples were a brownish pink color. He flicked his fingers over her nipples and felt them tighten under his touch.

He drew one finger down the center of her body as she'd done to him, circling her belly button, flicking the tiny gold hoop that she had there. From memory, he knew that playing with her piercing turned her on. She shifted her hips against his thighs, parting her legs as she did so. He continued to tease her belly button, needing her to be as ready as he was.

Every touch of her hands drove him closer and closer to the edge, and they both weren't even naked yet.

She pulled his head to hers and, as their lips met, part of him wondered if this was nothing more than a fevered summer dream. This woman he'd wanted for too long but hadn't realized until this moment.

One thing about Logan was that he wasn't just driven in business; his passion applied to every aspect of his life. He made love to her with the same intensity that he negotiated a deal in the boardroom. No part of her body was overlooked, no detail was too small to escape his attention. And, surprisingly, he seemed to remember everything that had turned her on all those years ago.

She pushed his shirt off his shoulders, which made him stop fondling her belly button piercing. But her body was still throbbing and even though he'd said he wanted to take it slow, she was ready to have him inside her. She wanted to forget everything except this man and make this night one she'd always remember.

Quinn reached for the button on his shorts but he stopped her again; this time she pushed his hands away. She got that he wanted the slow tease but she wanted him *now*. She undid the button and then lowered his zipper, reaching into the opening to take him in her hand and stroke him. He groaned her name, a guttural sound that seemed to be drawn from inside the depths of him.

"Oh, I'm not going to last, Ace," he said. "And I have it on good authority women like it to be longer than thirty seconds."

She couldn't help the laugh he drew from her. "That's true, but I want to touch you. I want you naked on the blanket so I can enjoy every second of you."

"You have to be naked too. Equality and all that," he said.

"Fine with me," she said, standing and stepping out of her underwear. She was momentarily glad it was night because she hadn't had a bikini wax recently. But then Logan's hands were on her legs, caressing his way up the length of them as he stood next to her. He cupped her naked butt and drew her forward, rubbing his erection against her center, and she had the feeling he didn't really care if she'd had a bikini wax or not.

She pushed his shorts down with his underwear and the tip of his erection bumped her stomach as he stepped out of his shorts. He put one hand between her shoulders and kept the other on her butt, tugging her to him. His mouth came down on hers hard, his tongue pushing into her mouth and his cock rubbing against her mound. She held on to his shoulders and realized he hadn't been joking when he'd said he might not last.

He'd gone from smooth, sophisticated lover to a man with an unquenchable need, and she loved it. This was what she wanted from him. Not the playing at being a gentleman when she knew that underneath his civilized exterior beat the heart of a warrior. A man who was fighting to take everything the world had—and tonight, everything that she had— to give him.

She met his passion with her own. No longer having to temper herself because he wasn't tempering himself. She grabbed his shaft, stroking his length, reaching lower to cup him. She squeezed gently before she tore her mouth from his and kissed her way down his chest. Biting at his pec, which flexed as she did so. He made that groan that sounded like her name again. His hands were in her hair as she moved lower on his body. She kept stroking him with her hand as her mouth drew nearer and she licked the tip of his erection, sucking him into her mouth as his hands tightened in her hair. He reached for her breasts, cupping them in his hands as she sucked him deeper into her mouth. He flicked his fingers over her nipples, and she felt the warmth between her legs.

Quinn was so hot for him, needed him now, but didn't want to stop sucking him. He pulled his hips back and lifted her into his arms, falling to his knees while cushioning the landing for her. They were facing each other again and he framed her face with his hands. In the moonlight, she couldn't see the expression in his eyes but had no doubt of what he wanted next. He pulled her down next to him on the blanket.

She reached for his body, not done with caressing him, but he caught her hand and drew it up above her head. He captured her other hand and held both wrists lightly in his grasp. He knelt next to her torso, his big body crouched and ready, his cock shooting out toward her, his breaths sawing in and out as he looked at her. He drew his free hand down the center of her, starting at her forehead. She sucked his finger into her mouth when he brushed it over her lips and then felt the wetness as he continued his path along her chest.

He ran his damp finger around each of her nipples before moving lower, flicking her piercing before he placed his palm over her mound. He pushed down with the heel of his palm, rubbing his hand over her clit, and then she felt his finger parting her. The air was cool for a moment against her sensitive flesh but then his finger was there. Flicking and rubbing against her. Her hips lifted as she tried to get more but he wouldn't be rushed. He drove her slowly toward the edge of her control. She felt her orgasm, right there just out of her reach, and struggled against his hold on her wrists, trying to touch him. Instead he just brought his mouth to hers as he plunged two fingers into her and drove her over the edge.

Logan felt a drop of precum on the tip of his cock and knew he was going to spill himself all over Quinn if he didn't get inside her now. But watching her orgasm, driving her to the edge, was the biggest turn-on of all. She was always the one in control. Always the one who kept part of herself back. Except just now. Just now he'd taken it from her and, after a long day when he'd felt like nothing was in his power, he'd needed that.

He leaned over her and kissed her, petting her between her legs until her orgasm subsided. She shifted underneath him, spreading her legs open and tugging her hands free from his grip. He let her go, moving so he was on top of her, shifting his hips until the tip of his erection was at the opening of her body. She was moist and soft and ready for him.

He almost hesitated but she grabbed his ass, pushed her feet into the blanket and drove herself up against him. He thrust deep inside her. She was tight and he hoped he didn't hurt her as he entered her. He kept himself fully seated inside her until he felt her body soften around him and then he pulled back and drove inside again.

She kept one hand on his butt and drew the other up his back. Her fingers softly moved along his spine as her mouth was on his, sucking his tongue deep into her mouth. He rocked against her harder and harder. He felt his own orgasm building and wanted to make it last, wanted her to come again with him, but wasn't sure he had any power to slow down. He reached between their bodies, flicking her clit with his finger, and she sucked harder on his tongue. Her hips moved urgently against his, his own moving like pistons as he tried to get to the edge and then over it. He kept pumping into her even as his orgasm hit. She bit his tongue and then tore her mouth free of his as she called his name out loud. He buried his face in her neck as his orgasm slowly passed, bracing himself on his hands and knees to keep from crushing her with his weight.

Logan felt her hands in his hair, twirling it through her fingers as he slowly came back into himself. He rolled to his side, pulling her with him, and she cuddled close to him. His breathing slowed and so did hers. He knew he should say something, needed to talk to her, but he had no words.

Didn't want to ruin this moment by trying to explain it or justify it. He wanted to just hold her with the summer stars above them and not think for a few damned minutes. And he could. He felt her drop a kiss on his chest and then she shivered as the breeze blew. He reached for his shirt with his free arm, draped it over her, and she smiled up at him.

As their eyes met, he knew that the words he didn't want to say were right there hovering, ready to come out. But he wasn't a man to make fake promises and he knew until everything was out about what he'd done to Williams, Inc., he couldn't ask her to let him back in her life. He couldn't reach out and take her with him because he was in a car that was going too fast and had no brakes. And if this night had proven anything to him, it was that Quinn mattered to him.

She had calmed his monkey mind and given him a chance to breathe. She'd made it okay to forget for just a little while and he wanted...well, something that he didn't dare take because she deserved better.

Hell, she always had.

"Don't," she said.

"What?" he asked. But he knew. That moment he'd had right after they'd come was gone. The world was waiting and there was no denying it.

"Think. Don't think, Logan. Lie here with me for just a little bit longer," she said softly, but even in her voice, he could hear that she knew it was too late.

He laid back because he was stubborn that way. He hated this part of himself. The part that always managed to break things even when he was trying to be careful. He could broker deals and increase profit margins, but when it came to the personal, he had no subtlety. That was glaringly obvious as he heard Quinn sigh and then sit up, reaching for her clothes.

"I need a shower. Want to come back to the house I've rented for the week and clean up?" she asked. "Or are you heading back to the bonfire?"

"I'm with you, Ace, if you'll have me," he said. "I know I—"

She put her fingers over his mouth to stop him from talking. "Let's just get dressed, go to my place, and then we can talk or dissect or whatever it is you think we need to do."

They both got dressed and as she started to walk toward the wooden walkway, he stopped her.

"I wanted to hold you and just forget for a little while longer. I'm just not sure how to do that, Quinn. Please, never think that I wanted this," he said, gesturing to them. "I just don't know how."

"Stop trying to make sure you win, and it will happen."

"This wasn't about winning," he said.

"Are you sure?" she asked.

He wasn't sure. Now that she'd pointed it out, he realized he hadn't wanted to seem like he needed her more than she needed him. And Quinn Murray never needed a man—especially Logan Bisset.

CHAPTER FIVE

ADLER WATCHED HER fiancé getting drunk and acting...well, like the man she'd fallen in love with. He'd never admit it, but he seemed to be bonding with his half siblings. The Bissets and his Williams siblings were taking their cues from him. In the Williams' family's favor, they'd always known Nick had had a different dad than Tad Williams. Of course, learning that it was August had thrown them all.

"He'd going to be so hung over tomorrow," Olivia said, coming up to her after Iris had left the bonfire. Quinn had disappeared as well, and Adler had tried to put on her big-girl panties and socialize as if she wasn't questioning everything. Looking at the young woman who was going to be her sister-in-law if this marriage went off, she smiled.

"He definitely is. I have the feeling he won't regret it," Adler said.

"I know I won't," Olivia said. "I recorded him and Zac singing earlier. I'm going to have blackmail material for years."

Adler laughed as she suspected Olivia wanted her to. Nick's youngest sibling and only sister had straight black hair that framed her heart-shaped face. She had dark brown, almost black eyes that were forthright. She was down for a good time, but she was also a very serious woman. She was young—twenty-eight—but everyone knew she was following in Nick's footsteps and would be a serious contender for CEO if he ever stepped aside.

"Are you okay?" Olivia asked as they both took a glass of white wine from the passing waiter.

"Yeah. I mean why wouldn't I be?" Adler really hoped it wasn't obvious how freaked out she was by the news that Nick wasn't who he thought he was. That the media was going to have a field day with the news two titans of industry shared a connection to Nick. It was the kind of juicy scandal the tabloids loved. And she'd always—*always*—hated that kind of media attention.

"We're going to be sisters," Olivia said. "After a lifetime with just guys, I had hoped we could talk and I wouldn't have to front all the time with you."

Adler turned to Olivia and realized what the other woman was saying. She and Olivia had spent some girl-time getting to know each other. She had craved having a close sister bond. She had a few half siblings from her father's numerous affairs, but he had a way with women that made them tend to hate him when he moved on so she'd never had a chance to get close to any of them.

"I do want that," Adler said. "I just don't want to ruin this night for you."

Olivia put her arm around Adler's shoulders. "You can't. We're sisters and I've got your back. So talk to me."

She looked at Olivia for another long minute and then took a deep breath. "I'm freaking out. I mean I wish I could get drunk, like Nick's doing, but I know that won't help, and I have to do some shooting in the morning for the reality TV show—which I'm not sure we should still do. But Quinn is counting on me. And maybe it's better to get ahead of this with some positive media..." She trailed off, realizing she was about to start rambling all of the fears plaguing her.

Olivia shook her head. "I get it. It's easy for Nick to drink because he can't begin to start sorting this out, but that's not you. It's not me either. Want to make a plan? I'm good at this and I'll help however I can. Iris will too. You don't have to worry about anything but your wedding. We can handle the other stuff," Olivia said.

The wedding was one of her chief concerns. Could she marry a man who wasn't who she thought he was? It seemed selfish for her to even be concerned about it, but she had never been the kind of woman who ignored her inner feelings. This was bothering her.

Adler knew the lie hadn't been Nick's, but she also realized this was going to change him in ways she couldn't even begin to guess. She certainly wasn't going to say any of that to Olivia, who watched her as if waiting for something. "You're right. I think it's just so new that I was overwhelmed. I'll make a list and then we can divvy it up."

"Great. Want to do it tonight?"

She started laughing. Olivia was a bit of a bookworm and didn't normally like socializing, so Adler wasn't surprised she wanted to do it now. "No, let's enjoy this party. I think once the word gets out, things aren't going to be like this again."

"You're right. This is the last moment where we know that Nick is both ours and the Bissets. All my life, Dad has told us August Bisset was the boogeyman and I sort of always believed him and thought that his kids, especially Logan, were the same. But now they are related to me..." Olivia let her words fall; she was probably as mixed up about everything as Adler was, albeit from a different perspective. And at that moment, Nick came running over to Adler, scooped her up in his arms and spun her around.

"I love you, Addie. Nothing else matters but you," he said, letting her slide down his body until their lips met and they kissed.

Nothing else mattered. She wanted to believe it as he deepened the kiss and cupped her butt, but she knew no matter how much they both wanted that to be true, the outside world would interfere.

Nick had a way of making that all fade as he pulled her into his arms and danced with her as her father sang about the simple life. She remembered her advice to Olivia and decided to enjoy this moment when everything seemed perfect, because she knew perfection was an illusion.

Juliette Bisset stood on the widow's walk looking out at the horizon. Her husband was in the study with Carlton forming some sort of plan. Tad and Cora Williams had left an hour ago and her mother had retired. She was alone on the walk, wearing the same shawl she'd wrapped Logan in when she'd brought him home from the hospital as a baby. She took a deep breath.

She'd had no idea that Logan was really August's son. She'd just claimed him in her heart as hers. But seeing Bonnie— Cora!—today had thrown her.

On that fateful night when she'd met a young single mother in a small rural hospital, she'd had no idea who the father of the other woman's baby—babies—was. But today she knew.

August Bisset. Her own husband.

After all these years, it felt like everything had been laid to rest. She'd had her dark little secret that she carried with her until today. Without even a hint of irony, she had to wonder how she could have missed that Logan was Auggie's son. They were like two peas in a pod. Auggie was being overly contrite and saying and doing all the things that...well, frankly, he'd done over the course of their marriage every time she'd found out he was cheating.

Juliette had seen in his eyes real sorrow this time. This was the one thing she hadn't expected to see. Their marriage had been good since Mari's birth. They'd slowly made their way into a relationship where they were both honest with each other, and that was what hurt the most. Auggie was finally the man she'd always wanted him to be. The way he'd been treating her since the revelation that Nick was his son was evidence of that.

Yet she knew it wouldn't last.

It couldn't.

There was no way, once he realized that she'd lied about Logan all these years, that he could forgive her. The baby she'd carried had been stillborn and she'd made a deal with the single mother who had expected one child and not twins. A deal to help save her rocky marriage. But looking back was probably going to not only ruin her marriage but also break her family. How could she have been so blind?

She was racked with guilt. Over the secret that had seemed so innocent until this afternoon when Cora Williams had shown up and revealed herself to be one and the same as Bonnie Smith. The woman who'd worked for Bisset Industries all those years ago, who'd had an affair with August. And with whom Juliette shared a secret that could be her undoing.

Frankly, Juliette had never paid any attention to August's business since she had carved her own life with her charity work. But now Juliette wished she had. Heck, she'd even avoided meeting Adler's future in-laws because...well, she hadn't wanted any part of August's sharklike behavior to spoil things for Adler. But now she wished— Heck there was a long list of things she wished she'd done.

And they didn't start with meeting Nick's mom. They started back in that hospital room in 1983. The place where she'd first met Bonnie. They'd both just gone through labor, and each was facing the hardest challenge of her life. The deal...it had seemed a simple solution at the time. Juliette would help out the destitute single woman who'd just given birth to twin boys by funding her education and giving her a lump sum of money to set herself up in exchange for one of the twins becoming hers. Replacing the stillborn baby that she'd brought back here to Nantucket and buried in that unmarked grave in the family plot.

She'd loved Logan from the second she'd held him. Had

never thought of him as anyone else's son but hers. And bringing the new baby home, the child everyone believed was hers and August's, had given her and August a new start until his eye had wandered again.

Someone cleared his throat and she glanced toward the open sliding-glass door to see August standing there with a tray that had two snifters on it. He stood tall almost six feet, five inches, but he'd lost a bit of that height in the last few years. His once jet-black hair was shot with gray, which only made him seem more distinguished. His jaw was still as strong. His nose a sharp blade that gave him an intense look.

"May I join you?" he asked. His voice was deep, and she closed her eyes as she felt tears burning at the backs of them.

"Baby, I'm sorry. Please let me try to make this right," he said.

She opened her eyes and realized that he'd moved onto the platform and was now crouching in front of her chair. She put her hand on his shoulder. She wanted to let him make it right, but she was torn. Should she just make her confession now? Would it come out? She was pretty sure that Bonnie aka Cora wasn't going to spill it, but if this afternoon had proven anything, it was that secrets had a way of coming out of the shadows.

"It's okay," she said, touching his cheek and feeling the stubble underneath her palm.

He turned his head and kissed her before standing and taking the chair next to hers. "It's not okay. I'm sorry I didn't know about Nick or even that Bonnie had been pregnant. What kind of man was I?"

She reached out for one of the snifters. "A selfish asshole."

"Agreed. I hate that I hurt you twice with this same indiscretion. You know I've changed."

"I do know," she admitted. "It's not for me to forgive. As you said, this indiscretion is something we covered a long time ago.

The kids are going to struggle. Especially Logan, as he hates the Williamses as much as you do."

Auggie took a sip of his brandy, rubbing the back of his neck with his free hand. And as she looked at him, she saw what she'd missed earlier: the strain around his eyes. He was taking this hard. Harder than she'd seen him take any news they'd ever received.

"Are you okay?"

He shook his head. "I have a son I didn't know about. I've been in meeting rooms with him over the years and never recognized him...how could I not have?"

Juliette reached over and took his hand in hers, squeezing it. "You weren't looking for a son. You were looking at a rival, so that's what you saw."

He lifted her hand to his mouth, his lips brushing her knuckles. "I really did hit the jackpot when I met you, Jules. I know I haven't always acted like it, but you are the greatest treasure of my life."

She couldn't stop the tears that fell when he said that. He put his snifter down and lifted her onto his lap, holding her and apologizing. But she knew the tears weren't for what he'd done but for what *she'd* done and the impact it was going to have on her family and this man she loved.

Quinn's rented house was two streets over from his gran's place. As they walked, Logan held her hand and they both took sips from the bottle of Jack. Most of the homes were dark but he could hear the sounds of music and laughter from the backyards. It was a quiet kind of night in this tranquil setting.

Usually being on Nantucket made his skin feel too tight. He wasn't a downtime guy and this trip wasn't really any different. Quinn didn't say much as they walked and she'd kept his shirt on over her dress. He wanted to say something that would make this seem like it was something more than a hookup. His mom always said to be honest and shoot straight.

"What are you thinking?" Quinn asked. "You keep looking over at me as if you want to say something."

"I do. But I'm not sure how to say it," he admitted. As with all deep truths, it was hard to actually voice.

"Then just say it."

He smiled. "My mom would say the same thing."

"Your mom has given you advice on women?"

"Inadvertently. You know today wasn't the first time we've had to confront my dad's infidelities. One time when I was about ten, I thought they were going to break up for good. She was so pissed. She cries when she's mad. She was in the garden deadheading plants and Dare and Leo and I went out to help. She turned to the three of us, with those wilted flowers in her gloved hand and tears in her eyes, and said, 'Don't lie. Never lie to a woman you love because that just makes the truth hurt that much more.' I didn't have a clue what she was talking about."

"So what are you trying not to lie to me about?" Quinn asked, cutting to the point in that blunt way of hers. Had the magic of the evening faded for her? He was still drifting in the summer evening in a haze of whiskey and regret that he'd ruined their cuddle on the beach.

"Nothing. I don't want to lie about anything. I think we both know that hooking up wasn't what either of us planned, but it feels like more than a hookup to me," he said. Damn, why was he talking so much? He should stop drinking. He saw a trash can near the sidewalk and walked over to throw away the bottle.

"It wasn't what I planned," she admitted. "But I don't regret it or I wouldn't have asked you back here. I know you're not in a good place, Logan. I'd have to be an idiot to read this any other way than we were hot for each other and you needed a distraction."

A distraction.

"No. I mean yes, but you are not just a distraction," he said, rubbing the back of his neck as if that would make things clearer.

She opened the door to the cottage she'd rented and they stepped inside.

He leaned back against the door as he closed it. "I wish we'd done this a few weeks ago. Before..." He stopped himself. Before what? Before he'd set about undercutting his rival who also happened to be marrying into his extended family? No. What he'd meant was before he'd become this guy. The man he was today, who never let anyone get the better of him. He wished... stuff hadn't happened. That somehow he'd have been different in college so that the two of them would have— No, that wasn't it either. He wouldn't change the man he was for anything. He knew that.

"Hey," Quinn said. She stood on the natural woven runner just watching him. "Let's just not lie when it comes up. I want to spend the night with you because I know this is it. You and me are never doing this again, so I want to get every second with you until the sun comes up. What do you want?"

He stared at her. Wondered how he'd ever been lucky enough to call her his, and knew that he wanted that exact same thing. She was the oasis in the crazy that was his family and this wedding of the year.

"The same. And maybe a shower. I have sand in places that it isn't meant to be."

She threw her head back and started laughing. "Me too. This place has a large master bathroom with a two-headed shower stall and a huge garden tub. Want to join me?"

He followed her down the hall to the master bath and stood there enjoying the sight of Quinn stripping and singing to Taylor Swift's "Lover" as she did so. He had his buzz from drinking but he was certain it came more from being with Quinn than from the alcohol.

He stripped off his clothes and followed her into the shower. He took his time soaping her body, running his hands over her freckled skin and making sure he didn't miss an inch. In the morning, when he had to walk away, he wanted this night to have been enough to last for the rest of his life. Because as Quinn had said, this was it. They weren't going to fall into each other's arms again.

She was a distraction, and he knew she wouldn't approve of what he'd done to Nick's business deal before he'd learned they were half brothers. She wouldn't approve of him at all, he thought. Behavior like that was why they were no longer a couple.

But for this one night none of that mattered.

CHAPTER SIX

LOGAN WAS STILL hung over from last night. He looked around Gran's den at his family and realized the rest of them were in misery, too. His mother was…well, not herself. His father sat in the corner, nursing one of the Bloody Marys that Gran's butler, Michael, had made for them. Zac had a tortured look on his face. Right before coming here, he'd had a confrontation with Iris, his date for the wedding, and was in real hot water.

It turned out that a private conversation Zac'd had in the lobby of his hotel, in which he'd confessed that Iris had paid to date him, had been recorded and the video had gone viral. Iris was angry at Zac, and Logan didn't blame her. But it was just another piece of kindling thrown on the fire that was slowly burning down the Bisset name.

The only silver lining—or silver-plated lining—was that Zac's problem was a welcome distraction from thinking about the situation with Nick Williams—and about Quinn. But his brother was broken. His feelings for Iris had intensified over the course of the weekend, and now his chances with her were virtually nil. Normally, Zac was carefree, looking at the horizon and longing to get back on his yacht and sail away. But even the ocean seemed to be closed to him now. He sat in the den at Gran's house where Carlton looked like he was going to implode if another one of them revealed something scandalous.

"Is this it? Are we all here?" Carlton asked.

Mari breezed into the room alone. Her fiancé, Formula One driver Inigo Velasquez, was racing this weekend. She pushed her Wayfarers up on her head and surveyed them all. "Who died?"

God, Logan loved his little sister.

"Um, Zac was caught on tape saying Iris paid him to be her date. There's been some fallout from that," he said. "I think what you are seeing is that shell-shocked look that comes from being hammered by hurricane-force waves."

"Geez, Zac, are you kidding me?" Mari asked, going over to Michael and taking one of the drinks he'd prepared. "Can I have something to eat, please, Michael? I'm starving."

"Yes, Miss Mari. Anyone else?"

"I'm hungry too," Zac said.

They all joined in asking for food and Michael left to prepare something. It had been a long time since the family had been together in one room. The family he'd grown up a part of and thought he'd known so well until yesterday's revelations.

"What are we going to do?"

"Zac, you have to apologize to Iris. To be honest, this is probably going to be a nice distraction for the paparazzi from the entire Nick thing. But she's not going to see it that way," his mom said. "Then we need to be prepared to present a unified front on… Nick."

"I agree," Carlton said. "I have a statement ready to release and I think that will help to mitigate most of the speculation. I want to stress that Cora Williams kept the name of Nick's father to herself. And it was only when they were forced into the same room that she admitted the truth. We need to continue to stress that there was no ulterior motive in keeping the secret, just two lives that went on separate paths."

Logan wanted to believe things would be that easy, that one

statement would make the paparazzi go away. But he knew it wouldn't. As soon as his business deal hit the papers—and it would on Monday—there would be more interest.

"Great. What about business? Are we going to mention that Nick is the CEO of our biggest rival?" Logan asked.

"And that Logan and he hate each other?" Leo asked. "I mean I think most people know that."

"You're not helping, Leo," Dare said. As a politician, he was usually the one to find the most diplomatic way of saying things. Logan realized that he needed his big brother's advice before the news broke on Monday.

"I'm just saying the kind of stuff that's going to crop up on social media. The kind of comments we are going to have to address," Leo pointed out. "Carlton, you know your stuff when it comes to the legitimate press but influencers are going to come for Iris and for Logan once the news breaks. I think my PR team could help Iris with that since I work with influencers all the time."

"I like that idea," Zac said. "Iris isn't talking to me so, can I reach out to her and tell her?"

"Sure," Leo said. "Dad? Should I call my PR team up here?"

His dad looked at Carlton, who nodded. "Do we have time to wait or should we video conference?"

His father put down his drink and stood, and Logan realized the old man was taking control of the situation.

"All of us in this room have a vested interest in making sure that the spin goes our way. Zac, your comment and your decision were unfortunate. We will help you fix it because that's what this family does. Leo and Carlton will work on the message. Everyone needs to smile and stay on message. Adler is your mother's only niece—her last connection to her sister—we are not going to allow anything to ruin her wedding."

His mom rose and walked to his father's side. She seemed motivated now and, while her smile wasn't as bright as it usually was, she was making the effort. "I will make sure that Adler is protected from this as much as I can. Her wedding needs to be her focus."

"Perfect," his dad said. "Logan, reach out to Nick and try to see if you can partner for the golf scramble together. Carlton will try to get some publicity photos of the two of you so we can allay the fears of both boards that this news is going to shake things up."

"How will that help?" Logan asked. "We're still going to be rivals with Williams, Inc."

"We want to look friendly," August said.

"I don't think that's the right message," Logan said.

"I just told you it was," his father shot back.

Logan clenched his jaw. "You're not the CEO anymore, Dad. We need to talk about this."

"Good idea," Mom said. "You two can have a chat on Monday. For now, let's focus on fixing Zac's mess and the wedding."

Iris was a mess and Adler was only a little better. Both of them were struggling to deal with fallout from dealing with the Bissets.

Quinn kept it to herself that she'd slept with Logan last night. But seeing her friends and how being connected to the Bissets had this kind of impact sharpened her desire to ensure that last night was a one-off.

They were in a private suite at the hotel and her production team had set up to film the manicures and pedicures the bridal party were having this morning. It was just for cutaways later. "Are you doing the golf scramble this morning?"

"Yes," Adler said. "Nick and I want to keep to the schedule. I mean I think that's what we want. He was sleeping when I left, but I asked Olivia to make sure he was at the golf club at eleven. I'm worried about everything falling apart."

"Me too," Iris said. "I'm so sorry, Adler, that everything with Zac has been leaked."

Adler hugged Iris, and Quinn sat there watching the two of

them. Just a day earlier she would have said her friends had it all. Men they loved and relationships that were solid. If anything, it just demonstrated that there was no such thing as a perfect one. She'd always known that. Had seen her parents' example: two people who married in a white hot fit of passion and were like fire and water. But she'd thought if she were smarter—like Iris and Adler—she'd be able to find a man who could be a partner to her.

Though, of course, falling into Logan's arms wasn't part of that plan.

"I'm sorry for you," Adler said. "But honestly, I think it will help distract from the scandal of Nick being a Bisset. It's so crazy right now. He's pretending it's not a big deal but he grew up hating August. When he first found out that he was my uncle, I thought it would be a deal breaker for us. Now it turns out August is his father."

"Me too," Iris admitted. "To be fair I know the Williams family way better than the Bissets, but from what I've observed, they aren't that different."

Iris had been friends with Nick in college and had been responsible for introducing him to Adler, who had been her roommate.

"In what way?" Quinn asked. "Logan is so driven, and my impression has always been that his family all have to be number one."

"It's the same with Nick's family. I mean Tad is nicer about it. More of a 'rising tide raises all ships' but he definitely wants them all to rise, if you know what I mean," Iris said. "Also, Tad has always hated August but no one knows why...do you, Adler?"

"No. I mean Nick said that he thought his dad and August had a falling out long before he was born. Interesting that Tad didn't know Cora had an affair with August or that she'd worked for Bisset Industries," Adler said.

"Yeah. I would hate to be her right now," Iris said. "I feel bad about it. But how did she think it would go when Nick met August?"

Adler shook her head and shrugged. "To be honest, I think she thought August wouldn't come to the wedding because he and I aren't close and he hates the Williams family as much as they hate him. He only decided last minute. I'm pretty sure she intended to never be in the same room with him if she could help it."

"I don't blame her," Quinn said. Her phone started pinging. Most of it was from her network wanting to discuss the scandalous rumors coming out of Nantucket. "Adler, who is releasing a statement about Nick?"

"I think it's going to be a joint one later, but I don't have the details. Why?" Adler asked as she glanced down at her painted toenails.

"The network wants deets and I'm stalling, but I am going to have to give them something," Quinn said.

"Let me text Nick and see what he knows," Adler said. She grabbed her phone and Quinn glanced at Iris, who was sitting so stiff and still, as if by keeping her posture perfect, she could hold herself together.

"Iris, you okay?"

"Yes, of course," she said. "I'll weather this. My parents are coming out today to be with me for the rest of the weekend. Mom said keep my head high. Leta told me not to respond to any of the gossip and just pretend that I didn't hear it."

"Does she think that will work?"

"No, but she said it will piss off the gossip sites who want more dirt. Zac is so apologetic, I think he'd say anything to make up for this, but it's too late. Mari said she would stand by me, which means a lot, but some of the other influencers that I've been working with have dropped me."

Iris was a popular influencer who had started a blog in college and transitioned it to a chronicle of being a single-girl-in-the-city as she'd left, growing her audience and her influence.

She had hired Zac to pose as her boyfriend because her fiancé had dumped her before the wedding and she had a collab with a couples brand for the weekend.

Quinn got up to hug her friend. This was the reality of the 24/7 lifestyle they were all living. For herself, Quinn knew she was outside the spotlight but still close enough that she was on the radar for some of the paparazzi because they knew she had friendships with Iris and Adler. This weekend was going to shine the spotlight on everyone and the only way she would survive it was to be strong for her friends and to stay away from Logan.

He was in the middle of the spectacle, which he hated. But she knew he'd manage, and it didn't matter if he hated it or not, because he wasn't her man. He was a guy she'd hooked up with for old times' sake. That was all.

Really.

And she wasn't going to let it be more than that. She couldn't. Because if she did, she might end up like her best friends. And really who wanted to feel like that?

Logan waited until Nick was paired up with one of his grooms- men before he walked into the clubhouse to be paired for the golf scramble. His mother stood to one side, looking elegant and smiling like her world wasn't falling apart.

"Mom, do you have a partner yet?"

"No, honey, I don't. What about you?" she asked.

He'd been planning to find Quinn and pair up with her, but she was busy with her film crew. He had a new respect for Quinn and the job she did. She'd been running around since they'd all gotten here and one of her crew had let it slip that she'd been working since seven this morning. Given how he'd felt when he'd woken up and slipped out of her rented house this morning, he really admired that.

"I don't. Want to join me and we can kick some butt?" he asked her.

"Whose butt?" Leo asked, coming over to stand next to them. "I don't have a partner yet. Are we making it interesting?"

"I'm game," Logan said. "Let's play for bragging rights and, let's say, ten voting shares in the company."

"Boys," Mom cautioned.

"I like it," Leo said.

"I don't. Never wager the company," Mom said. "Pick something else."

"Okay. Once Leo gets his partner, we'll decide. You know Mom and I won the Bridgehampton Scramble for the last three years."

"I do," Leo said. "But I suspect that's because I wasn't competing. And Mom has been carrying you for a while."

"Boys," Mom said, putting her arms around them both and hugging them, "it's because we are Bissets that we win."

"Exactly," Leo said. "Let me go get partnered up and then we can make a wager."

Leo walked away and Logan turned to his mom. She was smiling after his younger brother. "Leo's such a suck-up."

"Because he said I was carrying you?" she asked. "He knows it's not true. He just thinks it's funny. Your dad likes to needle you the same way."

"He does. Has it ever occurred to you that Dare and I are the most like you?" Logan asked.

Her smile dipped for a moment and then she nodded. "You are both a lot like your father too."

"Yeah, but you have a subtlety that he lacks and that I think I inherited."

"You and Leo are determined to make me blush today," she said.

"We just want you to know how much we love you," Logan said.

"Oh, boyo," she said, using her childhood nickname for him and hugging him close. "I love you so very much too."

Logan hugged her back, holding her longer than he needed to because he sensed that this latest thing with his dad was hurting her more than she let on. He knew how he'd feel if he and Quinn were a couple and some dude showed up saying she was his. And that wasn't even half of what his mom was dealing with.

And he wasn't a couple with Quinn, he reminded himself firmly.

He heard Leo cursing and stepped away from his mom to see what had his brother upset.

Juliette shook her head. "He's making a scene."

"I think you should have spanked him more when he was little. He's a bit of a brat."

His mom playfully punched Logan in the arm. "You all are. Let's go see what the problem is."

He followed her over to the table where the partner assignments were being managed.

"What's the problem, little Leo?" Logan asked.

"Nothing. There's no problem. Just found out I've been paired with Danni Eldridge."

"Why is her name familiar?" Juliette asked.

"She's a small business owner whose company is being compared to Leo's," Logan said with a smile. "Oh, I think we should make a healthy wager."

"She's not my competition. She's a startup working out of her garage. I have a large warehouse and factory where I produce hand-made quality products."

"So there isn't a problem, right?" Logan asked. His brother's defensive tone belied the notion that her little startup didn't bother him. Leo had started the same way. Hand-making products in his home and growing his business. "Where is she?"

"I don't know," Leo said. "I've never met her and don't know what she looks like."

"Surely you looked her up online," Logan said.

"I did. Her profile picture is a Singer sewing machine," Leo said.

"I'll go and find her," their mom said, moving toward the crowd of wedding guests congregated by the golf carts.

"I think we should wager shares," Logan said.

"Forget it. I don't know her at all. I thought I'd get Dare, but he's paired with some girl I've never met either."

"This just isn't your day, Leo," Logan said.

Before Leo could answer, their mom started back toward them, her arm looped through another woman's. The stranger had dark brown, curly hair and a heart-shaped face. Her eyes were brown and her gaze direct as she got closer to them.

Logan noticed that Leo was staring at her the way Logan was pretty sure he'd been looking at Quinn last night. "Maybe the competition isn't as bad as you thought," Logan said.

"Maybe," Leo said, walking over to the woman and holding out his hand. "Are you Danni? I'm Leo. Leo Bisset," he said. "I've been wanting to meet you for a while now."

"I bet you have," Danni said. "That's why you told the press that you thought my startup was just me trying to hang on to your coattails as you forge a new path."

"Damn," Logan said.

His mom elbowed him in the ribs. "Let's leave the two of them to talk. Leo, we'll meet you at the golf carts."

Logan followed her to the line, trying not to smile too much. There were a lot of times that Leo reminded him of himself. They both had a way of opening their mouths and making things a million times harder. No matter how much he thought he'd changed, there was a part of him that knew if he tried to get serious with Quinn he'd probably put his foot in it with her too.

CHAPTER SEVEN

THE NANTUCKET GOLF CLUB was busy with the wedding party and guests all playing eighteen holes. Nick and Adler had hired staff to be at each of the holes with beverages and snacks, and there were photo booths at the odd-numbered holes. Quinn had her camera crew set up on the most picturesque hole to capture everyone who played through. She had been filming some confessional video that she was going to edit as a gift to the couple, so had used her own personal camera.

So far, she thought it was going to be a nice video package to go along with the live wedding coverage. The day was sunny and perfect for June. Quinn wasn't a sentimental person but if she were, she'd think that Mother Nature was giving Adler a nice day to make up for everything that had happened the day before.

Adler was all smiles when she showed up at the hole partnered with her dad, along with Nick and his sister, Olivia, who were also partnered. Toby Osborn was the first one to the tee and Nick was offering his soon-to-be father-in-law some tips while Olivia stood off to the side snapping pictures with her SLR camera.

"How's it going?" Quinn asked Adler.

"Not too bad. I think things are dying down. Carlton has a

statement he's going to release to the press this afternoon. Do you want me to have him send it to you too so you can incorporate it into the wedding broadcast?" Adler asked.

Quinn realized that though Adler was smiling, she seemed fragile, like she was barely holding it all together. Quinn hugged her and Adler shook her head and put her hand up.

"Don't. You'll make me cry, and Nick and Dad will both want to know why… Like, honestly, if I have to tell them, will they even get it?"

"Sorry. Yes, have Carlton send it to me. Also, what do you think about you and Nick offering a personal little taped segment that deals with it? Just a quick it-was-a-surprise-but-whatever type thing?" Quinn asked. She was walking a delicate balance here because Adler was one of her best friends. Yet, as a producer, she'd be foolish if she didn't try to get them to talk about the issue on camera. It was the kind of thing that would make viewers who were hungry for gossip tune in, and could be a ratings boon.

"Sure. Can we do it before the rehearsal dinner? We'll both be dressed. Let me check with Nick on the timing," Adler said, going to talk to Nick.

Quinn noticed that Toby had finished taking his shot and waved him over. "I'm making a little video gift for Adler and Nick. Would you mind giving me a message in the booth over there? Just whatever you want to say to them," Quinn said.

"Love to, Q. But my girl looks like she's about to shatter. Is she okay?" Toby asked.

"She's as okay as she can be. I don't know what to do to help," Quinn confessed.

"Me neither. My gut is to do something scandalous to take the spotlight off Nick but… I'm finally with a woman who I think is the one. Is that selfish?" Toby asked.

Quinn shook her head. Toby had left a trail of lovers and scandals behind him and while Quinn knew she couldn't really speak for Adler, she was pretty sure her friend wanted her dad to have the happiness he'd found with Sonia, his latest girlfriend. "She'll be ticked at you if you do. She likes Sonia."

"All right. I'll just stay in a holding pattern for now. Where do you want me to do the taping?"

"That little area over there with the camera." Quinn gestured at the booth. "My PA, Tillie, will take you over."

As Tillie escorted him to the area, Adler came back over to Quinn. "Nick said if we could do the filming around four forty-five that would work with his schedule. He has to do something with his family at four fifteen. We're going to be on a tight clock."

"It will work," Quinn said. "Go tee off."

Adler went back to take her shot and Quinn managed to get Olivia over to the taping area after Toby finished. Nick stood to the side, watching Adler, and she saw a similar...well, *fragility* wasn't the right word for Nick, but he wasn't okay either.

"Hey, Nick, how are you doing today?" she asked.

"Okay," he said.

He reminded her so much of Logan in that moment. There was something about his smile that teased a memory at the back of her mind. The way he was using his natural confidence to mask the fact that there were many things out of his control right now.

"I guess that's the best you can say," Quinn added. She was tempted to mention something about Logan but then stopped herself. She'd had one night with her ex, and that was all it was. She didn't need to try to help Logan become friends with his new half sibling and longtime business enemy.

"Ad told me you want us to discuss the announcement about my real father. What do you have in mind?" Nick asked.

"Whatever you both feel comfortable discussing. I figure we'd look ridiculous if we don't address it. And it will give you both a chance to do it on your terms. Just whatever you want and, if you don't like it, we'll scrap it," she said.

"Really? That doesn't seem like it would be in your best interest."

"It's not, but Adler is one of my closest friends and I approach being a reality TV producer with an absence of malice. I don't want to become successful and win the ratings because I hurt either of you and made your lives worse."

"You're one in a million, Quinn. I know Adler values your friendship and I can see why. I hope we can continue to get to know each other and become friends."

Spontaneously, she hugged Nick. As the party left the hole, she wondered why Logan hated Nick so much. From everything that Quinn had seen, he was a decent man and one she thought Logan would respect.

Logan couldn't help but chuckle as he watched Leo trying to be chill and failing miserably. It was clear to him that he liked Danni. Their mother was doing her charming thing and keeping the conversation moving but his brother was flirting for all he was worth and getting nowhere. As his mom and Danni went to get drinks for the four of them, Logan couldn't resist needling Leo.

"So how's it going with Danni?" he asked as they walked over to the tee to set up their shots.

"I think you know how it's going," Leo said. "And I'm sure it's amusing to you."

"It is," Logan admitted. "After yesterday, it's reassuring to see that some things never change."

"How do you mean?" Leo asked.

"You and women you actually like," Logan said. "You just can't lower your guard and be real."

"Like you're such an expert at that," Leo said.

"I'm not. I suck at it too. As much as we both hate it, we are very similar in a lot of ways."

"I don't hate to admit it," Leo said. "I've always tried to be like you...but better."

Logan shook his head. His youngest brother never gave an inch. Actually, now that he thought about it, Danni Eldridge probably didn't stand a chance once Leo decided he was going after her.

"You try. That's all you can do," Logan said. "I wish Dad had come today. I know he thinks it's better if he stays away, but he loves golf, and it might have been good for him and Mom to be partners."

"You think so? She still looks like she's upset with him," Leo said as he glanced over at her. "I don't blame her. I'm mad at him and it's not even close to being the same."

Logan nodded. "Dad screwed up. I wonder if he thought he was doing the right thing when it happened."

"He didn't know Nick's mom was pregnant," Leo said. "He probably just figured his affair had ended, and Mom was pregnant with you, so he might have been happy to have it be over."

Logan nodded. Was that what his father had felt? It was always so hard to judge. His siblings all thought that he and August were the closest and, to be fair, they were close when it came to leading Bisset Industries. But personally he doubted he knew his father any better than the rest of his siblings. To be honest, his father never revealed much.

Logan thought his father had a certain charm, but he could also be very brusque—even with their mother. How did a woman love someone like that? Could she? He realized he wasn't just thinking about his dad but, really, he wondered if Quinn could find something inside of him—no. He wasn't going to go down that path. It was just that since he'd left her bed, he'd been missing her.

He could say that one night was all he wanted but being surrounded by all these couples, not just Adler and Nick, but the other couples here, had an effect on him. Even seeing Iris and Zac together, who were paired up and not speaking to each other as they played, made Logan long for more with Quinn.

Logan had always prided himself on being an island. On

not needing anything but the next win. But for the first time he saw the price that winning had on personal relationships. He didn't say it out loud to Leo, though he was pretty sure his father had thought that he'd won by having his affair, not getting caught, and moving on. He ate up that kind of conquest. Logan tried not to dwell on the fact that he'd been that kind of man too at one time.

Logan hadn't ever cheated on Quinn when they'd been together in college, but there had been times when he'd thought about it. It would have just been a subtle dig at her because she was smart and clever, and part of him had wanted to see if he could fool her. Luckily, he'd been intelligent enough to know that was a losing path.

How had his father not seen that?

Leo left to flirt with Danni again and his mom came over to take her shot. "You're looking so serious, boyo."

"I'm just thinking about Dad and wondering why he does the things he does," Logan admitted. "I mean—"

"Don't worry about it. I wonder the same thing all the time. I think sometimes he does it just to see if he can get away with it. Other times I think…well, he might stumble into something and though he regrets it when it's over, he never can admit he made a mistake."

"What good would admitting it do?" Logan asked. He had a feeling he might be in a situation where everyone was going to hate him in a few days, and he wasn't sure how to handle it. He should probably just come clean but he was embarrassed by his actions. As he always was. He hated that he had to win at any cost and it was only after he crossed the finishing line or put a tick in the win column that he looked back to see how it affected those around him.

This wasn't going to be easy for anyone to hear and at this moment he didn't want to make them all angry with him.

"It lets everyone around you know that you acknowledge you screwed up and that the hurt you caused wasn't your intention.

After the affair and before Mari was born, things changed with your dad and I. It was the first time that he realized by using arrogance to brazen his way through it, he was hurting me, and he was hurting you and your brothers. He decided at that moment that we meant more than his pride," she said.

"Did he?"

"I thought so," she said. But in her tone, he could tell that she wasn't so sure anymore.

Logan wanted to find the words to tell her that everything would be okay, but he didn't know that for certain. Their family was being ravaged by something even he couldn't figure a way out of.

The clubhouse was abuzz with guests sharing stories of their triumphs on the golf course. Quinn stayed toward the back of the room, filming with her crew, but as the crowd thinned out, she sent her team to lunch and asked them to meet back at her rented house around three. Though she was working, she was also a guest and wanted a few minutes to enjoy her friend's wedding as a guest. Also she'd noticed Logan making his way toward her and she wasn't sure she wanted her coworkers to see them chatting.

She'd hoped to be over him, but just the few moments she'd seen him today had proven that it would be difficult. That last night hadn't closed anything for her but instead had reopened emotions she'd thought had long ago subsided.

She should have known better.

It had taken her too long to get over Logan.

"Done working for the day?" he asked as he stopped next to her.

"For the moment. The crew is grabbing lunch," she said. "How'd you do?"

"Okay. Beat Leo, which is all that I cared about," Logan said.

She found that hard to believe. There were so many people

here that Logan saw as rivals even if she just started with the Williams family. "Really?"

"No, not really, but I'm trying to be gracious. I beat everyone except Nick…we tied," Logan said.

"The two of you are very similar. Probably comes from all those years of battling each other and watching your fathers battle—"

"Yeah, about that," Logan said sardonically. "You're not wrong. Regardless of DNA, Nick is still a Williams through and through, and it's going to take some time before I can see him differently."

She had suspected as much. "Does Williams still mean enemy?"

"Yes," he said then shoved his hand through his hair, ruffling it. He looked almost boyish with the thick blond hair sticking up. "I know it shouldn't. I mean even before we learned about the half sibling thing, he was marrying my cousin. But at the same time, we've been fighting them in the boardroom for as long as I can remember. The first summer Dare and I went to work with Dad, he was setting up a deal that Tad Williams undercut him on and won. It's hard to change years of thinking overnight."

"No one's asking you to," she said.

"I am. I'm asking myself to change, but it's hard, Quinn. Also…"

She waited to see if he was going to continue but he stopped as he watched Adler and Nick standing together. Nick had his arm around her.

"I'm an ass," he said. "I mean, how could I not see how much Adler loves him? I—I have to get out of here. Can you leave?"

She could. But did she want to? Of course, she didn't want to let him go alone when he'd asked to be with her, but at the same time, if she did go… There was no pretending any more that she wasn't starting to care about the man Logan was today.

Not the vestiges of what he'd been in college but the man before her, who was so much more complicated.

"Quinn?"

"Yeah, I'll go with you," she said.

They stepped outside and it was almost as if he took a huge breath. "Sorry about that. I did something before I came here that I regret," he said as they walked away from the clubhouse.

"What?"

"A business thing," he said. "It's complicated and probably boring, but Nick is going to be very unhappy, as will most of my family now that he's 'one of us.'"

"What did you do?"

"Just ruined a deal he has spent the last few months putting together," Logan admitted.

"Why would you do that?" she asked. "He's marrying your cousin."

Logan shook his head. "I don't know."

But she knew he did. "You hate to lose, right? Doesn't matter if there is human roadkill on the side of the superhighway that is Logan. You know that Adler is going to be devastated by this. And it's going to put a strain on things with her and Nick days into their—"

"Do you think I don't regret it?" he asked. "I do. You're right. I didn't think it through, and I thought it was sort of a moral victory because him marrying Adler felt like he got one over on us."

"Honestly, you make me crazy. Not everything is a competition," she said. How had she thought that he'd changed?

"Yeah, I know. I realized that when I walked into Gran's house and saw the devastation that my father had caused by being selfish. I thought it was just a friendly rivalry with Nick, but it wasn't. I was just trying to make sure I came out on top, just like you said, regardless of who I hurt to do it."

He turned away, his hands on his hips and his head bowed. "I can't stop it. What I've set in motion can't be changed. But I wish it could. I think until I saw how Dad's actions were hurting us all, I never got the effect my actions could have on my family."

She stood there for a moment, seeing him this way, knowing that he'd shown her this vulnerability because he trusted her. And…well, it drew her to him. She knew Logan wasn't perfect and, as much as it might make her seem like she wasn't smart, she always knew that it was his imperfection that got to her. His flaws made him human and real to her, and that was something she couldn't resist.

She went over to him and hugged him. He hugged her back. They didn't say anything else and, really, what else was there for either of them to say?

CHAPTER EIGHT

LOGAN'S QUIET MOMENT with Quinn didn't last long. His father texted him to discuss the business ramifications of the upcoming announcement dealing with the scandal of Nick's parentage. He left Quinn to head to his gran's house and found his father sitting not in the study as he usually was but on the sweeping back porch that overlooked the ocean in the distance.

"How was the golf?" his dad asked when he arrived.

"I beat Leo and tied Nick. Mom and this new girl, who is in Leo's field of business, played fair games."

"Your mom didn't play well?" his father asked.

"No, Dad, she didn't. She is doing a good job of being the perfect hostess, but we both know she's not on her A game."

"I know," his dad said. "I have no idea how to fix this."

"Me neither," Logan said. "Dad, what were you thinking?"

August rubbed the back of his neck, got up from the rocker and moved to the porch railing. "I can't say. When I was younger, the challenge drove me."

It wasn't much of an answer because Logan knew his father still liked a challenge. So did that mean he wouldn't rule out cheating on Juliette again?

"You wanted to talk business?" he asked.

"Yes. Carlton is already working on the spin, but I saw something…an article in a small paper about someone buying the patent to a new energy-efficient, low carbon emissions grain turbine."

"What about it?" Logan asked. His dad couldn't possibly know that he'd been the one to buy it. He'd done it through a small company he'd purchased under an LLC he'd started in college. There was no connection to Bisset Industries.

"Just thought it was curious as that patent had been one that I know Williams, Inc., has been trying to purchase for a long time. Just seemed odd that it would be snapped up from under them," August said.

"It is odd, but you know business is business."

"Until it's family," August said.

His dad knew. Somehow his father seemed to know it was him. "Yeah, well, things happen. I'd say that Nick didn't get as many of your genes as he should have if he let it slip away."

"You think?" August turned to face him. His appearance was just as intimidating as it had always been. His hair might be salt-and-peppered now and there were more sunlines around his eyes despite the fact that he had skin care treatments to stay younger looking.

"Dad, if you have something to say, just say it," Logan said.

"Confession is good for the soul," August said.

"Is it? Then why did you wait so long to tell us you'd had an affair while Mom was pregnant with me?" Logan asked. The rise of anger inside him was almost unstoppable. He turned away from his father to stop himself from blurting out all the other things he wanted to say. He was pissed. They all were. Their father had always been a strong and domineering force in their family but now… Logan looked at him and saw a man who wasn't who Logan had always believed he was.

"That's none of your business. It was between Mom and me. I'm asking you about a business deal. Did you buy up the patent?"

"Yes."

"Damn it, Logan. He's family now."

"He wasn't when I did it. And he's an ass. Just because he's suddenly my half brother doesn't change all the times he's dicked us over in business. I'm not going to just smile and shake hands. Sorry if the timing of my purchase isn't ideal for whatever you and Carlton have planned."

"Kid, it's not ideal because your cousin is marrying him on Saturday. She's family. This is going to hurt her."

He knew that. He'd wrestled about that very fact for longer than anyone would believe, even his father. But his need to beat Nick had outweighed Adler's possible hurt feelings. "I don't think Adler cares about business."

"Me either, but she does care about our rivalry with his family."

Logan shook his head and almost walked away. "Would you have made a different decision? If the opportunity had come to you instead of me, would you have passed?"

"No," August said. "I wouldn't have. But I always thought you had some of your mom's kinder side."

"I do. I'm definitely more charming than you are," Logan pointed out.

"Yes, but you're just as dangerous as I am," August said. "I think we need to let Nick know before it comes out on Monday."

"He'll be on his honeymoon," Logan said. "It can wait until he gets back. I mean he sort of has enough to deal with at this moment."

August looked at him and Logan stared right back. No matter what his dad wanted to do with this situation and the new son he'd found, Logan couldn't change a lifetime of animosity overnight. He'd been willing—hell, not willing, but had thought he'd try for Adler's sake—but if he were being honest, he hated that Nick was related to them.

He hated that the man who'd been his rival in business for more than a decade was his half brother. He kept using *half* in his mind to make the relationship seem more distant, but it didn't change the fact.

Nick Williams was now a blood relative.

"It's your decision," August said. "But from a man who's just had a secret explode when he wasn't ready for it, I can tell you, it's better to confront things on your terms instead of trying to manage the fallout."

His dad turned to head back into the house and Logan was going to just let him leave. But Logan reached out and touched his shoulder as he walked past.

"I'm sorry, Dad. I don't know what it is about me, but I just can't stand to lose. And if I see a chance to win, I have to take it."

His father nodded. "It's the Bisset in you. You get that from me."

"The golf scramble was really successful," Quinn said as she met up with Adler and Iris in the afternoon. Adler looked less stressed than she had been earlier. It was as if the bride-to-be had entered some sort of numb zone. The only reason Quinn thought that was from her years of filming destination weddings. Some brides just got tighter and tighter the closer they got to the ceremony and then others, like Adler, chilled out and nothing fazed them.

While Quinn normally preferred the chilled-out bride over a bridezilla, she wasn't sure this was healthy for her friend. "Did anything else happen?"

"When?" Adler asked as one of Iris's glam squad hovered around her doing her hair for the rehearsal dinner.

"At the family meeting?" Quinn asked.

"No. They just finalized the press release. Which is so bizarre. Nick's mom wasn't at the meeting. Nick said she's freaking out. I don't know her that well, so I'm not sure if I should reach out to her or just ignore the entire thing," Adler said. "Olivia's been cool, but she always has been. Carlton wanted everyone to pose for a picture, but Tad Williams refused. I thought it was going to get dicey, but then everyone just sort of moved on."

"I'm sorry you are dealing with this," Iris said.

"It's not your fault. Dad sort of said that it was ironic that I thought I was marrying someone so solid and stable and then this happened. I think he was trying to help," Adler said.

"I'm sure he was. He mentioned to me that he could do something outrageous if I thought it would help you," Quinn said.

"Oh, God, no. I'm not sure I'm ready for that," Adler said.

"I know. I told your dad you were handling it fine and that you liked him happy and...well, father-like," Quinn said.

"I do. I need something to be consistent and steady in all this," Alder said. "I know I shouldn't make this all about me—"

"You're the bride, you're totally allowed to," Iris said.

"Agree," Quinn added. "It is all about you."

"Nick is freaking out. He keeps trying to be all, *I'm cool with it*. But he really hates Uncle Auggie. He was willing to be cordial for this weekend but learning that he's his real dad has him thrown."

Quinn's phone started vibrating like crazy where she'd set it on the table. "I bet."

She wanted to be a good friend and just stay focused on Adler. Like, was that a hard thing to do? Her dad always said it wasn't like she was a brain surgeon; she could have a conversation without looking at her phone. But...

"Just answer your phone," Adler said. "I hope it's not anything urgent."

She smiled at her friend. "I'm sure it's not. I want to be here for you."

"Honestly, Quinn, you being the producer of the wedding show is huge for me. I think I would have bolted last night if it had been anyone else," Adler said. "Go ahead. I'm going to try to text Dad and make sure he knows I'm okay."

Iris was deep in discussion with one of her glam squad, so Quinn picked up the phone and turned her back on Adler.

She glanced at the first text, which was a link to a news story push from one of the wires. Skimming it, she saw it was the news that Nick was August Bisset's biological son. "It's just that press release Carlton sent."

"Good," Adler said. "Any reaction?"

She scanned the newsfeed and realized that it was pretty tame. "No, but it has just gone out. I was waiting to alert my boss. Do you mind if I go and call in? I want to let them know we are on top of the situation."

"'Situation,'" Adler said. "That's what my wedding has become."

Quinn turned around and walked over to her friend, pocketing her phone as she went. "No. It hasn't. Not for you and not for Nick. To the outside world, it might be, but who cares about that. Everyone who matters to you will know—"

"I know that," Adler interrupted. "Dad says a version of that all the time, but the truth is I hate it. I want people to not notice me, not talk about me. But from the moment I was born, everyone has."

Quinn hugged Adler. She didn't know what to say to help her friend. Words weren't going to fix that bit of brokenness deep inside Adler. Words couldn't change how much she hated to see her photo or her name in the press. Words couldn't help, but a hug could. Friendship could.

"I know I'm so blessed and so lucky and I have Nick. He's my rock, but... I just wanted a quiet, simple wedding. I mean I know I agreed to have it televised, but that's because I thought I could control the narrative that way," she said. "I'm not whining... I mean I am a bit. I'm feeling sorry for myself, I guess."

"You're allowed to. Honestly, you're way better than a lot of the brides we film and you've had a lot more thrown at you."

"Thanks for saying that. I'm sorry I sort of lost it a second ago. Go call your boss. I don't want you to get into hot water because of this," Adler said.

"You're welcome. You can lose it as many times as you want. It's all about you, Ad, I mean that. I won't get into hot water. I just like to keep on top of my boss, so she thinks I'm efficient."

"Then go. Do that. I'll be fine. Iris made me glam, I'm going to sit here and enjoy that," she said.

Quinn took her friend at her word and stood. She noticed that Iris looked over at her when she did so, and Quinn nodded at Adler. Iris walked over to sit with the bride-to-be as Quinn walked out to do her job. She was a friend first, but she was also there to work.

Something she kept forgetting, between Adler and Logan.

Cora Williams hadn't shown up at the meeting at her mother's house and Juliette couldn't decide if that was a good or bad thing. The two of them weren't friends and had nothing in common. Except for that one secret. The one that was getting closer to being revealed the more time they spent together. Now it seemed foolish that she'd never made an effort to meet Adler's soon-to-be mother-in-law.

What would she have done if she had? Somehow tried to convince her niece to break off her engagement? God knew she'd never been a great sister, and Mari would argue that she hadn't always been a good mother, but Juliette had tried. She'd done her best.

But she had a feeling that wasn't enough.

She took a sip of the gin and tonic that Michael had made for her and then sighed. The press release was done, so there was nothing else to worry about, right? Juliette knew differently but for now she was going to have to put on her hostess smile and act like everything was good.

The announcement was just one more little chink in the image of their "perfect marriage" she'd fought so hard to project since Mari's birth. It was like it was okay for her to see the ugly cracks from the inside but she had hated when one of August's affairs was made public. She could only fake smile for so long before she crumbled.

And this time...well, this time was worse. Everyone—especially Auggie—was being so sweet to her. They were treating her as the injured party almost the same way they were acting toward Nick. But she knew that if the truth really came out, no one was going to look at her with sympathy.

Maybe she was borrowing trouble.

"What are you doing out here all alone?"

She turned to see Vivian standing there watching her. Her mom was the strongest woman Juliette knew. She'd buried a husband, a child, and withstood financial ups and downs. Yet she still managed to seem untouchable. Juliette envied her mother that.

"Thinking."

"And drinking?"

"Yes, Mom."

"Should I join you?" she asked, moving closer to her. Her mother always smelled faintly of Chanel No. 5. Her hair was now more gray than blond, but her eyes were forthright and she held herself with the strength of a woman who could handle anything.

"If you want to."

She rang a little bell on a table near the door of the sitting room and a moment later Michael appeared with a martini. He refreshed Juliette's gin and tonic and then left.

"Remember when you came home and told me you were engaged to Auggie?"

Juliette sighed. She'd been so in love with him. He'd been tall, dark and handsome. A forceful man with an easy smile and the kind of charm that made everyone like him. He was top of their class at college and they'd started out as friends and then fallen in love.

"Yes. You weren't sure about him."

"I wasn't. I could tell he was a little too smooth," Vivian said. "But you knew he was the one. I tried to warn you, but you got your back up—rightly so—and I let it be. I've held my tongue when he had affairs and even when they went public."

"I know, Mom," she said. "Is that about to change?"

"I'm not sure. I don't know what I can say to you that you don't already know. Auggie has always had a wandering eye and I guess you should be thankful that it's taken this long for a child of his to show up—"

"Mom!"

Oh, God, were there more? She should have put an end to the philandering a long time ago or, at the very least, left. Except she loved him. It didn't matter that this hurt, or that he'd embarrassed her by cheating. What mattered was that he'd apologized. That they'd shared a lifetime together and she wasn't ready to walk away from that. But would he feel the same?

"Well, it's true," Vivian said. "But I was going to say I think there is more to this than an affair. You have weathered those before. And given that Auggie was surprised about the boy, you normally would have been…more forgiving toward him. It makes me think… Is there something more you want to tell me?"

No.

Hell, no.

Juliette had promised to take the secret to her grave and she knew that once it was out, it would spread. She took a long sip of her drink. She shook her head, but a part of her wanted to tell her mom. To let go of the secret that had been a dark blot on her soul for too long now.

She wouldn't. But she wanted to.

"I won't push," Vivian said. "Remember when Musette came back from rehab the first time?"

She nodded. Where was her mother going with this? She had never been able to understand her sister's addiction or how she couldn't break it.

"I knew she was using again," her mom said. "I knew she was going to have to be the one to decide to stop, that it had to come from inside her, so I held my tongue. But watching her struggle and eventually fail was one of the hardest things I've ever done as a mother. Watching you try to deal with this is very similar. You look like you're about to implode and I don't know how to stop it."

"I—"

"Don't. Save the stories for the others you are telling them to. Just know I'll be here when it all falls apart."

She watched her mother walk away, wishing it were easier to tell her than it actually was.

CHAPTER NINE

THE DAY FELT like it had gone on forever. Logan had been on Nantucket for three days and it felt like a lifetime. His father's point about Adler wasn't lost on him and he felt like the worst kind of douchebag ever. He'd avoided mingling with the rest of the family after the announcement had been sent to the press and gone for a walk on the beach to clear his head. He'd thought about texting Quinn, but honestly, he knew that as much as he wanted to see her, it wasn't the right thing.

For her.

It would be selfish, and right now he was trying to be a better man. But could he be? He'd always thought he was a Bisset 2.0, not as harsh and uncaring as his father about the companies and people he gobbled up in his quest to grow the business. He wanted to believe he was better than his father. But he wasn't. He'd been deluding himself.

He could say all he wanted that he had inherited his mother's grace and charm, but at the end of the day, he never opted to use those qualities. He always went for the kill in true Bisset style.

He shoved his hands through his hair. He should have skipped the wedding. He would be happier in his office working on deals, and just physically not being here would have been much better.

"Logan, wait up!"

He turned to see his oldest brother, Dare, calling him. Dare had an easy smile and though he was almost forty, seemed much younger. He had dark hair and their father's gray eyes. He was taller than their dad by an inch and always had an air of authority about him. He was the most levelheaded of all the siblings. As cantankerous as Logan's relationship with Leo and Zac was, his relationship with Dare was the opposite.

"Hey, sorry about leaving like that. I just…well, I've had enough of this," Logan admitted.

"Me too. I am happy for Adler, but this wedding has turned into the kind of situation I think we all would avoid if we could."

"Definitely. Also, I screwed up," Logan blurted.

"What? How?" Dare asked, falling into step beside him.

"I ruined one of Nick's business deals…it's a big one," Logan said. "Before you ask, I did it after I knew he and Adler were getting married. But news about it is about to break next week."

Dare put his hand on Logan's shoulder and squeezed. Unlike his father, who came in hot with consternation, Dare just got it. Got him. "I think that's not going to be a big deal. I mean now that Nick is our brother, surely business will change."

Logan shook his head. "It will matter to Nick. And I highly doubt that a man who was raised as Tad Williams's son is going to suddenly want to merge with Bisset Industries, if that's what you were thinking."

"I was. Actually, I have reached out to Nick and his family to see if I can open some kind of negotiation between our families," Dare said. "I've sat on some highly volatile committees in the senate, so I figured I was probably the only one who might be able to broker something between us."

"I doubt that anything you encountered in Washington will be as bad as this. I mean Dad and Tad hate each other. It's not just me who wants to beat the other guy. Dad has been trying to ruin Tad since he opened his business," Logan said.

"I wonder why," Dare said. "I could see if he'd realized that

Tad's wife was his former lover, but I'm pretty sure Dad didn't know. So it has to be something else. Has he ever mentioned it to you?"

"No. I brought it up one time and he told me it was none of my business, so I dropped it," Logan said. He'd never seen his father react that way until the moment he'd seen Cora Williams in the room two days ago.

"I guess we'll have to wait and see what happens," Dare said. "Last night was totally crazy. Zac was funny. I'm glad he's back. I mean I know he's made a mess of things with Iris, but to be honest, I don't believe for a second the only reason he's with her is because she offered to invest in his yacht team."

"Me neither. That boy is in love. He'll figure it out. I've never seen him like this with a woman," Logan said. "Do you think it's just wedding vibes?"

"What do you mean?"

"That he thinks he's in love? That it's real?" Logan asked.

"I don't know," Dare said. "Before Mari fell in love with Inigo, I would have said that we Bissets weren't really meant for romantic relationships. We're better at friendships and just socializing. Making connections for business or politics. But now Zac…it seems genuine to me."

"Me too," Logan said, shaking his head. Quinn had been right when she'd said he liked to compete. And he knew from watching Zac this morning that love didn't leave room for winners. He doubted he'd ever be comfortable with that.

His phone vibrated in his pocket and Dare's beeped. "Family text."

"Another meeting," Logan said. "Honestly, I am done with these. I miss the days when the biggest scandal was Mari partying too hard and wearing skimpy clothing."

"I know she doesn't. She's loving that, after all the meetings to deal with the Mari problem, it's now about the Auggie problem. I never would have thought that Dad would cause this kind of scandal," Dare said. "After all the shit he gave us growing up, there is a part of me that is relishing it."

"Yeah. I'm torn. Part of me is glad he's human and can screw up like the rest of us, but I've always been the most like him, D. What if that's my future?"

Dare stopped him. "The fact that you're worrying about it tells me it won't be."

"I hope you're right."

Iris and Adler had left and Quinn had a few minutes to herself. She thought about texting Logan but in the end decided not to. Today at the golf club she'd almost dropped her guard. Almost let him back into her life. When he'd walked away, she'd been reminded that almost was all she could safely allow.

Instead she went back to her rental house and downloaded the footage she'd shot for the personal video for Adler and Nick. She poured herself a Fiji water and just stared at the video screen. She'd been filming weddings for the last four years and as she'd gotten closer to thirty, she'd started thinking about marriage. Maybe it was time to look for a guy and settle down.

Iris had been...well, making mistakes as she tried to find a man to be her life partner. Quinn didn't need a man to move her career forward. Not that Iris really did, either, but Quinn had noticed that her friend's peers had all moved on to marriage or motherhood. Iris had said she was too old to be single-girl-in-the-city and Quinn felt that sometimes. Especially when her younger crew members were going out and she just wanted to go home, change into her comfy clothes and binge watch something on Netflix...honestly, she usually chose *Gilmore Girls* or *the latest rom com*.

Her mom warned her that she was getting too settled in her eccentricities. Somehow her mother thought if she didn't find someone who got her weird side then she was going to be alone forever. That, to be honest, didn't sound all that bad, given how

Juliette Bisset was dealing with the fallout of her husband's affair thirty-five years ago.

But at the same time, it would be nice to have someone to curl up with on cold nights and to talk about the latest gossip, and to feel just comfortable that they had each other. She shook her head.

Weddings did this. She knew it. She'd seen so many couples hook up at the destination weddings she'd filmed. Couples— like herself and Logan—who made no sense back home. Back in real life.

She needed to shake herself out of this mindset.

She knew part of the blame belonged squarely on Logan's broad shoulders. If he had gotten a little chubbier since college, if he'd somehow lost his charm or maybe become some kind of dull businessman, she could have resisted him.

Yeah, that was what she needed, she thought. He was just still…too sexy. Too attractive, and not just physically. And part of it was the challenge.

Her phone buzzed and she grabbed it, glancing down to see it was another news push from the wire. She scanned it and almost dropped her phone.

There was more to the story…

A nurse from a rural hospital had released a statement saying that Nick wasn't the only child born that day to Cora Williams, aka Bonnie Smith. Nick had a twin and the twin had been swapped just after birth with Juliette Bisset's stillborn baby boy.

Holy hell.

Was the nurse talking about Logan? She had to be. He and Nick were the same age. They didn't look alike but they were similar in height. And not all twins were identical. But still…

This couldn't be right. Why would the nurse wait so long to come forward?

Either way, this news was going to shatter Logan's world. He had always prided himself on being the best mix of his mom and dad. If Juliette wasn't his biological mom— Quinn wondered if she'd seen this story before the family. She started to text Logan but he needed to hear this in person so she raced over to his gran's house. There were a lot of cars in the driveway, which was to be expected given that Adler was getting married on Saturday.

Now that she was there, Quinn didn't want to just go into the house and blurt the news out. She texted Logan to meet her outside.

He was quick to respond.

Can't. Family meeting. Talk later.

This is important, she frantically typed.

I can't leave now. We can talk about sleeping together later.

Ok. It's about a news thing involving you not us hooking up.

Shit. But I can't talk now. Thanks for trying to warn me.

She realized that the news must have been delivered to the family. Quinn wasn't sure what to do. As the wedding video producer, this didn't affect her job. Sure, Nick and Adler would be upset, but the wedding details still needed to be filmed and everything needed to go on.

She'd focus on work.

She wasn't Logan's girlfriend, she told herself as she walked back to her house. But she was his friend. That hadn't changed over the years. And with his family in shambles, whether this story was true or just someone trying to make a quick buck off the Bisset and Williams names, didn't matter. Logan's sense of self was his rock. It was how he defined himself. And she knew, with his competitive nature, this kind of revelation would deeply affect how he viewed himself.

Quinn got together with her team and made sure that everything was ready for the wedding rehearsal and then the dinner afterward. Given all of the recent bombshells dropping about Nick and the Bisset family, she wanted to make sure her shoot went smoothly. That at least a small part of the weekend would go as planned.

She texted Iris to see if she'd talked to Adler, and Iris called her back.

"Hey, is something up?" Iris asked. "I'm with Adler. She and her dad are talking about the walk down the aisle. She wants to make sure that he plays the right song. Apparently, he wrote something new last night. Anyway, what's up?"

She debated telling Iris about the news story she'd read, but right now it was all unconfirmed and, for the first time since Quinn had gotten to Nantucket, Adler was doing just bride stuff. "Nothing. I was just checking on you both. Can I bring a cameraman over?"

Iris conferred with Adler and got the okay.

Quinn would do her job. If anything came of the news report then she'd be with Adler, the friend she'd actually come to Nantucket to celebrate and support.

The entire family, including Logan's grandmother, were in the study as Carlton read them the wire story. Logan couldn't believe what he heard. He turned to his mom, as did everyone else, and her face was ashen. From what felt like a great distance, he heard Carlton say that he'd dispute the nurse's claim. But Logan knew that wouldn't be necessary.

The look on his mother's face told him the story was true.

"Jules?" his father said. "How is this possible? Nick and Logan don't look like each other. Is it true?"

She took a deep breath, wrapping her arms around her waist as she stood there in the corner next to the floor-to-ceiling bookcases lined with books that had been in his mother's family for generations. Though now Logan realized that wasn't his family. There was no part of him connected by blood to his mother's family, the Wallises. He was a Bisset, though. Maybe he should feel better about his cutthroat instincts because he might need them in this crisis.

But he didn't.

Logan hated every second of this and as much as he wanted to rage about this secret having been kept from him, he also needed all of the details. He wanted every bit of information so that it couldn't be used against him again.

"You know I was alone when I went into labor. Dare, you were here with Gran, and Auggie, you were away on a business trip. I met Bonnie— I mean… I guess she goes by Cora now. We were in the delivery room together. The hospital was very small and we were talking before the births. I was trying—"

"Skip to the part where you swap your dead baby for me," Logan said.

Everyone turned on him. He knew it had been a mean thing to say, but he wasn't interested in the long, drawn-out story with all the emotion. He was after facts. That was all he could handle at this moment.

"Don't be such a dick," Leo said.

"I'll be whatever I want, she's not my mom," Logan said. "Right? That's true, isn't it?"

August cursed and turned on him, but when their eyes met, Logan knew his father understood his anguish. His dad started toward him, but he just shook his head.

"Finish the story," Logan said, glancing back at his mom—at Juliette.

"My birth was quicker, and I was in the recovery room," Juliette said. "I was crying when Bonnie—I mean Cora—came back in. She was crying too. She had anticipated having one child but two was too many for her to handle. She'd gotten a partial scholarship to go back to school and thought she could manage with one child but with two she was going to have to skip college.

"I told her that my marriage would probably be over when

my husband learned about the stillborn baby. The pregnancy had brought us back together. But I knew without that baby, your father and I would struggle to stay together."

"That's not—"

"Don't say it's not the truth, Auggie. We both know that we were barely keeping ourselves together as a couple then. Bonnie said she was going to have to give up one of the babies or maybe it would be better if she gave them both up," Juliette said.

"So you offered to raise one as our son," August said.

"I did. I also gave her money to support herself and get some help for the son she kept," Juliette said. "We swapped the bracelets and Logan became my son. I nursed you, you became my baby at that moment. I never thought of you as anything other than my son."

"So how did the nurse know?" Logan asked.

"She knew my son was stillborn and had gone away to do the paperwork. Even though Bonnie and I told her that she was mistaken, she knew the truth. I offered her a bribe, which she was reluctant to take but then Bonnie—I mean Cora—said that no one would ever find out, there were only the three of us. This way the boys would both be raised by mothers who could afford them and who wanted them. The doctor had already signed the paperwork and it was simply down to us filling it in. Bonnie took it from her and signed it. I thought that was it."

"You should have brought this to me," August said. "I could have—"

"What? What would you have done?" his mom demanded, but Logan could tell that she was angry and sad.

He got that. He felt the same way. But this lie was bigger than her or his father. This lie had, in one moment, stolen everything from him. Leo and Dare were on either side of him. Zac and Mari sat quietly across the room. They were all watching him and he felt like he was going to explode.

Logan stormed from the room. He heard his brothers calling for him to come back, but he just kept on walking and left his gran's—not his gran's, not really. He just left and got into his car and drove as far away from the house as he could go. That wasn't far, considering how Nantucket wasn't a huge island. But he needed to get away. He pulled into the parking lot for the ferry.

He pounded his fists on the steering wheel, but the angry energy inside him wasn't abated. He screamed and wanted to kick something. He needed a fight. He needed to figure out who he was because he'd been living a lie for thirty-five years. Everything he believed about himself was false. And he wished there were a way he could unknow that. Wished he could go back to being the man he'd been this morning.

But he'd never put much stock in dreams and he knew he was a man of facts. He had the truth now and he was the only one who could decide what to do with it. He was still a Bisset, thanks to his father's cheating ways, so he did the one thing he always fell back on: work and doing deals.

CHAPTER TEN

QUINN PLAYED A HUNCH. When she was done filming Adler, she went to the ferry to wait and see if Logan would show up. After about fifteen minutes, she saw his black sports car with the vanity plate Bsset1 pull into the lot. He drove to a corner. She watched him pound his fists on the steering wheel. Her heart broke.

She hated to see him like this.

She had no idea how to help him, if she even could, but she also couldn't walk away. Couldn't let him leave like this. The man she'd started to know over the last day and a half was different from the boy she'd known in college. Logan had changed, matured into someone she liked.

She didn't want to see him do something rash. Make a decision out of anger that he'd regret.

Why did it matter to her? Quinn asked herself. She didn't bother answering.

It mattered because it was Logan and a part of her had always been vulnerable when it came to his happiness. She knew that she couldn't make him happy. She knew that as well as she knew he couldn't make her happy. But she had always tried.

Quinn walked over to the car. If he rejected her, told her to leave, then she would. But she had to try.

He stared at her for a second as she stepped up to the driver's-side window. She saw the tears in his eyes, and he didn't bother to wipe them away. He just hit the button to lower the window.

"You know?"

"I know," she said. "I'm sorry."

"Yeah, well, it is what it is," he said. His words weren't rageful or bombastic, as she'd expected after witnessing his outburst with the steering wheel, but they were subdued and almost numb.

"I got the news when I texted you. I didn't want to type that out. I thought you should hear it in person," she said.

"Yeah, thanks for that," he said.

"So, are you leaving?"

"I don't know. I just don't want to be around my family, and they are everywhere on Nantucket."

"Can I get in?" she asked.

"Why?" he asked. "I know you can't leave."

"I don't think you should either," she said. "And it's okay to tell me it's none of my business, but I think you need a friend and someone you can just be real with. You know I won't judge."

"I do know that," he admitted. "But you have to stay here. It's your job."

"I know. Stay with me. Don't do the wedding, don't see your family, if that's what you want. Stay with me like we just hooked up and you're on vacation. Take a few days to figure this out."

He gave a snort as he shook his head. "It's going to take a lot more than a few days to sort this out. But I think I would like to stay with you. Are you sure? I know you said one night only."

"I did. And I'm not sure what will happen between us. Come with me as a friend," she said.

He nodded. "Hop in."

She walked around the car and got in. He didn't bother to put it in gear but just rested his arms on the steering wheel and stared at the ferry port. If she'd just learned she wasn't who she thought she was, she'd be looking for a magic genie to make this all go away. But Logan had always been more practical. The kind of man who faced things head-on.

"I don't know what to do next," he said. "This isn't like a business hit where I can regroup and go after the person responsible…it's my mom…oh, God, Q, my mom isn't my mom," he said, putting his forehead on the steering wheel.

She put her hand on his shoulder and squeezed. "She's still your mom. She raised you and she loves you. She's always going to be your mom."

"I get what you're saying but how can I look at her the same way?" Logan asked. "Everything's changed."

"It has. And there's no going back. I don' t know how you'll move forward, but I know you will."

"How? How do you know?"

"Because you're not someone to run away from a problem," she said.

He clenched his jaw and then nodded. "You're right. But I can't begin to think of a solution."

"Give yourself the day," she said.

"Just one day?" he teased.

"As many as you need. But I know you, Logan Bisset. You aren't one to wallow for long," she said.

He wasn't. It was funny that the woman he hadn't seen in over ten years would still know him so well, but he realized that he'd been more honest in his relationship with Quinn back in college than he'd been with any other person in a relationship since.

He knew part of it was that he'd been hurt when things had ended, and he'd decided never to allow someone to get close enough to make him feel like that again. And until today, when he'd learned of his mom's deceit, he hadn't. He'd protected himself well from feeling this kind of emotional pain.

Maybe Quinn was the only one to help him make sense of this and figure out how he was going to handle being a twin to a man he hated.

He hadn't forgotten about that. He'd been dwelling on the

betrayal he felt with his mom, but Nick was his twin. How was that even possible? Nick was everything he hated.

"Don't think about anything else," Quinn said. "I can see it building in you."

"I don't think I can shut it off," he said. "Nick can't be my twin. I hate that man."

"He is," she said.

"How can you be so sure?"

"If he wasn't, you wouldn't be upset," she pointed out. "You don't know him outside of the boardroom. I think there is a lot more to him than you realize."

"Fuck. I don't want to like him," Logan said.

"You don't have to," Quinn said.

And that was enough. For this moment, he was okay with that.

Logan took a shower when he got to Quinn's house. He had his gym bag in the trunk of his car so he changed into a pair of basketball shorts and a T-shirt that he'd had in there. Quinn was on a conference call when he came out of the bathroom, so he just put on his headphones and went to sit on one of the loungers at the back of her house. He put on his sunglasses and tried to let the music distract him, but he couldn't control his thoughts.

They kept returning to that moment when he'd learned that his mom wasn't his mom. That he was a twin who had been given up by his biological mother moments after he was born. The one she didn't want. But Juliette had wanted him. She'd loved him. Raised him with so much love that he knew he'd be able to forgive her for keeping her secret. But it would be down the road.

For as long as he could remember, everyone had made him feel loved. His parents, his siblings, his friends. His life had been full of people who cared about him, and he couldn't help but wonder about Cora Williams, who had looked down at two babies and chose to get rid of him.

He'd never ask her. Hell, if he had his way, he'd never speak to her again. But that thought was there in the back of his mind.

He hadn't realized his fists were clenched until Quinn sat next to him and lifted one of them, slowly prizing his fingers apart. She pulled his headphones out of his ears with her other hand.

"What are you thinking about?"

"I'm trying not to think of anything but it's hard. I mean, why did Cora pick me to give away? Isn't that stupid of me?" he asked. "I mean...until a few hours ago I didn't even know she was my mom."

"It's not stupid," Quinn said. "It's natural to wonder that. Do you want to meet with her and talk to her?"

"No," he said. "She's nothing to me. If she hadn't given me to my—to Juliette—she would have put me up for adoption. Who knows who I'd be..."

"I do," Quinn said.

"You do?"

"Yes. You didn't just turn into a super-competitive, driven man by mistake. You were born that way, Logan. Even Dare has said you were determined to be your father's successor from a very young age."

"That's true. I guess there's no arguing I'm a Bisset through and through."

"There isn't. Just think how much harder this news would have been—"

He stopped her by putting his fingers over her lips. "Don't. I can't even bear to think of that. I hate that these thoughts are circling around in my mind. Like I don't know who I am anymore. When that's the one thing I've never questioned."

"I wish I could show you that you're still the same man," Quinn said.

"You can't. I'm always going to know there is a part of me that's a lie. You know I hate that the world knows it too," Logan said.

"I do. But don't think of it that way," she said.

"How else should I view it?" he asked. "The board will have questions."

"They might, but they know you're not going to suddenly be less effective…unless you decide that you no longer want to be," Quinn said. "This might not be what you want to hear, but perhaps you should look at this as a clean slate. As an opportunity to change the things you didn't like about yourself."

"Are you trying to tell me something?"

"Like what?"

"Is there something about me that's unlikable?" He wondered what she'd say. He knew he was too driven, too competitive, too determined to prove himself. This news wasn't suddenly going to make him less so. In fact, now he had more of a determination to make sure that no one questioned who he was.

"You know what I mean," she said. "You had mentioned cutting Nick out of a deal, maybe you will take a different approach in the future."

He doubted there would ever be a time when he and Nick weren't adversaries. Nick had been pretty clear that he considered Tad Williams his father, and rightly so. Tad had raised him. The same way Juliette had raised Logan.

Neither of their parents had been bad to them. Well, he couldn't speak for Nick, but from what he'd heard, Tad was an okay dad. "This is so complicated."

"It is," she said, shifting around to sit on his lap. He pulled her close, wrapping his arms around her.

"Do you have to leave soon?"

"I do. I'm taping Adler and Nick and then the wedding rehearsal," she said. "Then I have the rehearsal dinner… I think Zac is planning something special to make things up to Iris. Tomorrow I'll be busy all day but, starting Sunday, it's just you and me."

He wondered why he'd stayed on the island. He should have left; it would have made more sense. Quinn had work to do and couldn't just sit around with him. But he also knew he wouldn't have wanted that.

"Okay. I'll go with you to the rehearsal...will you be a guest or working the entire time?"

"I'll be working for a bit but then I'll be a guest," she said.

"I don't know how I'm going to face everyone."

"Like you always do," she reminded him. "You're Logan Bisset and everyone knows you rule the world. No one is going to pity you or feel sorry for you."

No one except himself. He felt sorry for himself that Juliette wasn't his biological mom. That he wasn't the man he'd always believed himself to be. But other people's pity wasn't something he felt comfortable with and neither was hiding out.

August was locked in the study with Carlton, and Juliette's mom hadn't left her side since Logan had left the house. Now they were in the kitchen, drinking a cup of tea, and Juliette's kids were all sitting at the table with her. No one had said a word since Michael had served them and left them alone.

Juliette knew she needed to do something to help her kids get through this but she had no idea what to say. She'd always been able to smooth over the mistakes that Auggie made. To figure out a way to guide her kids and keep them focused on moving forward. But this...she had had no idea.

"Has anyone heard from Logan?" she asked. It was on her mind. She hated that one of her sons was out there, alone. From that moment in the hospital when she'd held him he'd always been her son. She might have known the truth in her mind but her heart had always claimed Logan as her son. It didn't matter that he was a grown man and that he was upset with her. She was worried. She knew how he could be; he needed someone to talk to, but who would he discuss this with?

"I haven't," Leo said.

"He texted me to say he's with Quinn," Dare said. "Sorry

I didn't mention it. I wasn't sure if he wanted anyone else to know."

"That's okay. I'm glad he's with her. Are they getting back together?" she asked.

"Mom. Don't act like everything is normal," Mari said. "We need to talk about this. I'm not going to pretend you haven't been keeping this a secret from us."

"I know things aren't normal, Marielle. I'm just trying to keep from breaking into a million pieces. I'm trying to keep the rest of us together," she said.

"Well, it's not working," Leo said. "I can't believe you did that. I mean I'm glad Logan was raised with us, but you should have—"

"Should have what?" Mari asked. "Told Dad? Told us? That would have gone really great."

Mari's sarcasm was strongest when she was hurting, and Juliette realized that she'd done a lot of damage to the heart of their family. She hated to see the kids fighting and knew she was to blame.

"I'm sorry."

Dare got up and came to sit next to her, putting his arm around her shoulder and hugging her close. She hugged him back and felt tears burning her eyes as she did so. Her first-born had always been a rock for her. She remembered the hot mess she'd been as a young mother, so unsure of herself. She'd screwed up a lot with Dare, but he'd turned out okay.

She had thought she'd done okay with all of the kids but this thing with Logan had proven otherwise. "No one was ever supposed to know."

"Secrets have a way of coming out," Vivian said. "No matter how well you think they are covered."

"Thanks, Mom. That helps."

Vivian shrugged and took a sip of her tea. "Don't snap at me. This was your secret, but as I see it, I don't think you could have done anything differently."

Juliette nodded.

She didn't either, but at the same time she regretted that she'd never said anything. Still, she'd justified putting it off. She'd been busy raising five kids, running her charities and keeping her marriage together. There had been a few moments when she'd let a thought creep in about that single mother who'd given her Logan, but it had always been a moment of gratitude that she had her wonderful son. Each of her kids was so different. So unique. And she loved them all. She didn't want to lose Logan now.

"I agree," Zac said. "Sometimes the secret gets bigger on its own. The circumstances change and you are stuck keeping quiet."

She looked over at her middle child. The one who was in a mess of his own making at the moment. "I never thought of Logan as anything other than my child."

Her other kids just nodded. They didn't need to hear this. Logan did. But he wasn't responding to her calls or her texts. She knew it would take time, but she didn't want to wait. She needed to make this okay. She needed her son back in her home, close to her, so she'd know he forgave her.

What if he never did?

"Does Nick know?" Leo asked. "I mean that he and Logan are twins?"

"I haven't been in touch with Adler," Juliette admitted.

"I talked to her a few minutes ago," Vivian said. "She sounded fragile. I offered for her to come over here or for me to go and see her but she said she needed to be alone."

"I'm so sorry. We should all be getting ready for the rehearsal. I feel like we've ruined her wedding."

"You have," Vivian said. "You and August have always played your little power games without thinking of the cost. We've barely had time to process the fact that August is Nick's father before your news comes out about Logan. It's like tit for tat."

"Mom," she said.

"It's true. It took you until last year to finally have a decent relationship with Mari because your anger at August got in the way."

"I never meant for it to end up like this," Juliette said. "Mari, you know I love you very much."

"I do," Mari said. "And Dad can drive us all up the wall at times. I'm not sure what you meant, Gran, but I'm pretty sure Mom didn't know about Nick and hadn't been plotting to one-up Dad with her secret about Logan. I think Mom just wanted another son to love. Maybe you should cut her a break."

Juliette was surprised that Mari had come to her defense. She wasn't sure she deserved it but Mari definitely understood her better than Vivian did. "Thank you, Mari. I'm so lucky to have you as my daughter."

"I know," Mari said with a wink. "This isn't a great situation to be in or a great time to have this come out, but it has and I think we should remember that all Mom ever did was love us and raise us the best she could."

"I agree," Dare said. "We'll make sure we are there for Logan and he'll find his way back to us."

She hoped her kids were right. But having them in her corner, she felt luckier than she probably had a right to feel.

CHAPTER ELEVEN

LOGAN COULD FEEL himself going down the moody, self-loathing, angry route as the afternoon wore on. Quinn left to do her job and he jogged to the grocery store, bought two bottles of Jack and dodged several paparazzi who weren't fooled by his sunglasses and Bisset Industries' baseball cap.

Go figure.

He gave them the finger as he left the grocery store and then gave them the slip at the hotel. Walking through the lobby of the hotel where a lot of his extended family and all of the wedding guests were staying wasn't his brightest decision, but it was safe to say that he wasn't firing on all cylinders at this point.

Reeling from his parents' revelations and wanting nothing to do with reality wasn't like him. He went up to his hotel room, packed a suitcase and then realized he was going to have to walk back to Quinn's.

Why was he going back to her? He had originally gone to her place to spend time with her but she had to work. And, really, did he want Quinn to witness this? Hell, he was living through it and he didn't want to see it. He texted her that he'd gone back to his hotel in case she came home and worried.

Then he opened the bottle of Jack and poured himself a couple of fingers of whiskey. He sat on the couch in the junior suite he'd rented for the weekend.

He couldn't do it. Couldn't deal with the fact that the woman who'd raised him wasn't his mother. He knew the arguments— that she'd loved him, that she'd raised him—but at the same time she'd betrayed him.

It wasn't that he wouldn't have been able to deal with being adopted— Well, maybe he wouldn't have, but it would be different if he'd grown up believing that about himself.

But he hadn't.

At least Nick, that lucky bastard, had always known Tad wasn't his father.

There was a knock on the door and Logan ignored it. He wasn't really in the mood to do anything but drink until he was numb.

The knock came again. "I know you're in there. Open up."

It was Quinn.

Images of the two of them from the other night on the beach danced through his mind. She'd always been too...he wouldn't say good for him, but just too nice for him. She cared about other people, something he'd always struggled with. Hell, now that he knew his biological mother had given him up minutes after his birth, he might have his explanation. He hadn't inherited her kindness gene because they weren't related by blood.

"Logan."

"Go away. I'm wallowing."

"No," she said. "People are coming off the elevator. Let me in."

Her words were low, terse, and he could sense she was getting angry at him. Angry Quinn he could handle. A fight might be good. He didn't want to deal with Caring Quinn. The woman who looked at him and saw past the façade of confidence and arrogance to the man beneath.

He opened the door and glanced down the hall to the area by the elevator, which was empty.

"Where'd they go?"

"Must have decided not to get off on this floor," she said, pushing past him. She had on a silk bomber-style jacket and a tank top with a pair of skintight black jeans. She had headphones around her neck and her smartphone in her hand.

"Are you supposed to be working?"

"I am working. We're taking a ten-minute break before I do an interview with Adler and Nick," she said. "I was worried about you. Are you drinking?"

"I am."

"Stop," she said. "That's going to make you feel worse."

She walked into the suite, opened the minibar, took out a bottle of Diet Coke and then turned to face him. He'd followed her, plopped back down on the couch and poured himself another glass of whiskey. "Tomorrow."

"Tonight. You shouldn't be drinking alone. Zac's got his own issues to deal with but surely you can call Dare and Leo."

"No, I can't, Ace. I don't want them to know that I'm..." He stopped. Any word that he could use to describe what he was feeling right now, he didn't want to say and he definitely didn't want either of his brothers to see him that way.

"Logan."

"Quinn."

He knew she was trying to help, and in a way she was. She was distracting him from the dark spiral his mind was all too willing to take him down. Never in his entire life had he been unsure of himself like this. There were times when he had used bravado to convince himself that he was okay. But he'd always been confident. Very certain about his place in the world.

And now he wasn't.

"Please don't do this. I have to go back and finish filming and I don't want to leave you this way."

"I'll be fine. I'm an adult, remember?"

She smiled. "I do. I seem to recall you saying if you have to tell someone that fact then maybe you're not as mature as you think you are."

"A very wise man," he said, recalling the conversation they'd had back in college. "Or just a guy trying to sound clever so he could score."

"You failed," she reminded him.

"That was just my opening salvo," he said. "I got there in the end."

"You did," she said. Her phone started vibrating in her hand and she glanced at the screen. Her brow furrowed and she tapped out a message before looking back at him.

The look on her face made him put down the whiskey. She was worried, and not just a little bit. She had that nervous look that he'd often seen on other's faces when he walked into a boardroom during a corporate takeover.

He stood and faked a smile the way his mom—Juliette—had taught him. "I'm fine. Go work."

He walked her to the door of his suite, kissed her and then opened the door and nudged her on her way. He'd be fine because he never wanted anyone to look at him that way again.

Quinn's team was all back by the time she walked into one of the small breakout rooms where they would be filming the interview with Adler and Nick. When they were done, she and her team were going to review the footage. They'd set up a small editing suite in a hotel room on the same floor for that purpose. Since the wedding would be broadcast live, all of the stuff they'd shot so far was going to be used as an intro and B-roll stuff.

"I like what we have. For now it almost seems as if the scandal isn't an issue, which I think you want us to keep that way, right?" Joe the editor said. "The network said to keep it classy. I think they are worried that we'll seem too tabloid-y."

"I got the same sort of warning from my boss," Quinn replied. "Let's send them the interview once we're done filming it and I've approved the cut—so they can see what we're doing.

That it's tasteful and all that. Our viewers are mostly tuning in to get ideas for the own weddings."

"Sounds good. I'll start working on the golf footage from this morning and the clambake from last night. You got some good stuff with the different guests. Also can we use Toby Osborn's song and the footage of Nick and…the other dude singing?"

"I have Abby working on that. She's talking to licensing—we might have to just use license-free music. We should know before tomorrow. Just go ahead and edit it as if we can use the songs for now."

"I will."

Joe left and Quinn went over to the love seat and checked the lighting with her camera guy before Nick came in. His hair was tousled, as if he'd been running his hands through it, and that wasn't something he normally did. "You okay?"

"Yeah. I guess you heard that Logan is my twin," he said without preamble. "I don't want to discuss that right now. I think we can just say that I found out who my biological dad was and it hasn't changed the way I feel about Adler. Will that be okay?"

"Yes. Honestly, Nick, whatever you want to say will be fine. And we can cut it out if you don't like it. I just think that it might be nice for you two to be able to control the narrative here."

"Me too," he said. "It would be so nice to control something at this point. I swear, if one more secret about my birth comes to light, I'm not going to be able to handle it."

"Yes, you will," Adler said as she came into the room. She was dressed in a jumpsuit that was slim-fitting on top and then flared out into palazzo trousers. She had her hair pulled back in a low chignon with tendrils framing her heart-shaped face. She looked beautiful and composed, but her eyes betrayed her and her lips trembled a little when she tried to smile.

Nick nodded and then just pulled her into his arms. Quinn turned away to give them privacy but also looked over at her camera man to make sure he was filming. This was the kind of moment their viewers loved. Those little behind-the-scenes intimacies between the bride and groom.

Nick cleared his throat and Quinn turned back around, smiling. "I think we're ready."

They both had their microphones on and took their seats. Quinn would be off camera asking questions to lead the interview and direct them so they stayed on topic.

"No wedding goes to plan, and yours has had a few bumps. Do you want to discuss that?"

Adler smiled and this time she exuded confidence as she held on to Nick's hand. "Well, Nick always knew that Tad Williams wasn't his biological father, but we just found out that he's the son of business tycoon August Bisset. My aunt is married to August, so it was a bit of shock all around."

"It was surprising, but it changes nothing between me and my parents. I'm still the man I always was and I think you still like me, right?" Nick looked down at Adler and smiled. It was a sweet moment.

"Yeah, I do," she said.

"Can't wait until you say that tomorrow," Nick said.

"Me neither," Adler responded.

"Tell us some of the ways that you're incorporating family into your ceremony," Quinn said, happy that they had at least addressed the scandal and then moved past it.

"Adler's dad wrote a song for us that he'll be performing at dinner after the ceremony and, actually, last night I got to duet with him at the bonfire," Nick said.

"Yes. Dad's music will be a big part of the ceremony and my mom wrote a song about me before she died that my dad's girlfriend is going to perform at the ceremony," Adler added.

Adler was really touched that Toby's girlfriend, Sonia, had offered to perform it. It was going to be a nice way to honor the memory of Adler's mom as part of the ceremony.

Quinn asked them a few more questions and as they talked she couldn't help but look for signs that Logan and Nick were twins. But it was hard to see it on the surface. Obviously they both looked very different. Logan was blond and a few inches shorter than Nick. But they both had that square jaw, like August, and they both were men who went after what they wanted.

It was easy for Quinn to see how much Nick wanted Adler, how much he loved her. And her mind drifted to Logan. Did he see her that way?

Adler thought Nick had handled himself really well during the interview. But that had just been the two of them. Now that she was at the rehearsal with all of the people responsible for the scandals that kept dropping she was having a moment where she wanted to throw a massive bridezilla fit or just sit in a corner and cry. She was so ready for this weekend to be over—something she'd never thought she'd feel about her wedding.

Her aunt Jules had tried to call her, but Adler had shut her down. She couldn't deal with any of the Bisset family right now. Mari had left a voicemail saying she was there if she needed to talk, but Adler didn't think raging at her cousin about how her parents were the worst people on the planet was going to really help.

Iris wasn't too happy about having the fact that she'd paid Zac to be her date revealed to the world, but her friend had found her peace with it. Adler wished she could likewise find peace with the revelations about Nick. But she knew part of her was looking at Nick differently now.

He was her touchstone. Her safety net. The love of her life. But now he was different. He might have said in the interview that nothing had changed, but it had. He wasn't speaking to his mom, which only added to the tension of the rehearsal. And for her part, Adler was ignoring Aunt Jules.

"Hey," Quinn said, pulling her aside. "I get that you're mad at Juliette, but I need some kind of footage where you aren't glaring at her or Nick's mom. I think it might be better if we just have you and Nick and maybe your dad and the bridal party for the filming. I know how difficult this is for you—"

"Do you?" Adler snapped. "My dream wedding has turned into one crazy-ass scandal after another and I'm supposed to smile and act like nothing has happened."

"I know it's hard. I'm sorry. But I have to film this. And I want to do it in a way that you'll be happy with," Quinn said, turning away. "Take a few minutes while we set up for some different angles and then we can try again."

Adler realized she was turning into a bridezilla. "Q!"

She ran after her friend and hugged her. "I'm sorry. I'm just losing it."

"I know. It's not personal. I have to have something, and if we use what I've filmed so far, you're not going to like it."

"Fair enough. Give me a minute to talk to Aunt Jules and Cora," Adler said.

"Okay. Want me to send Iris over so you're not alone?" Quinn asked.

"No. I need to do this by myself," she said.

Nick was standing in a group with the groomsmen, which included her cousin Zac, who had filled in last moment for a no show. Nick's brothers and father were with them. August Bisset hadn't come to the rehearsal, which Adler was glad about. Cora was talking to Olivia, and Aunt Jules was over by Mari and Iris.

She took a deep breath. She couldn't let the actions of these two women more than thirty years ago ruin her wedding. And she knew they didn't want them to.

"Aunt Jules? Cora? Could I have a word with you both?" Adler asked.

Olivia and Mari both looked at her, their eyes wide. But the older women just nodded, and Adler turned to walk toward the back of the church where they could have some privacy.

"Adler, let me—" Cora started once they were out of ear-shot of the others.

"Please don't, Cora. Let me just say this. I'm not happy with either of you right now. A part of me knows that's unfair, but it's how I feel," she said. "You both seem angry with each other as well, and since this wedding is being televised, I think we need to clear the air before we let them film another minute."

"I agree," Aunt Jules said.

"Of course, Adler, it's your special day and Nick's. I don't want to ruin it for either of you," Cora said.

Both of them were so contrite, quiet and almost sad that she felt wrong saying anything, but she knew she had to. "Thank you both for agreeing. The thing is, I am struggling to forgive you both for what you did. I know I'm not the one who needs to forgive you but there it is. I hate that you both kept this a secret until my wedding weekend. Even the fact that you feel bad for what you did isn't enough.

"Nick isn't himself. The paparazzi are swarming around him. And my dad, who is finally clean and in an actual healthy relationship, is contemplating doing something outrageous to draw the spotlight off of Nick's parentage. This isn't right."

"I'll speak to Toby," Aunt Jules said.

"That's not the point," Adler said. "I can't figure out how to not be angry with you."

"Don't," Cora said. "You're completely justified in being upset. We both are as well. We aren't going to magically all form some family. Juliette and I will stay in the background and give you space to be the center of attention."

"Yes," Aunt Jules added. "This is your chance to celebrate your love for Nick and the life you two are building. No one wants to intrude on that."

Adler nodded. She wasn't getting the closure she needed but Cora had been right when she'd said it was too soon for any of them to really achieve that. They would just all make the best of the situation. "Thank you."

"You're welcome," they both said at the same time.

Aunt Jules reached out to hug her and Cora looked like she wanted to as well. In that moment, Adler realized that as much as this weekend might have been for her, it wasn't anymore. She was caught in the middle of two warring families and she either had to figure out how to broker peace or decide if she wanted to peace out.

She hugged them both and noticed Nick watching them. He lifted one eyebrow at her, the way he did when they were at a party and he wanted to make sure she was okay. She tried to smile but she realized she wasn't just angry at these two women. She was also mad at him.

CHAPTER TWELVE

LOGAN WAS STANDING by the window in the hallway outside the ballroom when Quinn found him as she left the rehearsal dinner. She had decided to wear a cute sundress with wide shoulder straps and a flared skirt that made her feel very feminine. Like she wanted to twirl. That was precisely the reason why she usually wore jeans.

She'd expected Logan to cave and show up, so had been disappointed when she hadn't seen him there. She'd gotten dressed up for herself and her friends, not for him, or so she'd told herself when she'd left her bungalow. But a part of her knew she wanted to see him. Wanted to find a bit of the romance that was swirling around the events at the Nantucket Hotel despite the fact that the past was rearing its ugly head.

She'd stepped out of the hotel ballroom as Zac got up on the stage to sing to Iris, probably well on his way to winning her back. The Bisset men knew how to bring out the romance when it suited them. And after today, when she'd talked to Adler and Nick and Logan about all the different emotions that the news of August and Cora's affair and the results stirred up, she just wanted to be with Logan.

She wanted to be with this man who was dressed in a Tom

Ford suit and staring out the window like he'd lost his center and didn't know how to find it.

The look on his face as he stood there stirred all those feelings she'd been denying he made her feel. All that love and need and the desire to wrap him in her arms and do whatever she could to soothe the savage beast inside him. Except that she knew he didn't want to be soothed. He wanted to savage something. Someone. She wouldn't let him ruin Adler's wedding and she knew Logan well enough to know that he wouldn't want to do that.

He was probably readying himself for something she knew he'd regret after the fact. Like stealing the business deal out from under Nick. He always lashed out when he was angry and took the revenge he thought he deserved. But when the time passed and he had a moment to breathe and reflect, he always regretted it.

Had he changed enough for her to feel safe being with him?

"Quinn."

He'd turned to her while she'd been ruminating on whether she should stay or leave. The anguish in his eyes coupled with the way that suit fit him just brought her to her knees. He looked strong, sexy and so alone, that she couldn't help walking over to him.

She just stood there trying to tell herself she wasn't falling for him while knowing it was a big lie. There was no way she could resist Logan like this. She knew it, so why wasn't she wanting to run for the ferry and go back to the mainland to get as far from him as she could?

She didn't want to.

She liked her life; she wasn't going to pretend she didn't. But she wanted Logan. She craved the feelings that only he stirred in her. And he'd changed. She felt it all the way to her soul. He was a better man now.

And...

The biggest reason of all...

He needed her.

She saw it in his eyes and in his body when he reached one arm out to her. He needed her to come to him. And she did.

She didn't question it or try to justify it.

This wasn't a thinking thing.

This was a feeling thing.

This was a Logan thing.

This was a Quinn pretending it would be okay thing.

She nestled against his side, tipping her head to look up at his profile. He went back to staring out the window and she shifted her gaze to see what he was looking at. Then her breath caught in her throat.

August and Juliette stood in the hotel parking lot. From this distance, it was hard to see what was happening, but it looked like they were arguing.

"Oh, Logan."

"It's got to be about me. All her life she had the high ground in arguments with him. She's always put the family first, always put her smile on and stood next to him regardless of what he'd done and now...me."

"That's between the two of them. No matter how it feels right now, she'll still always put the family first," Quinn said. "Come on. Come with me and dance and forget about this."

"I can never forget this, Ace. This is who I am," he said. "I don't want to dance and smile. I'll probably take a swing at Nick because without him we'd never be here."

"I'm not sure that logic works," Quinn pointed out gently.

"I don't care. I know it makes no sense, but I don't want to be here, I don't want to know the truth or see it on everyone's face. I want to go back to the way it was before this stupid wedding," Logan said.

Quinn realized that he wasn't going to be okay. She thought time would heal him, but this cut seemed too deep.

"Want to go to your room?" she asked.

"Can you come with me?" he asked. "Are you done working?"

"Yes," she said.

He took her hand in his and led her down the hall to the bank of elevators. His parents entered through the side door as they approached. She slipped her hand under his arm and squeezed.

"Logan."

"Dad. Juliette," he said to them, and punched the elevator call button with more force than was necessary.

"You don't call your mother by her first name," August said.

Quinn was struck by how he might have been arguing with Juliette in the parking lot but he had her back with Logan.

"She's not my mom, is she?" Logan asked.

Tears rolled down Juliette's face and August lunged for his son. But Juliette held him back and Quinn grabbed Logan's arm, forcing him down the hall, away from his parents.

Losing Logan wasn't something that Juliette ever thought she'd have to face, but as her son walked away, she knew she had. August, even after all his anger in the parking lot, turned to her and, for the first time in a very long time, he didn't seem like he was holding part of himself back.

"I'll make him—"

"You can't make him," she said. "I never thought this would come out."

"You told me the truth always does," he reminded her. His tone was gentle; one he didn't use very often.

This was the man she'd fallen in love with. Not the one who could charm the room or who could broker billion-dollar deals before breakfast, but the man who had a deep well of empathy and used it sparingly. Just on a special few.

"I wish I'd told you, but we weren't in a good place," she admitted.

"It's my fault," he said. "Your actions were your own but they were motivated by me and the way that I was at that time. If I'd never had an affair and left you alone, maybe our son wouldn't have been stillborn. There are a million possibilities, but we are on the path that you and I have made. We have to trust that we raised Logan well enough that when he calms down from this betrayal, he'll come back to us."

"Us?" she asked. "He's not mad at you, is he?"

"I think it's safe to assume everyone knows I'm the one to blame. If I hadn't been so busy trying to prove I was the biggest, baddest asshole in the room and been more present with the family...maybe things would be different," he said. "I have to be honest, Jules, I anticipated a lot of things happening this weekend, but not what's actually come about."

She gave him a weak smile. "Same. How ironic is it that I end up in the same delivery room as your lover?"

"I think fate was playing tricks on us. Logan and I have both been in the same room with Nick and Tad, and I have to tell you those two men are nothing alike. I can see your influence in Logan's upbringing. Hell, Leo's just like him."

Juliette nodded. She knew her husband was trying to make her feel better and though her heart ached to go after Logan, she had to admit that Auggie was helping.

Someone cleared his throat. They glanced toward the ballroom where the rehearsal dinner was being held and saw Dare.

Her eldest son. She'd screwed up so much when she'd been a new mom, she knew she should be grateful he'd turned out as well as he had. A politician known for his fairness and bipartisan cooperation, he was truly the best of her and Auggie.

"Yes?" Auggie asked.

"Adler needs you, Mom. She's not sure she's going to go through with the wedding and just told Nick in front of the entire dinner party," Dare said.

"Oh, dear. This just keeps getting worse. Musette is probably cursing me from the afterlife," she said, rushing past Dare and into the room where Adler was just walking away toward the kitchens in the back.

Juliette wove her way through the partiers, trying to catch up to her niece. Cora, Olivia and Mari were right behind her as well. They didn't have to go far. Adler had only made it to the staff hallway and was leaning against the wall, tears streaming down her face.

Juliette went to her and pulled her into her arms. Adler resisted for a moment but then buried her head in Juliette's shoulder and cried.

"It's okay." She just rubbed Adler's back and kept murmuring to her.

"I think we just need to take a breath," Cora said.

"I agree," Juliette said, looking at the other woman. They shared so much but were both essentially strangers. Mari looked at her and Juliette nodded, indicating she should come and take care of Adler.

Then she pulled Cora aside. "I think we need to get the two of them in a room to talk this through. Can you try to talk to Nick?"

"Yes. I can. I know he's not handling August being his father very well and I'm afraid his dislike of Logan hasn't really helped with the other news," Cora said.

"I know. Logan's not even talking to me. But we can remind Adler and Nick that they love each other," Juliette said.

"Will that be enough?" Cora asked.

"I don't know. Frankly, I'm out of ideas. Do you have any other suggestions?" she asked the other woman.

Cora shook her head, chewing on her bottom lip. "Nick adores Adler. I think I'll try to remind him what's important. Maybe you can do the same with Adler?"

"I will. We can't let them go to bed until they have made up," Juliette said.

"Agreed. Olivia, come with me," Cora called to her daughter. "I'll text Mari after I've talked to Nick."

"Sounds good," Juliette said. The two women didn't have each other's cell numbers.

Cora and her daughter left, and she turned to Adler and Mari. Adler's mascara hadn't run, but her nose was red and her eyes were still watery. "Why did I think I wanted to get married to him?"

"Because you love him," Mari said. "And he loves you. Don't forget men can be dumb sometimes...not saying women can't too, but Inigo has done some really stupid stuff. Our wedding is stressing me out and it's just going to be a small affair in Texas at his family's estate."

"That's right. Mari's situation is a good example of this," Juliette added. "This wedding is a party to celebrate the couple that you are with your friends. All of these events are just icing on the cake. Right now, it seems like the cake tipped over in the back of the truck and the icing is smeared and pieces of cake are showing through, but the cake is still good. You and Nick are still good. He's still the man you fell in love with."

"Is he?"

"Yes. He's struggling and you're nervous because nothing is going according to the plans you've made. But the two of you are meant for each other, Adler," Juliette reminded her. "If you want to send everyone home and cancel the film crew, then we will do it. But I feel like you'll regret letting Nick go."

Adler appreciate her aunt and cousin trying to reassure her, but this wasn't something either of them could understand. Their fiancé hadn't turned from a sweet great guy into someone they didn't recognize. Nick was out of control. He'd been drinking way more than he normally did since he'd learned that August was his biological father.

And the thing with Logan had really sent him into a spiral. She was trying to be understanding, trying to give him the benefit of the doubt and let him have space to come to terms with it, but they were getting married tomorrow.

There wasn't time for him to fall to pieces and put himself back together the way he needed to. She needed him here and present.

"Darling girl, what can I do? Do you need me to go and talk

some sense into Nick? Do something outrageous so everyone gives you both some space?" her dad said as he came in to the hall. Sonia was behind him, wearing her trademark long flowy skirt and her bangles, which jangled as she moved.

"Don't do any of that, Dad," Adler said.

"Cora is talking to Nick," Aunt Jules added. "I'm sorry for my part in this, Adler. I wish... I just wish this wasn't happening now."

Adler took a deep breath. She wasn't mad at her aunt anymore. She was more upset by how Nick was acting and changing. Jules had done the best she could with the hand she'd been dealt. The coming-out timing could have been better for Adler, but she wasn't going to worry about her aunt right now. She was worried about Nick.

He wasn't acting like himself and seemed to have completely shut down on her. She'd wanted to force him to show her what he was feeling, and her outburst hadn't been planned, but once the words had left her mouth and he'd let her go, she was beginning to wonder if this wasn't what she should have done yesterday.

Marriage was a big step. Her father had been married so many times that she'd lost count. Not really, but it felt like that. He'd had eight wives, and that didn't count the number of live-in partners he'd had while she'd been growing up. For her, marriage was a one-time thing.

Adler had thought that Nick got that. That he was on the same page as she was. But tonight...when he'd let her walk away and hadn't followed her...well, she wondered if he was ready for a life with her.

"Everyone is wondering what's going on," Sonia said.

"Let them," her dad said. "Adler's what matters."

"I agree, but I thought if we went out there and rocked the house, maybe they'd forget about Adler for a while and that will give her some time to get things worked out," Sonia said. "Unless you're not working things out?"

Sonia had reddish blond hair that was shot with gray and

warm, brown eyes. From the moment she'd started dating Toby, Sonia had been caring and motherly toward Adler. That was something she'd really appreciated, and right now her suggestion sounded perfect. "Can you do that, Dad? It would give me a moment to breathe and think of what I should do next."

"Of course I can, darling girl," Toby said. "I'll do whatever you need."

"Thanks, Dad," she said, hugging him. "Go rock out and I'll... I guess I need to find Nick."

"Not yet," Mari said. "Cora's texting me after she talks to him."

Adler took a deep breath as her dad and Sonia left, and then turned to her cousin. "If his mom can't get through to him, then no one will be able to."

"I think everyone just wants to bring the focus back to the wedding," Aunt Jules said.

"I know you do," Mari said. "Ad, listen, you've been out of the spotlight for a while and I'm happy to give you some tips to help you manage it."

"Like what?" she asked.

"Don't listen to her. She was very antagonistic with the press, and had to resort to extreme measures to make them go away," Aunt Jules said.

Adler remembered all those angry photos of Mari giving the camera the finger and more than one lawsuit over when her cousin had verbally assaulted paparazzi after it was revealed she'd had an affair with a married man.

"It made them go away for a while," Mari said. "The thing is we need someone not related to the wedding to do something over the top, you know?"

"I do, but it seems like I'd be inviting bad karma to wish that on someone else," Adler said. "My dad has offered but he's finally..."

"I know," Mari said. "Karma is a bitch and when it comes for you, there is no dodging it, right, Mom?"

Juliette looked at her daughter for a minute. "I hadn't thought of it that way, but you are right. Payback doesn't always come the way you expect it to. I mean I wanted Auggie to understand how betrayed I'd felt every time he cheated on me and I guess hiding the fact that Logan wasn't my biological son did that."

Adler shook her head. She wasn't going to wish anything bad on anyone. She didn't want to add to the mess they were all currently stuck in. And while her aunt and cousin were distracting, her heart ached at the fact that Nick hadn't come after her or even tried to find her. Was there any hope for the two of them?

CHAPTER THIRTEEN

LOGAN KNEW HE should be alone, but Quinn had followed him up to his room. He was so close to punching something. Punching the wall would be good. It would give him the satisfaction of hitting as hard as he could as well as some resulting pain, which he could channel his anger toward.

He couldn't believe what he'd said to his mom. He'd known how badly those words would wound her and had chosen them for that purpose, but he hadn't expected to feel that backlash of pain, guilt and shame.

"Logan, are you okay?"

Quinn's voice was softer than it normally was, as if she knew he was a wounded animal and trying to soothe him. That only served to make him angrier. He didn't want to be soothed or pitied. Yet everything this weekend was forcing him into a position that demanded that.

"Yeah."

"Liar," she said, teasing him.

He didn't know if she felt like he was more able to handle it or if she was scrolling through a bunch of ways to treat him, trying each to see which one worked.

"You're right," he said, pivoting on his heel to face her. He shoved the sides of his jacket back and put his hands on his hips. "I am lying. I'm not okay. I just said the worst possible thing to my mom, and you know what? I would say it again. I almost wish she'd let my dad hit me because I'm mad at him too. And I know I'll regret all of this later, but for this moment I just feel...like I'm going to explode. Like I need to explode because maybe then I won't feel so fragile."

Quinn kicked off her high heels as she walked over to him. The skirt of her dress swooshed with each step she took. Her reddish-brown hair had been curled and swung around her shoulders. She tipped her head to the side as she got closer, narrowing one eye and studying him. She took his tie in her hand and tugged on it.

He stayed where he was for a moment before he gave in and let her pull him toward her.

"Fighting never helps," she said. "But maybe you need a competition to distract you."

Yes. "What'd you have in mind?"

"A little game of teasing. First one who cracks loses."

"Or wins," he said. "Depending on how they crack."

"Exactly. You game?" she asked.

"Are you sure, Ace?"

"Scared you can't keep it together?" she asked. "I mean you know what's underneath these clothes and it might be too much temptation for you."

He needed this. Needed her more than he'd realized until this very moment. "Oh, I think I'm up to the challenge. What are the rules?"

"Anything goes," she said. "First one to ask for something from the other one loses."

"Fair enough," he said, putting his arm around her waist and lifting her off her feet. He brought his mouth down on hers, not hard but just forceful enough to let her know he was here for this. Here for her. He kissed her long and deep, and shoved the thoughts of everything and everyone else out of his head.

It was just him and Quinn and that big king-size bed behind him. Win or lose, he knew he needed nothing more than this.

Sex wasn't a solution—or was it? Would it be his salvation? None of that mattered at this moment. He felt her fingers on the back of his neck, slowly caressing her way to his ear. She traced the outer shell and then pinched the lobe and he felt a jolt all the way down his body as he hardened.

She flicked the lobe of his ear with her finger again and he fought to keep from groaning out loud.

The stakes got a little higher as he realized how many of his turn-ons Quinn knew and was willing to exploit. She pulled her mouth from his, kissing his jawline and then sucking the lobe of his ear into her mouth and biting on it. Then she pulled back and whispered into his ear.

Her breath was hot, her words steamy. "Remember that time you and I were in the hot tub on winter break in Aspen? And you were determined that we wouldn't do it while others were around? And I ended up on your lap, sitting and talking to our friends while stroking your cock?"

He hardened a little bit more. As if he could have forgotten that.

"I remember that I had my hand in your bikini bottoms and my finger deep inside you. And you kept rocking against my touch as if you couldn't get enough."

She nipped at his ear again. "That was a nice night."

A nice night, indeed.

He turned away from her, shrugging out of his suit jacket and walking slowly across the room to hang it up on the valet in the corner. He felt the weight of her gaze on him as he moved. Knew she liked the way he looked in a suit and that this one fit him to a tee.

He turned back around and she waggled her eyebrows at him. "I do love a sharp-dressed man."

"I know," he said. "And I like that dress you're wearing. You don't wear them very often, but you have great legs."

"Thank you," she said, turning slightly from side to side, letting the skirt swish around her legs. "I love dresses, but no one takes me seriously when I wear one."

"I can see why," he said. "All I want to do is take *you*."

"That's because you're always thinking about sex," she said, reaching up underneath her skirt. A moment later her panties dropped to the floor and she stepped around them.

He groaned as he felt himself hardening even more. She looked so sophisticated and together, and now he knew she wasn't wearing underwear. It was almost too much and he had to force himself not to grab her and shove his hands up underneath that skirt.

"Care to dance?" he asked. He was going to take this slow and easy. He was playing this game to win; he always played to win. And tonight, he could use a tick mark in the W column.

"What'd you have in mind?"

"I'm not sure. Let me see what I have on my playlist," he said. He was stalling for time, trying to pull himself back from the edge.

Quinn felt like she might have won that round by dropping her panties. She knew Logan was just taking a breather, and she could use one too. She hadn't expected that just watching him walk across the room would get her so hot. To be fair, that kiss had started the slow melt inside her. She was hot and horny and ready for him. But she also knew this wasn't a competition she was prepared to lose. Logan needed a good, long fight, not some easy win.

While she knew she'd feel like a winner either way, Logan needed this score. She wanted it for him. And, to be honest, for them both. But there was a part of her that wanted the win too. She needed to know that these emotions swirling around inside her since they'd had sex on the beach weren't one-sided.

She wanted to know that he was starting to think about her

as more than a weekend sex romp. When she went back to real life on Monday, she was afraid she didn't want this to end.

She heard applause and then the riff of electric guitar, and shook her head. "Shake For Me." It was like playing dirty. She loved Stevie Ray Vaughan; the first time she'd danced with Logan this song had been playing. They'd been at a party at a frat house and one of the Texas boys had put it on.

Quinn threw her head back and laughed, remembering the smells of beer spilled on the floor from the keg, and smoke, and then Logan's expensive, woodsy cologne as he'd come over to her and asked her to dance.

He winked at her. "Will this do?"

"Bring it, boy," she said, slowly dancing her way over to him. She put her hands on his ass, grinding against him to the music as he put his hands on her waist and did the same. Logan had a natural rhythm and while some men might struggle to feel comfortable in their skin when they danced, he didn't.

When the chorus came, Logan started singing along, his voice low and gravelly, mimicking Stevie Ray, inviting her to shake like wild.

And she did. Shaking for him as they both danced to the song. Each brush of his body added fuel to the fire burning inside her. His erection nudged her stomach and she wished she was wearing a pair of jeans and a tank top instead of this dress. But the dress worked.

She pushed her leg between his, felt the strength of his thigh as he cupped her butt, drawing her up his thigh and then letting her slide back down. The next song on the playlist was "Pride and Joy." Another classic *Double Trouble* song. And actually, her favorite. They'd had sex the first time while this was playing in the background. It had been three weeks after that first dance.

He brushed his fingers over the swoop of her neck and shoulder and she realized she was limited to caressing him through his dress shirt and pants. But the sundress she wore left her arms, most of her chest and her sensitive nape bare. He ran his finger slowly along the back of her neck.

"Am I your little lover boy?" he asked.

She groaned. "You know you are. I guess that makes me your sweet little baby?"

"Hell, yes. It makes you mine, Ace."

His.

She wanted to be his. She twined her arms around his neck and pulled his head to hers, dancing against him while they kissed. She sucked his tongue deep into her mouth and moved against him. Every nerve ending she had was so sensitized and ready for his touch. She was ready for this game to end. She wanted to touch his skin. Caressing his back through his shirt was fine, but she wanted the heat of his flesh. She wanted to see him instead of just remembering how muscly and firm he was under his clothing.

He pulled away then rested his forehead on hers as he looked down into her eyes. His hands still cupped her butt and he was swaying back and forth as "Texas Flood" started to play. The jazzy blues music continued to enflame her and the fact that it was this music, the music that had been the soundtrack to the start of their relationship, was making it hard for her to stay focused on the game she'd suggested they play.

Looking into Logan's blue eyes, she forgot everything. Everything but this man who she knew wasn't as perfect as he felt to her at this moment. At this moment, she had the feeling that they could make this work.

"I could do this all night," he said. "Just hold you in my arms and remember the past. When we were both young and it seemed like we could do whatever we wanted in life."

"Me too," she said, putting her hand on the side of his face. She felt the faint stubble there. She ran her finger over it, enjoying the roughness against the tip of her finger. "I'm sensing a but..."

"I want you, Ace. I like this, but I want to hold you naked

in my arms, taste your hard nipples in my mouth, feel those bare limbs wrapped around me. I want that more than I want anything else."

The words were nothing more than the truth, and he knew he was a second away from shoving her skirt aside and cupping her naked ass. But he also didn't want to lose. He needed to make this last-ditch effort to get her to break first.

"I want that too. I love the feel of your naked chest rubbing against my breasts and the way your legs feel when they are tangled with mine as you drive up inside of me," she said.

He groaned and shook his head. She was on to him. "Not going to break first, are you?"

"Nope," she said with a grin.

A shot of something like love went through him. Quinn got to him in a way that no other woman ever had. God, he needed her. He needed more than he'd realized he did until this moment when her brown eyes were full of joy and desire.

She reached between them and he felt her hand wrap around his erection through his pants. He was already so hard that he knew it wasn't going to take much to push him over the edge. She ran her hand up and down his length and he tightened his muscles to keep from thrusting against her touch.

Logan tried to remember the rules she'd put in place but all he could think about was her naked and getting inside her. He lifted her off her feet and walked her back to the couch, sitting hard on the cushion. She bounced on his lap and he winced as he moved around, adjusting his legs and trying to make himself comfortable.

He reached for his zipper and drew it down, letting out a sigh of relief as he finally had room to get comfortable. She sighed too. Her fingers wrapped around him through the fabric of his briefs and stroked him. He lifted his hips and then reached his hand up under her skirt. Felt the smooth strength of her thighs and then the moistness at her center.

She shivered in his arms and then shifted until she was straddling him. She pushed his underwear down until his cock was free. He reached and made sure he was comfortable before she shifted around. He felt the heat of her center against him, the moist heat of her body rubbing against him, and knew that there were no losers in this moment.

He shifted his hips until the tip of his erection was at the entrance of her body. She put her hands on his shoulders and he cupped her naked butt.

Their eyes met and she pursed her lips. "Draw?"

"Draw," he said. He could live with that result as long as he didn't have to wait another second to get inside her.

Quinn lowered herself slowly onto him. She sucked her lower lip between her teeth as she took all of him and then paused, waiting for them both to adjust to him inside her. He drew his finger along her crack and felt her shiver in his arms, arching her back and thrusting her breasts forward as she let her head fall back.

He kissed her neck, suckled at that spot where her pulse beat strongly, and then urged her to start moving on him. She shifted backward, then thrust back down, riding him hard and taking everything he had to give. He was so close to the edge, so ready to come, that he couldn't wait another second. He reached between her legs, found that tiny bud, and rubbed it.

She pulled his head closer to hers, her mouth finding his as she rode him harder and faster. Then she ripped her mouth from his and cried out his name as she came, her hips moving more frantically against his. He rode the wave of her orgasm, driving up into her again and again until he came long and hard. She collapsed against him. He wrapped his arms around her and held her.

She had her head on his shoulder, her arms around his shoulders, and her breath brushed his neck each time she exhaled. He stroked her back up and down. Just holding her and hoping that this moment wouldn't end.

He'd never been the kind of man to hide from the world. But with Quinn in his arms and his life in tatters, he could easily stay here for the rest of his days and count himself content.

He knew that wasn't reality and that she'd have to go back to her job. That the real world was waiting for both of them. Dimly, he realized that Stevie Ray Vaughan was still playing from his smartphone. That music was so deeply ingrained in the soul of their relationship, he wondered if he'd been cheating at their game when he'd put it on.

"You okay?" she asked.

He glanced down, realizing she'd been watching him. Her brown eyes were fixed on him and he hoped she couldn't see the turmoil still swirling inside him. But this was Quinn, so she had probably already guessed it.

"Yeah," he said. What was one more lie from a Bisset? Apparently, that was something they were all very good at.

"Want me to stay the night?" she asked.

"If you want to," he said, trying not to seem vulnerable and ask her to stay. But he knew that he was vulnerable anyway.

Vulnerable to Quinn, who had always been able to see past all of his barriers to the heart of the man who always needed a win. The heart of a man who wanted her for himself and also wanted to beat her at the game they were always playing.

"I do."

CHAPTER FOURTEEN

WAKING UP IN Logan's arms was something she could get used
to. It fit with where she was in her life to have a man, and Logan
wasn't just any guy. He was the man she measured other men
by, she realized.

He was the yard stick she'd always used. Most men didn't
measure up. They weren't as driven, as fun, as sexy, as smart,
as able to poke fun at themselves. And she'd never realized she'd
been doing that until she was here with him and there was no
comparison with other guys.

There was just Logan.

There always had been, which made her feel scared and
shaky. He wasn't a sure thing; he never had been. She'd taken
a risk and she had to hope that he'd taken the same one. Last
night, he'd needed her and she'd allowed herself to believe that it
was the step toward building something together. And watching
him sleep, seeing his face relaxed instead of tense, feeling his
arms holding her to him, cuddling her to his side, it was easy to
believe that this was the first morning of the rest of their lives.

If she allowed herself to forget that it was Logan Bisset, she
could relax and just go with it.

But when had Logan ever done anything the easy way? He'd
broken her heart once and she didn't want to believe she was

the same woman who would fall for him again. But she knew she had. She could dress up however she wanted, say it was hot sex, or he needed her, and she liked that, but she knew deep down in her soul that she loved him.

Maybe...she always had.

She carefully rolled out of the bed and walked as quietly as she could to the bathroom, picking up her phone as she went. It was Saturday. Adler's wedding day.

She had a lot of work to do, and losing herself in her job was going to be a much-needed distraction. But another part of her, the part that she liked to bury deep inside—the romantic part— wanted Logan to wake up and beg her to stay.

She shook her head as she washed her face with cold water. She needed to snap out of this. She had to get her head in the right place. A woman who wasn't on her A game couldn't compete with Logan. He liked the competition and as much as he loved to win, she knew he also loved the challenge.

And Quinn knew that Logan was never going to stop the game. Never going to take a break and let someone get the better of him. Even her. Even if he did care for her. She didn't need to get the better of him, she just wanted him. *Damn.*

She knew he cared for her. That was part of this. Part of why she'd fallen again. She could feel the emotions he had for her. Saw it in the way he'd wanted her to stay last night but had been reluctant to say it out loud. She gave him so many chances, but she had to, for herself. If she ever walked away, she'd always have some doubt that she'd left too soon.

This wasn't like college when they'd been young and still figuring out who they were going to be. They were in their thirties now and she was pretty damn sure of who she was. Still a hot mess on some days but killing it on others.

She reached for Logan's toothbrush and dug around in his overnight bag until she found his toothpaste. As she brushed her teeth, she tried to give herself a firm look in the mirror. It was hard to be serious when she was brushing her teeth. But she needed to be. If she ever needed to listen to that inner voice in her head, it was now.

This was Logan.

He hadn't magically changed into a domesticated man, he was still the driven alpha male he'd always been. He was wounded right now, which made him vulnerable and dangerous. It could go her way but, just as easily, she could end up hurt by him.

The way his mother had been last night.

Logan didn't pull punches and Quinn didn't want to be beat up by him. Not physically. He'd never lay a hand on her in anger, but he could rip her heart out if she let him.

How could she protect herself when her body and soul wanted him for her own? When she wanted to just open her arms and say that she was his.

Her phone pinged and she saw it was Adler. She was heading to the room they'd rented for the bridal party to get ready. The hair and makeup artists should be arriving soon.

Quinn typed out a response.

Hey. I'm at the hotel, need to run back to my place before I meet you. My assistant and the film crew will be there. You okay?

Nervous AF. Nick and I had it out last night. I think we are okay. Not sure.

What happened?

Just more Bisset BS. Also, if you want my advice, never fall in love with a guy.

You're not okay. Give me ten minutes or so and I'll meet you. Where are you?

Pulling into the hotel parking lot. Meet in the makeup room. There's nothing you can say to fix this.

That's not what I wanted for you today.

Me neither but that's where I am.

"You ever coming out, Ace?" Logan yelled through the closed door.

She rinsed, spit out the toothpaste, and went to open the door. He stood there totally naked and she just took a moment to appreciate how good he looked. He smiled at her and it felt genuine.

This was good. They were good. Everything was going to be okay, she thought.

"I have to run," she said. "Things are going to be busy today. But I'll see you at the wedding and then at the reception."

"Uh, I'm not going. I really don't want to be there."

Surprised she wrinkled her brow. "It's Adler's day and she needs her family. You should go and socialize with everyone. It will make you feel better."

"Thanks, Quinn," Logan said sarcastically. "But I don't need your advice. I invited you up last night to screw not to be my shrink."

Quinn's face went white and then he saw her get pissed. He knew he was being an asshole. He shouldn't have said that to her but he wasn't going to just head down to the wedding like nothing had happened. Last night had been an oasis of calm in the middle of the craziness his life had become. But that was it. Nothing had been resolved and he'd slept for a few hours with Quinn in his arms, but most of the night his mind had been busy running through all the scenarios that would play out today.

He'd been cruel to his parents, he'd set in motion a business deal to ruin Nick's honeymoon, and his cousin probably would be happy if she didn't see him on her special day. Right now, he felt like the lowest of the low and he knew he deserved to feel that way.

Some of it, he placed on his mom's shoulders but since he'd stabbed her in the heart with his words last night, he knew that the blame had to come back to him. And the last thing he wanted was to wake up feeling like he did for Quinn.

He wasn't in any shape to be in a relationship with her, but no matter how he looked at it, they weren't just hooking up at the wedding. It felt like more. And unless he missed his guess, she felt it too. He wondered if he shouldn't have played Stevie Ray Vaughan last night. Maybe bringing up the memories like that was why he'd woken up this morning feeling like…well, feeling. Just all the emotions. And Logan hated that. He was a man who prided himself on keeping his life together.

And emotional men made mistakes.

His dad was a prime example of that. A kid he didn't know about…hell, twins he hadn't known about.

He scrubbed his hand over his face. "What, no snappy comeback?"

"I'm waiting for an apology," she said. "That was uncalled for and we both know it."

"Keep waiting, Ace," he said.

She blinked and her jaw got tight. She took a deep breath through her nose and he knew that this time there'd be no getting back together with her. This time when Quinn walked out of his life, she wasn't coming back.

He'd had his second chance and once again he was going to let her go. It was the smart thing to do and God, please let him still be smart. He didn't know what he'd do if he lost that edge.

"Damn it, Logan. Every time I think you're anything more than a cold-blooded shark, you remind me that I'm wrong," she said.

"I never said this was anything more than you and me and the summer heat."

She shook her head. "The summer heat? Are you freaking kidding me?"

She turned on her heel and he watched her go, forced his eyes off her ass as she moved around his suite collecting her clothes and putting back on the dress she'd worn last night.

It was still crisp and pretty in the light of day. Her hair was tousled but she still looked good. And angry. Really angry.

"You cheated last night, so you think you won. You didn't," she said.

"Fine," he said. He didn't really want to talk about that anymore. He wanted her out of his room and out of his life so he could continue being himself. Stop trying to be the kind of man that Quinn would want by her side. Because he knew now that was what he'd been doing. Trying so hard to pretend that he could be a better man when he wasn't. He was just Logan Bisset.

And now he knew he didn't have any of Juliette Wallis-Bisset's genes. None of her kindness and charm. He was just the blunt businessman his father had raised him to be.

Quinn had all of her clothes back on and came toward him, barreling for the bathroom. He stepped back, not sure what she was going to do.

"I need my phone."

She reached the counter and took it before turning back to him. "I thought you felt lost and maybe you weren't sure who you were anymore now that you found out that Juliette isn't your mom. But that's not it, is it? You're still your dad's Mini-Me. Still the man who needs no one but himself and, hey, congrats, that's exactly what you're going to get from me and probably every other woman you have a relationship with."

Her words hurt and, as much as he knew he deserved them, they weren't the kind of words Quinn usually said to anyone. He'd hurt her that much that she was starting to be more like him. Cold, calculating. *Congratulations,* he thought, *you've made Quinn into a nasty person just like you.*

"I'd tell you I hope you'll be happy, but that's not really your thing, is it?" She didn't wait for an answer but just walked straight through the suite and out the door. And he stood there wondering if he'd made the biggest mistake of his life or not. He knew that Quinn would be happier without him and, as she'd pointed out, he was the kind of man who liked to be alone.

He'd be fine.

As he got ready to take a shower, he pretended that whatever else happened today, he was okay with her leaving the way she had. He almost convinced himself it was true too until he went to the balcony and saw her walking across the parking lot. Her steps were clipped and angry.

He knew that he was never going to be okay with how things ended. And he didn't deserve to be.

Adler took one look at her best friend's face and realized she'd been with a guy. It had to be Logan. He was the only man who had ever put Quinn off her stride. Of course, the man she'd have said had nothing in common with her fiancé except for their business acumen would be able to hurt Quinn deeply.

"Come on, let's talk," Adler said, looping her arm through Quinn's and dragging her to the second bedroom in the suite. She closed the door behind them, so they'd have some privacy.

Quinn wore a pair of black jeans and a black T-shirt under her silk bomber jacket. She was ready to work; she had her hair pulled back into a ponytail and hadn't bothered with makeup. Her creamy complexion complete with freckles made her seem younger than her age.

"Why didn't you say you were with Logan again?" Adler asked.

"How'd you find out?"

"You look ready to spit nails and like you've been crying. He's the only one I've ever known to affect you like that," Adler said. "Plus, given all the shit that's going on this weekend, it's logical."

"There's nothing logical about me and Logan. It's just hormones and stupidity."

Adler gave a shout of laughter before she shook her head. "What has he done?"

"Nothing. It's not important. You and Nick are fighting? That's what Mari texted Iris who texted me."

"You guys need a better way to communicate. That is so last night. Nick and I sort of made up."

"How do you sort of make up?" Quinn asked.

Adler was wondering the same thing herself, but Nick had come to her this morning and said that they shouldn't let the events of the last few days derail their wedding. He still wanted to marry her. But he hadn't said he'd loved her when she'd left and she couldn't help but wonder if he was going through the ceremony because he needed a distraction from the scandals swirling around him.

"We're getting married. We still haven't sorted everything out, but with the ceremony being televised and all the family stuff, we just have to go through with it."

Adler hated the way that sounded. She hadn't been looking to get married just to be a man's Mrs. She'd thought she'd found her soul mate and the man who'd be her partner through the rest of her life. That she'd made a better choice than her dad, who had taken a long time to find Sonia. But maybe she'd been a little too big for her britches by thinking that way.

"Oh, no, Ad, you guys are the perfect couple. I'm sure this is going to blow over."

She smiled at Quinn but could see on her friend's face that she didn't believe it. Too much had happened for any of them to go back to where they had been before. She hoped that the wedding would be a step to her and Nick finding the way forward, but frankly he was drinking a lot and brooding. That wasn't the kind of man he'd been before. He was driven but he'd always been sort of open and upbeat, unlike the men in her family.

"No one is perfect," Adler said. "We're going to figure it out. What about you and Logan?"

Quinn shook her head. "There is no me and Logan. There's Logan, and he's pissed at the world. And there's me, who tried to make him see that this too shall pass."

Of course, Logan didn't want to hear that. Adler knew her cousin well enough to know he wouldn't be appeased by that. "He probably wants his pound of flesh."

"He got it last night. He said some really mean things to his mom and his dad," Quinn said. "I thought he was hurting and that he just needed some time— Never mind. You don't need to hear that."

"I'm sorry," Adler said. And she was. She wanted her friend to find happiness and the only man she'd been interested in seriously in a long time was Logan. There was something between the two of them that Adler didn't get, but that was love, wasn't it?

"Love is so weird. Aunt Jules still loves Auggie. Cora and Tad had their secrets and yet they are still together. Is it just the years keeping them united at this point or is some of it real emotions?" Adler asked. Once she'd believed that only the strong bond of love could keep a couple together, but now she didn't know. Who could love another person who kept those kinds of secrets?

"It is weird. And I'm not in love with Logan. I was in lust and I'm cured. What about you?"

"I'm still in love despite the fact that I'm ticked at Nick. He's the only man I want to be with. I guess that's why I'm going through with the wedding. I am upset, and he's unsure of himself right now, but I don't want to let him go. I still have hope that we can find our way back to each other."

Quinn gave her a sweet look and then hugged her. "I know you two will. You have to or else that means that the older generation and their machinations won. And that's not right. They were trying to hurt each other and you two are pure love and joy."

Adler shook her head. "I don't know about that, but I do know I'm not going to let their actions influence us any more than I have to. I'm going to marry Nick and we are going to start our life away from the craziness that is the Bisset-Williams feud."

"Good plan. Ready to start getting your hair and makeup done?"

"Yes. I want to do all the bride things and just get this day over with."

CHAPTER FIFTEEN

LOGAN LEFT THE hotel and ended up at his grandmother Vivian's house. But after his behavior, he wasn't sure he'd be welcome there. At the last minute, he took a detour, starting down the path to the beach. He found himself sitting on the sand watching the waves when his brothers found him. Dare, Zac, Leo and… Nick. His half sibling—wait, his twin. The brother he didn't want to have.

"Thought we'd find you here," Dare said.

"Your powers of deduction are working overtime," Logan said sarcastically.

"Don't be more of an ass than you already have been," Leo said. "Adler texted Nick and told him that you and Quinn were a thing and you broke her heart. Again."

"Is that why you're here?" he asked. His brothers weren't the type to meddle in his affairs. They pretty much all kept the ups and downs of their love lives to themselves and he, for one, appreciated that.

"Yes and no," Dare said as he sat next to him. "I can't speak for the others, but I needed to get away from Mom and Dad and all the wedding stuff. No offense, Nick."

"None taken," Nick said, sitting next to Dare.

Zac walked to the water's edge, looked out at the horizon and then down at the beach, bending to pick up a shell. He used the incoming wave to wash the sand off it.

He walked back over to his brother, pocketing the shell as he did so. "I'm here to give you some advice, bro. I have no idea if you were just hooking up with Quinn or if you thought it was something else and the stuff with Mom and Dad threw you off. But if you have even the slightest feeling that she's the one, don't let her slip away. I have never felt worse than when I'd thought I'd lost Iris," he said.

"You were hung over," Logan pointed out.

Leo punched him in the shoulder. "Don't be a jerk. Do you feel like that for Quinn?"

He shrugged. This wasn't something he was going to discuss with them. "I don't know. Nick, can I have a moment of your time?"

He might not like Nick but the two of them had been fucked over a lot this weekend. And Logan didn't want to be responsible for another shock. He felt like it was only right to give his adversary a heads-up to what he'd done.

Nick arched an eyebrow at him and then nodded. "Sure. Alone?"

"Let's take a walk," Logan said, standing.

Nick fell into step beside him as they walked down the shore. Logan realized that he knew nothing about this man aside from his business practices and that they usually were going after the same prize.

"First of all, I'm not sure about the twin thing," Logan said. "I don't like you. I'm pretty sure you feel the same about me."

"You're not my favorite person," Nick said drolly. "But I appreciate you coming to the wedding for Adler's sake."

Logan shook his head. He was a grade-A asshole and it was time that Nick knew it. "I didn't come here for Adler. I did it because my mom—Juliette—told me that I would let the family down if I didn't come."

"Well, still you showed up," Nick said. "I'm not sure I would have."

Fuck him. "I had to get a little bit of myself back though. Couldn't give in and show up at your wedding and let you win."

Nick tipped his head to the side, a hard look coming over his face "Let me win? What did you do to get back at me?"

"I undercut you on the patent deal you've been working on and on Monday FuturGen is going to announce a new partnership with an LLC I own. That happened way before I learned any of this stuff about you being my twin."

Nick clenched his fists. "The patent? How did you even know I was interested in that?"

Logan wished the other man would punch him. God, he'd turned into the worst version of himself. Nick was getting married to Adler today. A better man would have— He cut himself off. He wasn't a better man.

"I have connections. Plus, I was watching the stocks you've been buying up," Logan said. "I'm sorry. I shouldn't have done it, but I'm August Bisset's son."

Nick nodded. "I get it. We've never been friendly."

"No, we haven't. But I am sorry. I don't know why I do things like that," he admitted. "I just can't stand to feel like I've lost. After the deal goes through I'll transfer the patent to you. I want it to be my wedding gift to you and Adler."

Nick nodded. "I used to be like that before Adler. But having her by my side, no one can best that. She…she makes me stronger than I am on my own."

"I doubt that," Logan said. Though he remembered Quinn pulling him from his parents before he'd made things worse last night.

"Maybe stronger is the wrong word. She makes me smarter. Now I normally think things through because I know that if I do the wrong thing… I'll lose her."

"Normally? Not this weekend, right? I mean, how could you handle this? I'm weirded out but it must be even worse for you."

"I don't know that it's worse for me than for you, but I'm struggling. My dad has been a rock. We always knew that I was someone else's son, just not that it was August. So Dad and I have a solid relationship."

He looked at the other man. Nick was taller than Logan and had dark hair where Logan was blond. He searched Nick's face trying to see something that would confirm they were twins, but there weren't really any physical signs. "That sounds nice. Normally, Dad and I are solid, but this whole thing with my mom… it's just pushed me over the edge. I said some shitty things to Quinn this morning. Like, even bad for me, and I know I should apologize but I can't figure out if that would be better for her."

Nick put his hand on Logan's shoulder and Logan looked at the other man, who had always been his enemy but somehow no longer was. "I've been screwing up left and right with Adler this entire weekend, but I do know that I will do anything to keep her by my side. There's not another woman in the world who I'd do that for. If you feel even close to that for Quinn, don't let her go."

Logan nodded. "Yeah, thanks. Aren't you afraid that what you feel for Adler is a liability? That she'll cause you to lose your edge?"

Nick stopped walking and put his hands on his hips as he turned to look at the ocean. "Without her I'd still be working sixteen-hour days and not have much of a life. Williams, Inc., is more profitable than it ever has been before and I have to say I think me being in a good place with Adler has a lot to do with it. Even your little stunt outmaneuvering me with the patent isn't going to really be a bad hit," Nick said with a wink before he turned and walked back toward his brothers. "I finally realized that there is more to living than work."

"Like what?"

"Having someone to share it all with."

Logan watched the other man—his twin—leave and thought about all he'd said. Quinn had always made him want to be a better man but there was a part of him that had resisted. Afraid to give up any of the things he'd believed made him who he was. But now that he was back to square one, why not remake himself as a better man? One who wanted Quinn by his side and could be the man she needed by hers.

"Make sure that we have cameras at the front of the church and that they are focused on the bride. I'll use some of the drone footage for the guests and their reactions," Quinn said. "I know that everyone is tired. It's been a long day already and it's not even lunchtime. But we need to get this right."

"We will," her assistant said. "I've given the crew a forty-minute lunch break. The bride asked if you would join her and the bridesmaids off camera. She's in the suite still. The moms are...totally awkward. It's all frozen smiles and tension. But I think we can work around it. I'd hate to be the photographer for this gig."

"Me too," Quinn said. She bet it was awkward between Juliette and Cora. Both of them hadn't spoken since that day in the hospital when they'd made their deal and swapped babies.

She left the command center where her team was headquartered knowing Tillie had everything under control and went to find Adler. After their talk this morning, she was still ticked at Logan, but she'd pushed him to the back of her mind. He was in full-on corporate-jerk mode to her way of thinking. Knowing him, he wouldn't be at the wedding. In fact, she wouldn't be surprised if he had left Nantucket.

Her phone was quiet for once, which was a blessing, and she skimmed her social media feed as she walked to the elevator. She heard a familiar voice and glanced up to see Nick and Logan chatting with the other Bisset brothers. She took a moment, shaking her head. She would never have thought Logan could be civil to Nick. A lot had changed. But not enough.

She turned sharply into one of the staff hallways to avoid dealing with him.

Her heart hurt when she heard his voice, and she'd never been that good at hiding her feelings. In fact, the last time they'd broken up, she'd gone away for weeks to find herself again.

This shouldn't feel as intense as it did. It made her mad that she'd taken a chance on Logan and he'd been just...what? She really couldn't justify being mad at him for his actions. He'd never promised her anything. Never made it seem like he was hooking up with her to start a relationship.

It wasn't his fault that she'd fallen in love with him.

It was her own.

She should have known better than to think she could toy with Logan and not fall for him. But she hadn't. Also, he'd needed her. No matter what he might have said this morning, he'd needed her last night, and that had been the one thing that had driven her into his arms and lowered her guard.

Quinn took a deep breath. She wanted to believe she could be cool and that when she saw him again it wouldn't hurt. But love didn't work like that. And she was honest with herself, acknowledging she was always going to care for him no matter how he felt for her.

She had to figure out how to live with that. But not today. Today all she had to do was be Adler's friend and produce the best damned destination wedding episode that she could. And, honestly, she was happy to do that. Those things, in her wheelhouse, would give her something other than Logan to worry over.

She went back into the lobby; the men were gone, and she took the stairs up to the third floor where the suite Adler was using was located and knocked on the door.

Iris opened the door. Her friend was beaming. She'd been weathering the viral backlash from the news that she'd paid Zac to be her date this weekend and she and Zac had made up. As much as Quinn's own heart was aching, she was happy for Iris. Her friend deserved all the happiness she'd found when she'd fallen in love with Zac.

"About time you got here," Iris said. "Adler has something for us and she wouldn't let me have mine until you got here."

"Presents? I have something for her too, but it's downstairs."

"Same. Come on in. Are you any better? Adler told me what happened with Logan. I can't believe you..."

"Slept with him again, knowing he is love intolerant?"

Iris started laughing. "I wouldn't have put it that way, but yes."

"Me neither," Quinn said, looping her arm through Iris's as they made their way over to Adler.

"I'm so glad my besties are here," Adler said.

Quinn noticed that the room was empty except for the three of them. Adler was wearing a white robe embossed with her initials, as was Iris. The three of them went to sit on the love seat together.

"I got these for you...and okay, I got one for myself as well."

She handed them jewelry boxes. Quinn and Iris opened them and found Tiffany & Co. necklaces with the standard platinum heart charms. "I had no idea that I would be leaning on you two so hard this weekend. Thank you for having my back," Adler said.

Quinn turned the charm over and saw that it was engraved. *Sisters of the Heart.*

Logan stood at the back of the church watching Adler and Nick's wedding. It changed something inside him, making him reexamine the thoughts that had been stirring in his head all day and forcing him to face hard truths about himself. Forcing him to face how he felt about Quinn. He saw her working; she'd pretty much ignored him except for one heartbreaking moment when he'd walked into the church by himself and their eyes had met.

He'd wanted to go to her and had started to but she'd held her hand up and shaken her head before turning away. He'd seen the look on her face, known that she needed to work, and had left her to it. He hated to think that he was responsible for the dim light he'd seen in her eyes. But he knew he was.

His parents were seated in one of the front rows with Toby and his girlfriend. The Williamses were on the other side of the aisle. Cora Williams caught his eye, looking as if she wanted to talk to him, and Logan realized the woman was his biological mother. Looking at her, all he saw were the similarities between her and Nick. Was that why she'd given him up and kept Nick? Was it because Nick looked more like her? What a strange, irrational thing to think, but at the same time there it was.

But a few minutes after birth, would that have been obvious?

All the questions he had were swirling inside him again, but he glanced away and saw Quinn. Her back was to him. She wore a pretty, cream-colored dress that made her red hair and fair complexion even more eye-catching than normal. Just seeing her made him feel calmer. Better. He knew he loved her. He had been dancing around the thought since he'd woken alone in bed this morning. Hearing her in the bathroom, he'd thought about telling her. How happy he was to have her back in his life. Until the reality of his life had crashed around him.

He was trying to move forward. But how could he when the past was right there stinging him every chance it got?

Somehow, the ceremony was over, and he didn't remember any of it except Nick and Adler walking out of the church. Nick had looked at him and tipped his head toward Adler as if to say, *This is what matters.*

Logan hung back, not sure if he should find his brothers or his parents. He just didn't feel like he fit in anywhere.

Cora came over to him by herself. "Do you have a minute to chat with me?" she asked. She had a quieter personality than his mom—than Juliette. She had thick black hair and kind blue eyes. His eyes, he realized.

"Um, sure. What did you want to talk about?"

She swallowed and then said, "Well, I imagine you have some questions for me."

Did he? Of course, he did. But this woman was the wife of one of his fiercest business rivals. Could he let himself be vulnerable in front of her? He knew he had to if he wanted to move past the feelings that were swirling inside him. "Why did you give me up?"

"I didn't pick Nick over you," she said. "You were the baby closer to Juliette and it was easier for us to swap you. I was so overwhelmed by having twins...there was a moment when I thought about giving both of you to her."

He didn't know what to say to that. Fate had given him to his mom—and he now acknowledged that Juliette was his mother, even if she hadn't given birth to him. There had been no rejection from Cora or choice on Juliette's part. Just fate pushing him to the family he needed to be raised in. "Thank you for telling me that. I... I don't know how we will go forward. I mean I'm pretty sure Tad isn't too pleased to hear that I'm related to you."

"He was surprised about August being the father. I had told him about having twins and the swap I'd made in the hospital," she said. "He's always hated August because of the way August cut him out of Bisset Industries, so I knew mentioning that I'd had an affair with August would...well, not be something he wanted to hear. And, honestly, I hadn't thought we'd see him at the wedding at all. Adler's not close to him."

"It was just the perfect storm," Logan said.

"Exactly. If you want to get to know me, I'd love that. And if you don't, that's fine too," she said. "I'm so happy to have the chance to get to see you as a man. I've thought of you often and hoped you'd ended up in a happy home."

"I did. I had a very good upbringing."

Cora reached out and hugged him. It was awkward at first because he was standing so stiffly. But he returned the embrace and heard her sigh. He couldn't imagine what it had been like for her to live with the decision she'd made. "Thank you."

"You're welcome. It's the least I could do," Cora said.

The photographer was calling for the groom's parents and

Cora smiled at him as she turned away. He watched her go. His life would have been different if he'd been raised by her and Tad, but he didn't know that it would have been better.

He saw his mom watching him and realized he owed her an apology. He started toward her and she motioned that she'd come to him.

"Mom, I'm so sorry for what I said last night," he said the moment she got to him.

Juliette pulled him close for a hug. "It's okay. I deserved it."

"No," he said firmly. "You didn't. I was being a jerk. I was raised better than I behaved, and I can only blame it…actually I have no excuse."

"You're a Bisset, Logan. No matter what, you react strongly to everything. Emotions are hard for you and I get that. You remind me a lot of your father," she said. "You always have. You're stubborn and brash."

"I am," Logan admitted. "Why have you stayed with him all these years?"

"Because he is always trying to be a better man. He loves me and I love him, and it's not easy, but each of these things we've lived through has brought us closer," she said.

"Mom, I could use your advice. I hurt Quinn and I need to win her back," he said. "Will you help me?"

"Yes, son," she said.

CHAPTER SIXTEEN

HIS BROTHERS DRIFTED over to them in the back of the church. Zac was at the front with the bridal party, but Leo and Dare were with him. Mari had gone outside to take a call from Inigo. And his dad was nowhere to be seen.

"You know it's not that your father and I ignore the mistakes, we just try to find a way to use them to make us stronger as a couple. I hope you boys know that," his mother said.

"I don't necessarily understand it, but it seems to work for you two," Logan said.

"It does," Dare added, and Leo nodded.

"What works?" August said as he came up behind them. "Did you two have your talk, Logan?"

"Yes, sir. I already apologized to Mom for my behavior last night, but I owe you one as well," he said as he turned to face his father.

His dad clapped him on the shoulder. "Apology accepted. I would have said something similar in your shoes. I am sorry that my past actions have caused so much strife for you lately. I hope you know that I have never regretted being your father. No matter the circumstances of your birth, I've always loved you."

"I know, Dad," he said. "I love you and Mom too."

"Damned straight. You got the best parents," he said.

"I wouldn't go that far," Dare said. "You do have exacting standards."

"Which has served you well in your political career," August said. "As a matter of fact, I have a lobbyist I want you to talk to. Got a minute?"

"Sure," Dare said.

"I'm going to check on Adler. I feel so bad that her mother's not here to share this special moment, and that my actions caused her extra stress," his mom said. "It was a beautiful ceremony though."

"It was," Logan agreed as his mom walked away.

"There's Danni," Leo said.

Logan saw the woman Leo had been unsuccessfully trying to woo all weekend. "Go and see if you can work your magic today."

"I pretty much have no game with her, Logan. I'm not sure why."

"Because you're not the player you think you are. Stop trying to front, and be yourself," he said.

"Myself?"

"Yeah. It will work a lot better than whatever you've been doing," he said.

Leo nodded and then walked away. Logan realized how lucky he was to be a part of his family. He had thought that learning about his true biological mother had changed him but, fundamentally, it hadn't. He was still the man he'd always been. But he could be better. He'd been working toward being a better man from the moment he'd seen Quinn again.

At the bonfire.

When he'd realized that he wanted her. He'd sold it to himself as a distraction because that had been easier to handle at that moment, but he knew it had never been that. One look and he'd started to fall for her again.

He'd regretted losing her, and she'd be the first to point out that was because he couldn't stand not winning, but the truth was, he hadn't meant to hurt her or to let her leave once much less twice.

He'd always believed he was stronger on his own, but his parents had proven that wasn't the case. Even Nick had said he thought having Adler by his side had given him an edge in business.

Quinn could do that for him. She was already showing him that he could have a life away from work. That there were other parts of his life that he couldn't keep ignoring. Watching Adler and Nick pose together and seeing Quinn off to the side watching them, Logan knew what he had to do.

He walked over to her. She shook her head, but he came closer. "I need to talk to you. Can you take a break for a few minutes?"

"Please don't do this right now. I'm trying to work," she said.

"I can wait. Just tell me when."

"When?" she asked. "How about never?"

"That won't do," he said.

She grabbed his wrist and turned, pulling him to the back of the church and out the door. They faced off in the deserted parking lot; the guests had gone on to the reception and the bridal party and family were inside.

"What are you doing?" she asked. "I'm not ready to be chill and just say yeah, everything's cool. And you seem like you just want some closure so you can move on. I can't do that. Not today."

He shook his head. "I know that. I was a jerk earlier and I have no excuse except that I didn't know how to tell you that I'm falling in love with you. That I wanted you to stay with me and I knew I had no right to ask. Everything felt like it was shifting, that my world was turning into something new."

She put her hand on his jaw. "Oh, Logan. I know that. I get that you're not yourself right now. But I expected you to treat me with respect. I can't be with a man who doesn't understand that."

Logan nodded. He'd hurt her in a way she wasn't going to

just forgive, and he didn't blame her. He was going to have to show her he'd changed and that was going to take more time than he had this afternoon.

"I'm sorry, Ace. I wish I'd never said those things, but you know the man I am. I can't even promise that I'd never behave that way again. But I will tell you that I will keep trying to change and to show you how much you mean to me."

She shook her head. "Don't. Don't make rash statements like that."

"Why?"

"I might believe them and I'm not sure that I should. In fact, I know I shouldn't because you're not the kind of man who is capable of that kind of gesture."

Logan was saying all the right things and Quinn wanted to believe him. She loved him, so that made her see him in the way her heart wanted her to. But her mind wasn't having it. Just this morning he'd turned from the sexy lover of the night before into a man who'd cut her to ribbons. She didn't want to be the kind of woman who ended up in a relationship like that. As much as it hurt to say no, she knew she had to. Because if he hurt her again, she wouldn't be able to forgive him or herself.

"Fair enough," he said. "I don't really deserve a second chance from you, but would you consider giving me some time to prove I'm not the man you think I am? That I have changed for the better?"

"How would you do that? I live in California and Bisset Industries is here on the East Coast. I think it's best if we both just walk away. Take this as a little P.S. from our affair in college and leave it there."

He watched her with an inscrutable expression on his face. His jaw clenched and his hands moved restlessly at his sides, as if he wanted to touch her but didn't trust himself.

"I can't do that. I'm my best self when I'm with you. And this morning was a lifetime ago. I had to come to terms with all of the changes in my life, and I'm not going to lie and tell you that I'm one hundred percent there yet. But losing you, watching you walk out, woke me. Showed me that I don't want a life without you, Quinn. I know it's asking a lot of you, and I don't expect to change your mind. But I have to try. I've never felt this way about anyone before. I love you."

She shook her head. "That's not fair. You can't say that. Not now. I told you—"

"That you'll believe me? I hope you do. Because I'm not a man to lie to anyone. You know that about me. I'm not saying this because I think it will make you come back, I'm saying it because it's true. Whether you let me back into your life or not, my feelings for you won't change. Love doesn't work that way. And it took losing you for me to understand that."

She was struggling to keep her guard up, to keep the walls in place. But this was Logan. He had never been the kind of man to not speak his truth. He'd never been someone to use falsehoods to woo her. He'd been honest from the beginning.

"I want to believe you."

"That's a start," he said. "Will you take a chance on me? Let me prove to you that this morning was just me reacting badly to events I couldn't control."

Torn, she could just stare at him.

His expression changed and he sighed. "I don't blame you if you say no."

Say no.

Could she live with herself if she did? She'd always regret it if she didn't give him a chance. She wanted a chance too. With Logan. The man she loved.

He took her hand in his. "Please."

She stared into his bright blue eyes, not sure she'd heard him right.

"I'm begging you to give me another chance," he said. "I don't want to live the rest of my life knowing that I let you get away—twice."

"Is this because you feel like, if I do, you won't win?" she asked. She had to ask. He hated losing so much, he'd undercut Nick to prove that he wasn't giving in to a Williams.

"No. It's not because I want to put a tick mark in the win column. I need you with me because I love you. You make life fun and exciting. You make me engage in things when I'd rather just sit and sulk. My life is so much better with you in it. I love you."

"I love you too," she admitted.

Her assistant came out, followed by the rest of the bridal party, and Logan moved so that he was standing between her and them. "I know you have to work but I can't leave it like that. Will you give me a second chance? Can we be a couple?"

"Yes," she said.

He pulled her into his arms and kissed her long and deep. There was the sound of applause, but she could only hear Logan whispering in her ear how much he loved her and how lucky he was to have her by his side.

She went back to work, finishing up filming a few more church shots, and Logan just waited for her. She knew that his life wasn't always going to enable him to wait on her while she was working, but she appreciated that he had.

They went to the reception hand in hand. He stopped before they walked inside.

"I don't know if I can always be perfect," he said.

"I know you can't be, Logan. That's part of what I love about you. As long as we're partners and you're not trying to compete with me, we can make this work."

"We can. I want that more than anything," he said. "I love you, Ace."

"I love you too," she said.

Adler came out of the hall by herself, tears streaming down her face.

"What's the matter?"

"Auggie and Tad are fighting. Nick punched Auggie in the eye."

Logan ran into the rehearsal hall and Quinn and Adler followed. The two older men were having a standoff and Nick was between them. Logan raced to their sides, standing by Nick. He looked over at Quinn and Adler and then nodded.

"You two are going to have to figure out a way to get along. Nick and I are twins, Dad. You're now related to each other by Adler's marriage. The rivalry has to end or you are going to both lose everything."

* * * * *

A Life-Saving Reunion

Alison Roberts

Books by Alison Roberts

Harlequin Medical

Christmas Eve Magic
Their First Family Christmas

Wildfire Island Docs
The Nurse Who Stole His Heart
The Fling That Changed Everything

A Little Christmas Magic
Always the Midwife
Daredevil, Doctor…Husband?

Harlequin Romance

The Wedding Planner and the CEO
The Baby Who Saved Christmas
The Forbidden Prince

Visit the Author Profile page
at millsandboon.com.au for
more titles.

Dear Reader,

How far back can you remember?

My earliest memory is of a pair of red shoes that I had when I was three years old. (I still love red shoes!) And my love of big ships came from traveling from New Zealand to England when I was five years old. It took six weeks and I loved every minute of it.

I lived in London for eighteen months. My dad, who was a doctor, had a job at Hammersmith Hospital and we lived in a basement apartment on Prince Albert Road—so close to the zoo that we could hear the animals at night sometimes. I started school there and a favorite place to play was on Primrose Hill.

Setting a story in a place that was such an important part of my early life is such a treat and I even got to play in Regent's Park and on Primrose Hill again. :)

Working with my talented colleagues at Harlequin Medical is also a treat and the threads in this series are very strong and so emotional that it was, at times, a heart-wrenching story to write.

What a privilege to bring those threads together and not only complete a story that gives two people the chance of a love that will last for the rest of their lives, but also celebrate the finale of all the other stories and the resolution of the conflict that runs through the Paddington Children's Hospital series.

Happy reading!

With love,

Alison

**Praise for
Alison Roberts**

"The author gave me wonderful enjoyable moments of conflict and truth-revealing moments of joy and sorrow… I highly recommend this book for all lovers of romance with medical drama as a backdrop and second-chance love."
—*Contemporary Romance Reviews* on
NYC Angels: An Explosive Reunion

"This is a deeply emotional book, dealing with difficult life and death issues and situations in the medical community. But it is also a powerful story of love, forgiveness and learning to be intimate… There's a lot packed into this novella. I'm impressed."

—*Goodreads* on
200 Harley Street: The Proud Italian

CHAPTER ONE

He'd known this wasn't going to be easy.

He'd known that some cases were going to be a lot harder than others.

But Dr Thomas Wolfe had also known that, after the very necessary break, he had been ready to go back to the specialty that had always been his first love.

Paediatric cardiology.

Mending broken little hearts...

And some not so little, of course. Paddington Children's Hospital cared for an age range from neonates to eighteen-year-olds. After dealing only with adults for some years now, Thomas was probably more comfortable interacting with the adolescents under his care here but he'd more than rediscovered his fascination with babies in the last few months. And the joy of the children who were old enough to understand how sick they were, brave kids who could teach a lot of people things about dealing with life.

Or kids that touched your heart and made doing the best job you possibly could even more of a priority. It had to be carefully controlled, mind you. If you let yourself get too close, it could not only affect your judgement, but it could also end up threatening to destroy you.

And Thomas Wolfe wasn't about to let that happen again.

He had to pause for a moment, standing in the central corridor of Paddington's cardiology ward, right beside the huge, colourful cut-outs of Pooh Bear and friends that decorated this stretch of wall between the windows of the patients' rooms. Tigger seemed to be grinning down at him—mid-bounce—as Thomas pretended to read a new message on his pager.

This had become the hardest case since he'd returned to Paddington's. A little girl who made it almost impossible to keep a safe distance. Six-year-old Penelope Craig didn't just touch the hearts of people who came to know her. She grabbed it with both hands and squeezed so hard it was painful.

It wasn't that he needed a moment to remind himself how important it was to keep that distance, because he had been honing those skills from the moment he'd stepped back through the doors of this astonishing, old hospital and they were already ingrained enough to be automatic. He just needed to make sure the guardrails were completely intact because if there was a weak area, Penny would be the one to find it and push through.

And that couldn't be allowed to happen.

With a nod, as if he'd read an important message on his pager, Thomas lifted his head and began moving towards the nearest door. There was no hesitation as he tapped to announce his arrival and then entered the room with a smile.

His smile faltered for a split second as Julia Craig, Penny's mother, caught his gaze with the unspoken question that was always there now.

Is today the day?

His response was as silent as the query.

No. Today's not the day.

The communication was already well practised enough to be no slower than the blink of an eye. Penny certainly hadn't noticed.

'Look, Dr Wolfe! I can dance.'

The fact that Penny was out of her bed meant that today was

one of her better ones. She still had her nasal cannula stuck in place with a piece of sticky tape on each cheek, the long plastic tube snaking behind her to where it connected with the main oxygen supply, but she was on her feet.

No, she was actually standing on her tippy-toes, her arms drooping gracefully over the frill of her bright pink tutu skirt. And then she tried to turn in a circle but the tubing got in the way and she lost her balance and sat down with a suddenness that might have upset many children.

Penny just laughed.

'Oops.' Julia scooped her daughter into her arms as the laughter turned to gasping.

'I can...' Penny took another gulp of air. 'I *can*...do it. Watch!'

'Next time.' Julia lifted Penny onto her bed. 'Dr Wolfe is here to see you and he's very busy. He's got lots of children to look after today.'

'But only one who can dance.' Thomas smiled. 'Just like a Ballerina Bear.'

Penny's smile could light up a room. Big grey eyes turned their attention to the television on the wall, where her favourite DVD was playing and a troupe of fluffy bears wearing tutus were performing what seemed to be a cartoon version of *Swan Lake*.

'I just want to listen to your heart, if that's okay.' Thomas unhooked his stethoscope from around his neck.

Penny nodded but didn't turn away from the screen. She lifted her arms above her head and curled her finger as she tried to mimic the movements of the dancing bears.

Thomas noted the bluish tinge to his small patient's lips. Putting the disc of his stethoscope against a chest scarred by more than one major surgery, he listened to a heart that was trying its best to pump enough blood around a small body but failing a little more each day.

The new medication regime was helping but it wasn't enough. Penny had been put on the waiting list for a heart transplant weeks ago and the job of Thomas and his team was to keep her healthy for long enough that the gift of a long life might be possible. It was a balancing act of drugs to help her heart pump more effectively and control the things that made it harder, like the build-up of fluid in her tissues and lungs. Limiting physical activity was unfortunately a necessity now, as well, and to move further than this room required that Penny was confined to a wheelchair.

The odds of a heart that was a good match becoming available in time weren't great but, as heartbreaking as that was, it wasn't why this particular case was proving so much more difficult than other patients he had on the waiting list for transplants.

Penny was a direct link to his past.

The past he'd had to walk away from in order to survive.

He'd met Penny more than six years ago. Before she was even born, in fact—when ultrasound tests had revealed that the baby's heart had one of the most serious congenital defects it could have, with the main pumping chamber too small to be effective. She'd had her first surgery when she was only a couple of weeks old and he'd been the doctor looking after her both before and after that surgery.

He'd spent a lot of time with Penny's parents, Julia and Peter Craig, and he'd felt their anguish as acutely as if it had been his own.

That was what becoming a parent yourself could do to you...

Gwen had only been a couple of years older than Penny so she would have been eight now. Would she have fallen in love with the Ballerina Bears, too? Be going to ballet lessons, perhaps, and wearing a pink tutu on top of any other clothing, including her pyjamas?

The thought was no more than a faint, mental jab. Thomas had known that working with children again might stir up the contents of that locked vault in his head and his heart but he knew how to deal with it.

He knew to step away from the danger zone.

He stepped away from the bed, too. 'It's a lovely day, today,' he said, looping the stethoscope around his neck again. 'Maybe Mummy can take you outside into the sunshine for a bit.'

A nurse came into the room as he spoke and he glanced at the kidney dish in one hand and a glass of juice in the other. 'After you've had all your pills.'

'Are you in a rush?' Julia was on her feet, as well. 'Have you got a minute?' She glanced at her daughter, who was still entranced by the dancing bears on the screen. 'I'll be back in a minute, Penny. Be a good girl and swallow all those pills for Rosie, okay?'

''kay.' Penny nodded absently.

'Of course she will,' Rosie said. 'And then I want to know all the names of those bears, again. Who's the one with the sparkly blue fur?'

'Sapphire,' Thomas could hear Penny saying as he held the door open for Julia. If she had concerns about her daughter's condition, they needed to go somewhere else to discuss it. 'She's my favourite. And the green one's Emerald and...the red one's Ruby...'

The relatives' room a little further down the corridor was empty. Thomas closed the door behind them and gestured for Julia to take one of the comfortable chairs available.

'Are you sure you've got time?'

'Of course.'

'I just... I just wanted to ask you more about what you said yesterday. I tried to explain to Peter last night but I think I made it sound a lot worse than...than you did...' Julia was fighting tears now.

Thomas nudged the box of tissues on the coffee table closer and Julia gratefully pulled several out.

'You mean the ventricular assist device?'

Julia nodded, the wad of tissues pressed to her face.

'You said…you said it would be the next step, when…*if*… things got worse.'

Thomas kept his tone gentle. 'They sound scary, I know, but it's something that's often used as a bridge to transplant. For when heart failure is resistant to medical therapy, the way Penny's is becoming.'

'And you said it might make her a lot better in the meantime?'

'It can improve circulation and can reverse some of the other organ damage that heart failure can cause.'

'But it's risky, isn't it? It's major surgery…'

'I wouldn't suggest it if the risks of going on as we are were less than the risks of the surgery. I know Penny's having a better day today but you already know how quickly that can change and it gets a little more difficult to control every time.'

Julia blew her nose. 'I know. That last time she had to go to intensive care, we thought…we thought we were going to lose her…'

'I know.' Thomas needed to take in a slow breath. To step away mentally and get back onto safe ground. Professional ground.

'A VAD could make Penny more mobile again and improve her overall condition so that when a transplant becomes available, the chances of it being successful are that much higher. It's a longer term solution to control heart failure and they can last for years, but yes, it is a major procedure. The device is attached to the heart and basically takes over the work of the left ventricle by bypassing it. Let's make a time for me to sit down with both you and Peter and I can talk you through it properly.'

Julia had stopped crying. Her eyes were wide.

'What do you mean by "more mobile"? Would we be able to take her home again while we wait?'

'I would hope so.' Thomas nodded. 'She would be able to go back to doing all the things she would normally do at home. Maybe more, even.'

Julia had her fingers pressed against her lips. Her voice was no more than a whisper. 'Like…like dancing lessons, maybe?'

Oh…he had to look away from that hope shining through the new tears in Julia's eyes. The wall of the relatives' room was a much safer place.

'I'll tell Peter when he comes in after work. How soon can we make an appointment to talk about it?'

'Talk to Maria on the ward reception desk. She seems to know my diary as well as I do.' He got to his feet, still not risking a direct glance at Julia's face.

From the corner of his eye, he could see Julia turn her head. Was she wondering what had caught his attention?

He was being rude. He turned back to his patient's mother but now Julia was staring at the wall.

'My life seems to be full of teddy bears,' she said.

Thomas blinked at the random comment. 'Oh? You mean the dancing kind?'

'And here, look. This is about the Teddy Bears' Picnic in Regent's Park. Well, Primrose Hill, actually. For transplant families.'

The poster had only been a blur of colour on the wall but now Thomas let his gaze focus.

And then he wished he hadn't.

Right in the middle of a bright collage of photos was one of a surgeon, wearing green theatre scrubs, with a small child in her arms. The toddler was wearing only a nappy so the scar down the centre of her chest advertised her major cardiac surgery. The angelic little girl, with her big, blue eyes and mop of golden curls, was beaming up at her doctor and the answering smile spoke of both the satisfaction of saving a small life and a deep affection for her young patient.

'That's Dr Scott,' Julia said. 'Rebecca. But you know that, of course.'

Of course he did.

'She did the surgery on Penny when she was a baby—but you know that too. How silly of me. You were her doctor back then, too.' Julia made an apologetic face. 'So much has happened since then, it becomes a bit of a blur, sometimes.'

'Yes.' Thomas was still staring at Rebecca's face. Those amazing dark, chocolate-coloured eyes which had been what had caught his attention first, all those years ago, when he'd spotted her in one of his classes at medical school. The gleaming, straight black hair that was wound up into a knot on the back of her head, the way it always was when she was at work.

That smile...

He hadn't seen her look that happy since...well, since before their daughter had died.

She certainly hadn't shown him even a hint of a smile like that in the months since he'd returned to Paddington's.

Had Julia not realised they had been husband and wife at the time they'd shared Penny's care in the weeks after her birth?

Well, why would she? They had kept their own names to avoid any confusion at work and they'd always been completely professional during work hours. Friendly professional, though—nothing like the strained relationship between them now. And Julia and Peter had had far more on their minds than how close a couple of people were amongst the team of medics trying to save their tiny daughter.

'She was just a surgeon, back then.'

Thomas had to bite back a contradiction. Rebecca had never been 'just' a surgeon. She'd been talented and brilliant and well on the way to a stellar career from the moment she'd graduated from medical school.

'Isn't it amazing that she's gone on to specialise in transplants?'

'Mmm.' Sometimes the traumatic events that happened in life could push you in a new direction but Thomas couldn't say that out loud, either. If Julia didn't know about the personal history that might have prompted the years of extra study to add a new field of expertise to Rebecca's qualifications, he was the last person who would enlighten her.

Sharing something like that was an absolute no-no when you were keeping a professional distance from patients and their families. And from your ex-wife.

'It's amazing for us, anyway,' Julia continued. 'Because it means that she'll be able to do Penny's transplant if we're lucky enough to find a new heart for her...' Her voice wobbled. 'It might be us going to one of these picnics next year. I've heard of them. Did you see the programme on telly a while back, when they had all those people talking about how terrible it would be if Paddington's got closed?'

'I don't think I did.' The media coverage over the threatened closure had become so intense it had been hard to keep up with it all, especially since Sheikh Al Khalil had announced last month that he would be donating a substantial sum of money following his daughter's surgery.

'Well, they had a clip from last year's picnic. They were talking to a mother who had lost her child through some awful accident and she had made his organs available for transplant. She said she'd never been brave enough to try and make contact with the families of the children who had received them, but she came to the picnic and imagined that someone there might be one of them. She watched them running their races and playing games and saw how happy they were. And how happy their families were...'

Julia had to stop because she was crying again, even though she was smiling. Thomas was more than relieved. He couldn't have listened any longer. He was being dragged into a place he never went these days if he could help it.

'I really must get on with my rounds,' he said.

'Of course. I'm so sorry...' Julia had another handful of tissues pressed to her nose as he opened the door of the relatives' room so she could step out before him.

'It's not a problem,' Thomas assured her. 'I'm always here to talk to you. And Peter, of course. Let's set up that appointment to talk about the ventricular assist device very soon.'

Julia nodded, but her face crumpled again as her thoughts clearly returned to something a lot less happy than the thought of attending a picnic to celebrate the lives that had been so dramatically improved by the gift of organ donation. The urge to put a hand on her shoulder to comfort her and offer reassurance was so strong, he had to curl his fingers into a fist to stop his hand moving.

'Um...' Thomas cleared his throat. 'Would you like me to find someone to sit with you for a bit?'

Julia shook her head. 'I'll be fine. You go. I'll just get myself together a bit more before I go back to Penny. I don't want her to see that I've been crying.'

Even a view of only the woman's back was enough to advertise her distress, but it was the body language of the man standing so rigidly beside her that caught Dr Rebecca Scott's attention instantly as she stepped out of the elevator to head towards the cardiology ward at the far end of the corridor.

A sigh escaped her lips and her steps slowed a little as she fought the impulse to spin around and push the button to open the lift doors again. To go somewhere else. It wasn't really an option. She had a patient in the cardiology ward who was on the theatre list for tomorrow morning and she knew that the parents were in need of a lot of reassurance. This small window of time in her busy day was the only slot available so she would just have to lift her chin and deal with having her path cross with that of her ex-husband.

How sad was it that she'd known it was Thomas simply because of the sense of disconnection with the person he was talking to?

He might have returned to work at Paddington's but the Thomas Wolfe that Rebecca had known and loved hadn't come back.

Oh, he still looked the same. Still lean and fit and so tall that the top of her head would only reach his shoulder. He still had those eyes that had fascinated her right from the start because they could change colour depending on his mood. Blue when he was happy and grey when he was angry or worried or sad.

They had been the colour of a slate roof on a rainy day that first time they had seen each other again after so long and she hadn't noticed any difference since. He was as aloof with her as he was with his patients and their families.

She'd known it wasn't going to be easy. She'd known that some cases were going to be a lot harder than others but, when she'd heard that he'd agreed to come back and work at Paddington's, Rebecca had believed that she could cope. She'd wondered if they could, in fact, put some of the past behind them and salvage some kind of friendship, even.

That hope had been extinguished the first time their paths had crossed when nothing had been said. When there had been no more warmth in his gaze than if she'd been any other colleague he'd previously worked with.

Less warmth, probably.

The old Thomas had never been like that. He'd had an easy grin that was an invitation for colleagues to stop and chat for a moment or two. He would joke and play with the children in his care and he'd always had a knack for connecting with parents—especially after he'd become a father himself. They loved him because he could make them feel as if they had the best person possible fighting in their corner. Someone who understood exactly how hard it was and would care for their child as if it were his own.

This version of Thomas might have the same—or likely an improved—ability to deliver the best medical care but he was a shell of the man he had once been.

Part of Rebecca's heart was breaking for a man who'd taught himself to disconnect so effectively from the people around him but, right now, an even bigger part was angry. Maybe it had been building with every encounter they'd had over the last few months when they had discussed the care of their patients with a professional respect that bordered on coldness.

Calling each other 'Thomas' and 'Rebecca' with never a single slip into the 'Tom' and 'Becca' they had always been to each other. Discussing test results and medications and surgery as if nobody involved had a personal life or people that loved them enough to be terrified.

It was bad enough that he'd destroyed their marriage by withdrawing into this cold, hard shell but she could deal with that. She'd had years of practice, after all. To see the effect it was having on others made it far less acceptable. This was Penny's mother he'd been talking to, for heaven's sake. They'd both known Julia since she'd been pregnant with her first—and only—child. They'd both been there for her a thousand per cent over the first weeks and months of her daughter's life. He'd been the old Thomas, then.

And then he'd walked out. He hadn't been there for the next lot of surgery Penny had had. He hadn't shared the joy of appointments over the next few years that had demonstrated how well the little girl had been and how happy and hopeful her family was. He hadn't been there to witness the fear returning as her condition had deteriorated again but now he was back on centre stage and he was acting as if Penelope Craig was just another patient. As if he had no personal connection at all…

How could he be walking away from Julia like that, when she was so upset she had buried her face in a handful of tissues, ducking back into the relatives' room for some privacy?

Rebecca's forward movement came to a halt as Thomas came closer. She knew she was glaring at him but, for once, she wasn't going to hide anything personal behind a calm, professional mask.

'What's going on?' she asked, her tone rather more crisp than she had expected. 'Why is Julia so upset?'

Thomas shifted his gaze, obviously checking that nobody was within earshot. A group of both staff and visitors were waiting for an elevator. Kitchen staff went past, pushing a huge stainless steel trolley. An orderly pushing a bed came towards them, heading for the service lift, presumably taking the small patient for an X-ray or scan. The bed had balloons tied to the end, one of them a bright yellow smiley face. A nurse walked beside the bed, chatting to the patient's mother. She saw Rebecca and smiled. Then her gaze shifted to Thomas and the smile faded a little.

He didn't seem to notice. He tilted his head towards the group of comfortable chairs near the windows that were, remarkably, free of anyone needing a break or waiting to meet someone. Far enough away from the elevator doors to allow for a private conversation.

Fair enough. It would be unprofessional to discuss details of a case where it could be overheard. Rebecca followed his lead but didn't sit down on one of the chairs. Neither did Thomas.

'I was going to send you a memo,' he said. 'I'm meeting both Julia and Peter in the next day or two to discuss the option of Penelope receiving a ventricular assist device. It's only a matter of time before her heart failure becomes unmanageable.'

'Okay...' Rebecca caught her bottom lip between her teeth. No wonder Julia had been upset. A VAD was a major intervention. But she trusted Thomas's judgement and it would definitely buy them some time.

His gaze touched hers for just a heartbeat as he finished speaking but Rebecca found herself staring at his face, waiting for him to look at her again. Surely he could understand the effect of what he'd told Julia? How could he have walked away from her like that and left her alone?

But Thomas seemed to be scanning the view of central London that these big, multi-paned old windows provided. He could probably see the busy main roads with their red, double-decker buses and crowds of people waiting at intersections or trying to hail a black cab. Or maybe his eye had been drawn to the glimpse of greenery in the near distance from the treetops of Regent's Park.

'You've had experience with VADs? Are you happy to do the surgery?'

'Yes, of course. It's not a procedure that happens very often but I've been involved with a couple. Do you want me to come to the meeting with Penny's family and discuss it with them?'

'Let's wait until it's absolutely necessary. I can tell them what's involved and why it's a good option.'

Rebecca let her gaze shift to the windows, as well. She stepped closer, in fact, and looked down. The protesters were still in place, with their placards, outside the gates. They'd been there for months now, ever since the threat of closure had been made public. It hadn't just been the staff who had been so horrified that the land value of this prime central London spot was so high that the board of governors was actually considering selling up and merging Paddington Children's Hospital with another hospital, Riverside, that was outside the city limits.

Thanks to the incredible donation a month or so ago from Sheikh Idris Al Khalil, who'd brought his daughter to Paddington's for treatment, the threat of closure was rapidly retreating. The astonishing amount of money in appreciation of such a successful result for one child had sparked off an influx of new donations and the press were onside with every member of staff, every patient and every family who were so determined that they would stay here. Even so, the protesters were not going to let the momentum of their campaign slow down until success was confirmed. The slogans on their placards were as familiar as the street names around here now.

Save Our Hospital
Kids' Health Not Wealth

The knowledge that that announcement couldn't be far off gave Rebecca a jolt of pleasure. Things were looking up. For Paddington's and maybe for Penny, too.

'It is a good option.' She nodded. 'I'd love to see her out of that wheelchair for a while.'

'It would put her at the top of the waiting list for a new heart, too. Hopefully a donor heart will become available well before we run into any complications.'

The wave of feeling positive ebbed, leaving Rebecca feeling a kind of chill run down her spine. Her muscles tensed in response. Her head told her that she should murmur agreement and then excuse herself to go and see her patient, maybe adding a polite request to be kept informed of any developments.

Her heart was sending a very different message. An almost desperate cry asking where the hell had the man gone that Thomas used to be? Was there even a fragment of him left inside that shell?

'Yes,' she heard herself saying, her voice weirdly low and fierce. 'Let's keep our fingers crossed that some kid somewhere, who's about the same age as Penny, has a terrible accident and their parents actually agree to have him—or *her*—used for spare parts.'

She could feel the shock wave coming from Thomas. She was shocked herself.

It was a pretty unprofessional thing for a transplant surgeon to say but this had come from a very personal place. A place that only a parent who had had to make that heartbreaking decision themselves could understand.

She was also breaking the unspoken rule that nothing personal existed between herself and Thomas any more. And she wasn't doing it by a casually friendly comment like 'How are you?' or 'Did you have a good weekend?' No. She was lobbing a verbal grenade into the bunker that contained their most private and painful history.

In public. During working hours.

What *was* she thinking? Being angry at the distance Thomas was keeping himself from his patients and their parents was no excuse. Especially when she knew perfectly well why he had become like that. Or was that the real issue here? That she had known and tried so hard to help and had failed so completely?

'Sorry,' she muttered. 'But, for me, it's never an anonymous donor organ that becomes available. I have to go and collect them so I get involved in both sides of the story.'

Thomas's voice was like ice. He really didn't want to be talking about this.

'You *choose* to do it,' he said.

He didn't even look at her as he fired the accusation. He was staring out of the damned window again. Rebecca found that her anger hadn't been erased by feeling ashamed of her outburst.

'And you choose to shut your eyes.' The words came out in a whisper that was almost a hiss. 'To run away. Like you always did.'

There was no point in saying anything else. Maybe there was nothing more to say, anyway.

So Rebecca turned and walked away.

CHAPTER TWO

'THE LINE HAS been crossed.'

'Oh?' Thomas had opened the file he needed on his laptop. He clicked on options to bring his PowerPoint presentation up and sync it to the wall screen he had lowered over the white-board in this small meeting room. 'What line is that, Rosie?'

He certainly knew what line had been crossed as far as he was concerned. It had been a week since Rebecca's astonishing outburst and he still hadn't recovered from the shock of how incredibly unprofessional she had been.

What if someone had overheard? Members of the press were still all over any story coming out of Paddington's. Imagine a headline that revealed that the leading transplant surgeon of Paddington Children's Hospital described her donor organs as 'spare parts'?

Anyone else could well have taken the matter elsewhere. Filed a formal complaint, even. And was Rosie now referring to it? Had it somehow made its way onto the hospital grapevine?

No. Her expression was far too happy to suggest a staff scandal. He tuned back in to what she was saying.

'...and now that the bottom line's been crossed, thanks to the flood of donations, the government's stepping in to make up any shortfall. It only needs the signature of the Minister of

Health and Paddington's will be officially safe. There won't be any merger.'

'That's good news.' Thomas reached for the laser pointer in its holder on the frame of the whiteboard. '*Very* good news,' he added, catching sight of Rosie's disappointment in his lack of enthusiasm.

'Mmm.' Rosie looked unconvinced. 'Apparently there's going to be a huge party organised in the near future as soon as everything's finally signed and sealed but some of the staff are planning to get together at the Frog and Peach over the road on Friday to celebrate early. Guess we'll see you there?'

She was smiling but didn't wait for a response. Other people were arriving for the meeting now and there were bound to be far more acceptable reactions from anyone who hadn't heard the big news of the day. One of the physiotherapists, perhaps. Or Louise, who was the head dietician for Paddington's. One of the staff psychologists had just come in, too, and Thomas nodded a greeting to the head of the cardiac intensive care unit, who came through the door immediately after her.

Everybody in the team who had—or would be—directly involved in Penelope Craig's case had been invited to this meeting, including Rosie as one of the nurses that had provided so much of her care over the many admissions the little girl had had. One of the only people missing as the clock clicked onto the start time of eleven a.m. was her surgeon.

Rebecca Scott.

He hadn't seen her all week, come to think of it. Not that he'd wanted their paths to cross. The shock of their last interaction hadn't been only due to her lack of professionalism. Or that she had so unexpectedly crossed the boundaries of what their new relationship allowed.

No. Thomas had not been able to shake the echo of that vehement parting shot. That he chose to shut his eyes. To run away. And that he had always made that choice.

Did she really think he was such a coward?

He *wasn't* a coward. Had Rebecca had no understanding of how much strength it had taken to deal with what they had gone through? How hard it had been to keep putting one foot in front of the other and keep going?

Obviously not.

No wonder their marriage had fallen apart so easily.

No wonder he had been left feeling such a failure. As a husband *and* as a father.

But to drag it out again and hurl it in his face like that…

It had been uncalled for. Unhelpful. Insulting, even.

And so, yes, he was angry.

'Sorry we're late…' The door opened as Rebecca rushed in to take a seat at the oval table, followed by her senior registrar.

Thomas could feel himself glaring at the late arrivals.

Rebecca was glaring right back at him. 'We got held up in Recovery after our last case. I couldn't leave until I was sure my patient was stable.'

'Of course you couldn't,' someone said. 'We wouldn't expect you to.'

Thomas looked away first. Just in time to notice the raised eyebrows and shared glances that went round the table like a Mexican wave.

'No problem,' he said evenly. 'But let's get started, shall we? We're *all* busy people.'

The tension in the room behind him felt like an additional solid presence as he faced the screen and clicked the pointer to bring up his first slide.

'As you know, we're here to discuss a case we're all involved with—that of Penelope Craig, who's currently an inpatient in our cardiology ward. For those of you who haven't been so directly involved in the last few years, though, here's a quick case history.'

The slide was a list of bullet points. A summary of a clinical case reduced to succinct groups of words that made one crisis after another no more than markers on a timeline.

'The diagnosis of hypoplastic left heart syndrome was made prenatally so Penelope was delivered by C-section and admitted directly to the cardiac intensive care unit. She underwent her first surgery—a Norwood procedure—at thirteen days old.'

He had been in the gallery to watch that surgery. Rebecca had been a cardiothoracic surgical registrar at the time and it had been the most challenging case she'd assisted with. She'd sat up half the previous night as she'd gone over and over the steps of the surgery and Thomas had stayed up with her, trying to make up for any lack of confidence she was feeling. Even as he paused only long enough to take a breath, the flash of another memory came up like a crystal-clear video clip.

He had been in the front row of the gallery, leaning forward as he looked down at the tiny figure on the operating table and the group of gowned and masked people towering over it. Over the loudspeaker, he had heard the consultant surgeon hand over the responsibility of closing the tiny chest to Rebecca. As they changed positions, she had glanced up for a split second and caught Thomas's gaze through the glass window—as if to reassure herself that he was still there. That he was still with her with every step she took. And he had smiled and nodded, giving her the silent message that he believed in her. That she could do this and do it well.

That he was proud of her...

His voice sounded oddly tight as he continued. 'A hemi-Fontan procedure was done at six months to create a direct connection between the pulmonary artery and the superior vena cava.'

Rebecca had been allowed to do most of that procedure and she'd been so quietly proud of herself. They'd found a babysitter for Gwen and they'd gone out to celebrate the achievement with dinner and champagne and a long, delicious twirl around the dance floor of their favourite restaurant.

Those 'date' nights had always had a particular kind of magic. It didn't matter how frantic the hours and days before them had been or how tired they were when they set out. Somehow they could always tap back into the connection that had been there from their very first date—that feeling that their love for each other was invincible. That there could never be anyone else that they would want to be with.

The idea that the night after that surgery would be the last 'date' night they would ever have would have been unthinkable at the time. As impossible as losing their precious child.

Thomas didn't actually know if it had been Rebecca who had done the final major surgery to try and improve the function of Penelope's heart. He'd walked out by then, taking a new job in adult cardiology at a major hospital up north in the wake of that personal tragedy that had torn their lives apart.

He'd run away...like he always did...

Thomas cleared his throat as he rapidly ran through the list of the more recent admissions.

'April of this year saw a marked deterioration in Penelope's condition following a series of viral infections. She's been an inpatient for the last ten weeks and was placed on the waiting list for a heart transplant about two months ago. This last week has seen a further deterioration in her condition and there's an urgent need for intervention.'

The next slide was a set of statistics about the availability of transplant organs and how many young patients were unlikely to make it as far as receiving a new heart.

The slide after that sombre reminder was a picture of a device that looked like a tiny rubber plunger with a single tube attached to the top and two coming out from the base.

'For those of you not familiar with these, this is a ventricular assist device—an implantable form of mechanical circulatory support. Parental consent has been given and it's our plan for Penelope to receive a VAD as soon as theatre time can be arranged.' Thomas sucked in a longer breath. 'Dr Scott? Perhaps you'd like to speak about what the surgery involves?'

Using her formal title caused another round of those raised

eyebrows and significant glances. Was it his imagination or did this meeting feel really awkward for everybody here?

'Of course.' Rebecca's gaze quickly scanned everybody at the table. It just didn't shift to include himself. 'To put it simply, it's a straightforward bit of plumbing, really. The device is a pump that uses the apex of the left ventricle as the inflow and provides an outflow to the aorta, bypassing the ventricle that's not functioning well enough.'

Thomas could feel himself frowning. It was fine to describe something in layman's terms for the members of the team with no medical background, like the dietician and the psychologist, but to his own ears it was simple enough to be almost dismissive. Like describing a donor organ as a spare part?

His anger had settled into his stomach like a heavy stone. No wonder he hadn't been that interested in eating in the last few days. Was it going to get even worse when he had to work so closely with Rebecca on Penelope's case? Perhaps the unwanted memories that had ambushed him during his brief presentation had been a warning that it was going to become increasingly difficult to work with his ex-wife. The prospect was more than daunting, especially given that everybody else here seemed to be aware of the tension between them.

David, the cardiac intensive care consultant, was giving him a speculative glance as if he was also having concerns about how this particular combination of the lead carers in this team was going to work. With an effort, Thomas erased the unimpressed lines from his face.

'Of course it's not quite that simple in reality,' Rebecca continued. 'It's a big and potentially difficult surgery and there are complications that we have to hope we'll avoid.'

'Like what?' The query came from one of the physiotherapists.

'Bleeding. Stroke. Infections. Arrhythmias.' Rebecca was counting off the possible disasters on her fingers. 'Some might not become apparent immediately, like renal failure and liver dysfunction. And some intraoperative ones, like an air embolism, are things we will certainly do our best to control. I guess what I'm trying to say is that there *are* risks but everybody agrees that the potential benefits outweigh these risks in Penny's case.'

Rebecca's smile was poignant. 'As most of you know, Penny Craig is one of those patients you just can't help falling in love with and we've known her all her life.

'I'm sure we're all going to give this case everything we've got.' Her smile wobbled a fraction. 'I know *I* am...'

The murmur of agreement around the table held a note of involvement that was very unusual for a clinical team meeting like this. Heads were nodding solemnly. Rosie was blinking as if she was trying to fight back tears.

For heaven's sake... Did nobody else understand how destructive it could be to get too involved? Was the staff psychologist taking this atmosphere on board and making a mental note that a lot of people might need some counselling in the not-too-distant future if things *didn't* work out the way they all had their hearts set on?

Thomas raised his voice. 'It's certainly all about teamwork and it's to be hoped that we will see a dramatic improvement in this patient's condition within a very short period of time.' He glanced down at the laser pointer in his hand, looking for the 'off' button. 'Thank you all for coming. I look forward to working with everybody.'

A buzz of conversation broke out and more than one pager sounded. David came around to his end of the table. 'I'm being paged to get back upstairs but come and see me when you have a moment? I'd like to go over the postoperative care for Penny in some more detail so I can brief my staff.'

'Sure. I'll be heading up there shortly. There's a four-year-old who was admitted to ICU with severe asthma last night but now they're querying cardiomyopathy. We might need to transfer her to your patch.'

'I heard about that. Page me if you need me in on that consult.'

'Will do.'

The rest of the room was emptying during the brief conversation with David. Everybody had urgent tasks waiting for them elsewhere, including himself. Thomas shut down the programme on his laptop and picked it up, his thoughts already on the case he was about to go and assess. Severe breathlessness and wheezing in children could often be misdiagnosed as asthma or pneumonia until more specific tests such as echocardiography were used to reveal underlying heart disease.

It was a complete surprise to turn and find he was not alone in the room.

Rebecca was standing at the other end of the table.

'We need to talk,' she said.

Thomas said nothing. Given how disturbing their last private conversation had been, he wasn't at all sure he wanted an opportunity that could, in fact, make things worse.

'I'm sure you agree that we can't work together with this kind of tension between us. Especially not on a case like this. Everybody's aware of it and it's destructive to the whole team.'

He couldn't argue with that. And, to his shame, he knew he had to take part of the blame. He had no reason to feel angry with Rebecca for anything to do with her involvement in Penelope's case. He was letting personal baggage affect his relationship with a colleague to such an extent, it was actually difficult to make eye contact with her right now.

He looked down at the laptop in his hands.

'So what do you suggest? That we call in a different cardiologist? In case you hadn't noticed, they've been short-staffed around here ever since the threat of the merger got real. That's why I agreed to take on a permanent position again.'

A brief upwards glance showed that Rebecca's gaze was on him. Steady and unrelenting. He held her gaze for a heartbeat. And then another as those dark eyes across the length of the table merged with that flash of memory he'd had during his presentation—when they'd been looking up at him for reassurance that she had his support when she'd been facing one of her biggest challenges.

A different lifetime.

One in which giving and receiving that kind of reassurance and support had been as automatic as breathing. When success for either of them had created a shared pride so huge it could make it hard to catch a breath and when failure was turned into a learning experience that could only make you a better person. A lifetime that had been iced with so much laughter.

So much love...

It had been a long time since that loss had kicked him quite this hard. A wave of sadness blurred the edges of any anger he still had.

'That's not what I'm suggesting,' Rebecca said quietly. 'Penny deserves the best care available and, on either side of the actual surgery, you are the person who can provide that.'

'And you are the person who can provide the best surgical care,' he responded. 'She deserves that, too.' He closed his eyes in a slow blink and then met her gaze again. 'So what is it that you *are* suggesting?'

'That we talk. Not here,' she added quickly. 'Somewhere more...' She cleared her throat. 'Somewhere else.'

Had she been going to suggest somewhere more private? Like the house they'd lived in with Gwen that Rebecca had refused to sell?

He couldn't do that. What if she still had all those pictures on the walls? That old basket with the toys in it, even?

'I'm going for a walk after work,' Rebecca said quietly. 'Through Regent's Park and over to Primrose Hill. It's a gorgeous day. Why don't you come with me?'

A walk. In a public place. Enough space that nobody would be able to overhear anything that might be said and the ability to walk away if it proved impossible to find common ground without this horrible tension.

Except they had to find that common ground, didn't they, if they were going to work together?

If they couldn't, Thomas would have to add a failure to remain professional to the list of his other shortcomings and this one wouldn't be private—it would be fodder for gossip and damaging for both their careers.

And his career was all he had left now.

'Fine.' He nodded. 'Page me when you're done for the day. I'll be here.'

Out of one meeting and straight into another.

Rebecca only had time to duck into her office and grab a folder from her desk before heading down to the coffee shop on the ground floor where the committee members in charge of organising the Teddy Bears' Picnic would be waiting for her.

The countdown was on for the annual event that Rebecca had been instrumental in setting up four years ago and this one promised to be the biggest and best yet.

The committee president, a mother of a child with cystic fibrosis who had received a double lung transplant six years ago, waved excitedly at Rebecca and she weaved her way through the busy café opposite the pharmacy on the ground floor.

'We had to start without you, I'm afraid.'

'No problem, Janice. I'm so sorry I'm late.' It seemed to be becoming the theme of her day today, but at least she didn't have anyone glaring at her. Janice was beaming, in fact.

'I've got *such* good news. Your suggestion to contact the president of the World Transplant Games Federation really paid off. We're going to have trouble choosing which inspirational speakers we want the most.'

'Oh? That's fantastic.' Rebecca smiled up at the young waitress taking orders. 'I'll have a flat white, please. And one of your gorgeous savoury muffins.' The way her day was shaping up, it was highly likely to be the only lunch she would get.

'We've got an offer from a man called Jeremy Gibson. He

got a liver transplant when he was in his early thirties and had three young children. He's competed in the games for four years now and, last year, he led a sponsored hike in the Himalayas to raise awareness for organ donation and advertise how successful it can be.'

Rebecca nodded but she wasn't quite focused on this new meeting yet. The way Thomas had looked at her—after he'd asked if she wanted to call in a new cardiologist for Penny's case...

The tension had still been there. That undercurrent of anger that she knew had been caused by her telling him that he always ran away was still there. But there'd been something else, as well. A sadness that had made her want to walk around the edge of that table and simply put her arms around him.

To tell him how sorry she was.

For everything.

That was a bit of a shock, all by itself. She was over the breakup of her marriage.

She was over Thomas.

Who, in their right mind, would choose to be with someone who simply wasn't there when the going got too rough?

'And then there's Helena Adams,' Janice continued. 'A double lung recipient who's a champion skier and...' She consulted a notepad on the table in front of her. 'And Connor O'Brien—a young heart transplant recipient who ran in the London Marathon last year.'

'They all sound amazing,' Rebecca said.

'Maybe they could all come,' their treasurer suggested. 'They don't all have to speak. They could just mingle and join in some of the fun and chat to parents and kids. And the press, of course. We're going to get way more coverage this year, what with the threat to Paddington's already getting so much publicity.'

'We've got three television crews coming,' the secretary added. 'We're going international, apparently.' She fanned her face. 'This is all getting so much bigger than we ever thought it would.'

'Okay.' Janice's deep breath was audible. 'Let's get on with everything on the agenda. We've got a lot to get through. Has the bouncy castle been booked?'

'Yes. It's huge. And it's got turrets and everything. I've got a picture here...'

'Oh, it's perfect,' someone said. 'And how appropriate, given that Paddington's nickname is "the Castle"?'

An old redbrick Victorian building, Paddington Children's Hospital did indeed have its own turrets—the largest of which was a distinctive slate-roofed dome that loomed above the reception area of the main entrance.

'What's more important is to decide where it's going to go. I'm not sure the layout worked as well as it could last year and we've got so many extra things this time. The zoo has offered to organise and run pony rides.' Janice looked around the table. 'I know the London Zoo is one of our biggest sponsors and that's why we go over the road to Primrose Hill but is it going to be big enough? Do we need to consider a shift to part of Regent's Park?'

'I'm going to go there this evening,' Rebecca told them. 'I'll take the draft plan for the layout with me and walk it out but I think it'll be fine. We had tons of extra space last year and it was lovely to be on top of the hill and see everything that was going on. Some of the photos were fabulous, weren't they?'

She caught her lip between her teeth, her thoughts wandering again as the other committee members reminisced about last year's success. Should she have told Thomas the reason she was planning that walk in the park after work today?

No. If he'd known it had anything to do with the children and families of both donors and recipients of transplanted organs, he would have run a mile.

They really needed to talk if they were going to be able to work together and he didn't need to know the real reason she was there, did he? It was summer and the evenings were long. She could always stay later than him and sit on the top of the hill with the plan in her hands and make any notes she needed for changes.

It was important that they spent this time together. Before things got any more difficult between them.

And she was looking forward to it. Kind of. In a purely professional sense, of course. She'd feel better when she'd had the chance to apologise for that verbal attack. Thomas hadn't deserved that. She knew he was doing his best in the only way he knew how. That he had probably been doing that all along. It was just so sad that he couldn't see that he'd chosen such a wrong path.

That he, above everybody else, was suffering more because of it.

In retrospect, however, there was another reason why inviting Thomas to share this walk might have been a bad idea. It hadn't occurred to her at the time that a walk up Primrose Hill was an echo of their very first date.

Maybe he wouldn't remember. It wouldn't matter if he did. Just breathing the same air as Thomas was an echo of so very many things and, somehow, they had to find a way to deal with that.

CHAPTER THREE

THE WARMTH OF the summer's evening did not seem to be doing much to thaw the chill that surrounded Thomas and Rebecca like an air-conditioned bubble.

The virtual silence for the brisk walk to Regent's Park had been largely disguised by the sounds of the busy city streets but it became increasingly obvious as they followed a path into the vast stretch of green space.

'Thanks for agreeing to come,' Rebecca offered, finally.

'As you said, we need to find a way we can work together. Without letting our personal baggage interfere in any way with patient care.'

It sounded as though Thomas had rehearsed that little speech. Maybe it had been something he'd said to himself more than once today. Because he'd been arguing with himself about whether or not he could bear to spend any time with her?

Rebecca took a deep breath and did her best not to let it out as a sigh. He was here, walking beside her, so that was a good start. Maybe it was too soon to open the can of worms that was their 'personal baggage.' If Thomas could actually relax a fraction, it could make this a whole lot easier. And who wouldn't relax on a walk like this?

The boat lake beside them was a popular place to be on such

a warm, sunny evening. It was crowded with boats—classic wooden rowing boats and the bright blue and yellow paddle boats. The grassy banks were dotted with the rugs and folding chairs of groups of families and friends who were preparing for a picnic meal. There were dogs chasing balls and children playing games on the shore of the lake.

And there were ducks.

Of course there were ducks. How many times had she and Thomas come here with Gwen on those precious days when she wasn't with her caregiver or at nursery school? They'd started bringing her here to feed the ducks way before she was old enough to walk or throw a crust of bread.

Not that she was about to remind Thomas of those times. Or admit that she still automatically put crusts of bread into a bag in the freezer until it was so full it would remind her that she never had the time or motivation to feed ducks any more. No one seeing them would ever guess at the kind of shared history they had. They would see the tall man with his briefcase in his hand and his companion with the strap of her laptop case over her shoulder and assume that they were work colleagues who happened to be sharing a walk home at the end of their day.

Exactly the space they were in, thanks to the boundaries that had been put firmly in place from the moment Thomas had set foot in Paddington's again.

Except that Thomas was smiling. Almost. He had his hand up to shield his eyes as he took in the scene of the boating activity on the lake and his lips were definitely not in a straight line.

His breath came out in an audible huff that could have been suppressed laughter.

'Nobody's swimming today,' he murmured.

It wasn't a lake that anybody swam in. Unless they were unfortunate enough to fall out of a boat, of course.

Like she had that day...

Good grief. She had deliberately avoided opening that can

of worms labelled 'shared memories' but Thomas hadn't even hesitated.

Okay, it was funny in retrospect but it hadn't been at the time. Thomas had been inspired by the romantic image of a date that involved rowing his girlfriend around a pretty lake and Rebecca had been dressed for the occasion in a floaty summer dress and a wide-brimmed straw sunhat.

It had been a gloriously sunny day but there'd been a decent breeze. Enough to catch her hat and send it sailing away to float on the water. Thomas had done his best to row close enough for her to lean out of the boat and retrieve the hat but he hadn't been quite close enough. And she'd leaned just a little too far.

The water had been shallow enough to stand up in but she'd been completely soaked and the filmy dress had been clinging to her body and transparent enough to make her underwear obvious. The shock of the dunking had given way to helpless laughter and then to something very different when she'd seen the look in Thomas's eyes. Getting out of those wet clothes and into a hot bath hadn't been the real reason they couldn't get home fast enough.

And now, with Thomas pulling that memory out to share, Rebecca had the sensation that shutters had been lifted. There was a glint in his eyes that made her feel as if she'd stepped back in time.

As if everything they'd had together was still there—just waiting to have life breathed into it again.

It was the last thing Rebecca had expected to feel. It was too much. It wasn't what she wanted. She didn't want to go anywhere near that kind of space in her head or her heart and that made it…what…terrifying?

She had to break that eye contact. To push that memory back where it belonged—firmly in the past.

'Nobody sensible would,' she heard herself saying. 'But we all make mistakes, don't we?'

She hadn't looked away fast enough to miss the way that glint in his eyes got extinguished and her words hung in the air as they walked on, taking on a whole new meaning. That the mistake that had been made encompassed their whole relationship?

The soft evening air began to feel increasingly thick with the growing tension. This was her fault, Rebecca realised. She'd had the opportunity to break the ice and make things far more comfortable between them and she'd ruined it because she'd backed off so decisively. Maybe it was up to her to find another way to defuse the tension. At least she was no stranger to tackling difficult subjects with her patients and their families.

She had learned it was best to start in a safe place and not to jump in the deep end as Thomas had—perhaps—inadvertently done.

'I did that consult you requested on your new patient this afternoon. Tegan Mitchell? The thirteen-year-old with aortic stenosis?'

'Ah…good.' There was a note of relief in his voice as he responded to stepping onto safe, professional ground. 'What did you think?'

'Classic presentation. Even my junior house surgeon could hear the ejection click after the first heart sound and the ejection murmur. It was the first time she'd come across an example of how the murmur increases with squatting and decreases with standing. She's got some impressive oedema in her legs and feet, too.' Rebecca's lips curled into a small smile as she glanced up at Thomas. 'Tegan, that is, not my house surgeon—*her* legs are fine.'

Thomas didn't smile at her tongue-in-cheek clarification. 'I've got Tegan booked for an echo tomorrow morning. We've started medication to get her heart failure under control but I think she's a good candidate for valve replacement surgery, yes?'

That tension hadn't been defused enough to allow for a joke, obviously. Rebecca nodded. 'Absolutely.'

He didn't see her nod because he had turned his head as the path forked.

'Do you want to go through Queen Mary's Garden?'

'Why not? It'll be gorgeous with the roses in full bloom.'

Thomas took the lead through the ornate gates and chose a path between gardens with immaculately trimmed hedges surrounding waves of colour. Rebecca inhaled the heady scent of old-fashioned roses but Thomas didn't seem at all distracted by the beauty around them.

'How's your theatre list looking for later this week?'

'Not too bad but it can always go pear-shaped at a moment's notice if a transplant organ becomes available—especially if I have to fly somewhere for the retrieval. I've got two cystic fibrosis kids on the ward now who are desperate for new lungs and I can get called in for other cases, too. I started my transplant training with kidneys and livers, way back. I still love helping with those surgeries when I'm needed.'

'Way back? Five years isn't so long ago.'

'Mmm.' The sound was neutral. Five years could seem like for ever, couldn't it?

As if to push her thoughts where they probably shouldn't really go, a young couple passed them on the wide path. The woman was pushing an empty stroller. The man had a safe grip on the legs of the small child on his shoulders who was happily keeping his balance with fistfuls of his father's hair.

Five years ago she and Thomas would have looked more like this couple than a pair of colleagues. They had been happily married with an adorable three-year-old daughter. They were both juggling careers and parenthood and thriving on their lifestyle even though it frequently bordered on chaotic.

They hadn't intended to have a child so soon, of course, but the surprise of her pregnancy when Rebecca was studying for her finals in medical school had quickly morphed into joy. It had been meant to happen—just like they'd been meant to meet and fall in love so completely. They'd announced the pregnancy to the gathering of friends and family who'd come together to celebrate their low-key wedding and brushed off any concerns about how they would manage those busy early years of hospital training with a baby in their lives.

'We'll cope,' they had both repeated with absolute confidence. 'We've got each other.'

And they *had* coped. They had known exactly what specialties they had set their hearts on and Rebecca was chasing her dream of being a cardiothoracic surgeon with as much passion as Thomas put into his postgraduate studies in paediatric cardiology. The firsthand experience of being parents only confirmed what they also already knew—that they were destined to always work with children.

So yes, right now, five years was a lifetime ago. And it had been a long time since Thomas had turned his back on the specialty he'd worked so hard to get into.

'How are you finding being back at Paddington's?' she heard herself asking.

The look she received was almost bewildered.

'I mean, working with children again,' she added hurriedly. 'It must be very different to what you were doing up north...' Oh, help! This wasn't exactly staying on safe ground to get a conversation going, was it?

'It was...a big change...' It sounded as though Thomas was treading carefully—unsure of how much he wanted to say. 'I knew it wasn't going to be easy...'

Wow.

The step he'd voluntarily taken onto personal ground was as unexpected as him referring, however obliquely, to that date when she'd fallen out of the boat. Rebecca had no idea what to say in response. Should she offer sympathy which might immediately lead the conversation into the reasons why it hadn't been easy? To tell him how hard it had been for her, too—to be around children in those grief-stricken months after losing Gwen?

Even now, it could stir the threat of tears that had always been barely below the surface of her existence back then. How often did she have to fight for control? Whenever she heard the cry of a child and the soothing sound of a mother offering comfort. Or she saw the smile of a toddler or heard the delicious sound of a baby giggling. And the hardest thing of all was when she was holding one of her tiny patients herself. Or when a small child held their arms up, expecting the cuddle she would never refuse.

No. She wasn't ready to talk about that. And it would be the last thing Thomas would want to hear about. He had only agreed to this time together in order to clear the air enough for them to be able to work together. Perhaps what was really needed was a way to put more effective boundaries around the past so that they could both move on with their lives.

'No,' she finally said quietly. 'But everybody's delighted that you've come back.'

There was a moment's silence. Was he wondering if she was including herself in that 'everybody'?

'And you're here at such an important time for Paddington's,' Rebecca added quickly. 'You arrived right at the point where we all thought it was the end and then, thanks to the huge drama of that fire at Westbourne Grove Primary School, the media got on board and things started to turn around.'

'Yeah... I did think I might be accepting a permanent job at a hospital that wasn't going to be around much longer. Seemed a bit crazy at the time.'

'But now it looks like it's going to be all right. I know it's not really official yet but it sounds like it's going to be signed and sealed any day now. Are you going to the party at the Frog and Peach on Friday?'

Thomas shrugged. 'I'll have to see how the day goes.'

'Me, too. I often seem to be pretty late getting away once I've caught up on paperwork and things.'

'Same.'

Did they both work such long hours because there was nothing to make them rush home? Rebecca hadn't heard the slightest whisper of gossip that there might be someone else in Thomas's life now. She didn't even know where he was living, in fact.

'I hope this isn't taking you too far out of your way,' she said politely. 'Or keeping you from something you'd rather be doing on a nice summer's evening.'

'It's not a problem,' Thomas said. 'And it's not far to get home. I've got an apartment in South Hampstead.' He cleared his throat. 'And you? You still in Primrose Hill?'

'Mmm.' It was another tricky subject. Buying the basement flat in such a good area had been a huge step in their lives together and they couldn't have done it without the windfall of the legacy from Rebecca's grandfather. Thomas had refused to accept any of that money in the divorce settlement so he'd walked away with almost nothing.

'Keep it,' he'd said. *'Keep everything. I don't want any reminders.'*

Which reminders had been on the top of that list?

The night they'd taken possession and had a picnic on the bare floor of the living area with fish and chips and a bottle of champagne? Had either of them even noticed the discomfort of the wooden boards when they'd made love as the final celebration of getting the keys to their first home?

They'd decided later that that had been the night Gwen had been conceived and that had been as perfect as everything else in their charmed existence.

A sideways glance gave her a moment of eye contact with Thomas and she saw the flash of surprise in his face. Oh, help! Had he seen what she'd been thinking about just then? The way she'd known he'd been remembering how she'd looked with that dress plastered so revealingly to her body after her dunking in the lake?

It was too easy to read too much into those glances. There were too many memories. And yes, some of them were the best moments of her life but they had been buried under far more overwhelming ones.

Maybe the biggest reminders of sharing that house were the ones that included Gwen after her birth? Walking round and round that small space, trying to persuade their tiny human to go to sleep. A floor that was an obstacle course because it was covered with toys. The sound of a little girl's laughter that echoed between the polished floorboards and the high ceilings...

She'd had to live with those reminders and, for the longest time, tears had done little to wash away the pain they caused. But gradually—so slowly Rebecca had barely noticed it happening—something had changed and sometimes there was comfort to be found in them.

Gwen's room might have become an office but occasionally, when Rebecca was working there late at night, she would remember going in just to watch Gwen sleep for a moment. She would take that warm, fuzzy miracle of loving and being loved so much and wrap it around herself like the softest blanket imaginable. Sometimes, Thomas would come with her and they'd stand there hand in hand and the blanket would be wrapped around them both. And it would still be around them when they went to sit on the big, old couch that dominated the small living room. Or it would be an extra layer on the antique brass bed that was big enough to almost touch both sides of their bedroom.

The couch was still there.

And the bed.

Were the memories that lingered even after all this time something else that Thomas had been so desperate to get away from?

Rebecca had chosen to stay. To live with those memories.

To cope with the loneliness of losing all that love...

CHAPTER FOUR

THEY'D BEEN WALKING in silence for a long time, now.

Thomas stole a sideways glance at Rebecca. What was she thinking about?

What had they been talking about?

Oh, yeah, where they were living.

She was still in that house they'd chosen together. Had he imagined it or did she still remember the way they'd celebrated when they'd picked up the keys and had finally been alone together in their first, real home? The idea that he'd caught a glimpse of that memory in her eyes when their gazes had touched might have been purely projection but even if she had forgotten that particular night, there was no way she could escape all the other memories.

He couldn't begin to imagine being able to have done that himself. How could you escape from memories that made you feel as if your heart was being ripped out of your chest when they were all around you? When even the walls had soaked up the sounds of a newborn baby's cry and an infant's laughter and the first words of a toddler?

It was just as incomprehensible as choosing to take your career into an area that held memories that were still too raw to go near. To actually take a child into an operating theatre to harvest organs when you knew the kind of grief the parents were experiencing had to mean you could shut yourself away completely.

To stop caring to the extent that it was possible to think of those organs as 'spare parts'?

Thomas could feel the muscles in his jaw tensing so much they made his teeth ache.

No wonder their marriage had failed.

Maybe they'd never really understood each other.

Their route had taken them right through Regent's Park now and they were walking past the perimeter of London Zoo. A screech of some excited animal could be heard—an orangutan, perhaps? Thomas hadn't been near a zoo for five years and he wasn't comfortable being this close. There were memories everywhere, here. A lazy Sunday afternoon, pushing Gwen's stroller down the paths and stopping to try and capture her expressions when she saw the animals and birds. The penguins had been her absolute favourite and she'd shrieked with laughter every time they waddled close to the fence.

They'd bought a stuffed toy penguin in the zoo shop that had been almost as big as she was but it had to be tucked into bed with her that night. And she'd fallen asleep, still smiling...

Thomas waited for the jolt of pain that always came with memories like that. He could feel his muscles tense and his face scrunch into a scowl, as if that would somehow protect him.

Rebecca seemed oblivious. She was heading for the other side of Prince Albert Road, clearly intent on getting to Primrose Hill and that was good. The further away from the zoo they got, the better. He wouldn't have to mentally swat away more memories.

Like the way Rebecca's face would light up with pleasure when they watched the otters which were *her* absolute favourite.

Or that photograph that someone had offered to take of them as a family, beside the huge, bronze statue of the gorilla just inside the entrance to the zoo. He'd been holding Gwen with one arm and had his other arm around Rebecca. Their heads had both been level with his shoulders and he must have said something funny, because they'd both looked up at him as the photo was taken and they were all grinning from ear to ear.

Looking so happy…

His scowl deepened as they reached the entrance to Primrose Hill Park because now they were going past the children's playground.

For a split second, his gaze caught Rebecca's as they glanced at each other at precisely the same moment. He knew they were both thinking the same thing—that the last time they'd been to this playground, they'd been with their daughter.

They'd probably both looked away from each other in the same moment, as well.

There were more memories, here. More jolts of pain to be expected.

Except…that first one hadn't arrived yet.

That was weird. How could he actually have such a clear picture in his head of something like Gwen being tucked up with her toy penguin and not feel the same crippling blast of loss that he'd had the last time his brain had summoned something like that from that private databank of images?

As if he needed to prod the wound to check whether it was possible that it had miraculously started healing, Thomas let himself think about it again. He could see Gwen's dark curls against the pale pillowcase, her cheek pressed against the fluff of the penguin. He could see the sweep of her dark lashes become still as sleep claimed her and he could see the dimples that came with even the smallest smile.

And yes, he could feel the pang of loss and a wash of sadness but it wasn't really pain. He could—almost—feel his own lips trying to curl up at the corners.

Instead of relief, this awareness that something had changed brought something far less pleasant with it.

Guilt?

Was he somehow failing Gwen by being less traumatised at being reminded of her loss?

Maybe grappling with a sense of failure was familiar enough to be preferable to something strange and new.

He'd been over this ground often enough in the past few years. How he'd failed Gwen as a father because he hadn't been able to keep her safe.

How he'd failed Rebecca as a husband because he hadn't been able to keep their marriage alive.

But how could it have worked when they were such different people? People who had never really understood each other?

'Do you mind if we stop for a moment?'

'Not getting puffed, are you? We're not even at the top of the hill.' Unbidden, another memory ambushed him. 'I seem to remember you ran up here the last time we did this. Faster than I managed.'

Rebecca's face went very still.

She hadn't forgotten that moment in time, had she?

Their very first date. A walk in the park and the decision to get to the top of the hill to admire the view.

'Race you!'

'Last one there is a rotten egg!'

She'd won that race but she'd had to throw herself onto the grass to try and catch her breath. And Thomas had lain down beside her and neither of them had bothered to look at anything more than each other between those lingering kisses. The walk down the hill had been much, much slower. Holding hands and exchanging glances so frequently, as if they needed to confirm that they were both feeling the same way—that they'd found a hand to hold that would get them through the rest of their lives...

Oh, man, this walk together really hadn't been a very good idea, had it? It was doing his head in. This was all so hard and exactly what he'd been determined to avoid when he'd chosen to come back to Paddington's.

But Rebecca was staring down the hill, her face still expressionless, seemingly focused on something that had nothing to do with any memories of their first date.

'I just need to check something.'

'What?'

'Um…' Rebecca's eyes were narrowed against the glare of the sun as she looked down the slope. 'We need a flat area for both the pony rides and the bouncy castle…'

Thomas blinked. 'You've lost me.'

'I'm on the organising committee for a big picnic that's happening soon. It's our fourth year and it's going to get a lot more publicity this year because of Paddington's being in the spotlight with the threatened closure. We need to make sure there are no glitches, so I'm checking out the plan.'

Something like a chill ran down Thomas's spine.

'I saw the poster in the relatives' room. It's for transplant patients, yes?' He could hear the chill in his tone. He didn't want to start talking about any of this. Except that this was the reason they couldn't work well together, wasn't it? And that was why they were here now.

They *had* to talk about it.

'Not just the patients. It's to celebrate everything that's good about organ donation in the hope of getting people more aware and making it easier to talk about.' Rebecca's tone was cautious enough to reveal that she, too, recognised they were approaching the real point of this time together. 'It's for the patients and their families, of course, but also for all the people who devote their working lives to making the success stories happen. And… and it's for the people on the other side, too. Some people have contact with the recipients of their child's organs and…and even if they don't, it's a day where they can celebrate the gift of life they were able to provide.'

Julia had said something about a parent like that but it was in the 'unthinkable' basket for Thomas. To see another child that was having fun at some amazing picnic with pony rides and a bouncy castle because they had a part of *his* daughter?

The chill in his spine held an edge of horror now.

Did *Rebecca* know a child like that?

He wasn't going to ask. *He* didn't want to know.

Refreshing that smouldering pile that was the anger that had been ignited last week was a preferable route to feeling either so disturbed by unexpected memories or guilty about things he had or hadn't done in the past.

'Yes,' he heard himself saying aloud. 'I guess you need to drum up a good supply of those *spare* parts.'

The silence that fell between them was like a solid wall.

Impenetrable.

It stretched out for long enough to take a slow breath. And then another.

They weren't even looking at each other. They could have been on separate planets.

And then Rebecca spoke.

'I should never have said that. I'm sorry. It was completely unprofessional. And…and it was cruel.'

'I couldn't agree more.'

'It's not what I believe,' she said softly. '*You* know that, Tom.'

It was the first time she'd called him Tom since he'd come back and it touched a place that had been very safely walled off.

Or maybe it was that assumption that he knew her well enough to know that she would never think like that.

And, deep down, he had known that, hadn't he? It had just been so much easier to think otherwise. To be angry.

'So, why did you say it, then?'

'You've been so distant ever since you came back. So cut off. I don't even recognise you any more.' There was a hitch in Rebecca's voice that went straight to that place that calling him 'Tom' had accessed. 'I guess I wanted to know if the man I married still exists.'

His words were a little less of a snap this time.

'I haven't changed.'

'Yes, you have.' He could feel Rebecca looking at him but he didn't turn his head. 'Something like what we went through changes everyone. But you…you disappeared. You just…ran away.'

There was that accusation again. That he was a coward.

The reminder of how little she understood came with a wave of weariness. Thomas wanted this over with. He wanted to put this all behind them effectively enough to be able to work together.

He wanted…peace.

So he took another deep breath and he turned his head to meet Rebecca's gaze.

'Everyone processes grief differently. You should know as well as anybody that it's not a good idea to make assumptions.'

'But that's the problem,' Rebecca whispered. 'It always was.'

'What?'

'That you *didn't* process it. You shut yourself away. Emotionally and then physically. You left me. You left Paddington's.'

That was unfair.

'I didn't *leave* you. It was *you* who asked for the divorce.'

'You did leave me.' Rebecca's eyes were bright enough to suggest gathering tears. 'You started walking away the day Gwen died and I felt more and more alone until the idea of staying in our marriage was worse than escaping.'

Thomas was silent. He had a horrible feeling that those words were going to haunt him from now on and that they would be harder to deal with than an accusation of cowardice.

'You don't even want to talk to me any more. You've been here for months now and you've avoided anything that doesn't have something to do with a patient. You can't even ask whether I've had a good day, let alone talk about something like the Teddy Bears' Picnic. And…' Rebecca was clearly struggling to hold back her tears now. She sniffed inelegantly. 'And you never smile. And you call me Rebecca. Or Dr Scott. Like I'm…a complete stranger.'

Thomas closed his eyes for a moment. It was true. He'd created as much distance as he could to try and make their first meeting easier and he'd kept it up. For months…

'I… I'm sorry.'

Rebecca nodded. She sniffed again and then scrubbed at her nose with the back of her hand.

'Excuse me. I don't have a hanky,' she said.

'Neither do I.' Thomas wished he did. Offering one could have been an olive branch. And they needed an olive branch.

'You're right,' he said slowly. 'I have been distant. I knew it was going to be hard working with children again. I thought I'd be making it a whole lot harder if I spent time with you, as well.'

'You don't have to spend time with me to be friendly. Just a smile would do. Or saying something friendly that made me feel like a person and not just a surgical consult.'

Thomas nodded. 'I could do that. Something like "Have you had a good day?"'

It was Rebecca's turn to nod. But then her breath escaped in a huff of sound that was more like a sob. 'Actually, I've had a horrible day. Ever since you glared at me for being late for the meeting this morning and everybody was reminded of how much you hate working with me.'

'I don't hate working with you. You're the best surgeon I have available. I think…your skills are amazing.'

'But you'd rather it was someone else with my skills.'

'You probably found it easier to work with the cardiologist I replaced.'

She shook her head this time. 'Not professionally. You're the best, too.'

'But personally,' Thomas persisted, 'you don't find it any easier than I do.'

'Only because you hate me.'

Thomas sighed. 'Oh, Becca… I could never *hate* you.'

The short version of her name had slipped out, as Thomas turned to look at her directly, so he could see the effect it had.

Her face became very still but something in her eyes changed. Became softer. Like a smile that didn't reach her lips.

And something softened inside Thomas, too.

'Come here,' he said gruffly. 'Friends can have a hug, can't they?'

CHAPTER FIVE

THOMAS WOLFE WASN'T the only person in the gallery to watch
this particular surgery.

Rosie Hobbes was sitting beside him, alternatively watching
the screen that gave a close-up view of what was largely ob-
scured by the gowned and masked figures below and leaning
forward to watch the whole team at work.

'I've never seen the insertion of a VAD before.'

'No. It's not common. Especially in children.'

'Do you think it'll work?'

'It will certainly buy us some time. The only thing that could
guarantee more time is a transplant. This is a bridge which
should give her a much better quality of life while we're waiting.'

Rosie was looking down into the theatre again. At the small
chest now open and so vulnerable.

'Life's so unfair sometimes, isn't it?' she murmured.

'Mmm.' Thomas couldn't argue with that. He had firsthand
experience of exactly how unfair life could be. So did the surgeon he was watching so intently.

The last time he had watched Rebecca operate had, ironically, been on this same patient, when Penny had been only
about six months old.

Life wasn't only unfair, it had patterns to it. Circles. Or were they spirals? A kind of pathway, anyway, that could take you back to places you'd been before. Places where memories could be looked at through a lens that changed with increased distance or wisdom.

Did you choose to follow those pathways with the familiar signposts, Thomas wondered. Or were they somehow set in place by fate and always there, waiting for you to step back onto them? Spirals could go either way, couldn't they? They could go downwards into tight loops that sucked you into a place you didn't want to be. Or they could lift you higher into loops so wide that the possibilities were no more than promises.

He was, very unexpectedly, back on one of his life pathways. Ever since that walk with Rebecca the other day when they'd reached some kind of truce and sealed it with that hug.

Or maybe he'd stepped back onto that path the moment he'd agreed to come back to Paddington's.

It still felt weird.

The way the memories had begun to rush at him from every direction but without the pain he would have expected.

He could think of Gwen and find himself ready to smile.

He could remember Rebecca falling out of that boat and how unbelievably sexy she'd looked in that wet dress…

He had even found himself reliving that hug on the top of Primrose Hill and how it had reminded him—again—of their very first date.

'We're ready to go on bypass.' Rebecca's voice was calm and clear through the speaker system. 'And the pocket for the pump is all set. How's the pump preparation looking?'

The surgeon working on the back table to prepare the device looked up and nodded. 'Ready when you are.'

'Stand by.' Rebecca and her registrar started the task of getting Penny onto bypass. Despite her obvious focus, she kept her audience involved. 'Because we know that this surgery is a bridge to transplant, I'm being careful to leave space for re-cannulation at the aortic cannulation site.'

It took long minutes to get Penny onto bypass and to the point where the heart was stopped. Her life now depended on the oxygen being circulated by the cardiopulmonary bypass machine. It was a procedure that was common and relatively safe these days but it still gave Thomas a sense of wonder at what medicine was able to achieve, along with a dollop of pride that he was able to be a part of this astonishing world.

He was proud of Rebecca, too. He had been perfectly sincere when he'd told her that she was the best surgeon he had available and that her skills were amazing, but he hadn't realised how much better she had become in the last few years. So confident but, at the same time, so exquisitely careful of every tiny detail. His gaze was fixed on the screen again as she inserted a suture.

'This marks the site of the core,' she said, for the benefit of the observers. 'I've used the left anterior descending artery to identify the intraventricular groove. We're going to core anteriorly due to the small size of the left ventricle.'

We. It was Rebecca who was doing the actual task but she'd never shown any sign of developing the ego that some surgeons were famous for. She'd always seen herself as part of a team.

And now Thomas felt like he was part of that team, too. As difficult as it had been to step onto personal ground during that walk, they had found a space just within the perimeter that was apparently going to make it possible to work together without the awful tension of the last months.

Maybe it would even allow them to become friends one day.

It had also given him rather a lot to think about. The quiet conversations between the surgeons, nursing staff and technicians below were only catching the surface layer of his attention as his thoughts drifted back to what was becoming a familiar route.

He'd known that her heartfelt words would haunt him.

I felt more and more alone...

He'd felt alone, too. They might have been walking the same

path back then, in those dark days, but they had been nowhere near each other and the distance had only increased.

Looking back, he could see that it had been Rebecca who'd made the effort to reach out time and time again.

'I've kept some dinner for you. It's in the oven.'

'I'm not hungry.'

The bed, where they would lie side by side, should have made them feel less alone but those sleepless hours had been the worst. The slightest contact with her skin would make him flinch and move away.

'It's been a long day. I'm tired.'

But he'd *been* there. He hadn't been running away. He'd been desperately sad. He'd needed more time to try and put the shattered pieces of his life back together and it was something that Rebecca couldn't help with. Not just because she was fighting her own battle but because she was so much a piece of what had been shattered.

His family.

The family that he had failed to protect.

She'd been right to accuse him of being distant ever since he'd returned to Paddington's. Was she also right that he'd coped with his grief by initiating that distance all those years ago? Had he been the one to push them so far apart that there had been no hope of connecting enough to help each other?

How could he have let that happen to the person who'd been his whole world until Gwen had arrived? The only woman he would ever love like that...

'Look at that,' Rosie whispered beside him. 'That's the inflow cannula going in and getting secured to the sewing ring. Dr Scott's incredibly neat, isn't she?'

Rebecca's size had often led people to make incorrect assumptions about her abilities but having such small hands with those long, delicate fingers was a bonus for a surgeon who often had to work on tiny patients. Being so much shorter than he was had always seemed another bonus because it made it easier for children to be drawn to her. At six foot one, Thomas towered over his small patients. And when was the last time he had crouched down to talk to one of them? Had he forgotten the difference that could make in his years of working only with adults?

Maybe he'd forgotten how tall he was, along with ignoring so many other personal things that only intruded on his focus on his work.

Hugging Rebecca on Primrose Hill had made him acutely aware of his height because of the way her head only reached his shoulder. Not that that had ever been a bad thing. As if it was a step from a well-remembered dance, she had turned her head so that it fitted perfectly into the natural hollow beneath his collarbone. It probably wasn't such a good thing that holding her that close had also reminded him of how soft her curves were...

With an effort, Thomas refocused on what he'd come here to watch. Brooding about how much he had failed Rebecca to leave her feeling so unbearably alone that she'd had to escape her marriage was not only inappropriate, it wasn't going to help anyone. The past was simply that—the past. They could only move forward and now they seemed to have found a way to do that.

At least he'd been the one to reach out this time.

To offer that hug that was a physical connection on top of an emotional one.

And it had felt good.

More than good.

As if there was a promise in the air he was breathing now.

The promise of finding peace?

She knew he was watching her.

Not that she'd looked directly up at the gallery at any point but she'd caught movement from the corner of her eye as she'd entered the theatre—her arms crossed in front of her, keeping her scrubbed and gloved hands safe from contact with anything— and she'd known it was Thomas, simply from the impression of height and that measured kind of movement he had these days.

Rebecca wasn't about to let anything disturb her focus. She did allow herself a heartbeat of pleasure that he was there but the only other irrelevant thought that escaped that part of her brain before she closed it down was that the last time Thomas had been observing her work had been during the second cardiac surgery that Penelope Craig had had, when she was still so tiny—only a few months old.

Or maybe the thought wasn't completely irrelevant. The surgery had been a success that time. She was going to do her utmost to make sure it was this time, too.

Finally, it was time to find out. The ventricular assist device had been meticulously stitched into position and Penny had been weaned off the cardiopulmonary bypass.

'We'll start the device at the lowest setting and keep the aortic clamp on to get rid of the last of the air.' Rebecca turned to one of the Theatre technicians. 'I'll need the transoesophageal echo soon, so I can check the final position in the chest without the retractors.'

She took plenty of time to gradually increase the flow of the device while the heart's function and pressures were closely monitored.

'We may not decide on final settings for a few days,' she said, for the benefit of everyone watching. 'Some people leave the chest open for a day to allow for stabilisation but I would only do that if I was concerned about something like ongoing bleeding. This is looking great, so I'll be happy to close. Let's get these cannulas removed and some chest drains in.'

There was movement again in the gallery and Rebecca glanced up to see that some people were leaving now that the procedure was all but over and it had clearly been successful. Thomas was still there, however. He acknowledged her glance with a nod and the hint of a smile.

A smile…

Things had certainly changed in the last few days.

That hug on Primrose Hill had been a turning point. A starting point, perhaps, of a new relationship. One of colleagues who could work together without causing discomfort to themselves and those around them.

Maybe it could even be the start of a friendship?

Rebecca turned back to coach her registrar through the placement of the chest drains. She had to admit that the idea of being friends with Thomas might be pushing things and getting closer than colleagues might not be a good idea, anyway. It had messed with her head more than a little, that hug. Especially coming in the wake of so many memories that had been undisturbed for so long. Not that she'd ever forgotten how it had felt to be held in his arms with her head nestled in that hollow beneath his shoulder but she'd never expected to actually feel it again.

But, like the memories that they'd shared, that hug had stirred up feelings that might be far better left alone.

Like how much she had missed Thomas in her life.

How much she *still* missed him…

No. She missed having a partner but Thomas would never be that man, again. You couldn't rewrite history and too much damage had been done.

Minutes ticked past to add another hour to the long stint in Theatre but Rebecca wasn't about to leave her small patient under the complete care of others. Even when the surgery was completely finished and she had stripped off her gloves and mask and hat to dispose of them in the rubbish, she stayed in the room, keeping a close watch on all the monitors as the team tidied up around Penny and prepared her for the transfer to Recovery. And then she went with them, still watching for any change in pressures or heart rhythm.

It was no surprise that Thomas arrived by her side almost immediately.

'She's stable,' Rebecca told him. 'It's looking good.'

He was scanning the bank of monitors himself. 'You did a fantastic job,' he said quietly. 'Julia and Peter are waiting in the relatives' room. Do you want to come with me to tell them the good news?'

'Of course.' She stayed a moment longer, however, moving to the head of the bed. She put her forefinger against her lips and then reached down to touch Penny's cheek gently. 'Be back soon, pet. Sleep tight.'

Sleep tight, don't let the bedbugs bite...

Had Thomas remembered the final goodnight she had always given Gwen? That soft touch that transferred a kiss and the whisper of an old rhyme that was irrelevant except that it was remembered from her own childhood.

When had it become something she had started to do with her youngest patients?

She couldn't remember. Somewhere in the last few years, it had just become one of those automatic, preferably private things. Like a good luck charm? No. She was too much of a scientist for something like that. It was because she worked with children and you couldn't help connecting with them at a level that was never appropriate or possible with adults.

And maybe it was because she knew, better than most, how precious these little lives were.

If Thomas remembered, he didn't show any sign of it. He was still looking at the monitors, in fact, rather than the small person attached to them. Rebecca's heart sank a little as she followed him from the Recovery area. They might have made a breakthrough in their own relationship but was Thomas ever going to step any closer to his patients? Allow himself enough of an emotional connection to share the joy that came with success?

He certainly had a smile for Penny's parents.

'I'll let Rebecca tell you how well the surgery went but it was all I could have hoped for. You'll be able to go in and see her very soon.'

Julia burst into tears. Peter put his arms around her and ignored the tears rolling down his own cheeks.

'She'll have to go to intensive care after this, won't she?'

'Yes. But probably not for long. It's amazing how quickly children can bounce back from even open heart surgery.'

'And she's going to be better?' Julia lifted her head from her husband's chest. 'She won't need the wheelchair or to be on oxygen all the time?'

'That's what I expect.' Thomas nodded. He smiled again but the glance at his watch told Rebecca that he was already preparing to move on to his next patient. Stepping back from this emotional encounter with his patient's parents?

Perhaps he wasn't ready for the kind of connection that would allow him to share their intense relief with its glimmers of joy that would become hope. And she could understand that. If you were distant enough not to buy in to the joy, it meant that you were protected from the pain when things didn't go well. With many of the cases doctors like she and Thomas had in their care, the long term outlook wasn't good, so that pain was inevitable. Rebecca had learned to deal with it. To remind herself that it was worth it because of the heavier balance of the joy.

Thomas had chosen to step back.

To run away...

But he had come back. Surely being willing to work with children again was a sign that something big had changed. And there'd been moments during that walk when she could believe that the man she'd married really did still exist somewhere behind those barriers.

Baby steps...

Like the fact that he could smile at her again.

It wasn't as if the distance he kept made the care he provided any less thorough. He went above and beyond what most doctors did which was why it was, again, no surprise to find him in the intensive care unit late that evening, when Rebecca went back for a final check on Penny.

'I met Julia by the elevator. She's finally gone to get something to eat in the cafeteria and then she's coming back to stay the night with Penny.'

Thomas nodded. 'Are you still happy to lighten the sedation level as early as tomorrow morning?'

'Yes. She's been stable ever since the surgery. The VAD is working perfectly. We'll keep the pain control up, of course, but I wouldn't be surprised if she wakes up and wants to get out of bed and put her tutu on. Like Sapphire, there.'

Thomas glanced at the end of the bed where the sparkly blue, soft toy bear that Julia had bought as Penny's post-surgery gift was waiting for her to see as soon as she woke up. But he wasn't smiling. Did he know how desperately Penny wanted to be a ballerina? Did it matter?

'It's very late,' she added. 'What are you still doing at work?'

Had his career become his whole life, the way hers had?

Did he not have someone to go home to?

The thought had occurred to her before, but she'd never heard any hint of what Thomas's life outside the hospital contained these days. It had been five years. It shouldn't be surprising if he did have someone else in his life by now but Rebecca knew how much of a shock it would be.

She wasn't ready to find out.

'It is late,' he agreed. 'I was catching up on some work. Trying to decide whether or not to go to that thing at the pub over the road.'

'Oh, the Frog and Peach. I'd completely forgotten about the celebration drinks.' Rebecca looked at her watch. 'It's only ten p.m. The party should be only just getting going.'

How good would it be if she and Thomas could go to a work function together? To have a drink with their colleagues and make it obvious that they'd found a way to work together again?

'Saving Paddington's is definitely something to celebrate,' she said, looking up to catch his gaze. 'Shall we pop in? Just for a quick drink?'

He hesitated and she could almost see him following the same train of thought she'd just had.

'Sure,' he said. 'Why not? Give me a few minutes to sort what I've left on my desk and I'll meet you in Reception.'

CHAPTER SIX

WEIRDLY, THERE WAS almost nobody from Paddington's still at the Frog and Peach by the time Rebecca and Thomas arrived.

There were plenty of people, and an enthusiastic game of darts going on in one corner, but the only two remaining staff members were Matt McGrory, the burns specialist at Paddington's, and Alistair North, a paediatric neurosurgeon. They were standing at the bar, their glasses almost empty.

'Where is everybody?' Rebecca asked. 'What kind of party is this?'

'We started early,' Matt said. 'On the dot of six p.m. Some people are working tomorrow and others had families to get home to.'

'I was sure Quinn would be here. She's been so involved in the campaign to save the hospital.'

'Oh, she was.' Matt's smile reflected the kind of glow that only newfound love could bring. 'Simon's babysitter could only stay till ten, so she had to go home.'

'How *is* Simon?' Like many of the staff members at Paddington's, Rebecca's heart had been caught by the case of five-year-old Simon, who was Quinn's first foster child, when he'd been badly burned in the fire at Westbourne Grove Primary School.

But Matt was still smiling. 'He's doing great. The scars on

his face are looking brilliant thanks to the wonders of spray-on skin. His arm will take a bit more work but the best thing is that his self-confidence seems to be growing by the day.'

'Maybe it's because you and Quinn are together?' Alistair suggested. 'Giving him a real family?'

'I'd like to take the credit but I reckon Maisie has to take most of it.'

'Who's Maisie?' Thomas asked.

'She's a rescue dog we rehomed. Gorgeous collie-cross. Simon adores her, and it's helping in ways we never expected. Like when we went to the park the other day. These kids about Simon's age came over and wanted to pat his dog and help throw the ball for her and I swear they didn't even notice his scars.'

'Oh, that's brilliant,' Rebecca said.

'Claire was here to start with, too,' Alistair said. 'It was the perfect opportunity to share the news that we've decided to stay in London.'

'That's great news,' Thomas said.

'She was looking forward to catching up with you,' Alistair said to Rebecca, 'but she's getting tired pretty easily these days so she went at the same time as Quinn.'

'I'm not surprised she's tired.' Rebecca smiled. 'Didn't I hear a rumour that you've got twins on the way?'

'Yes.' Alistair had the same kind of glow that Matt did. 'Not sure how that news got leaked so fast. It's very early days so we're being careful.'

Rebecca felt a pang of something poignant. She remembered what it was like to be so in love. To be so sure that you'd found the person you wanted to spend the rest of your life with. To be expecting a first baby...

Hopefully, these new couples within the ranks of their colleagues would have the happy-ever-after that she and Thomas had missed out on.

'I'll have to catch up with them both some other time,' she

said. 'I wanted to tell Quinn what a great job she did. She put a lot of effort into that committee.'

'I'll tell her you noticed,' Matt said. 'She's over the moon about the result, that's for sure.' His smile broadened. 'I believe she's now on a new committee that's going to be organising the official celebration bash.'

Rebecca laughed. 'That sounds like Quinn. Any word on what sort of party it's going to be?'

'Black tie, from what I've heard. A big dinner with lots of speeches.'

'I'll look forward to it.'

'Me, too,' Alistair said. 'In the meantime, can I buy you guys a drink? It's good to see you out and about for once, Thomas.'

'Ah…' Thomas's gaze slid sideways. Towards the door? Was he thinking that the fact that this wasn't really a work function any more was a good reason to bail?

'I'll have a white wine,' Rebecca said quickly. 'Is it still red for you, Tom?'

Her heart skipped a beat. Unexpectedly, she wanted him to stay. She wanted time with him away from the hospital again, like they'd had on that walk through the park.

Maybe it wasn't the best idea but she wanted…what? To see a glimpse of the real Thomas again? The one that had called her 'Becca' and given her a hug?

'Sounds good,' he said. 'But I'll buy them. Can I get you something else, Matt? Alistair?'

'No, thanks,' Alistair said. 'I'll finish this but then I'd better head off, too. Got an early ward round tomorrow.'

They clinked glasses when the drinks had been poured.

'Here's to Paddington's staying exactly where it should be. For ever.'

'Paddington's,' Rebecca echoed. 'It's been quite a fight, hasn't it? Let's hope there's no final glitch that stops it becoming official.'

'How could there be?' Matt said. 'It feels like we've got the whole of London on our side now.'

'How amazing was it for Sheikh Idris to have made that donation?' Alistair said. 'We wouldn't be celebrating now if it wasn't for him. Can you imagine being *that* rich?'

'No.' Rebecca sipped her wine. 'But I can imagine loving my daughter enough to want to thank the people who helped her. And save the place where the miracle had happened.'

Oh, help! That was a heavy thing to say, given the company. No wonder Thomas was draining his glass of wine. The bartender noticed instantly and raised a bottle as well as his eyebrows. Thomas nodded and his glass was refilled. He glanced at Rebecca's glass and then caught her gaze and she nodded acceptance of the unspoken offer.

Why not? It had been a long day and they both had things to celebrate other than a successful campaign to save the hospital they both worked in. They shared a patient who'd come through some pretty amazing surgery today.

And they were making a fresh start on their new relationship.

It was already feeling easier and Alistair had obviously noticed a difference. She hadn't missed that glance he'd shared with Matt when they'd seen them come in together and he'd made a point of telling Thomas that it was good to see him being social.

It was Rebecca that he seemed to want to talk to now, however.

'I was looking for you earlier today. Sounded like you were tied up in Theatre for a long session. Interesting case?'

'It was. You don't often get to insert a ventricular assist device.'

'Ah, that's little Penelope Craig, isn't it? I heard about that. Did it go well?'

'It's working perfectly,' Thomas put in. 'We'll just have to hope that it buys enough time for her to get a transplant.' He turned away to respond to something Matt said and, within moments, the two of them were engrossed in conversation.

Alistair was looking thoughtful as he took a step closer to Rebecca. 'That's what I was wanting to give you a heads-up about.' He lowered his voice, even though nobody would have been able to overhear their conversation in this noisy bar. 'I've got a case in ICU at the moment. Six-year-old boy. We're going to repeat tests in the next day or two but I don't think we're going to find any signs of brain activity. He could become a possible donor in the near future.'

Rebecca's nod was solemn. 'I know the case,' she said quietly.

Who didn't? This little boy—Ryan Walker—had been the most seriously injured child in the dreadful school fire at Westbourne Grove that had been the catalyst to turn the attention of the media onto the plight of Paddington Children's Hospital's impending closure. Any real recovery from his severe head injury had always been unlikely and, only a few weeks ago, he'd had a major setback with a new bleed in his brain. He'd been on life support in the intensive care unit ever since.

If he was declared brain-dead, and his parents were willing to consider the idea of organ donation, then he would become one of Rebecca's patients. It was not often that she became involved at this stage. Retrieval of organs was usually somewhere else, from a patient whose family had already accepted that there was no hope for their own child and who had the generosity of heart to realise that their tragedy could provide hope for others.

'Have the parents been spoken to?'

'Not yet. They're still coming to terms with how bad things are. I think they're still hoping for some kind of miracle. I suspect that discussion is going to come after the next electroencephalogram. I was hoping to maybe include you in that family conference. To introduce the subject of possible organ donation?' Alistair sighed and then finished his drink. 'And now I really must get home and make sure that Claire's been putting her feet up.'

Matt followed Alistair's lead and Thomas and Rebecca found themselves alone at the bar when they'd really only started on their refilled glasses.

A waiter walked past, carrying plates from the kitchen and the smell of the hot food made Rebecca turn her head.

'Have you eaten?' Thomas asked.

'No. I didn't find the time. I'll grab a sandwich when I get home.'

'I've just realised I missed dinner, too. Not a good idea, drinking on an empty stomach.'

'No...' She'd wanted him to stay here and give them some time together, but dinner seemed like an intimate thing to do.

But friends could have dinner together, couldn't they?

Of course they could. It was what friends did.

'I think I saw some Yorkshire puddings with that roast beef that went past.'

'Oh.' Rebecca pushed any lingering doubts aside. 'I'll bet they have fish and chips with mushy peas on the menu, too.'

'Let's find out.'

Within a matter of minutes, they found themselves at a quiet corner table, menus in hand and, a commendably short time after that, they had delicious, hot meals in front of them.

And it was much easier than Rebecca had expected. They'd done this a million times together in the past and they could eat and chat without it being a big deal. They talked about Penny and the surgery.

'I'm glad you came to watch,' she admitted.

'So am I,' Thomas said quietly. 'You've come a long way, Becca. Did it occur to you that the last time I watched you operate was also on Penny? When she was about six months old?'

'Mmm...'

He hadn't been around for the last surgery on Penny, though, had he? He'd gone by then and had taken any hope of salvaging anything from the wreck their marriage had become.

A silence fell between them, which made the background

conversation of other customers and the music from the juke box increasingly noticeable. Rebecca took a sip of her wine. And then another.

When the Ricky Martin song with its strong Latino beat started playing, the silence between them suddenly became charged.

Some memories only needed something like a few bars of a song to make it feel like they'd happened yesterday.

Salsa dance classes had been a form of exercise Thomas had been dragged along to when they were at medical school.

'It'll keep you fit,' Rebecca had assured him. *'And it's the best stress relief. Just what we'll need when it comes to exam time.'*

Who knew what an excellent dancer Thomas would turn out to be? Or how much they both found they loved it?

Rebecca hadn't danced in more than five years.

From the look on Thomas's face, neither had he.

The wine had to be blamed for the lack of thought on Rebecca's part. For the crazy urge that she couldn't suppress. Maybe it was the memory of the kind of stress relief it could provide. A cure for the slightly awkward silence? A distraction from both memories she didn't want to sink into and the prospect of the kind of conversation she might have to have with Ryan Walker's family in the near future?

'I love this song,' she heard herself say as her smile grew. 'Are you up for it?'

Friends could dance together, couldn't they? Without it being a big deal? It wasn't that much of a step up from having dinner together and that had been fine until a few moments ago. Maybe she wanted to recapture that feeling of being comfortable in each other's company.

Thomas was looking stunned. It was clearly the last thing he had expected and just as obviously he had no idea how to react.

Rebecca helped him out. She put her glass of wine down and stood up, holding out her hand, already turning towards the tiny square of a dance floor that the pub offered.

It didn't matter if he was only being polite, so that she wouldn't be embarrassed by being the only person on the dance floor, but something inside Rebecca's chest melted as he hesitated for only a moment before following her. He touched her fingers, caught her hand in his and then pulled her close.

They could have been back in one of those Tuesday night dance classes. Or even at the one competition they'd entered, just for fun. The muscle memory came back within moments and they moved together as well as they always had. Thomas's lead was so smooth and so easy to follow that Rebecca could simply let the music flow over them and enjoy every step and twirl and dip.

It was over too soon. The next song was a slow one and the kind of dancing that would require was definitely not appropriate between friends. Rebecca didn't even risk a direct glance at Thomas as she headed back to their table.

'Thanks,' she said. 'Can't remember when I last had a dance.'

'Me, neither.'

Another silence fell. Were they both thinking back to when that might have been?

Thomas certainly was.

And it wasn't that difficult because he hadn't been anywhere near a dance floor in the last five years. Rebecca had been the last person he'd danced with.

The realisation released a flood of memories. Just snatches. How reluctant he'd been when Rebecca had come into class that day at med school, waving a flyer advertising the start of a new term for salsa classes.

The laughter and fun of those Tuesday nights when they'd both been complete beginners, fumbling their way through the steps and trying not to trip each other up.

The satisfaction of moves becoming automatic enough to be able to enjoy the music and hold Rebecca in his arms at the same time. To see the joy on her face and feel it in the response of her body.

Their wedding dance…

How much harder it had been to dance with her as her belly expanded in pregnancy but it hadn't stopped them.

There had always been music on when they were at home to-gether. How often had they paused for a moment as they passed each other? When a brief touch or hug could morph into a dance move or two?

Gwen had loved it. As a baby she'd beam at them from her bouncy chair. As a toddler, she'd demanded to join in.

Maybe that was actually the last occasion that Thomas had danced. When he'd held the small hand of his daughter in the air so she could twirl around. When he'd scooped her into his arms and then bent down to dip her head close enough to the floor to make her shriek with laughter.

Oh, God!

That memory hurt.

Was the pain the reason his gaze sought Rebecca's? Did he need the comfort of a connection with the only other person on earth who would understand how much it hurt?

He saw the moment that connection fused. The way her eyes filled with tears.

'Oh, *Tom*…'

Her lips were trembling. He saw the first tear escape and roll down the side of her nose.

How embarrassing would it be for her to break down in front of all these people in the pub? It would be worse than finding herself alone on the dance floor. Pulling out his wallet he put down more than enough cash to cover their dinner.

'Come with me,' he said, taking her hand. 'Time we got some fresh air, I think.'

She held it together until they were out on the street. Until they'd walked far enough to be away from the sound of the regulars at the Frog and Peach enjoying their Friday night out.

And then she stopped and pulled her hand from his, so that she could cover her eyes.

'I... I'm sorry,' she choked. 'It's just that I... I remembered the last time I saw you dancing...'

Thomas clenched his jaw. 'Me, too. With...with Gwen...'

The sob sounded like it was being torn from Rebecca's heart.

'Sometimes,' she whispered, 'I miss her *so* much...'

There was nothing Thomas could do other than take her in his arms. He needed to hold her. He needed someone to hold him back because those tears were contagious.

'Same,' he muttered.

They stood there for what seemed like the longest time. Against a wrought-iron fence, out of the way of people who passed with barely a glance at the embracing couple. Cars and buses and taxis thundered by on the busy road. The world continued to spin but, for Thomas, it had paused. There was nothing but this holding. And being held.

And then Rebecca shifted in his arms and looked up at him and her wet cheeks gleamed under the light of a nearby lamppost. Her eyes were huge and dark and...and so very, very sad.

There was nothing Thomas could do other than to dip his head and kiss her.

Gently.

Slowly.

With enough tenderness to let her know that he understood.

That he felt exactly the same way.

CHAPTER SEVEN

THIS WAS WHAT had been missing from her life for so long.

Being held when she felt so sad.

Knowing that someone else understood how she felt.

Rebecca closed her eyes and fell into that kiss. There was no way she was going to question the wisdom of what was happening or what the consequences might be.

She'd been waiting for this moment for ever. She just hadn't realised it.

That touch of lips on hers was so heartbreakingly tender it should have made her want to cry but, instead, it covered the source of the tears that had already been falling and smothered them like sand on the embers of a fire.

It was the feeling that someone genuinely cared about her.

Loved her, even…

No. Not *someone*. There was only one person who had ever made her feel quite like this. Only one person who could really understand exactly how she felt, because he had been there and he felt the same way.

Tom…

The name escaped her lips on a sigh but Rebecca didn't realise it was audible until she felt the change in the way she was being held. The tension in the muscles of his arms was instant—preparation for being taken away?

Yes. Thomas was letting her go as she opened her eyes. He was turning his head, too, but not before she'd seen the glint of tears in his eyes and something that looked a lot like…regret?

And then he ran his fingers through his hair, raising his face to the streetlamp above them. His eyes were tightly shut.

'Sorry,' he muttered. 'I shouldn't have done that.'

Why not?

Because it meant that he was throwing away the rule book about keeping so much distance between them?

Because he had another partner that he'd just cheated on? The lines of pain on his face suggested that that was the more likely explanation.

The chill that ran down Rebecca's spine actually made her shiver. But she was still aware of the warmth that kiss had delivered. The comfort of feeling that he still cared.

Did *she* still care? Judging by the urge to erase those lines of pain around his eyes and mouth, apparently she did.

'It's okay, Tom.' Rebecca touched his arm. 'We were both upset. It's my fault. I… I shouldn't have asked you to dance. Dragged us both back into the past like that.'

He opened his eyes and looked down at her and she could see nothing but sadness in his eyes.

'It never goes away, does it?'

'No.' But Rebecca pulled in a deeper breath. 'It does change, though. It gets less painful. There are good things to remember, too.'

His nod was slow. One corner of his mouth lifted a little.

'Yeah…like how much she loved to dance. She was such a happy little thing, wasn't she?'

Rebecca nodded. Gwen had been the happiest of children. She would wake up with a smile on her face and her arms outstretched to greet the people she loved and the new day that would always bring excitement. And she spread that happiness around her with such abundance that anybody nearby would catch it and then give it back and it would get bigger every time.

The world without Gwen had lost so much light. It was still dark in places and Rebecca knew it wouldn't help to step any closer to those corners. It wouldn't help her and it might well drive Thomas back to where he'd been—unable to find any way out.

'It's okay,' she said again. 'It didn't mean anything more than sharing a memory. It…it wasn't cheating or anything.'

'Cheating?' Had Thomas taken a step back or did it just feel like he had? 'What's that supposed to mean?'

Rebecca bit her lip. This was really overstepping boundaries. A shared past was something they couldn't avoid but Thomas had been very clear that his current personal life was out of bounds. They were just beginning to feel their way into what could become a friendship. Making a reference to his sex life was more than awkward.

It was excruciating.

He was still waiting for a response. Frowning, now, as if he was fitting pieces of a difficult puzzle together.

'Did you feel like *you* were cheating?' he asked quietly. 'Are you…*with* someone, Becca?'

'No!' The word came out more vehemently than she had intended. As if the idea of being with someone was shocking. She followed it with a huff that sounded incredulous. 'Not me, I thought *you* might be…'

There was a long moment of silence. Rebecca shivered again and wrapped her arms around her body. She didn't dare meet his gaze. Instead, she turned her head to look along the footpath. In the direction she needed to take to go home.

To escape?

Thomas cleared his throat. 'I'm not,' he said. 'Are you?'

Rebecca raised her gaze. 'No.'

Their gazes held. The question they both wanted to ask hung

like a cartoon bubble over their heads. Until they both spoke at the same time.

'Has there been…?'

'Have you…?'

Another pause. And then it happened again.

'No,' they said in unison.

The silence had a stunned echo to it this time.

It was Rebecca who broke it.

'Why not?' she whispered.

'Why?' he countered.

'Because…because it's been five years. And I know… I know how lonely it can get.'

Thomas looked away. 'Guess I haven't been ready,' he said. 'I focused on work enough for that to be all that mattered.'

'Me, too,' Rebecca admitted. 'And the time just kept going past. I'd forgotten how long it was until…until you came back to Paddington's. I guess I've just taken things day by day for so long, it's become engrained. I never look too far into the future.'

'And I discovered that it's better never to look too far into the past.'

Rebecca felt herself become very still. This was a huge admission, wasn't it?

She hadn't felt this close to Thomas since…well, maybe since the very early days of their relationship. When it had been so easy to say anything and trust that it would be accepted and understood. When anything seemed possible and glowed with the prospect of real happiness.

It had been a very different kind of closeness at the end— during those awful days when they'd sat in the intensive care unit beside Gwen's bed. Holding each other's hands so tightly that it could become painful—but never as painful as what was happening around them. That connection had been more powerful, perhaps, but far less happy.

With the embrace of that dance still lingering on her skin, Rebecca chose to tap into that first memory of the connection they'd discovered with each other. It made it feel so natural to say more.

'We're both stuck, aren't we?' she suggested softly. 'Living in the present.'

'It's not a bad place to be.'

'But we're still young. There's a lot more to life than work…'

Thomas moved his head in another one of those slow, thoughtful nods. He even offered her the ghost of another smile.

'Like dancing?'

Rebecca smiled back and mirrored his nod.

'I'll keep that in mind.' His faint smile vanished. 'It's getting late. I'll walk you home.'

'No need. It's out of your way. I can get a cab.'

'At this time on a Friday night? You'll be lucky.'

Rebecca wanted to agree. She wanted to walk with Thomas and keep talking. If they did, maybe she could find that connection that seemed to have vanished again.

Or had she imagined it?

Fate intervened in any case. A black cab was heading towards them, with its yellow light glowing to advertise its availability. Thomas raised his arm and it pulled into the curb.

'There you go. I was wrong…' His smile was tight. Relieved? He wanted to get away, didn't he? So that he didn't have to revisit any more painful memories? Or to admit he might have been wrong about anything else—like the way he'd abandoned her when she'd needed him more than ever?

Rebecca opened the back door of the cab. 'Want to share?'

She could feel his hesitation. She saw him open his mouth as if he was about to accept the invitation. And then his expression changed—as though he'd just walked into a mental brick wall.

One of those well-built barriers?

'I'll walk.' His voice had a gruff edge. 'I need the exercise after those Yorkshire puddings.'

She turned her head as the cab pulled away. She could see

Thomas through the back window, already heading in the opposite direction.

Alone.

Going back to his apartment where he would still be alone.

As she would when she got back to hers.

It felt wrong.

A lot more wrong than it would have felt last week. Or even yesterday.

She hadn't been wrong about finding that connection again, had she? It was bigger than simply the fact that they'd kissed each other. Or admitted that there'd been no one else in their lives since their marriage ended.

Something had shifted in the layers that had been used to bury what had been their marriage. Had Thomas seen the same glint of what had been uncovered?

Did he realise that the connection they'd had was still there?

That it was possible that it might actually be even stronger?

That wasn't the real question, though, was it?

Rebecca felt suddenly weary enough to rest her head on the back of the seat and close her eyes.

The real question was whether he would want to uncover any more of what had been buried for so long. Whether she wanted that herself.

'And I discovered that it's better never to look too far into the past.'

You wouldn't find anything if you chose not to look. And you could make it easy not to see by kicking the layers back into place.

She hadn't intended to force either of them to look tonight. Asking him to dance had been impulsive and the shared memories that it had provoked had been inevitable.

Had it made things harder?

Judging by the ache in her own heart, Rebecca suspected that it had.

That ache suggested that she'd never really stopped loving

Thomas. Getting closer to him again could mean that she was setting herself up for a whole new heartbreak—one that could mean she would be stuck for even longer.

Alone. With no partner in her current life or dreams of a family in her future.

Something like a groan escaped along with her sigh.

'You all right, love?'

Rebecca opened her eyes to see the cab driver watching her in his rear-view mirror.

'Almost there,' he added cheerfully. 'You'll be home before you know it.'

She summoned a smile and turned her head in time to see the signpost of her street flash past.

This was where she lived.

But it wasn't a home any more. Not really.

Work was failing to provide the complete distraction that Thomas Wolfe had come to depend on.

He'd spent most of his weekend at the hospital and most of that in his office, writing an article for a paediatric cardiology journal on the relationship between the diagnosis of asthma and dilated cardiomyopathy. He took his time over ward rounds on both Saturday and Sunday mornings but his visits to the intensive care unit were very brief.

Penny was the patient in most need of frequent monitoring but, theoretically, she was under the care of her surgical team at the moment and wouldn't be transferred back to the cardiology ward until Rebecca was happy with her condition. He was on call, of course, if any consultation was needed but, so far, everything was going very smoothly. They'd kept her asleep a little longer than planned but her sedation was now being gradually lifted and it was hoped that she would be awake and ready to move to the ward first thing on Monday morning.

His visits to the unit hadn't coincided with any that Rebecca might be making and that was probably a good thing because Thomas wasn't sure he was ready to see her again just yet.

What had happened on Friday night was still doing his head in. Thoughts kept intruding, even when he should have been completely engrossed in his writing.

A diagnosis of moderate persistent bronchial asthma was made in the four-year-old girl. A year later she was admitted with features of an acute exacerbation, including breathlessness, cough, sleep disturbances and poor response to nebulised salbutamol...

His gaze drifted to the series of chest X-rays he was planning to include in the next section, but he wasn't looking at the evidence of fluid build-up in the lungs.

It was that kiss that was the problem.

Or maybe it had been the dancing.

Then again, he kept remembering—with a slight sense of shock—that Rebecca had told him she was single. That she hadn't been with anyone else in the last five years.

Why not?

It couldn't have been because of any lack of interest on the part of the men she must have encountered. She was gorgeous. Clever. Funny. Such a positive person, too. That was where Gwen's sunny nature had come from. Rebecca had a smile that could light up a room and she automatically looked for the bright side of anything, no matter how bad it was.

Even when it was the worst thing imaginable. She'd been the one to bring up the awful subject of organ donation, when they'd been sitting so helplessly, day after day, beside the bedside of their critically injured daughter.

'If there's even the shadow of something good that could come out of this,' she'd said, *'maybe it's the fact that the lives of other people's precious children could be saved.'*

She'd been the one who had arranged Gwen's funeral. The

tiny pink casket with bright flowers painted all over it. The pink and white balloons that were released that contained little packets of wildflower seeds. The songs that had come from beloved television shows and Disney movies.

'It's the last party I can ever give her,' she'd said. *'I want it to be what would have made her happy.'*

Oh, God...

So many memories were coming out of the woodwork. He tried to shake them off before that lump in his throat made it too hard to breathe. Before he had to fight back tears, the way he had when he'd made the mistake of kissing Rebecca and could feel the grief of losing her—and Gwen—doing its best to wrap his heart in those vicious tentacles all over again.

But why was she still alone?

She hadn't blamed herself for the accident. She certainly hadn't blamed him. She hadn't even blamed the nursery school who had been responsible for Gwen's safety that day.

She'd moved on. She'd been able to keep working with children. More than that, she'd become involved with the whole transplant side of medicine and even changed the direction of her own career to become as involved as it was possible to get.

If she could handle the emotional side of that, why hadn't she moved on enough to find a new partner? To start a new family, even, which had always been her dream of the perfect future.

There was only one answer that Thomas could come up with.

He'd hurt her so badly, she simply didn't want to risk it again.

And yet, here she was trying to establish a friendship with him. She seemed to want to spend time with him and it had definitely been her idea to have that dance.

It didn't make sense.

She'd accused him of running away. Of leaving their marriage even while they'd still been together.

Did this mean that she was prepared to forgive him?

That it was possible there was more than friendship to be salvaged from the wreck of their lives together?

It had felt like that, when he'd been holding her in his arms while she cried.

When he'd kissed her and felt her kissing him back.

But it was doing his head in.

Part of him wanted nothing more than a second chance.

Part of him wanted to keep well clear of all those memories to protect himself.

But another part still cared enough to be determined not to hurt Rebecca again. He'd failed her once before and it certainly hadn't been intentional. How could he be sure that it wouldn't happen again?

It would be better for everybody if he dismissed the possibility.

He carried on writing.

Respiratory distress worsened to the point that mechanical ventilation was required. The most likely diagnosis considered at this stage included complicated severe asthma, infection, fluid overload and underlying cardiac disease...

His hands stilled again as he lost the thread of his next sentence. Shutting his eyes for a moment, Thomas tried to force himself to focus. This article was taking a lot longer than usual to pull together but he would get it done; he just needed more time.

And that was the answer to a lot of things, wasn't it?

More time.

He could step back from the confusion that a friendship with his ex-wife was causing. Given time, he would be able to think more clearly and decide what the best course of action might be. It seemed that trying to set her free by ending their marriage hadn't worked but something needed to happen so that they could both move on in their personal lives.

By finding new partners?

Thomas could feel himself scowling at a computer screen covered with words that were no more than a blur.

He didn't want a new partner.

Worse than that, the thought of Rebecca with someone else was…unacceptable?

Oh, man, his head really was a mess. And it was starting to interfere with his work.

How had he managed to keep his personal head space successfully separated from anything professional for the last five years?

Because he had been a long way away from Rebecca, that was why. He hadn't had to see her every day. To talk to her and watch her work. He hadn't spent any time with her alone.

And he hadn't even *thought* about dancing with her, let alone kissing her.

Okay, so that wasn't completely true.

With a sigh, Thomas saved his file and closed the programme. He needed some fresh air. A brisk walk or maybe a run that would not only distract him, it might tire him out enough to sleep properly tonight.

A long run. All the way around Regent's Park and Primrose Hill, perhaps.

No. Too many memories, including some very recent ones.

Hyde Park, then. It was closer, bigger and far less familiar.

Safer. For both himself and the woman he had loved so totally.

It was exactly what he had always vowed to do. To put Rebecca's needs above his own.

To keep her safe.

Any working week in a field of medicine that included critically unwell patients was a roller-coaster of good moments, worrying moments and—at the bottom of one of those loops—the really heartbreaking moments that made you wonder if you were up to the kind of stress this job could entail.

Rebecca was about to face one of those low swoops and she had to gather every ounce of her courage to do it.

Walking away from one of the good moments was making it harder. She had just come from the paediatric cardiology ward where her visit to Penelope Craig had coincided with Thomas doing his ward round.

The smile with which he had greeted her had been a relief. She'd barely seen him all week and had convinced herself that she'd wrecked any chance of friendship between them after that night at the Frog and Peach.

Dancing with him, for heaven's sake.

Crying on his shoulder. Was it really so surprising that he'd tried to comfort her by kissing her? It hadn't meant anything but it could well have been enough to have him raise those barriers between them again.

But he'd smiled at her as she entered Penny's room and it hadn't just been a polite greeting. There was a warmth in his eyes that said he was happy to see her. Had he noticed that their paths hadn't crossed in so many days?

Perhaps he thought she'd been deliberately avoiding him and he was relieved, as well. The truth was that Rebecca had been flat out. The Teddy Bears' Picnic was happening this coming weekend and the last minute organisation had taken up every spare second she'd had, and then some, including several very late nights.

So she was weary, and that always accentuated any emotional components of her job.

Everybody was smiling in Penny's room this morning.

'So she can come home next week?' Julia asked. 'And she doesn't need to be on oxygen all the time?'

'Not unless she's getting breathless or becomes unwell,' Thomas told her. 'And that's looking less likely every day.'

'And we can let her do whatever she wants? Go back to school?'

'Not just yet. We'll keep her in until after the weekend and see how she's doing and then we'll talk about school. Let her walk around as much as she wants to and you could take her to the playground.'

'I can dance,' Penny told Rebecca. 'Just like Sapphire Ballerina Bear. Want to see?' She scrambled off her mother's lap, put her arms in the air and turned herself in a slightly wobbly circle. She didn't seem to be in any significant pain as she bounced back from her major surgery. The grin on her face made everybody smile all over again.

'That's fantastic,' Rebecca said. She held out the object in her hand to Julia. 'This is for you. Keep it with you at all times from now on.'

'Oh...' Julia's gaze sought that of her husband and her glance was fearful.

'It's the pager,' Peter said.

'Yes. Penny's on the top of the transplant list now and a new heart could become available at any time. If it does, even if it's somewhere else in the country, you'll get paged and you'll need to come back to the hospital immediately. That doesn't mean that the transplant will definitely go ahead because sometimes unexpected things happen but you'll need to be here and be prepared. We repeat a lot of tests to make sure nothing's changed.'

Julia and Peter both nodded solemnly.

'In the meantime...' Rebecca smiled at Penny who was twirling again. 'Enjoy everything that you haven't been able to do for so long. I'll come back again before you go home in case you have any questions but you've got my phone number, too. Don't hesitate to call.'

'Thank you so much, Dr Scott,' Peter said. 'You have no idea how much this means to us all.'

'Oh, I think I do.' The glance in Thomas's direction happened without thinking and the look in his eyes was better than any smile. They both knew how precious for Julia and Peter this time with their daughter would be. They both knew they were providing a gift they'd never been able to receive themselves.

The connection was most definitely still there.

And, regardless of whether either of them would choose for it to happen or not, it seemed to be getting stronger.

So it was no wonder that her next appointment was a prospect that weighed down both her feet and her heart. She could feel both getting heavier as she slid away from the joy of Penny's visit to the sadness that she knew she would find in the quiet space of the most private room of the paediatric intensive care unit, where six-year-old Ryan Walker had been declared brain-dead late yesterday afternoon.

Alistair North was waiting for her outside the unit.

'Ryan's parents are with him at the moment. They were present for the second round of tests last night and they've been here ever since. I paged you when they were ready to ask about what's going to happen next.'

Rebecca nodded. As a doctor who worked in the field of organ transplants, she was not allowed to have anything to do with the range of tests conducted to confirm brain death. These were normally done twice, by two different doctors, spaced apart by at least twelve hours.

'No inconclusive results, then?'

Alistair shook his head, his face sombre. 'I think it was the angiography that hit them the hardest. The image is so clear when all you've got is a dark space inside the skull with absolutely no blood flow.'

Rebecca nodded. She knew exactly how devastating that kind of image could be.

'His grandparents are in one of the relatives' rooms, looking after his little sister, Gemma.'

Alistair introduced her to Louise and Colin Walker, Ryan's parents, who were sitting, their hands linked and their faces pale with shock, beside his bed.

Wisps of red hair showed under the bandages on Ryan's head and his freckles stood out on a pale little face. Only six years old, this was a tragedy that touched everybody's hearts.

'I'm so very, very sorry,' she said quietly. 'I haven't been involved with Ryan's care since his accident but I know that everything possible was done.'

They both nodded but Colin was frowning. He didn't understand why she was here.

'You asked about what happens next,' Alistair said. 'So there are decisions that need to be made. Difficult decisions.' He cleared his throat. 'I asked Dr Scott—Rebecca—to come because she's had a lot of experience with supporting people to make these kinds of decisions.'

'You mean about...about when we turn off the life support?' Louise's voice broke and she covered her eyes with her hands. 'And what...what happens then?'

'There's no hurry,' Rebecca said gently. 'We can give you all the time you need. And all the support you—and the rest of your family—might find helpful.'

'Rebecca is a surgeon,' Alistair continued quietly. 'There's never a good time to introduce a subject like this, but she's the head of our transplant team. She's come to talk to you about the possibility of Ryan being an organ donor.'

Colin Walker's face became even paler as he joined the dots. 'No,' he whispered. 'How could you even ask?'

'I understand,' Rebecca said into the horrified silence. 'I'm not here to do anything more than introduce myself at the moment. To leave you with some information and my phone number. You can call me anytime at all—day or night—if you have any questions or need to talk.'

Colin couldn't look at her and Louise still had her hands over her face.

'All I ask is that you think about it,' she added softly. 'And I can tell you that the gift of life *can* help—for both sides.'

She glanced at Alistair and he nodded. It was time for her to leave and not seem to be putting any pressure at all on these grieving parents. The subject had been raised and Alistair and the team in the intensive care unit would continue to care for Ryan until they were ready to make their decision.

Walking through the double doors to leave the unit, Rebecca could see a woman coming out of one of the relatives' rooms, holding the hand of a small girl who had bright red curly hair and a freckled button nose. About two years old, she had to be Gemma—Ryan Walker's little sister. Rebecca smiled at the grandmother but kept going. This wasn't the time to introduce herself to the wider family.

It was good that Ryan wasn't an only child. Not that that could change how devastating this whole situation was but Rebecca had thought more than once over the years she'd been involved in this specialty that it could make a real difference in the future. She'd seen it happen on the rare occasions when she'd become involved at this earlier stage of the process of organ donation. These parents were forced to carry on. To stay engaged with all aspects of life—including each other?

Every time, it made her wonder whether that would have made a difference to herself and Thomas and she would feel a beat of her own loss. Not just for Gwen, or for their marriage, but for the larger family that could have been.

She paused in front of the elevators, closing her eyes against the pain of it all.

Maybe Thomas hadn't been so wrong, after all, to distance himself from having to experience it again and again.

She wanted to tell him that. To tell him that she understood. More than she had at the time.

That she could forgive him…

No. Right now she didn't want to talk to him.

She just wanted him to hold her in his arms and comfort her. To remind her that they'd done the right thing when they hadn't hesitated to agree to donate Gwen's organs. When they'd known that they wouldn't be able to hold their precious daughter when she took her last breath.

They would only be able to hold each other.

CHAPTER EIGHT

'I UNDERSTAND.' REBECCA gave Louise Walker's hand a squeeze. 'It's okay.'

Louise looked up at the clock on the wall of this private room. 'Colin will be back soon. He's collecting his parents from the airport. They were on a cruise ship so we've had to wait until they got to a port.'

'He doesn't know that you asked to meet me?'

The distressed young mother shook her head. 'He doesn't want to talk about any of it. Turning off the life support is bad enough but the idea of organ donation is too much for him.'

'I do understand.'

'But I want to do it,' Louise whispered, tears streaming down her face. 'I keep thinking, what if Ryan was the one who was really sick and needed a new heart or lungs or something? If I was one of those parents who was hoping, every day, that a miracle would happen and that an organ would become available...'

'There are two sides to every story,' Rebecca agreed quietly. 'But everybody feels differently and it would be very wrong to try and force Colin to agree to something he can't handle.'

'Dr North says we can take a few days but...it's so hard. Part of me just wants it to be over, you know? So that we can start trying to put our lives back together.'

'I understand,' Rebecca said again. 'And I don't want you to feel guilty about not making a decision. Or making the decision for Ryan not to be a donor. It's something the whole family needs to be sure about.'

'I know my parents think it's a good thing—that something good could still come out of this whole horrible accident. All these weeks we've had hoping for the impossible.'

Rebecca had to blink away the sudden moisture in her own eyes. Along with the echo of her own broken voice from so long ago.

'If there's even the shadow of something good that could come out of this, maybe it's the fact that the lives of other people's precious children could be saved.'

'I think Colin's parents might, too,' Louise added. 'We're all going to come in and spend time with Ryan over the weekend. That will be the time to talk about it again.'

'You've got my number. If I can support you in any way—with whatever decision you make—please call me.'

'I will. And thank you.' She looked up at the clock again. 'I'd better get back. Mum wants to get home so they can take Gemma to the zoo this afternoon. Weird, isn't it? But life doesn't stop, even when it feels like the world should have stopped turning for a while.'

Rebecca let go of her hand, noting how pale and exhausted Louise was looking. 'Have you been away from here at all yourself?'

Louise shook her head. 'Every minute counts, doesn't it?'

The two women parted at the door. Impulsively, Louise hugged Rebecca.

'I think you do really understand,' she whispered. 'It means a lot.'

Rebecca hugged her back. This part of her job often entailed an emotional connection to patients and their families that went above and beyond normal boundaries. Not that she'd ever tell people that she'd been through the same thing herself because that could be a form of pressure to follow her example. That her understanding was genuine seemed to come through unspoken, however, and it was reassuring both to the families she worked with and to herself.

She brought something to this job that nobody else could. It was what she was meant to be doing and she was proud of the difference she could make in the lives of others.

That pride was normally a very private thing that came in moments like this. A public acknowledgement like the one that was to be celebrated at the Teddy Bears' Picnic was very different. Accolades were unnecessary—embarrassing, even—but any discomfort was outweighed by the joy of being with so many people who'd had their lives transformed by organ donation. There was a real need for public education, too, and this year was even more important given the spotlight that Paddington's was still under.

As the head of the transplant team, Rebecca knew that she would be under her own spotlight and she knew the responsibility that she carried. Transplant surgery entailed the kind of drama that people loved to hear about. Showcasing Paddington as an important centre with a track record of great success could confirm how necessary it was for this hospital to remain for generations to come. It could be the final push that would mean its safety was officially guaranteed.

It was a perfect day for the big event.

Not that Thomas had intended to go, but everybody had been talking about it when he'd been in at work doing his usual ward round.

'They want as many Paddington's staff members there as possible, to show how united we all are,' Rosie had told him as she accompanied him to Penny's room. Julia was apparently worried that her daughter was coming down with a cold or something that might delay the possibility of her going home.

'I'm going to meet Leo there, as soon as my shift finishes,'

Rosie continued. 'The twins have got their teddies ready for the "best dressed" bear competition at the end of the day and they're so excited by the prospect of a pony ride. It'll be such fun!'

'The Teddy Bears' picnic?' Julia Craig overheard the end of the conversation at they entered her room. 'I wish we could go. Next year.' She smiled at Penny. 'You could take Sapphire.'

'I want to go now,' Penny said. 'I want a pony ride, too.'

'Let's see how you are,' Thomas said. 'Mummy says you've got a sniffle.'

It wasn't anything to worry about but the Craig family wouldn't be attending the picnic this time. Maybe it was knowing that Rebecca would be there that tipped the balance as Thomas left Paddington's early in the afternoon.

It had been so good to see her yesterday when she'd given Penny's parents that significant pager. To see her return his smile and feel like it was still possible that they could be friends without his head getting so messed up.

That they could rewind a little? To forget that dance. And the kiss.

To start again with some better boundaries in place?

Besides, the day was too perfect to spend either in his office finishing that article or stuck in that shoebox of an apartment that had no view of anything green. Thomas pulled off his tie and opened the top button of his shirt. He rolled his sleeves up and kept walking, taking the same route that he and Rebecca had taken that first time they'd spent some real time together since his return.

The sun shone from a cloudless sky but the slopes of Primrose Hill caught a breeze that kept the temperature pleasant enough for the children to enjoy even the more strenuous activities available, like the egg and spoon races and the obstacle course. Thomas walked past the team of volunteers cooking sausages on barbecues and the gazebo that had a queue of children waiting their turn for face painting. He could see a trio of fat, little ponies that had another queue of excited children waiting and he could hear gleeful shrieks coming from inside the bouncy castle.

There were cameras and reporters everywhere, from television stations, both local and national newspapers and magazines.

And there was Rebecca, looking absolutely gorgeous in blue jeans and a white, short-sleeved shirt that had a teddy bear print on it. She had her long, dark hair tied back but it wasn't wrapped up into a knot like it would be at work. It hung down her back in a wavy ponytail that was being teased in the breeze.

She hadn't seen him, because she was focused on the woman she was talking to, and he was partly screened by the man with a huge camera balanced on his shoulder and a young lad who was holding a fluffy microphone on a stick close to the two women. Thomas was simply one of the group of interested onlookers who were watching this interview. He edged a little closer so that he could hear what Rebecca was saying.

'So three people in the UK die every day because of this shortage. At the moment there are over six thousand people on the transplant waiting list and about two hundred of them are children. And many of those children come to Paddington Children's Hospital because we're one of only a few major centres for paediatric transplantation.'

'But there are organs that could be available, aren't there?' the interviewer asked. 'Is it that people don't know it's possible to donate them? Or do they not *want* to?'

'It's complicated,' Rebecca said, 'and it's a difficult subject to even think about for people who are facing the heartbreak of losing a loved one.'

'What is it that you—and all the other doctors and medical staff here from Paddington's—want to happen? We've got a lot of people watching what's happening here. What would you tell them was the purpose of a day like today?'

'Today is about celebrating life.' Rebecca's smile lit up her face. 'Of letting the families that take that amazingly generous step of making organ donation possible realise just how much of a difference they can make to so many lives.' Her gaze shifted as she waved her arm towards the huge crowd of people around them and then it caught as she spotted Thomas.

She didn't break her speech. 'We want people to talk about it. We all think that the sort of terrible situations that lead to organ donation won't happen to us—that they only happen to other people.'

Her gaze was holding Thomas's.

'But, sadly, they do happen to some of us. And if we talk about it before they happen, it might help us make a decision that can change the world for others.'

'I'm Angela Marton and we've been talking to Dr Rebecca Scott.' The interviewer turned to face the camera. 'That's an important message for all of us. And now let's go and meet some of the children and their families here today whose worlds *have* been changed.'

She led her crew away and the onlookers drifted in other directions but Thomas stayed where he was. He was still holding Rebecca's gaze and neither of them were smiling. The moment was, in fact, very close to being tear-jerking.

He began stepping closer at precisely the same moment Rebecca did.

His voice, when he managed to find some words, was raw.

'We did do the right thing, didn't we?'

She knew that he was talking about Gwen. About the decision they'd made to donate *her* organs.

'Absolutely,' she whispered. 'I'm proud of it...aren't you?'

Thomas had to swallow the huge lump in his throat. 'I think I am,' he said softly. 'I've never thought of it like that before.'

Rebecca's smile was as soft as her gaze. In that moment, that look felt as tender and loving as he remembered it being when they were first in love.

'I'm so glad you came today,' she said.

Thomas cleared his throat. 'Me, too.'

He wanted to sink into that soft gaze. To pull it around him for comfort like the softest blanket on the coldest night.

'Want an ice cream? Or a sausage? They're really good.'

Her smile widened until it was as bright as the one she'd given the television crew when she'd said that today was about celebrating life. Their poignant moment of connection was still there, but—as always—Rebecca was finding something positive to move towards.

And he was happy to follow her lead.

'Actually, I'm starving. A sausage sounds perfect.'

How amazing was it that Thomas had come this afternoon?

This was huge.

A lot bigger than Thomas himself probably realised, despite his admission that he had gained a new perspective, but Rebecca wasn't going to allow the beat of fear to diminish the joy that this gathering always bestowed. Having Thomas by her side only made it all the more important to focus on the positive.

It wasn't difficult. Everywhere they went, people came to greet them, eager to share news.

'Dr Scott, remember Tyler?'

The sturdy boy wearing the colours of his favourite football team ducked his head, hiding beneath the brim of his baseball cap. An older brother slung a protective arm over his shoulders.

'Tyler! Of course I remember you. Didn't you move to Manchester?' Rebecca laughed. 'Silly me. I should have recognised the jersey.' She looked up at the boy's parents. 'It's been, what… three years since Tyler's transplant? How's he doing?'

'He made it onto the junior football team last season,' his dad said proudly. 'Got player of the week twice.'

'Wow.' Rebecca looked suitably impressed. 'And you've come all the way to London just for today?'

'We had a minibus,' Tyler's mother told her. 'We belong to a support group for transplant families and we all decided to come for a day out. Tyler and his brother here have been practising to enter the three-legged race. We didn't realise how big it would be, though. Isn't it amazing how many kids there are that probably wouldn't even be alive if they hadn't had transplants?'

'It certainly is.' Thomas joined the conversation. 'But I bet there aren't too many who are player of the week in a football team.'

She introduced Thomas to Tyler's family. A few minutes later, she introduced him to Madeline's family and they learned how her life had changed since her lung transplant two years ago. Stephen was another cystic fibrosis patient who'd received his heart and lung transplant only last year. Piper had been given a kidney as a live donation from her father.

And then there was Ava.

'Rebecca.' Ava's mother, Jude, enveloped her in a hug. 'It's been way too long.'

'I know, I'm sorry. I've been meaning to call you but life's been a bit crazy what with all the organisation for today on top of everything else.' Rebecca's heart skipped a beat as she turned to include Thomas. Would Jude guess? More alarmingly, would Thomas guess that this was anything more than a doctor/patient relationship?

'This is Thomas Wolfe,' she said, the light tone of her voice sounding a bit forced to her own ears. 'He's a cardiothoracic surgeon at Paddington's. He left London before you moved here so he doesn't know Ava yet.'

He doesn't know anything about Ava, she added silently. And he doesn't need to. Not now.

Possibly not ever…

'I think we've got an outpatient appointment coming up with you, soon.' Jude held out her hand. 'Pleased to meet you, Thomas.'

'Likewise. And you, Ava.' Thomas was smiling at the tall twelve-year-old who had long blonde braids and astonishingly blue eyes. 'That's a very well-dressed bear you've got there.'

'It was my grandma's,' Ava told him shyly. 'It was Grandee's idea to give him the waistcoat and monocle. She said he needed to be old-fashioned because he's an antique. Like Grandee.'

'He's going into the competition for Best-Dressed Bear,' Ava's father added. 'Hadn't we better go and get him entered?'

'We won't hold you up.' Rebecca hoped she didn't sound as relieved as she suddenly felt. 'The speeches are going to start soon, too, and I think I need to introduce some of the speakers.'

'You *are* going to come to my birthday party, aren't you?' Ava said as the family began to move on. 'It's a special one.'

'I know, sweetheart. Thirteen. How does it feel to be almost a teenager?'

Ava shrugged. 'Okay, I guess. At least I'll be allowed to get my ears pierced. *Finally...*' She rolled her eyes at her mother.

Rebecca and Jude shared a smile. Teenage angst starting already?

'It's not far away. What can I bring?' Rebecca asked.

'Nothing but yourself. It's just family.' Jude hugged her again. 'We'll have a proper catch-up, then.'

She got a hug from Ava, as well, and then Rebecca watched them walk away for a little too long. Because she could feel Thomas staring at her? Of course he was. How many patients' families made it clear that they considered their doctor to be a member of their family?

He walked with her towards the main stage where preparations were going on for the guest speakers.

'Ava looks well,' he said, finally. 'How long ago did she get her transplant?'

Rebecca's mouth went a little dry. She tried to keep her tone casual. 'Oh, quite a few years ago now.'

'Did you do her surgery?'

'No...um...they were living in Newcastle then so the transplant was done there. Ava's dad got offered a new—and much better—job last year and it was partly because she could continue her care at Paddington's that they took it.'

'How come you know them so well?' he asked then. 'How did you meet them?'

She couldn't tell him. Did Thomas even know that it was possible for members of a donor's family to initiate contact with organ recipients through the intermediary of the transplant association? That the families could meet if both sides wanted to? Would she ever be able to tell him what an emotional journey it had been to meet the little girl who had received Gwen's heart and how they had welcomed her into their family with such love?

How healing it had been for her?

Janice, the president of the picnic committee, was rushing towards them, a clipboard in her hand that she was waving over her head.

'Yoo-hoo! Rebecca!'

But Rebecca had stopped walking. Because Thomas had stopped and one glance at his face told her that he had put two and two together. He looked as if he'd just been punched in the gut and had frozen completely to try not to collapse from the pain.

'Oh, my God…' he said. 'You know who Ava's donor was, don't you?'

Rebecca said nothing. The noises around her faded to a faint hum. She couldn't say anything.

She didn't need to.

Thomas had gone as white as a sheet.

For a long moment they simply stared at each other. She could feel his shock. The unbearable pain of knowing that a part of his daughter was in another little girl who got to dress up her teddy bear and have a family day out in the summer sunshine.

When, if life was remotely fair, it should have been Gwen.

And then he simply turned and walked away, disappearing into the crowd before Rebecca even had time to blink.

'Oh, thank goodness,' Janice said behind her. 'I've been looking for you everywhere. Are you ready to introduce the speakers? There's a radio station that wants to interview you, as well.'

Desperately, Rebecca tried to catch a glimpse of Thomas. If ever there was a time they needed to talk, this was it. A time to talk. To hold each other and cry…

And it was impossible.

She had duties she had to attend to. Being the face of transplants at Paddington's wasn't an ego trip. She was representing a hospital in desperate need of the final green light for its survival and she had the chance to say something about that before she introduced those speakers. To thank so many people who had contributed to the campaign and made this an issue that was so much bigger than a local community.

She had to do her bit to save the hospital she loved and believed in.

But what about the man that she had also loved and believed in once? The realisation that this wasn't simply that she cared about him the way she might care for any close friend made her catch her breath.

She *still* loved him…

Still believed in him…

Even a glance might be enough to convey how important that connection still was.

But Thomas was nowhere to be seen.

He had to keep moving.

If he stopped, he'd have to think and Thomas didn't want to think. He didn't want to feel the horror of that realisation all over again.

He'd known there was something odd about Rebecca's connection to that family from the moment they'd spotted each other. She was a part of that family, wasn't she?

Literally. Some of her genes were part of that pretty little girl with the long braids and big, blue eyes.

Some of *his* genes were, too.

It was too much.

She should have warned him. If he'd known, he would never

have gone near that picnic today. Oh, he'd known that some-where out there were several children who'd received the gift of Gwen's organs and he genuinely hoped they were all doing well. But to know who any of them were? To be a part of their lives and watch them growing up, when you couldn't help but think about what your own child might be doing at the age she would be now?

The pain was unbearable and all he could do was try and walk it off.

An hour passed and then another. Thomas wasn't even no-ticing where he walked. Around the circumference of Regent's Park. Through city streets. Right around Hyde Park. Twice.

He was thirsty. His feet and his legs ached but his heart ached more. So he kept walking until the sun was low in the sky and this day was finally drawing to a close. A day he never wanted to remember.

Exhaustion was helping because he was too tired to think co-herently. Too tired to have taken any notice of where he'd been walking for the last hour but it was another shock to realise the automatic route his subconscious had dictated.

He was in his old street. Only a lamppost away from the rail-ings and steps that led down to that basement apartment where he'd lived with Rebecca.

With Gwen…

The pain felt more like anger now.

This was Rebecca's fault. She could have warned him. Could have saved him the agony of these last few hours.

'Tom?'

His name sounded hesitant but laced with a concern that also triggered an automatic response in his exhausted state. His steps slowed and stopped. He turned.

'How could you?' His voice felt rusty. Broken, almost. 'How could you do that to me?'

He could see his pain reflected in the dark pool of her eyes.

A man walked past with his dog and gave them both a curious stare.

'Not here.' Rebecca's touch on his arm was a plea. 'Come inside, Tom. Please.'

He was too tired to resist the touch. Nothing could be worse than what had already happened today but, if it was, he might as well get it over with.

And he wanted an answer to his question. So he wouldn't spend the rest of his life with it echoing in his head. And his heart.

How could you?

CHAPTER NINE

IT WAS WORSE than she feared.

Having forced herself to give her attention to representing a hospital that needed to stay exactly where it was to keep providing the superlative care that young transplant patients deserved, Rebecca had spent the rest of the picnic event and the long tidy-up afterwards worried about Thomas.

Where he was and what he was thinking. How much he might hate her for what had—unintentionally—happened when he'd been introduced to a recipient of one of Gwen's organs.

To find him virtually on her doorstep when she'd finally been able to make her way home had been astonishing. To see the sheer exhaustion in his body language and the anger in his eyes had been frightening. He'd been pushed well past any safety barriers he'd built up over the last few years. And he was blaming her?

At least he'd agreed to come inside. He would be facing ghosts that he'd done his best to avoid but maybe today had shown him that you couldn't avoid them. They would always be there so you had to accept them and, when you did, you didn't have to fear them so much. He was facing some of the grief he'd never processed. Perhaps this was the first step he needed to take to finally do that?

She'd never imagined him ever being here again. If she'd thought about it, she would have decided that it was the last thing *she* would ever want.

But here they were. And, who knew? Talking now might turn out to be the most honest conversation they would ever have.

Thomas said nothing as he followed Rebecca through the front door and down the tiny hallway. She saw him turn his head as they passed the two rooms on either side, one of which had been Gwen's bedroom and was now her office. The hallway led into the living room where the old couch was still in exactly the same place but she didn't stop there. She took him through to the kitchen and busied herself putting on the kettle and lifting the teapot down from its shelf. Thomas sank down onto one of the two chairs at the small table by the window that looked out onto the shared garden.

The garden where Gwen had taken her first steps...

He said nothing until Rebecca placed a steaming mug of tea in front of him.

'I don't understand. I can't begin to understand why you did any of this.'

Rebecca sat on the other chair. They were close enough to touch but it felt like they were a million miles apart. 'Any of what?'

'The job you do. Having to spend so much time with families who've been destroyed. How you keep it in your life every single day.'

'It *is* in our lives every single day,' she said softly. 'Isn't it?'

'I don't obsess over it,' Thomas said. 'I don't go looking for ways to make it harder. How could you have gone looking to find out who...who was out there...who was still alive because we lost our daughter?'

'I didn't go looking,' Rebecca told him. 'What I did do was to make myself known to the transplant association. I said I'd like to know if they were ever contacted by any of the recipients in the future because I thought it would help me to know that we hadn't made that decision for nothing. That there were lives that had been changed for the better. And...and they gave me a letter that Ava's mother had written more than a year before. It was waiting in the files, in case I ever asked for information. I've still got it, if you'd like to read it. It was addressed to both parents of their donor.'

She could see how painful it was for Thomas to swallow by the jerky movement of the muscles of his neck. He didn't say anything.

'Some of the words are blurry,' she added. 'Jude must have been crying when she wrote it. She wanted us to know that we'd given them a miracle. That they thought of us as part of their family and always would. That they would feel blessed if they could ever get a chance to thank us in person.' Rebecca swiped away the tears that were trickling from her eyes. 'I thought about it for a long, long time but I decided I wanted to meet her. Just Jude. Another mother who'd gone through the agony of facing the loss of her child.'

'But you didn't stop at that, did you?'

'No. The decision to meet Ava took a long time, too, and I was terrified about how I would feel. I cried all the way home. Most of that night, as well. But then I found that it had helped. That there was peace in knowing that we'd done the right thing. That a gorgeous kid like Ava has another chance at life. It really helped.'

'It's not helping me,' Thomas muttered.

'Not yet. But I think it will.'

'What makes you think you know how I feel?' Anger tipped each word, making them as sharp as arrows.

'I don't,' Rebecca admitted. 'But I want to help.'

'By throwing something like that at me? Without even warning me that it was a possibility?'

'That's not fair. I didn't know you were going to be there. We're only just getting to know each other again. Why would I have told you something that I knew you weren't ready to hear?

Something that would push you away? I'm sorry it happened like that but…but I'm not sorry I'm part of Ava's life.'

'I don't want to be.'

'You don't have to be.' But, perhaps, even considering that possibility would help him process some more of that grief that he'd just shut away and tried to ignore. The grief that was keeping his life even more stuck than her own?

Their mugs of tea were cold. With a sigh, Rebecca got up and opened the fridge. She took out a bottle of wine and Thomas didn't protest when she put a glass in front of him. The only sound to break the silence for a long while was glass against wood as they picked up and put down their drinks.

It was Rebecca that broke the silence.

'It happened to both of us, Tom,' she said quietly. 'And it was the worst thing that could have ever happened. Nothing's going to change that but it doesn't wipe out the good stuff.'

'What *good* stuff?'

'How much we loved each other. How much we loved our daughter. We were good parents, Tom. We're good people.'

'*Were* we?' Thomas drained his glass. 'Why didn't we keep her safe, then?'

'We weren't even there.'

'Exactly.' Thomas reached for the bottle and refilled his glass. 'We were so wrapped up in our precious careers. Paying other people to look after our kid. If one of us had stayed at home, it wouldn't have happened.'

Rebecca caught her breath. 'One of us? You mean *me*? Are you saying *I* was a *bad* mother?'

His head shake was sharp. 'No. I could have been at home. Or we could have taken turns.'

'What happened was *not* our fault. It could have happened anywhere. We *could* have been there. On a Sunday afternoon when we were going to the zoo, maybe. It was a freak accident, Tom. The footpath is supposed to be a safe place to walk. For anyone, including a class outing from nursery school. Nobody expects a car to go out of control and hit people who are on a footpath.'

'Oh… God…' Thomas covered his eyes with his hand. 'It feels like it happened yesterday.'

Rebecca's chair scraped on the floorboards as she moved it closer. Close enough for her to be able to wrap her arms around Thomas and hold him until the shaking and the tears subsided.

She was crying, too. And at some point Thomas began holding her as much as she was holding him. The daylight was rapidly fading from the room but neither of them thought to move and turn on a light. When they finally unwrapped their arms enough to pull back and see each other's face, it felt like the middle of the night. The way it used to sometimes, when they were in bed together. Naked and vulnerable but…but safe, as well, because they were with each other.

How could she have been so convinced that Thomas could never be a part of her life again? Doubts were being washed away by a flood of remembered feelings. Of that safety. That love…

They were overwhelming. She couldn't stop the whispered words leaving her lips.

'I still love you, Tom. I've missed you *so* much…'

It was so easy to lean closer again and touch her lips against his. Maybe he'd moved at the same time because the pressure was much greater than she'd expected it to be. Nothing like that gentle kiss of comfort they had shared that night after that dance.

This kiss had an almost desperate edge that was like trying to catch hold of something precious that had been lost and was fleetingly in sight again. Or maybe it was the aftermath of a deep, shared grief that was begging for an affirmation of life. Of love…

Whatever was behind it only got more powerful as lips and then tongues traced such well-remembered patterns. As hands moved to touch skin beneath clothes.

It was Thomas who stood up first, drawing Rebecca to her feet.

It was Rebecca who kept hold of his hand and led him through the darkness to the bedroom.

Had Thomas really believed that today would be one he never wanted to remember?

How wrong could he have been?

But the last thing he could have imagined happening was to be here, like this. In his old bed.

Cradling the woman he had always loved in his arms as she slept in the aftermath of such a passionate physical reconnection.

And how could something like sex have seemed so right when it had come from such a gruelling emotional roller-coaster that had been fuelled by grief and anger and…and bone-deep loneliness?

He adjusted the weight of Rebecca's head on his arm and she sighed in her sleep. Her breath was a warm puff against the skin of his chest.

This felt right.

Walking for all those hours yesterday hadn't dealt with any of those heart-wrenching emotions but it seemed that making love to Rebecca had done more than he could have believed was possible.

Because it had been making love and not simply sex. And for the first time since that terrible accident, Thomas felt at peace.

Exhausted, too, of course. And unsure enough of what his future looked like now to be unable to allow sleep to claim him just yet but he was happy just to be here. To feel as if a small piece of his shattered world had just been put back together.

No. Not a small piece.

The biggest part of it, maybe.

Was that being disloyal to Gwen's memory? From the moment of her birth, she had been the sun that their lives revolved around. The bonus that made them a family instead of a couple. The living promise of the future they'd both dreamed of.

Thomas found himself listening to the silence of the apartment around them. Could he hear the echo of childish laughter? The patter of small feet running across the floorboards?

They hadn't even thought of pulling the blinds down on the windows when they'd come into this room so there were shards of light from the streetlamp on the road above. If he turned his head just a little, Thomas could see the framed photographs on Rebecca's bedside table and he stared at them for the longest time.

There were three photographs.

One of them was the first photograph of Gwen ever taken. She was lying in Rebecca's arms, only minutes after her birth and mother and baby were gazing at each other as if nothing so incredible had ever happened in the world.

Another was the photograph of them beside the bronze gorilla at the zoo when both the girls in his life had been laughing up at him and he had the grin of the happiest man in the world.

And the last photograph had been taken years before they became a family. Before Gwen had even been a possibility. Newly in love, on a weekend away, he and Rebecca had gone into one of those automatic photo booths. He could remember the strip of black-and-white images, most of which had been them making silly faces. But then they'd kissed.

The tiny photo Rebecca had chosen to put into a heart-shaped frame had been the moment they'd broken that kiss. When their lips were only just apart and they were looking at each other as if there could never be anyone else on the planet who could make them feel like this.

Something tightened in his chest and squeezed so hard that Thomas couldn't take a breath.

Rebecca had been right.

There *was* good stuff that could never be wiped out.

Like how much they had loved each other and how happy they had been together.

He turned away from the photographs to press a gentle kiss to Rebecca's head.

'I love you, too,' he whispered. 'I'm sorry I forgot how much.'

And then he listened again. Yes. He could hear those echoes. And it did make him feel sad but sadness wasn't the only thing he was aware of. He could remember the love and the laughter. The *good* stuff.

The kind of stuff that another little girl's parents were being blessed with when they'd faced the prospect of losing it for ever. A little girl with long blonde braids and blue eyes.

That unexpected flush of pride returned.

Not that he was going to let the worst of those memories surface. It was enough to register this new perspective for just a heartbeat. They *had* done the right thing in making that agonising decision that day. He was proud of it.

Proud of them both.

Thomas let his eyes drift shut, his cheek resting against the softness of Rebecca's hair. In the final moment before he fell deeply asleep, he turned his head a fraction to press another soft kiss to her forehead.

It felt like far more than the start of a new week the next morning.

It felt like the start of a new life.

But new born was also fragile and Rebecca wasn't going to take anything for granted. Not even when their lovemaking at dawn had been so heartbreakingly tender. Something they had both chosen to do that hadn't been prompted by any need for release in the wake of being put through an emotional wringer.

Thomas didn't stay for breakfast.

'I need to get home and changed,' he said. 'What would people think if I turned up to work with you, looking like I'd slept under a hedge for a week?'

'They might think that it was the best news ever.' Rebecca followed him to the door and smiled up at him, her heart too full of joy to hold the words back. 'That Dr Wolfe and Dr Scott had found each other again.'

Thomas was smiling, too. 'Have we, Becca? Have we found each other again?'

The full glow of this reborn connection might be fragile but fragile things needed nurturing, didn't they?

'I hope so.' She reached up to touch his face. 'I don't think I ever stopped loving you, Tom.'

He bent to kiss her. A soft touch that clung for a heartbeat and then another.

'Same,' he whispered. 'But I still need to change my clothes.'

Rebecca watched him climb the steps and let herself dream for a moment. Maybe, soon, his clothes would be back where they belonged—in their wardrobe. And Thomas would be back where he belonged, too.

With her.

The sound of her mobile phone ringing brought her back to the present.

'Dr Scott? Rebecca?'

'Speaking.'

'It's Louise Walker. I'm sorry to ring you so early but… I've been awake all night.'

'That's fine, Louise. How can I help?'

'We decided. Last night. We talked about it with the whole family and we all feel the same way…'

Rebecca's heart squeezed at the pain in the young mother's voice. It didn't matter what the decision was, it had been hard won and she was happy that the whole family was in agreement. Louise couldn't see her nodding, or that she had closed her eyes as she waited out the silence as Louise fought for control of her voice.

'We're ready,' she whispered. 'We want Ryan to be a donor.'

CHAPTER TEN

THE NEEDLES OF hot water in his shower landed on skin that felt oddly raw.

As a young boy, Thomas Wolfe had been fascinated by arthropods—invertebrate creatures who had to shed their exoskeleton because it restricted growth—like grasshoppers and stick insects.

He felt like a human version.

The emotional shock of confronting the very real evidence that parts of his own daughter still existed had cracked the shell he'd been inside for years. Talking to Rebecca had painfully peeled more of that shell away. Being touched and touching with so much love had been the rebirth of the man who'd been hidden. The man he used to be.

Hermit crabs. They were another creature that could emerge from their old shell and start again and he'd definitely been a hermit in an emotional sense.

Was that part of his life over?

Could he start again, with Rebecca by his side?

How miraculous would that be?

The way the water stung was a warning to be careful, however, not to rush anything. Arthropods were at their most vulnerable when newly emerged. He was sure he remembered a statistic that moulting was responsible for something like eighty to ninety per cent of arthropod deaths. They needed time for their new shells to harden.

He needed time, too.

Arriving at Paddington's for the start of the new working week made things feel more normal and boosted his confidence.

There was no need to rush anything. Safety—for both himself and Rebecca—was paramount.

There was a television crew in the area near the main reception desk. Annette, one of the senior members of the team that staffed the desk, waved at Thomas.

'Dr Wolfe? I was just telling these visitors that you're just the person who might be able to answer this query.'

'What's that?' Thomas frowned, trying to remember where he'd seen the perfectly groomed blonde woman who was smiling as he approached. Oh, yes...she'd been the person interviewing Rebecca at the Teddy Bears' Picnic yesterday.

Good grief! With all that had happened since, it felt like a very long time ago.

'I'm Angela Marton,' she introduced herself. 'We're hoping to film a feature on a child that's waiting for a transplant. There was such an overwhelmingly positive response to our coverage from the picnic yesterday. We thought a more in-depth story would help raise awareness of the need for donors. And Paddington's needs all the good publicity it can get at the moment, doesn't it?'

'I can't give permission for something like that,' Thomas said. 'You'll have to speak to our CEO—Dr Bradley—about that.'

'Where is it that you work?'

'I'm in Cardiology.'

'Oh...' Angela's eyes lit up. 'You don't happen to have someone waiting for a heart transplant, do you? A family who might be prepared to share their story?'

'I'm afraid our patient information is completely confidential.'

'Mmm... Of course it is. I totally respect that.'

The look in her eyes suggested otherwise. People were always keen to talk if it gave them a moment of fame, weren't they? Penelope Craig was well-known around Paddington's. Who knew whether an orderly or clerk or even a kitchen hand had overheard things that they could share?

The need to protect Penny and her family from a possibly unwelcome intrusion in their lives made Thomas excuse himself. Hopefully, they could send Penny home today and he wouldn't feel so responsible if their privacy was invaded. His pager sounded at the same time, which added weight to his comment that he was needed elsewhere.

The pager message was to find a phone to accept an external phone call from Dr Rebecca Scott. Thomas felt a beat of excitement as Annette handed him a phone he could use. He couldn't wait to hear Rebecca's voice. He wanted to *see* her again, in fact—the sooner, the better.

It was more than hope that this new beginning was going to take them back to where they'd once been.

In love.

Married.

With a shared dream of a future together...

It was the strength of the *wanting* that made him so aware of how soft this new shell of his still was.

To want something this much and not achieve it had the potential to destroy him all over again. And there would be no coming back from going through that a second time.

He distracted himself from that fear by focusing on a much more mundane detail. It was high time they had each other's mobile numbers, wasn't it? Using a formal contact process like this was not appropriate for anything personal.

Except it wasn't anything personal that Rebecca wanted to talk to him about.

'I'm just on my way into work,' she said. 'I've had a call from the parents of a little boy that was declared brain-dead a few days ago and they've agreed to let him become a donor. I'll get onto the matching processes as soon as I get in. It's just possible that he could be a match for Penny so I thought I'd better give you a heads-up. It would be a shame to discharge her and then bring her straight back in.'

Thomas eyed Angela and her crew, who were now standing near an elevator looking for directions towards Dr Bradley's office. He lowered his voice, anyway.

'How far away is the donor? Will you have to travel for the retrieval?'

'No.' Rebecca's voice was quiet. 'He's in our own intensive care unit.'

'Oh...' Thomas blinked, taken aback. He remembered a snatch of conversation he'd overheard that night at the Frog and Peach, when Rebecca had been talking to Alistair North. He didn't want to know any more, though—like the name or age of this boy. In fact, hadn't he heard something not so long ago? About one of the children who'd been injured so badly in the school fire?

He didn't allow any additional information of who it might be to surface because it felt too close to home. Too personal. Keeping things as anonymous as possible was the sensible way to handle this.

'Fine,' he said then. 'Thanks for the heads-up. I'll keep things on hold until we know more and then I can either discharge her or initiate the final work-up.'

'Cool, thanks. I'll let you know as soon as possible.'

'Great. And, Becca...?'

Her tone changed, becoming suddenly softer and warmer. He could imagine her lips curving into a private smile. 'Yes?'

'Thanks for last night. For...everything.'

There was a moment's silence. 'I'll see you soon,' Rebecca said, and it sounded like a promise. 'And, Tom?'

'Yes?'

'Maybe you can give me your mobile number?'

His mouth curled into a smile of his own. 'I've got your number from this call. I'll text you mine.'

Penelope was wearing her pink tutu skirt. She also had a diamante, princess tiara on the top of her head. She was sitting, cross-legged, on the covers of her bed, her eyes glued to the latest adventures of the Ballerina Bears. Her toys and games and art supplies were all packed into suitcases in a corner of the room but her parents didn't look happy about any of it.

They looked totally stunned.

'But...' Julia's bottom lip trembled. 'But we were going to take her home today. That's why she's wearing her crown. She's going to be a princess for the day and we've got her carriage waiting. And she's looking so *well*...'

Peter took hold of her hand. 'But this is what we've been waiting for, hon. This could mean years and years of her being well.' His voice cracked and he cleared his throat, shifting his gaze from his wife to the two doctors in front of them.

'Are you sure? This is an exact match?'

'As close as we could hope for.' Rebecca smiled. 'We need to do another blood test on Penny. It's the final comparison of the donor's blood cells and Penny's blood serum to make sure that she hasn't created any new antibodies that might attack the donated organ. It's very unlikely, but we need to check.'

'And if it's okay?' Julia's eyes were wide and terrified. 'When...?'

'The sooner, the better,' Thomas said. 'We've got a hold on a theatre for about two this afternoon.'

Julia's head swivelled to look at her daughter. Penny didn't notice because she was staring at her hands, trying to follow the direction her beloved bears were giving each other.

'You use your thumb and your middle finger,' Sapphire was telling her friends. 'Like you're holding a tiny magic stone...'

Julia tried to hold back her tears. It was her loud sniff that attracted Penny's attention.

'What's the matter, Mummy?'

'Nothing, darling. I'm…happy, that's all.'

'Because we're going home?'

Thomas smiled. 'What is it that you want most of all, Penny?'

'To be a ballerina.' The little girl's smile stretched from ear to ear.

'And what is it that you need so that you *can* be a ballerina?'

'A new heart.' Her tone was matter-of-fact. As if it was a solution as simple as getting a new pair of shoes.

It was Peter who went close enough to the bed to stroke Penny's head. 'What would you say if we told you that you might be able to get that new heart today?'

Penny shook her head. 'But we're going home, today, Daddy. Can we do it tomorrow?'

Then she looked slowly around the room and the television programme was forgotten as the magnitude of what was going on around her sank in. The smile everybody associated with this brave little girl wobbled and her voice was very small.

'Do I have to have another operation?'

'Just one.' Rebecca sat on the chair beside Penny's bed and took a small hand in hers. 'And then we hope there won't be any more. Maybe ever…'

'And the new heart will make me better?'

Rebecca nodded and smiled. 'That's the plan, sweetheart.'

'And I can go back to school?'

'Yes.'

'And I can have ballet lessons?'

'Yes.' It was Julia who answered this time. 'Of course you can.'

Thomas watched the look that passed between Penny's parents as they gripped each other's hands. He could see the mix of fear and hope and he could feel it himself. The protective shield he'd kept between himself and his patients and their families just didn't seem to be there any more.

He looked back at Penny, who was smiling at Rebecca now.

'Okay, I guess it's okay if I don't go home today.'

And then Thomas let his gaze rest on Rebecca's face. That smile that he loved so much. That look she was giving Penny that told the little girl she was the most important person in the world right now. He could feel her determination that she was going to give Penny and her family what they wanted so desperately.

And he could feel his own love for Rebecca that was a big part of the emotional mix in this room. He wanted a successful outcome as much as anybody else here.

He could feel everything with such clarity, it was painful.

Because of his new, soft shell?

He'd forgotten what this felt like. Hope. The anticipation of something so joyful, it made the world look like a different place.

A much better place than he'd been living in for such a long time.

There was nothing more for him to do here. Penelope Craig was Rebecca's patient now, and would be until she was discharged with her new heart to return to the care of her cardiologist. He wanted to be there, though. He wanted to be in the gallery to watch the surgery. To let Rebecca know that she had his complete support and to meet her gaze if she chose to look up and seek encouragement. The way he had when the first surgery had been done on this very child.

How appropriate would it be for him to be there again, now, in what could be the definitive surgery that could give her many years of life? That he could celebrate their new connection by repeating history and letting her know that he believed in her.

That he—once again—believed in *them*?

He also wanted to be by her side when she went to tell Julia and Peter how well it had all gone.

It would be a long surgery. He needed to clear everything else on his agenda today to put the time aside.

The urgent call to the intensive care unit came shortly after the message from Rebecca that said the green light had been given to the suitability of the donor heart and its intended recipient. Penelope Craig was now in the final stages of her pre-theatre preparation.

The patient Thomas had been called to see was a six-month-old baby who'd been admitted and rushed to intensive care in a life-threatening condition. He arrived to see an alarmingly fast trace on the ECG monitor and a baby with a bulging fontanelle who was struggling to breathe and going blue. The baby's terrified mother was standing to one side with a nurse.

'Oxygen saturation is improving with the nasal cannula,' he was told. 'Up from eighty-four per cent on room air.'

Thomas looked at the ECG printout he was handed. 'Looks like a supraventricular tachycardia. Other vitals?'

'Respiratory rate of sixty-five, blood pressure is eighty on fifty and she's febrile at thirty-nine point four degrees.'

'Deep tendon reflexes?'

'Brisk.'

'We could be looking at meningoencephalitis, then. Or meningitis.'

'A spinal tap is next on our list. But we need to get this tachycardia under control.'

'I agree.' The heart rate was far too rapid to be allowing enough oxygen to circulate and it was a very unstable situation. Thomas had his fingers on the baby's arm. 'I've got a palpable peripheral pulse. Let's try some IV adenosine with a two-syringe rapid push. If that doesn't help, we'll go for a synchronised cardioversion.'

The drug therapy was enough to slow the heart rate to an acceptable level. Thomas stayed with the baby a little longer, as treatment to bring down her fever and improve oxygen levels was started. He wrote up lab forms to check electrolyte levels that could well need correction to prevent further disruptions to the heart rhythm.

And then he left, after a glance at his watch told him that Penny would be heading for the operating theatre within an hour or so. So would the donor of her heart. They would be in side-by-side theatres. Other theatres may also have been cleared and there could very well be a retrieval team from another transplant centre waiting to rush precious organs to other children in desperate need.

It was no real surprise, then, to see Rebecca up here.

What shocked him was that she had her arm around another woman who was sobbing quietly, her head on Rebecca's shoulder.

A chill ran down his spine at the realisation that this had to be the mother of the donor child.

He had to walk past them. Despite every ounce of willpower he could summon, Thomas couldn't prevent his head turning. The door to the room was open. His glance only grazed the scene within but it was instantly seared into his memory bank.

A small boy, so still on the bed, his head bandaged and a hand lying, palm upwards as though it had just been released from being held.

His father sitting beside him, his head in his hands and his shoulders shaking.

Rebecca didn't even see him going past, she was so focused on the woman beside her.

'There's still time,' he heard her murmur. 'Go and be with Ryan. And with Peter. He needs you. You need each other...'

The chill didn't stop when it reached the end of Thomas's spine. It seemed to be spreading to every cell in his body.

He was that father.

He could feel the utter desolation of knowing that, very soon, the final goodbye would have to happen. That they would walk beside the bed that their child was lying on until they got as close as they were allowed to Theatre. That they were about to lose even the appearance of life that the intensive care technology could provide.

He could feel his world crumbling around him all over again.

And Rebecca's words unleashed another cascade of terrible memories.

You need each other...

He hadn't been there for her when she'd needed him. Not in any meaningful way. He'd started to pull himself into his shell from the moment they'd taken Gwen further along that corridor that led to the operating theatre and he'd just made himself more and more unavailable.

Not because he'd *wanted* to. Hurting the woman he loved so much was the last thing he would have ever chosen to do. He just hadn't been able to survive any other way.

And who was to say he wouldn't do it again?

Even now, as he walked away from the paediatric intensive care unit, Thomas could feel himself frantically looking for some mental building materials, desperate to try and resurrect at least enough of a barrier to protect himself from this wash of unbearable emotion that seeing the donor's family had induced.

No, it wasn't just an anonymous donor any more.

His name was Ryan, and Thomas clearly remembered having heard the story. He was the little boy who'd gone to school, just like he would have on any other ordinary day. But the unthinkable had happened and he'd been badly injured in that fire at his school.

And he had parents who loved him as much as he and Rebecca had loved their little Gwen.

Thomas took the stairs. He couldn't stand next to anyone waiting for an elevator right now, let alone have the doors slide shut to confine him.

He needed space. A private place to somehow deal with this onslaught of memories that had been buried so deeply he'd thought he was safe from feeling like this again. So he headed up the stairs, instead of down. All the way to the top of the building and through the door that led to the helipad. Empty at the moment, with nothing more than the most amazing view of central London on display. He walked to the furthest corner he could find and stood there, staring at familiar landmarks.

Like the green spaces of the parks and the bump of Primrose Hill where he'd held Rebecca in his arms for the first time since they'd parted and this whole cascade of reconnection had begun. He could see the rooftop and signage of the Frog and Peach over the road where he'd danced with her that night. He could even make out the wrought-iron fences further along the road that marked the spot where he'd kissed her.

He couldn't do it, he realised.

He couldn't allow even a possibility of hurting Rebecca all over again.

Going to the Teddy Bears' Picnic yesterday had been a mistake but it paled in comparison to what had happened between them last night.

It couldn't happen again.

He wasn't going to allow Rebecca to risk her future happiness by being with him. He was the one who couldn't handle these memories.

He was the one who was really stuck. So he was the one who had to set her free to find a new future.

With someone else.

But how—and when—could he tell her that?

Maybe very soon, he thought as his mobile phone began to ring and he saw the name 'Becca' on the screen.

He swiped to answer the call but he didn't get time for any kind of greeting.

'Tom? Where are you?' Rebecca sounded alarmed.

'What's wrong?'

'It's Penny… She's gone missing…'

CHAPTER ELEVEN

'WHAT DO YOU MEAN—gone missing?'

'We can't find her. I came up to see her and check that everything was ready for her to go to Theatre and she's not in her room. She's nowhere in the ward.'

Thomas had already turned away from the view and from any thoughts remotely personal. His stride, as he headed back to the door leading to the stairwell, was verging on a run.

'I don't understand. How could she have gone anywhere? Who was with her?'

'That's just it. No one.'

'What?' Thomas hit the button to release the automatic door with the flat of his hand.

'It was only for a minute or two, apparently. Peter had gone to Reception to meet Penny's grandparents. Julia had dashed to the loo and Rosie responded to an alarm that signalled an emergency in the treatment room. She wasn't needed, in the end, and went straight back but Penny had disappeared. Rosie thought she'd gone to find her mum in the loo but Julia hadn't seen her.'

'She can't be far away. She's probably visiting one of her friends.' Thomas was taking the stairs, two at a time.

'She's not in the ward. We've checked. Everybody's looking for her. Rosie's beside herself. She thinks it's her fault but it was a cardiac arrest alarm and she said Penny promised to stay in bed.'

'Have you called Security?'

'Yes. They've been all over it for the last ten minutes. Nobody's seen her.'

Maybe Thomas hadn't completely banished personal thoughts. Penelope Craig was still his patient, even though her care was to be in Rebecca's hands for the next little while.

He could understand why Rosie was feeling so bad but Penny's safety was ultimately *his* responsibility.

Like keeping her family safe from the intrusion of that television crew had been, especially today of all days.

To see Angela and her camera and sound people milling around the space near the stairs as he exited on the floor of the cardiology ward was like a slap in the face. The lens of the camera was like a giant eye, swivelling to point straight at him as his presence was noted.

'Dr Wolfe? Is it true that a little girl's gone missing? One that was about to have a heart transplant?'

'No comment.' Thomas pushed past the reporter. How on earth had the news been leaked so quickly?

How hard should it have been to have stopped these strangers finding out anything about Penny? It felt like a personal failure.

And there was a list of other personal failures that it could be added to.

Like not having this special patient in the place that she was supposed to be in order to receive her life-saving surgery.

Like not having been in the right place at the right time to keep his own daughter safe.

And, above all, like not having been able to keep his marriage safe.

He hadn't even heard the last question Angela was calling after him but he raised his hand in a silent 'no comment' gesture. He could see Rebecca in the ward corridor through the double doors. She was amongst a cluster of people that included Penny's parents and grandparents and a man he recognised as Jim, the head of Paddington's security team. Rosie was also there, her face pale and desperately worried.

And, no matter what the odds had been for Penny surviving the surgeries and setbacks she'd already had in her short life, he'd never seen Julia Craig looking this terrified.

'She's probably just found a place to hide,' Jim was saying as Thomas joined the group. 'I expect she was frightened about having to go to Theatre again. We'll find her, Mrs Craig. Please try not to worry too much.'

Julia shook her head. 'She wouldn't just run away—it's not like her at all. And she said she'd stay in bed, didn't she?'

Rosie nodded. 'I was gone such a short time, Julia. I'm so sorry...'

'It's not your fault. I would have left her to go to the loo if you hadn't been there. I've done that a million times.'

'She hasn't been *able* to run anywhere before this,' Peter put in. 'Because she's been too sick. But now... Who knows how far she could have gone?'

'Somebody will have seen her,' Jim said. 'How many little girls do we see wearing a pink tutu and a princess crown? I've got my men everywhere. We're combing the entire hospital.'

'But what if she isn't in the hospital any more?' Julia whispered, 'What if someone's...?' Her breath hitched. 'What if someone's *taken* her?'

'I've got someone reviewing CCTV footage right now. And we've started with the main doors. We've also called in the police.' He turned towards Rebecca. 'How long have we got? When does her surgery have to happen by?'

'We've got a bit of time,' Rebecca answered. 'But that's not the point. What matters is *finding* Penny—as soon as we possibly can.' She ran her hand over her head. 'I can't just wait here. I'm going to start looking myself.'

Her gaze snagged Thomas's as she turned away and his own concern ramped up into real alarm as he saw the fear in her eyes.

Was it at all possible that someone *had* taken Penny? Had she wandered far enough away from the ward for some random predator to spot an opportunity?

It was so unlikely that he would have dismissed the notion as ridiculous up until now.

But, a long time ago, he would have said the same thing about a random car going out of control and mounting a footpath, wouldn't he?

Nothing was impossible, however horrible it might be.

And the fear in Rebecca's eyes was impossible to ignore. As much as he knew he couldn't allow her to depend on him for what she needed, he had to help.

'I'll come with you,' he said.

'We'll try the playground again,' Peter said. 'In case she's come back.'

'And I'll check under every bed,' Rosie added. 'And in every cupboard. She's *got* to be somewhere.'

Jim looked up, ending a call he'd been taking on his phone.

'CCTV from every exit has been checked. There's no sign of her having been taken anywhere and we've got every door covered by security now. She's here. *Somewhere…*'

They started in the wards closest to Cardiology and talked to everybody they encountered.

'Have you seen a little girl? Wearing a pink tutu?'

'No…sorry… We'll keep an eye out.'

'Do you mind if we have a look in the storeroom? She could be trying to hide.'

She was such a little thing, Rebecca thought, moving a laundry bag in its wheeled frame to one side in that storeroom. She'd be able to squeeze into the smallest place.

'I don't understand why she wanted to run away,' she said to Thomas. 'It's not as if this is her first operation. I'm sure I didn't make it sound scary.'

'I'm sure you didn't,' he agreed. 'But who knows what might make a six-year-old kid feel nervous?'

A six-year-old kid?

Just another child?

Thomas didn't seem to be feeling anything like the level of anxiety gripping Rebecca.

'This is *Penny* we're talking about, Tom.'

'Mmm... Maybe the wards are the wrong place to be looking. I wonder if anybody's checked an outpatient area like Physiotherapy. Or the X-ray department?'

He was already walking away from her and Rebecca stared at his back. It felt like she was being accompanied in this search by a member of the security team. Someone who hadn't known Penny for her entire life and had no personal involvement in her case.

The chill hit her like a bucket of icy water.

Thomas was running away again. Hiding behind those self-protective barriers. Pretending he wasn't involved so he could distance himself from the discomfort of anxiety—or worse. Because he felt guilty? Okay, Penny was his patient but it was ridiculous to assume responsibility for something that had happened when he was nowhere near her. When other people had accepted that mantle of responsibility.

That hadn't stopped him from blaming himself over Gwen's death, though, had it?

It hadn't stopped him believing he had failed as a father.

But how could he do this, when they'd been so close again only last night? When they'd talked about exactly how it *hadn't* been his fault?

Fear stepped in then. How could she have allowed herself to resurrect and sink into those feelings for Thomas? To dream about a shared life again?

This was a tough moment in their professional lives but she needed his support and he was creating a distance that hurt. If they got together again, how long would it be before something important went wrong and she really needed him again?

She couldn't do this.

Because—maybe—she couldn't trust Thomas enough.

But now wasn't the time to think about any of that. Not only was Rebecca desperately worried about the state of mind of a patient she loved dearly, there was a clock ticking. Penny wasn't going to be the only recipient of one of Ryan's organs and there were retrieval teams already arriving at Paddington's. Ryan's surgery would be going ahead whatever happened. If Penny couldn't be found, his heart might have to go to the next person on the waiting list.

Minutes flashed past as they raced along corridors and into every space that might be accessible to a newly mobile little girl. Thirty minutes and then sixty.

Rebecca answered a phone call that informed her that there had still been no sighting of Penny. And then another that confirmed that Ryan would be on his way to Theatre very soon.

'We're running out of time,' she told Thomas as they waited for an elevator to get down to Reception. It had been someone in X-ray who'd thought they'd seen a girl in a pink dress in the toy shop.

Rebecca had to close her eyes tightly to hold back tears of despair.

Surely Thomas could see how upset she was? Just a touch on her arm or an encouraging word would be enough. Maybe even enough to dispel the horrible feeling that he was as distant now as he'd been when he'd first come back to Paddington's.

But he hadn't moved any closer when she opened her eyes as the lift doors slid open.

And he hadn't said a word.

A very pregnant woman, with long, glossy dark hair, stepped out of the lift. She stared at Thomas for a moment and then smiled as she obviously remembered who he was.

'It's Thomas, isn't it? We met in A&E the day of the school fire.'

'And don't I know you?' Rebecca said. 'You're a paramedic, aren't you? And you and Dominic were a big part of the early publicity in the campaign to save Paddington's?'

The woman nodded. 'Victoria,' she said. 'Victoria Christie—but soon to be MacBride. Dom's persuaded me to marry him.'

She was smiling, but the smile suddenly faded. 'I've just come in for an antenatal check,' she said. 'But what on earth's going on around here? There are police officers and reporters all over the place. Reception is crazy...'

Rebecca glanced at Thomas. 'Maybe the toyshop isn't the best place to check, then. If there are already so many people down there, someone would have spotted a little girl in a pink tutu.'

'A pink tutu?' Victoria's eyes widened. 'Are you talking about Penny?'

Thomas had been holding the lift doors open by keeping his hand on them. A malfunction alarm began to sound.

'You know her?'

'I've transported her so often she's like a part of the family. And she's the only kid I know who would sleep in her tutu if she was allowed to.'

'She's gone missing,' Thomas said.

'And she's due in Theatre,' Rebecca added. 'We've got a heart available for her. A perfect match.'

'Oh, my God...' Victoria was looking horrified.

'We've got to go, but can you keep an eye out for her? I'm not sure if anyone's checked Ultrasound or Maternity, yet.'

'Of course I will. I'd spot that tutu a mile off.'

'She's got a crown on today, as well.' Rebecca had to swallow past the lump in her throat. 'She's being a princess for the day.'

Victoria nodded, moved out of their way so they could get into the lift, but then swung back towards them.

'That reminds me of something. Have you checked the turret?'

'What?' Thomas put his hand back into the gap as the doors were closing and they opened again with a jerk.

'We were talking about the turret one day in the ambulance.

The big one over Reception? I told her about how, when I was a kid, I'd always thought that a princess lived there but that, actually, it's only a dusty old storeroom full of ancient books and bits of paper.'

'I didn't even know you could get into it,' Rebecca said.

'You're not supposed to,' Victoria said. 'But there's a door. It looks like it's just a cupboard but then you find the staircase. I told Penny about that door. About the staircase...'

It was Thomas who caught Rebecca's gaze as the doors slid shut and the lift began to descend. She could see the hope in his eyes that maybe *this* was the breakthrough they'd been waiting for. A place that nobody would have thought to look because nobody even knew it was accessible?

The glance was unguarded only for the time it took for Thomas to blink. And then he was staring straight ahead at the blank metal of the doors.

'Don't get your hopes up too much,' he murmured. 'It would be a miracle if she'd found that door and hadn't been spotted by someone in Reception.'

As Victoria had warned, the area around the main reception desk was crowded. They showed their official IDs to a police officer who was directing the general public towards a temporary information kiosk that had been set up outside the pharmacy.

The television reporter, Angela Marton, was speaking directly into a camera.

'From what we understand, a child—a small girl who is desperately in need of a new heart—has gone missing, only minutes before her surgery was due to take place.'

At least they hadn't revealed her name, Thomas thought. He put his hand up to shade the side of his face. Angela knew he was a cardiologist and she certainly knew that Rebecca was a transplant surgeon after interviewing her at the Teddy Bears' Picnic. If she spotted either of them, they would have to fight their way through a media scrum to get where they needed to go.

But Angela seemed oblivious to any movement around her.

'This is what it's about, folks. This emergency situation—even more than the tragic fire at Westbourne Grove Primary School—is showing us what this hospital is all about. There isn't a single member of staff here who isn't searching for this little girl right now. Hoping that—any minute now—there will be an end to the dreadful worry her family is experiencing. Everybody cares...*so* much...'

The tiny break in her voice suggested that Angela cared as much as everybody else but Thomas knew that she would lead the pack that would snap at their heels if she sensed a new lead in the unexpected drama she was in the middle of. He tried to shield Rebecca with his body as he led them through the press of people and around the far end of the reception desk.

And there was the door. Inconspicuous enough to be simply part of the wall and tucked far enough behind a rack of filing cabinets that it couldn't be seen from the other side of the reception desk. It wasn't impossible that nobody would have noticed a small girl going through this door. A glance behind him showed Thomas that nobody was watching them as he waited for Rebecca to slip through the gap and then followed her.

The attention of the film crew—and everybody else—had shifted to a group of uniformed people, one of whom was carrying an insulated box. It had to be a retrieval team from another hospital but Angela made a very different interpretation.

'Oh, my... Could that be the heart *arriving*?'

How long would Ryan's family be able to remain anonymous? It was a blessing that the assumption was being made that the heart was arriving from an anonymous donor somewhere else in the country but Thomas could still feel the tension ramping up sharply as he shut the door behind him. Ramping up as steeply as this narrow, spiral, wooden staircase. Round and round they went, leaving the chaos behind them. By the time they got to the top, it was so quiet, they could have been miles away from Paddington's. In a forgotten library, perhaps, with a circular room stuffed full of archived paperwork. The tension was still there but it felt different. As if the whole world was holding its breath.

Dust motes floated in the shafts of light coming through small, latticed windows. The floor was thick with dust, as well, but it had been disturbed. There were tracks in it.

'They look like adult-sized footprints.' Rebecca was whispering as if she, too, felt like she was in a library. 'Who could have been in here? I didn't even know it was possible.'

'Victoria did.'

'Mmm…' Rebecca was staring at the floor. 'Oh, my God, Tom! *Look*…'

And there it was.

A tiny footprint. Of a bare foot. He could even see the outline of where small toes had left their mark in the dust.

He took a step further into the round space. And then another. Far enough to see past a tall stack of boxes. And there, curled up in the corner and fast asleep, was Penny. She had her head cushioned on one arm and her tiara was so lopsided it was almost covering one eye.

His overwhelming relief was echoed in Rebecca's gasp as she came past the tier of boxes but then it evaporated as fast as it had appeared.

Was Penny unconscious rather than asleep? Or *worse*… What if the device helping her heart to pump enough blood to the rest of her body had malfunctioned in some way because of an unexpected, additional stress—like climbing those steep stairs?

Thomas could feel the moment his own heart stopped because he felt the painful jolt as it started again with a jerk. He was crouching by then, his hand smoothing back one of Penny's braids to feel for a pulse in her neck.

A strong pulse…

Penny's eyes flickered open as she felt the touch. She looked up to see both Thomas and Rebecca bent over her and she smiled at them.

'Did you come up to see where the princess used to live, too?'

'We sure did.' It was hard to speak through the tightness in his throat. 'But it's time to go back now, sweetheart.'

'Okay.' Still smiling, Penny held up her arms. 'But I'm tired. Will you carry me?'

'Sure will,' Thomas managed.

'And I'm really, really *hungry*.'

'So you haven't had anything to eat? Or drink?'

His gaze caught Rebecca's as Penny's head was shaking a very definite and rather sad 'no.' At least that was another obstacle to getting her to Theatre that they wouldn't have to worry about.

By the time he'd scooped the little girl into his arms, she was sound asleep again. He stood up and turned and then stopped because he knew that Rebecca needed to touch this child herself—so that she could really believe that this crisis was over.

She had a tear rolling down the side of her nose and Thomas had to blink hard to hold back the prickle in his own eyes. And then Rebecca raised her gaze to his.

'You *do* care,' she whispered. 'As much as you ever did. You try and shut yourself away but it's not who you really are, is it?'

He could see more than relief in her dark eyes. He could see hope.

Hope that he couldn't allow to grow. But how could he destroy it?

'Of course I care,' he said quietly. 'Penny's my patient.'

'And she's fine. We'll get her to Theatre now. Everything's going to be all right.'

Thomas started moving towards the staircase. He would have to go very slowly and carefully. The stairs were narrow and steep.

It might not have been all right, he thought as they neared the bottom. *And it would have been my responsibility. My failure…*

'What?' Rebecca was ahead of him, her hand on the door handle, but her head turned sharply. She stopped moving.

Good grief! Had he spoken those thoughts aloud?

But Rebecca shook her head, as if she didn't believe what she might have heard. She turned the handle and, a moment later, he was stepping back into the real world of Paddington's. Penny stirred in his arms as she heard the exclamations of people around her that rapidly morphed from surprise to become a cheer. Undaunted by all the attention, she was beaming when she caught sight of her mother coming towards them and seemed oblivious to the flash of cameras around them.

'Make way, please.' Thomas held out his arm to clear a path towards the elevators. 'We don't have time for this...'

A hugely relieved Rosie was waiting in the ward to help give Penny a thorough check and get her ready for her trip to Theatre. Thomas and Rebecca worked together until they were both satisfied there was nothing to stop the surgery going ahead. Until the pre-surgery sedation had taken effect.

And, like she had after the VAD had been inserted, Rebecca touched her forefinger against her lips and then touched Penny's cheek to transfer the kiss.

'See you soon, pet,' she said softly. 'Sleep tight.'

It broke his heart how much he loved her for that tiny gesture that spoke of how much she cared, a promise that Penny wasn't going to be alone in what was to come.

It broke his heart to realise just how much he loved *her*...

And how much he was prepared to sacrifice to keep her safe.

Today's crisis could have had a very different ending and, even if it was irrational, he would still feel that at least part of it was a failure on his part.

He couldn't risk failing Rebecca again. Somehow, he had to tell her that but not yet. Not just before she was heading into Theatre for a surgery that was so crucial.

But he caught the glance she threw over her shoulder as she headed for the door and he knew she was picking up this new tension between them. He couldn't let her scrub up with that hanging over her, could he?

'Walk with me?'

'Sure.' Thomas walked by Rebecca's side towards the operating theatre locker rooms. He felt her glance at him more than once but it wasn't until they reached the storeroom that she finally said something.

'I can't leave it like this,' she said. 'I heard what you were muttering under your breath and I can't go into this surgery without saying something.'

Thomas had to lick his suddenly dry lips. 'About what?'

He got a loaded glance as a response to his being deliberately obtuse. Rebecca pulled supplies from the labelled shelves. A small-sized scrub tunic and pants, a cap and shoe covers.

'It wasn't your fault that Penny went missing,' she said. 'You've got to stop blaming yourself for things that you have no control over.'

This was it. A chance to say what he needed to say. Maybe Rebecca would understand.

'What about the things I should have had control over? Like being there for you when you needed me so much?'

Rebecca paused, the bundle of clean clothing in her arms. 'It takes two people to make a marriage work,' she said quietly. 'And maybe it takes two to make it fail. I didn't understand how bad it really was for you. Maybe I was too wrapped up in my own journey. I think I do now, though. When I had to go and speak to Ryan's parents that first time...' She took a slow inward breath. 'It was...really hard.'

Thomas was staring at the bundle of linen in Rebecca's arms but he was thinking of what he'd been holding such a short time ago. He could still feel the shape of Penny in his arms. How small and fragile she was. He could still feel the aftermath of that shock wave of thinking that she might not just be asleep. That they might have been too late. And that morphed into a different shock wave that he would never be able to erase from his memory.

Of arriving in the emergency department to see Gwen when she'd been brought in after that terrible accident. Barely alive. He'd certainly been too late, that time.

Rebecca could see that her words had triggered memories that Thomas was struggling with.

She needed to go. To get showered and changed and then start scrubbing in for the transplant surgery. Two lots of surgery, because she had to be the one to remove Ryan's heart to ensure the best possible outcome in reattaching the vital blood vessels.

And while she knew she could block out anything personal when she chose to focus completely on the tasks ahead of her, she couldn't leave Thomas looking so haunted. Not when it felt like she was losing him. She could feel everything they had found between them again—and everything they could find in the future—slipping away. Thomas was running again. Trying to find a safe place behind his barriers. She'd known it was happening during their search for Penny and it had rekindled all her doubts but then she'd seen the truth in his eyes when he'd been holding the little girl in his arms.

She'd seen the man she had always loved, who was capable of giving just as much love back, if only he could find a way past the burden of guilt he'd been carrying for so long. But the hope of that happening was also slipping away and what she said now might be her last chance of preventing that happening.

His next words confirmed her fears.

'I still feel like I failed Gwen,' he murmured. 'I was her daddy. I was supposed to keep her safe.'

'You were the *best* daddy.' Rebecca's voice was low but fierce. 'It wasn't your fault. There are no guarantees in life, Tom. We can only do our best. We can celebrate our successes and support each other if things don't go the way we hoped.'

'But I *didn't* support you. I can't risk that happening again.'

'So you're just going to give up? Run and hide?' The pain was sharpening her voice now.

'Maybe that's the only way I can keep *you* safe. To make sure I never hurt you again.'

Rebecca's breath came out in an incredulous huff. 'By staying away from me? Do you really think *that's* not going to hurt me?'

She couldn't deal with this now. Later, she would have to process the idea of losing Thomas all over again but, for now, it had to be pushed aside. Through the open door of the storeroom, she could see a bed being pushed along the corridor.

Ryan's bed.

The next few hours were going to test her to her limits. She not only had to use every skill she had to the best of her ability but she would have to ride that emotional roller-coaster from one end of the spectrum to the other.

She had to lose a tiny patient for ever.

And she had to give another one the gift of a new life.

She couldn't do it alone. She needed support and she needed it from someone who was trying to find a way to run away from her—and he believed that, by doing that, he was protecting her?

He couldn't be more wrong.

'Do one thing for me, Tom. Please?'

'What's that?'

'Be in the gallery. Not for this bit...' She would never ask him to do that—not when it would be like asking him to relive the final moments of his own child. 'Just for Penny's surgery?'

He'd been there for Penny's last operation. She could still remember how much confidence it had given her, knowing he was there simply to encourage her. To believe in her.

She needed him there for what would hopefully be Penny's final major surgery.

The bed and its entourage of medics were much closer now. Thomas turned his head and saw it.

Then he turned back to Rebecca. She could see so much pain in his eyes. But she could see something else, as well.

She could see how much he loved her...

'Yes.' His voice was no more than a whisper. 'I can do that. I'll be there.'

CHAPTER TWELVE

HE WASN'T RUNNING AWAY. But Thomas Wolfe *was* walking away. Temporarily.

He had no intention of not honouring his promise to be in the gallery for Penelope Craig's surgery but he couldn't hang around and wait knowing what was happening in Theatre Two right about now.

There were too many people here, as well. Theatre One was being prepared for Penny's surgery and Theatre Three had just been cleared for a child needing a new kidney. There were retrieval teams here for organs that would be rushed to other parts of the country adding to the congestion.

Thomas needed a space to centre himself. Maybe he needed to convince himself that he was doing the right thing.

That look in Rebecca's eyes when she'd asked him if he thought that removing himself from her personal life wouldn't hurt her...

He'd been so sure that it was the right thing to do.

So why did it feel so very wrong?

The rooftop could be a good place to go, although there might be helicopters waiting to transport those precious organs to their destinations as fast as possible. He needed to be careful which route he took to go anywhere, mind you. The media presence inside Paddington's right now was probably as big as it had been at any time during the whole campaign to save the hospital.

Bigger, even. They had a case that could highlight the importance of this beloved institution with the kind of drama people could lose themselves in. They already had the gripping opening of their story with Penny's disappearance and the frantic search. They had the tear-jerking reunion of the little girl with her parents and now the nail-biting tension of waiting to hear how the surgery had gone. They also knew who the two doctors were who were most involved in Penny's case and the last thing Thomas needed right now was to have a microphone or camera shoved in his face by Angela Marton and her colleagues.

His steps slowed as he neared the main doors that closed this floor of operating theatres and recovery areas from the foyer that contained the elevators and stairwells. Would there be cameras as close as right on the other side of those doors? He turned his head, even though he knew there was no other route to take. The only doors on either side of him led to a couple of small rooms that were used for things like meetings. Or for relatives that had been allowed to accompany a patient on the journey to Theatre but might not be able to cope with anything too clinical.

And that was when he saw them.

Ryan's parents.

They were sitting alone in one of the rooms.

Just sitting.

They were side by side but they weren't holding hands. They weren't talking to each other. At this precise moment, they weren't even looking at each other.

It was the sense of distance between them that hit Thomas so hard.

He knew they were both feeling utterly lost and that they each had to find their own way to start this most difficult of journeys but...

But if he could go back in time he would change the path *he* had taken.

He knew that this couple had probably asked for privacy after their final farewell of their son but something pushed Thomas to enter their space, uninvited.

To see if there was anything he could do to offer even the smallest amount of support.

They didn't seem to find his presence an intrusion. Maybe they needed something—anything—to give them a reference point in this bewildering new map of their lives. He pulled a chair out and perched on the edge of it, leaning forward as he spoke to them.

'This is the hardest part,' he told them. 'Taking the first steps into a life that's changed for ever.'

'No.' Peter Walker's voice was so raw it was painful to hear. 'The hardest part is knowing that I failed my son.'

It was tempting to break an unwritten rule and reveal something intensely personal but Thomas bit back the words. This wasn't about him.

Except, in a way, it was. Because he could hear himself saying the same thing. He could hear the echoes of it that had bounced around in his head for the last five years and he could see it inscribed in every brick of the walls he had built around his heart.

Where were those walls right now?

He could feel the pain of these young parents as acutely as if it was his own.

Because it still *was* his own?

But it was hearing someone who was the image of where he'd been five years ago saying his own destructive mantra aloud that made him realise how wrong it was.

'You *didn't* fail,' he told Peter. 'Neither of you did.'

Maybe it was the conviction in his tone that made Julia lift her head from her hands and stare at him with the same expression as her husband. Waiting for him to say something else. Something that might give them a glimmer of comfort?

'You loved Ryan,' he said quietly. 'I know exactly how much you loved him because you're going through this right now and you'd only be doing this to give the gift of life to other children because you understand how much *their* parents love *them*.'

Both Julia and Peter had tears on their cheeks. They had turned to look at each other as Thomas was speaking and now they reached out and took each other's hands.

'You understand because that's how much you loved your little boy,' Thomas added. 'And, in the end, that's what really matters. He was loved. And he will always be loved because that kind of love never dies.'

It could be damaged, though, couldn't it?

Poisoned by self-blame. By running away and hiding. It could be lost even though it still existed.

'Help each other.' Thomas could hear the crack in his own voice and he had to pause for a heartbeat to keep control. 'You've got tough times ahead but you'll get through them and—if you can help each other—you can be strong enough.'

It was time to leave them alone now. Thomas stood up but there was one more thing he needed to say.

'Believe that you were the best parents and that Ryan knew how much he was loved. And...' He had to swallow another lump in his throat. 'And be proud of what you're doing right now. Believe me, one day, you'll know it was exactly the right thing to do.'

Stepping out of the room, Thomas didn't even look at the doors that would have taken him away from this area.

He knew now, without the slightest shadow of doubt, that there was something else that was exactly the right thing to do.

And he was going to do it.

It was the last thing Rebecca Scott expected to see.

She surprised herself by even glancing up at the gallery, in fact, because nobody came to watch this kind of surgery. It was hard on everybody and the atmosphere was sombre. Respectful and sad and there were several people in the extensive team in Theatre Two that were openly tearful.

But glance up at the gallery she did.

And there was Thomas.

Standing right behind the glass wall.

His posture told her that he was as sombre as any of them. Probably tearful himself as he grappled with memories that no parent should ever have to experience.

But he was here.

For her?

For himself?

No. As Rebecca stepped in to do her part of Ryan's last surgery, she knew that it was something bigger that had brought Thomas so close.

He was here for them both.

She couldn't tell if he was still in the gallery when she walked out of Theatre Two because she was blinded by tears that didn't stop falling until she'd finished scrubbing in again—this time for Penny's surgery.

Looking up at the gallery in Theatre One was the first thing she did as she entered a space that had a very different atmosphere.

This one was full of hope…

And that was what filled Rebecca as she looked up for a much longer moment this time, her lips curving with just a hint of a smile.

Thomas didn't seem to be smiling but it was hard to tell because he was touching his forefinger to his lips.

Then he touched the glass between them with that fingertip.

And Rebecca could feel that fairy kiss just as surely as if it had been his lips touching her skin. Telling her how much he cared and that she wasn't alone…

From the instant she looked away, her focus was completely on her work. This was the ultimate in the specialty she had chosen to devote her professional life to. A long, painstaking procedure that had moments when it seemed like the most extraordinary thing any doctor could do.

To remove such a vital organ and have a tiny chest open in front of you that had an empty space where the heart should be.

To take another heart and fill that space.

And, best of all, to join it up to every vessel and allow blood to fill it and, with the encouragement of a small, electric shock, to see it begin to beat and pump that blood around its new body.

It had taken a little over five hours from the time Penny's chest had been opened until the final stitches were in place and Rebecca stood back, as yet unaware of her aching back and feet, simply watching the monitor screen for a minute. The green light of the trace was a normal, steady rhythm. Blood pressure and oxygen saturation and every other parameter being measured were all within normal limits.

There were some tears again now, from more than one person in Theatre One, but they were happy tears. This little girl had the chance of a new future. As Rebecca allowed the intrusion of personal thoughts to mix with this overwhelming professional satisfaction, the joy of the potential new future became her own, as well. Looking up, the surprise this time was that Thomas had vanished from the gallery but Rebecca was smiling as she stripped off her mask and gown and gloves and left the theatre.

She knew she would find him waiting for her just outside the doors.

Waiting to fold her into his arms?

He came with her to find the space where Julia and Peter Craig were waiting.

'It's good news,' were the first words they heard. 'Everything went as well as we could have hoped for. Penny has a new heart.'

There were still more tears then. Both Penny's parents needed time to cope with the onslaught of relief and then allow themselves real hope. There were lots of questions to be answered again.

'Where is she now?'

'In Recovery. You'll be able to see her very soon.'

'Where will she go then?'

'Into Cardiac Intensive Care—like last time. We'll keep her asleep for a few days while we make sure the new heart is working perfectly. She'll probably be in there for seven to ten days.'

'And then…?'

'And then we'll move her back to the ward and Dr Wolfe will take over to keep a very close eye on things, but in two or three more weeks, we fully expect you to be taking Penny home.'

It was a long time later that Thomas and Rebecca finally left their young patient in the care of the very capable team in the cardiac intensive care unit. Neither of them could remember the last time they had eaten anything but it was too soon to do anything as mundane as finding a table in the staff cafeteria.

'Let's get a bit of fresh air,' Thomas suggested.

Rebecca shook her head. 'I can't leave the hospital. I need to be close to the unit for the rest of tonight. Besides, you know how many journalists and television crews are camped out in Reception. One interview was more than enough for me.'

'I'm amazed Penny's parents agreed to it.'

'I think they needed to say thank you. To everyone who helped to search for Penny. To the whole surgical team. And mostly, they wanted to let their donor's family know how much this gift means to them. They did that so well, didn't they? Even that woman who was interviewing us was crying.'

Rebecca's eyes were shining too brightly now, as well. She needed a bit of time away from everything.

'I know just the place,' Thomas told her. 'Come with me…'

He took her by the hand and led her up the stairs. Up and up, until they found themselves on the rooftop of Paddington Children's Hospital—just in time to see the last of a glorious summer sunset gilding the windows and chimneys of buildings and leaving the tops of the trees in their nearby parks a dark silhouette against a soft glow of pink.

'What a day…'

'I know.' Rebecca closed her eyes for a moment. 'I've never

lost a patient when they were supposed to be on their way to Theatre before. I was so afraid Penny wasn't going to get her new heart.'

'But she did. Thanks to you. I can't tell you how proud I am of what you do, Becca. It's extraordinary. And brave, especially for you, but…but I think I understand *why* you do it, now.'

'*You* were brave,' Rebecca said softly. 'Being there for Ryan's surgery. I know how hard that must have been.'

'I'd just been with Ryan's parents. Talking to them.'

Rebecca's eyes widened. 'What did you say?'

'That they needed to believe they had been the best parents. That it was only because they loved their little boy so much that they were able to go through with giving the gift of life to others. That they should be there for each other and…and that they hadn't failed their son.'

'Oh, Tom…' Rebecca put her arms around him and pressed her forehead against his chest.

'That was when I *knew*,' he said. 'That we were the best parents, too. That what we did really is something to be proud of.' He kissed the top of Rebecca's head. 'I don't need to run any more. Or hide. I would never have chosen to get sucked back into the past the way Penny's case has taken me but it's the best thing that could have happened. I don't feel stuck any more.'

Rebecca lifted her head to meet his gaze. She opened her mouth but no words came out.

'We loved Gwen,' Thomas said softly. 'And we loved each other. And love that strong never dies, does it?'

'No, it never does.' Her voice wobbled. 'We'll always love Gwen. And remember her. And miss her.'

Thomas held her gaze. 'We will always miss her and we can't change that but I've missed you, too. I had no idea how much and I can't bear the thought of always missing you when that's something we *could* change. I love you, Becca. I need you—as much I need my next breath.'

'I love you, too, Tom. More than I ever have. You're still the person I fell in love with but there's so much more of you to love now. So many new layers. We've been through so much, haven't we?'

'We're older.' Thomas smiled. 'And wiser.' He dipped his head to place a gentle kiss on Rebecca's lips. 'But you're still the person I fell in love with, too. Just…more beautiful, inside and out.'

He kissed her again and, this time, there was passion to be kindled from within the tenderness. A promise of what was to come.

'I think I learned something important today,' he whispered, when they finally drew apart.

'I know you did.' Rebecca smiled. 'You learned not to hide.'

'And something else.'

'What?'

'That just because you didn't do something perfectly the first time doesn't mean that you failed. It means you can learn something so you can do it better the next time.'

A tiny frown appeared between Rebecca's dark eyes. 'But you know you didn't fail with Gwen. We didn't fail…'

'I failed our marriage.'

'We both did.' The frown disappeared and there was a new glow in her eyes. 'But do you mean that you think we could do it better if there was a next time?'

'Not if…' Thomas paused to kiss Rebecca again. 'When. If you'll say yes? Will you, Becca? Will you marry me again?'

'Yes,' she whispered. 'Yes and yes and yes!'

Maybe there would have been more 'yes's' but Thomas didn't need to hear any more.

Besides, he was too busy kissing her.

EPILOGUE

THIS WAS GOING to be an evening that nobody would ever forget.

'Oh, my goodness!' Rebecca had to pause for a moment to take in the scene through the doors ahead of them and Thomas smiled down at her.

'It's a bit of a step up from the Frog and Peach, isn't it?'

'Are you kidding? This is the *Ritz*...'

The magnificent dining room of the famous hotel looked like it belonged in a palace. A halo of chandeliers hung beneath the ceiling frescoes and the soft light glinted on the crystal and silver on the tables. Nobody had expected such a gala party to celebrate the official success of the campaign to save Paddington Children's Hospital but, once again, the generosity of people whose lives had been significantly touched over the many decades that the central London hospital had existed had resulted in an extraordinary donation.

So, here they were—a large group of the people who had been most involved in the campaign had been invited to gather and enjoy an evening to celebrate. They were all dressed in the kind of evening wear that befitted the programme of cocktails, dinner and dancing, along with speeches that would publicly acknowledge the contributions they had all made. The men's black tie outfits were a perfect foil to the splashes of colour in the gorgeous dresses some of the women had chosen to show off.

Rebecca had gone for a classic black dress, however. Maybe because it wasn't the dress that she wanted to show off. Glancing down, she straightened the fingers of her left hand. A tiny movement, but Thomas's smile broadened.

'How long will it be before anyone notices, do you think?'

Rebecca smiled back. 'Let's find out, shall we?'

It didn't matter if nobody else noticed, she thought as she took his hand and turned to follow him to where everyone was gathering for a cocktail before dinner. They both knew she was wearing it for the first time and that it had a special significance. It wasn't the same ring Thomas had given her the first time she had agreed to marry him but it was the same solitaire diamond that had been reset—because they both wanted to keep the best of the old but make a new start.

'Can I offer you the cocktail menu?' a waiter queried. 'Or do you know what you'd like already?'

'A champagne cocktail, please,' Thomas said. 'There's a lot to celebrate tonight.'

'Just mineral water for me,' Rebecca said. 'I'm the sober driver.'

'Och, I've got one of those, too.' The voice behind her with its distinctive Scottish burr sounded amused.

She turned, with a grin, to greet Paddington's paediatric trauma surgeon, Dominic MacBride.

'Not for much longer, Dominic.' Her smile included the woman standing beside him. 'I wasn't sure you'd even make it tonight, Victoria.'

'It's crazy, isn't it? This baby seems to be determined to stay put for as long as possible.' Victoria's eyes widened as she watched Rebecca take the tall glass of water from the silver tray. 'Is *that* what I think it is on your finger?'

Rebecca's smile felt misty now. 'Yes. Tom and I are engaged. Again...'

'I knew it.' Alistair North turned his head towards them from where he and Claire were standing with Leo and his fiancée, Rosie, and Matt McGrory and his fiancée, Quinn Grady. 'I had a feeling something was going on that night when you were so late at the Frog and Peach you both missed the first party. You thought so, too, didn't you, Matt?'

'It was obvious,' Matt agreed. 'Just a matter of time.'

'Oh, congratulations—this is awesome news.' Claire stepped closer to admire Rebecca's ring. 'Are you going to have a big wedding or just duck into a registry office like Alistair and I will?'

'We haven't got round to planning anything,' Rebecca said. 'But it's second time around so I imagine we'll keep it pretty low-key.'

'Low-key...' Rosie sounded wistful. 'You wouldn't believe the amount of organisation that goes along with getting married to an Italian duke. Not that I'm complaining or anything...' The smile she gave Leo suggested that it was all very well worth it.

'We haven't got round to planning anything, either.' Dominic sighed. 'And it's not going to happen until this little princess decides to make her appearance.'

Victoria looked down at her impressive belly. 'Hear that?' she said. 'Daddy's getting impatient and I need to be able to wear a dress that doesn't look like a circus tent. It's time to make a move.'

'The sooner, the better,' Dominic added.

Thomas laughed. 'Be careful what you wish for,' he warned. 'Unless you want to avoid all the speeches tonight?'

'I reckon the dancing will do something,' Victoria said. 'And that won't be until all the speeches are finished.'

'Good luck with that.' Rebecca smiled. 'It didn't work for me and we tried a pretty fast salsa when Gwen was due.'

A sudden silence fell amongst the group of colleagues as some cautious glances were exchanged.

Rebecca and Thomas shared a glance of their own.

'It's okay,' Rebecca said. 'You all know our story and we know that you've all been so careful not to say anything but things have changed...' She felt the touch of Thomas's hand as his fingers curled around hers. 'Our first child will always be a very special part of our lives and we want to be able to remember her. And talk about her...'

'*First* child?' Claire was standing close enough to Rebecca to lower her voice and still be heard. 'And is that water you're drinking—like me?'

'Oh, look...' Rosie didn't seem to have heard the quiet comment. 'There's a film crew setting up over there. I didn't think this was going to be televised.'

'Maybe Sheikh Idris and Robyn are making a grand arrival. He's one of the biggest stars here tonight, after all. Without his donation, the campaign might not have been anything more than a protest.'

'No... I don't think so.' Rosie was peering through gaps as people started moving towards the dining tables. 'It's... Good heavens! Is that Julia and Peter Craig—Penny's parents?'

Rebecca nodded. 'There's an ongoing documentary being made about Penny's journey as a transplant patient. It all began the day of her surgery when she went missing and the crew happened to be there to catch the action. Everybody wanted to know what was happening and how things turned out.'

'I was one of them,' Victoria said. 'I was glued to my phone in the ultrasound waiting room, trying to get the latest news.'

'She became the poster girl for saving Paddington's in those last days, didn't she?' Claire added. 'So many headlines. I read somewhere that that was the final pressure needed to get everything signed and sealed.'

'But why are they still following her? Surely the family's got enough to cope with—it's not that long since her surgery.'

'I think Julia and Peter look at it as a way to give back,' Thomas said. 'They want to do all they can to raise awareness of the shortage of organ donors.'

'The committee invited them as special guests tonight,' Quinn put in. 'They *did* become so important as the finale to our campaign. And they're representing all the parents who owe so much to what Paddington's has been able to do.'

'And Penny's doing so well,' Rebecca added. 'I think they're delighted to share that. She's started back at school part time already. And she's started having ballet lessons.'

'Oh...' Rosie looked as if she was blinking back tears. 'That's the best news ever. I'd love to see her dancing.'

'I expect you will—on the documentary. Oh, there's Idris and Robyn arriving and it looks like the official party's going in. That's our CEO, Dennis Bradley, with them. Hadn't we better go and find our table?'

There was a long table at one end of the room where the dignitaries like the CEO, people from Paddington's Board of Trustees and government officials were seated. Idris and Robyn were also at this top table, along with Julia and Peter Craig, but other guests were seated at round tables for six.

Thomas and Rebecca sat with Leo and Rosie and Matt and Quinn. The other tables quickly filled and a silence eventually fell as the Member of Parliament most closely associated with Paddington's stood up to say something. It was a short speech to start the evening where he welcomed everybody, thanked the owner of the Ritz hotel and Sheikh Idris Al Khalil for making this evening possible and finally offered a succinct toast.

'To Paddington Children's Hospital.'

The toast echoed throughout the room as glasses were raised and then a new buzz of conversation broke out. It wasn't often that these colleagues got together socially and none of them were short of things to talk about.

'I can see Robyn's engagement ring from here,' Rebecca said to Rosie. 'It's no wonder she can't wear it at work.'

'I love that she's wearing a dress that's the same green as the emeralds in that ring. And doesn't she look happy?'

'Over the moon happy. I think I'd be exhausted by all that

commuting she's doing. I'll bet she can't wait for the wedding and her final move to Da'har. And what about you guys? Didn't I hear that you're moving to Rome?'

'We've decided Florence is better,' Rosie told her. 'Leo's *palazzo* is in Tuscany, and we want to be near his mum.' Her voice trailed off as her attention was caught by Leo, who had been talking to Matt and Thomas but was now frowning at the screen of his phone. 'What's up, Leo?'

'I might just pop out for a moment.'

'Why?'

'I thought I'd ring the babysitter and check on the twins.'

'They're fine. She'd ring us if there were any problems. They'll both be sound asleep by now.'

'I'll just text her, then.'

Rosie shook her head. 'You know what, Leo?'

'What?'

'You're turning into a helicopter parent.'

They both seemed to find this amusing. Quinn was smiling, too.

'Maybe it's something to do with jumping in the deep end as a new parent. Matt and Simon are pretty much inseparable these days. They came up with a joint proposal for me, would you believe? We'd gone out for a picnic and they were both kneeling on the rug while they got things ready and then Matt proposed and Simon told me that I had to say "yes" because he wanted two parents for when he got properly adopted. And then they made me call Maisie and it turned out they'd tied my engagement ring to her collar.'

'Oh, that's so romantic. A real family proposal.'

'Mmm… What about yours, Rebecca?' Rosie had turned back as Leo put his phone away. 'Was it a romantic proposal?'

'Of course it was.' Thomas had overheard the question. 'A perfect sunset and a view of half of London.'

Rebecca laughed. 'We were on the rooftop of Paddington's— near the helipad.' Then her laughter faded into a smile that was purely for Thomas. 'But yes, it was as romantic as I could have wished for.'

'I know what you mean about jumping in the deep end as a parent,' Rosie said to Quinn. 'You should see Leo. I don't even get a look in as the reader of bedtime stories any more. Apparently I'm nowhere near as good at doing dinosaur voices.'

Laughter and stories continued as the dinner service began. The food served that evening was as amazing as everybody expected, with dishes that featured treats like Norfolk crab, roasted scallops, venison and veal. Dessert delights included a praline custard and a banana soufflé. The three courses of the dinner were separated by speeches and many people were asked to stand and be acknowledged—like Quinn, at their table, for her contribution to the campaign committee. Rebecca missed the last bit of the pre-dessert course speech, however. It was the smell of the banana soufflé that was suddenly too much.

'Are you okay?' Rosie asked. 'You've gone very pale.'

'Bit warm, maybe.' Rebecca fanned herself with her menu, fighting off what appeared to be her first wave of morning sickness. 'Excuse me for a moment...'

With her hand pressed to her mouth, she tried to maintain a dignified walk to the restroom and not break into a run. She was aware that Thomas was following her but there was no time to wait for him.

She only just made it. And when she emerged from the cubicle to splash some cold water on her face, there was someone else doing the same thing at the neighbouring basin.

'I was right, wasn't I?' Claire's smile was rueful. 'How far along are you?'

'We only just found out,' Rebecca said. 'It's too early to tell anybody yet.'

'Your secret's safe with me.' Claire reached for one of the soft handtowels. 'I should be over this after three months, but maybe it's worse when it's twins...'

The door opened and Victoria came in. She was looking as pale as both the other women.

Claire and Rebecca looked at each other.

'I don't think you've got a problem with morning sickness, have you?'

Victoria sank onto the edge of one of the upholstered armchairs in this luxurious restroom.

'I just needed to move. Those straight dining chairs were giving me the most awful backache.' She closed her eyes and blew a long breath out through pursed lips. 'That's better. It's wearing off, I think.' Opening her eyes she smiled at the others.

'Don't mind me. I'll be fine. Go back and enjoy your dessert.'

Except that almost immediately her face tightened into lines of pain again and she bent her head, her arms clasped around her belly.

'I'll stay with her,' Rebecca murmured to Quinn. 'Can you go and get Dominic?'

The door swung shut behind Claire, only to open again almost instantly.

Thomas looked concerned. 'Claire told me that it looks like Victoria's in labour. Shall I call an ambulance?'

'Yes,' said Rebecca.

'No,' Victoria said at the same time. 'It's a first baby—nothing's going to happen in that much of a hurry. I just need to go to the loo…'

'Not a good idea,' Rebecca said.

'Ohhh…' Victoria gripped the upholstered arms of the chair. 'That hurts!'

The door opened again and Dominic came in. One look at Victoria and his jaw dropped. He reached for his phone. 'I'll call an ambulance.'

'I'm not sure there's time.' Victoria's voice was strained. 'This is crazy but… I think I have to push!'

'Hang on a tick. Let's just check what's happening first. Tom? Can you take her other arm? Let's get her onto the floor.'

Claire poked her head around the door and saw what was happening.

'Oh, heck... I'll stay out here and make sure nobody else comes in, shall I?'

'Please,' Thomas said. 'And call an ambulance. We're going to need some transport very soon.'

It was Dominic who lifted the folds of Victoria's dress out of the way. Thomas knelt behind her so that she could lean on him and Rebecca was holding her hand—or rather, letting her own hand get squeezed in a painfully hard grip.

'What's going on?' Victoria gasped. 'Can I push?'

'There's no cord in the way.' Dominic's voice was shaky. 'And she's crowning. Go for it, hon...'

It only took two pushes and a beautiful baby girl was delivered straight into her father's hands. The first, loud cry of the healthy newborn made Victoria burst into tears. Dominic had tears running down his own face as he put their daughter into her mother's arms and against her skin. Rebecca gathered every soft towel she could find on the shelves to cover them both for warmth and Thomas moved to let Dominic take his position and support his new family. Dominic's hands were shaking as he took his phone out of his pocket.

'Not that we're ever going to forget this,' he said. 'But could you do the honours?'

So Thomas took the very first family photo. Victoria lay against Dominic's chest and he was leaning over her shoulder as they both gazed down at a tiny face with wide open eyes that were staring back at her parents.

Thomas had to clear his throat as he handed back the phone. 'The ambulance should be here in no time.' He caught Rebecca's gaze and she nodded. This brand new family needed a little bit of time all to themselves.

'We'll be just outside the door if you need any help before then.'

Claire was guarding the door on the other side and had Alistair beside her but a small crowd had gathered behind them.

Robyn and Idris were there. And Rosie and Leo, Matt and Quinn.

'We heard her cry,' Rosie said. 'Is everything all right?'

Thomas put his arm around Rebecca's waist and drew her close to his side. 'Everything's perfect,' he said.

It seemed like every couple there needed to draw each other close as they shared the joy of this unexpected event. To smile. To touch. To steal a kiss...

Rebecca leaned closer to Thomas and looked up to bask in the intimacy of eye contact.

'That will be us in the not-too-distant future,' she whispered.

'I can't wait,' Thomas murmured back. 'You?'

Rebecca smiled. 'Like you said...everything's perfect...'

And it was.

* * * * *

Keep reading for an excerpt of
The Price Of A Dangerous Passion
by Jane Porter.
Find it in the
Hot Italian Nights anthology,
out now!

PROLOGUE

New Year's Eve

SHE HAD RULES. Rules she never broke. There were no exceptions. Charlotte never mixed business and pleasure, never. She wasn't ever tempted, either…regardless of the value of her clients. All her clients were VIPs to her, clients who came to her for her sterling reputation. They trusted her to make the best possible decisions for them. They came to her because they needed her expertise in sorting out image issues, public relation snafus and social media nightmares. How could they trust her judgment, if her judgment was faulty?

If her judgment lost sight of the objective?

If she forgot why she was there in the first place?

Charlotte Parks knew all these things, and yet Brando Ricci was making it almost impossible to remember why these—*her*—rules were so important. She'd wrapped up business weeks ago, well before Christmas. All conversations and concerns with the Ricci-Baldi family had been handled, settled, put to bed. She was here at the Ricci family's grand New Year's Eve party because they loved to throw lavish parties and loved to include everyone who had helped them. And Charlotte had helped them, having spent the entire autumn in Florence, working to smooth tensions following intense, negative media attention arising from the family's struggles with power, and issues from succession.

Not all issues were completely settled, but much of the tension was gone, and the family had come together to present a unified face to the public once again. Tonight's party was part of that unified face.

She shouldn't have come tonight. Her part was done. She'd been paid—well paid, too. There was no justifiable reason to have returned to Florence for a party.

The music changed, slowed, and Brando pulled her closer, his hand settling low on her back, her breasts crushed to his tuxedo-covered chest. "You're overthinking," he murmured, his breath warm against her ear.

"I am," she agreed. "Or perhaps I should say, I'm thinking. And I should be thinking. You are dangerous."

"I would never hurt you. That is a promise."

And she knew that. She knew he'd be amazing—in bed, out of bed. The chemistry between them was electric and had been there from the moment they'd met last September. But the chemistry is what also troubled her, because she'd never felt a pull like this... She'd never even considered throwing caution to the wind. And yet here she was, a half hour from midnight, wrestling with her conscience, wrestling with desire.

"I shouldn't be here," she whispered, fingers curling around his, her heart thumping too hard, her body warm, sensitive, exquisitely aware...aroused. She hadn't made love in over a year... perhaps two years... She hadn't felt this attracted to anyone... ever. Part of her was so tempted to give in to the heat, while the logical, disciplined part warned that it was a mistake, a mistake that could jeopardize her career, her reputation...

Her heart.

She looked up into his handsome face again. He was gorgeous...truly handsome, but it wasn't just beautiful bone structure. He was smart, fascinating, compelling. During the months of working with the Ricci family, Brando was the one who drew her, time and again. Even though he was the youngest in his family, he had the most wisdom and insight, and she'd come to trust and respect his point of view, even going to him when Enzo, Marcello and Livia couldn't agree on anything, hoping Brando could find a diplomatic way to bring his fractious siblings together. And he had. And he did.

She'd returned tonight to Florence for him.

For this…

Whatever this was.

"What are you afraid of?" he asked now, his narrowed gaze sweeping her face.

His scrutiny made her face tingle, setting countless nerve endings alight. "Losing my head. Losing control."

The corner of his mouth lifted ever so slightly. His hand slid lower on her back, nearly cupping the curve of her butt. "We're two consenting adults."

She could feel his sinewy strength pressed against the length of her. His hard chest, his waist, the powerful thighs. "Yes, but business and pleasure should always be kept separate—"

"We're no longer working together," he reminded, his head dropping, his lips brushing the side of her neck.

She shuddered, and closed her eyes, trying to ignore how her breasts tightened, nipples pebbling, desire coiling within her. It was becoming increasingly difficult to keep a clear head. All she wanted was his mouth on hers, his hands teasing, exploring the length of her. It had been so long since she'd been with anyone and yet she wanted him…wanted his weight on her, wanted his body filling hers, wanted the pleasure she knew he'd give. The pleasure she craved…not from just anyone, but him. Brando Ricci. Vintner. Entrepreneur. Billionaire.

Lover.

No, not her lover, not yet.

"We shouldn't do this," she whispered, air catching in her

throat as his thumb stroked the side of her neck, lighting little tongues of fires just beneath the surface of her skin.

"We've done nothing wrong," he murmured. "We're simply dancing."

Done nothing wrong yet, she silently corrected, with *yet* being the operative word.

Charlotte tipped her head back to look up into Brando's mesmerizing silver eyes that were anything but cool, or cold. The heat in them scorched her now and she felt a shiver race through her. She'd fought this attraction for months, fought the sizzling awareness, suppressed the hunger, but tonight she was losing the battle. Just being in his arms was making her breathless and dizzy. Her body hummed, aching with awareness. Hunger.

"It's nearly midnight," she said, glancing over his shoulder at the enormous clock that had been mounted on the wall of the palace ballroom for tonight's New Year's countdown.

He glanced at the clock, too. "Ten minutes."

Her gaze took in the orchestra on the stage playing everyone's favorites, and the throng of beautiful people filling the dance floor. The seventeenth-century ballroom was packed with some of Europe's most glamorous, wealthy people. They were having a wonderful time, laughing, dancing, drinking, celebrating. When the clock struck midnight, the celebration would become deafening.

She'd always hated crowds, and normally avoided parties, but when the invitation came to attend the Riccis' party, she didn't say no. She couldn't say no.

"What are you thinking, *cara*?" Brando's deep voice was a caress.

Cara, darling. She felt another helpless shiver race through her.

She'd come tonight for him.

She wanted only him.

And yet, her rules. Her stupid rules.

She dampened her lips with the tip of her tongue. "I don't mix—"

"Business and pleasure," he completed for her. "I know. But tonight is not business. We're done with business, done with the family, done doing what others want us to do."

His lips brushed hers, a fleeting kiss that felt as if he'd set a thousand butterflies free inside her heart and mind. Wings of hope. Flutters of possibilities.

She always lived so alone, so controlled, so contained, but tonight… Tonight she felt as if maybe, just maybe, she belonged somewhere, to someone. Even if it were for one night only.

"Just tonight," she said hoarsely. "You must agree this is just one night, and nothing more than that. Promise me, Brando."

His lips brushed hers again. "Fine. Tonight is ours. Tonight belongs to us."

"And tomorrow—"

"We won't worry about. It's not here."

BRAND NEW RELEASE

Don't miss the next instalment of the Powder River series by bestselling author B.J. Daniels! For lovers of sexy Western heroes, small-town settings and suspense with your romance.

RIVER WILD

—R—
A POWDER RIVER NOVEL

PERFECT FOR FANS OF YELLOWSTONE!

In-store and online January 2025

Previous titles in the Powder River series

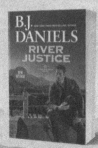

September 2023

January 2024

August 2024

Subscribe and fall in love with a Mills & Boon series today!

You'll be among the first to read stories delivered to your door monthly and enjoy great savings.

WE SIMPLY LOVE ROMANCE

MILLS & BOON

JOIN US

Sign up to our newsletter to stay up to date with...

- Exclusive member discount codes
- Competitions
- New release book information
- All the latest news on your favourite authors

> ## Plus...
> get $10 off your first order.
> *What's not to love?*

Sign up at **millsandboon.com.au/newsletter**